MORE PRAISE FOR *East*

★ "The stuff of epic tale telling, replete with high drama and compelling characterizations."
—*Booklist* (starred review)

"Lure[s] readers from one scene to the next faster than a great white bear can traverse the landscape... Readers will find themselves enchanted." —*The Bulletin*

"A saga of remarkable people and those who aren't quite human, an epic of love, beauty, loss and betrayal."
—*VOYA*

"The story itself is gripping, endlessly so... Pattou certainly has made a successful fantasy out of a simple fairy tale... and the details... come to life as she describes them." —*KLIATT*

"Full of absolutely enchanting characters and locations... eloquently written and impossible to put down. Pattou has brought the tale of an enchantment, a Troll Queen, a talking polar bear, and a fabulous ice castle so completely to life that it hardly seems
—Bank Stre

EDITH PATTOU

East

MAGIC CARPET BOOKS
HARCOURT, INC.
Orlando   Austin   New York
San Diego   London

First Magic Carpet Books edition 2005

Magic Carpet Books is a trademark of Harcourt, Inc.,
registered in the United States of America and/or other jurisdictions.

The Library of Congress has cataloged the hardcover edition as follows:
Pattou, Edith.
East/by Edith Pattou.
p.   cm.
Summary: A young woman journeys to a distant castle on the back
of a great white bear who is the victim of a cruel enchantment.
[1. Fairy tales.   2. Bears—Fiction.]   I. Title.
PZ8.P2815Eas   2003
[Fic]—dc21   2003002338
ISBN 978-0-15-204563-0
ISBN 978-0-15-205221-8 pb

Text set in Fournier
Designed by Cathy Riggs

Printed in the United States of America

I K M O P N L J

To my father,

for his love of stories—

from *Harold and the Purple Crayon* to *Doctor No*

And to my mother,

for her unwavering support

East

PROLOGUE

I found the box in the attic of an old farmhouse in Norway. It was large, the size of a footlocker, and there were markings on it; runes, I learned later.

When I opened the lid, it looked like the box contained mostly papers, a jumbled mass of them, in several different languages and written in different styles of handwriting. There were diaries, maps, even ships' logs.

As I dug deeper, under the papers, I found more: skeins of wool; small boots made of soft leather; sheaves of music tied with faded ribbon; long, thin pieces of wood with maplike markings on them; dried-up mushrooms; woven belts; even a dress the color of the moon.

Then I came upon what looked to be the mouthpiece of a very old reed instrument. I held it up toward the light coming through the small attic window. As the late afternoon sun caught it, a most extraordinary thing happened. I heard the clear, high note of a flute.

And it was coming from inside the trunk.

Other sounds came then—whispering, muttering, swirling around inside my head. Dogs barking, sleigh bells, the cracking of ice. Voices. *Hearing voices—this isn't good,* I thought.

Still holding the ancient mouthpiece in the palm of my hand, I lifted the top piece of paper out of the trunk. It was a handwritten note.

They want me to write it all down, though I'm not sure why.

It seems enough that Father and Neddy wrote down their parts. Especially Neddy; he was always the storyteller in the family. I am not a storyteller, not really. It takes more patience than I've got—or rather, than I used to have. I guess I did learn a little bit about patience in the course of the journey. But even so, I'd much rather set the story down in cloth. Well, actually I have. Hangs on the north wall in the great room, and the whole story is there. But words are easier to understand for most people. So I will try.

It isn't easy for me to walk the path back to the beginning of the story, even to know where the true beginning is. And telling a story, I suppose, is like winding a skein of spun yarn—you sometimes lose track of the beginning.

All I intended to do, when I began the journey, was to set things right. They say losing someone you love is like losing a part of your own body. An eye or a leg. But it is far worse—especially when it is your fault.

But already I'm getting ahead of myself. It all began with a pair of soft boots.

BOOK ONE

East

Once on a time there was a poor farmer
with many children.

Father

EBBA ROSE WAS THE NAME of our last-born child. Except it was a lie. Her name should have been Nyamh Rose. But everyone called her Rose rather than Ebba, so the lie didn't matter. At least, that is what I told myself.

The *Rose* part of her name came from the symbol that lies at the center of the wind rose—which is fitting because she was lodged at the very center of my heart.

I loved each of her seven brothers and sisters, but I will admit there was always something that set Rose apart from the others. And it wasn't just the way she looked.

She was the hardest to know of my children, and that was because she would not stay still. Every time I held her as a babe, she would look up at me, intent, smiling with her bright purple eyes. But soon, and always, those eyes would stray past my shoulder, seeking the window and what lay beyond.

Rose's first gift was a small pair of soft boots made of reindeer hide. They were brought by Torsk, a neighbor, and as he fastened them on Rose's tiny feet with his large calloused hands, I saw my wife, Eugenia, frown. She tried to hide it, turning her face away.

Torsk did not see the frown but looked up at us, beaming. He was a widower with grown sons and a gift for leatherwork. Eager to show off his handiwork and unmindful of the difficult circumstances of Eugenia's recent birthing, he had been the first to show up on our doorstep.

Most of our neighbors were well aware of how superstitious Eugenia was. They also knew that a baby's first gift was laden with meaning. But cheerful, large-handed Torsk paid no heed to this. He just gazed down at the small soft boots on Rose's feet and looked ready to burst with pride.

"The fit is good," he observed with a wide smile.

I nodded and then said, with a vague thought of warning him, "'Tis Rose's first gift."

His smile grew even wider. "Ah, this is good." Then a thought penetrated his head. "She will be a traveler, an explorer!" he said with enthusiasm. So he did know of the first-gift superstition after all.

This time Eugenia did not attempt to hide the frown that creased her face, and I tensed, fearing what she might say. Instead she reached down and straightened one of the boot ties. "Thank you, neighbor Torsk," she said through stiff lips. Her voice was cold, and a puzzled look passed over the big man's face.

I stepped forward and, muttering something about Eugenia still being weak, ushered Torsk to the door.

"Was there something wrong with the boots?" he asked, bewildered.

"No, no," I reassured him. "They are wonderful. Eugenia is tired, that is all. And you know mothers— they like to keep their babes close. She's not quite ready for the notion of little Rose wandering the countryside."

Nor would she ever be. Though I did not say that to neighbor Torsk.

That night after we had pried Neddy from Rose's basket and gotten all the children to sleep, Eugenia said to me, "Didn't Widow Hautzig bring over a crock of butter for the baby?"

"She was only returning what you loaned her," I said.

"No, it was for Ebba Rose. Her first gift, I'm quite sure." Her voice was definite.

Eugenia did like to keep her children close, but it turned out she wanted to keep Rose closest of all. And that had everything to do with the circumstances of Rose's birth.

Neddy

OUR FAMILY WASN'T ALWAYS poor. My grandfather Esbjorn Lavrans had a well-respected mapmaking business, and my father's father was a prosperous farmer. But Father had a falling-out with his family when he went to Bergen to be an apprentice to the mapmaker Esbjorn. My mother, Eugenia, was Esbjorn's daughter, which is how Father met her.

Father and Mother had eight children. Rose was the last-born and I was second to last, four years old when they brought Rose home from Askoy Forest. Some would say four is too young to remember, but I definitely have memories. Lots of them. I remember her smell, like warm milk and soft green moss. I remember the noises she'd make—gurgling like the creek we later took to calling Rosie's Creek because she fell into it so often; the clicking she made with her tongue, like a wren pecking at our chimney; the howls of frustration when she kept toppling over while learning to walk. Not that it took her long. She was running around on her short legs at just five months.

I also remember clearly the evening Mother and Father came home from an afternoon of herb hunting, and instead of herbs they were carrying a lumpy bundle that made funny noises.

My older brothers and sisters had been worried about Mother and Father because there had been a storm and they were much later than usual returning. I told everyone not to worry, that they had gone out to bring home the baby and that's why they were so late getting home.

My older sister Selme laughed. "Mother is still more than a month away from her lying-in time," she said. "And besides, everyone knows you can't just go pluck babies out of Askoy Forest," she added with a superior look.

But it turned out I was right after all.

When they finally came through the door, Mother looked very pale and sat down as soon as she could, holding the noisy thing on her lap. The others crowded around, but I hung back, waiting. When they'd all looked long enough, Father led me to Mother's side. When I gazed at the little scrunched-up face, I felt a peculiar glow of pride. Like I'd done something good. I knew it was Mother who'd brought this baby into the world (and she certainly looked worn out from doing it), but from that moment I felt like the wild little brown-haired baby was my very own gift—and that it would be my job to watch over her.

If I had known just how wild a thing she would turn out to be, I might have thought twice about taking her on. It's a funny thing. I think it was Mother and I who had the hardest time with Rose's wandering ways. But we both had different ways of living with it. Mother tried always to reel her in. To keep her close by. But for me, I knew it couldn't be done, so I just ached and felt sorry for myself when she'd disappear. That's the trouble with loving a wild thing: You're always left watching the door.

But you also get kind of used to it.

Rose

I COULD SAY THAT I FELT guilty and ashamed about the trouble I was always getting into when I was a child, driving my mother to her wit's end on a daily basis. But the truth is I never did feel either of those things.

I don't think it's because I was selfish or unfeeling. I just couldn't understand what all the fuss was about. What was a little spilled blood or a broken bone now and then?

I never set out to be disobedient. I just couldn't keep my thoughts, and then my feet, still. I'd see something— the azure flash of a butterfly's wing, a formation of clouds like a ship's mast and sails, a ripe yellow apple perched high in a tree—and I'd be off after it without a second thought.

Exploring ran in my blood. My grandfather Esbjorn was a mapmaker as well as an explorer. And my great-great-grandfather was one of the first Njordens to travel to Constantinople.

The only thing that gave me the slightest twinge of sadness was Neddy, with his exasperated, sorry-for-himself look when he found me after yet another time I'd run off without telling anyone.

"But I saw this rabbit with a tail so white it *glowed*," I'd try to explain (when I was old enough to put words to my feelings).

Neddy would just sigh and say that Mother wanted me in the kitchen straightaway.

"I'm sorry, Neddy," I'd say, wrapping my arms around his legs, watching the corners of his mouth for the smile I always managed to squeeze out of him. And then I'd go to the kitchen and Mother would scold me yet again.

Neddy

TO SAY THAT MY MOTHER was superstitious would be like saying the great blizzard of 1539 was naught but a light snowfall.

Every single thing a body did in our house was charged with meaning. To sweep dust out the front door was to sweep away all your good luck. To sing while baking bread was to guarantee the arrival of ill fortune. To have an itch on the left side of your body meant certain disaster. And if you sneezed on a Wednesday, you would surely receive a letter—good news if you were facing east and bad if facing north.

Father liked to tell the story of how he first learned of Mother's "birth-direction" superstition.

When Father and Mother announced their engagement to her family, the first words to come out of his future mother-in-law's mouth were "But Arne, we don't even know what your birth direction is!"

Father said that he gaped at her, totally bewildered.

"Yes, Arne, we must know right away, before you and Eugenia make any more plans."

"Oh, I'm quite certain he's a south, or a southeast," Mother said reassuringly.

"But we must know for sure," said her mother.

Father said he started to laugh then, thinking they were having some elaborate joke with him. But they weren't.

And Father would have us all doubled over with laughter as he described the pilgrimage to my grandparents' farm to interrogate them regarding the direction my father's mother was facing when she gave birth to him. It turned out that the direction his mother was facing when Father was born was southeast, which was a good thing according to Mother.

What wasn't such a good thing is that this turned out to be the last time Father saw his family. There had already been ill feeling between them that Father had hoped to heal during the visit. But if anything, the strange line of questioning from the "city folk" Father was marrying into seemed to make matters worse, and they parted with bad blood.

Father

MY EUGENIA'S FERVENT BELIEF in the birth-direction superstition was unusual to say the least. I have never come across anything like it during the course of my life, but it had apparently been handed down through many generations of Eugenia's family.

They believed that birth direction was of overwhelming importance. Not the alignment of the stars, nor the position of the moon, nor the movement of the tides, nor even the traits handed down from parent to child.

My theory was that this strange notion sprang from their preoccupation with mapmaking.

"And every child born in our family," Eugenia explained to me, "is given a name that begins with the first letter of their birth direction. So a north-facing baby might be called Nathaniel; a southwest-facing child, Sarah Wilhelmina; and so on. I myself was an east-facing baby."

"And what are the attributes of an east-facing baby?" I asked.

"Well, among other things, that I am tidy, a sound sleeper, and somewhat superstitious."

"*Somewhat?*" I countered with a grin.

It turned out that Eugenia went a little further with the birth-direction superstition than any of her forebears. On the night after we were wed, she announced to me that she wanted to have seven children.

"Seven is a good number," I replied. "But why seven? Is that a particularly lucky number?" I said with a teasing smile.

"No, it is that I want one child for each point of the compass," she replied.

Puzzled, I said, "But that would be four, or eight perhaps..."

"I have left out north, of course."

"Why not north?" I asked.

"Surely you know about pure northern children?" she responded in surprise.

"No," I said, refraining from reminding her that no one outside her family would even be engaged in such a conversation.

"Oh, they are terrible! Wandering and wild and very ill behaved. Northern people in general are that way. My own sister—surely I've told you this?—married a north-born (against the advice of our mother, needless to say), and he took off on a sailing ship when she was pregnant with their third child and has not been heard of since. I refuse to have a child I cannot keep my eye on."

I felt a sliver of worry at those words. "I hope you are not going to be an overprotective mother, Eugenia."

"Oh no, Arne," she reassured me. "It's just that norths are particularly wild. Always into trouble. But that is not the only reason I will not have a north bairn. There is another, of much more importance."

"And what is that?"

"Some years ago I went with my sister to a *skjebne-soke*."

Though *skjebne-sokes* were scarce in our region, I was not surprised that someone as superstitious as Eugenia had managed to find one.

"She was very gifted, this *skjebne-soke*. Why, she predicted to the day when Karin Tessel would have her first bairn! And she told my sister that she would lose her husband to the sea..." Eugenia trailed off, then fell silent.

I studied her face. "The *skjebne-soke* said something about you having a north bairn?"

She nodded, then said in a low voice, "She said that if I were to have a north-born, that child would grow up to die a cold, horrible death, suffocating under ice and snow." She shuddered and instinctively I drew her close to me. Because avalanches were not uncommon during the winter in our country, especially on the seven mountains that surrounded Bergen, I could see that Eugenia took this ominous prediction quite seriously.

I myself considered such prophecy and superstition to be nonsense, and perhaps if I had tried to reason with Eugenia, taken a stronger stand against her many superstitions right from the beginning, I might have averted much of the ill fortune that later befell us. But I did not. I saw her ideas as harmlessly eccentric, even charming at the outset, and I indulged her. I, too, wanted a large family, and seven seemed as good a number as any. . . .

But even Eugenia's own mother thought that methodically *planning* the birth directions of each of her children was ill advised. Before she died she had cautioned Eugenia against it.

"'Tis meddling in the affairs of God and fate, and only disaster can come of it," she had said.

Eugenia herself had been born due east. Her mother went into labor unexpectedly on a boat that was traveling down the Rauma River, which was notoriously twisty. Fortunately, Eugenia's mother had had a *leidarstein* and needle with her (she carried both with her at all times during her pregnancy), and the owner of the boat brought a pail of water. While his wife labored, Esbjorn magnetized the needle and floated it in the water, so it turned out that they were able to calculate the birth direction without much difficulty. "To think I might have been a north, had the boat taken a sudden turn!" Eugenia would mutter darkly.

Eugenia began our family with northeast, Nils Erlend. Her reasoning was that she would tackle the most difficult direction first, when she was youngest and most vigorous; and the next most difficult (Neddy Wilfrid) at the end, when she was at her wisest and most experienced as a parent.

It all went just as Eugenia had planned, from northeast to northwest.

Nils Erlend, who liked to roam but had a frugal, organized side.

Elise, the quiet, perfect east; practical and obedient.

Selme Eva, who was comfortable and kind.

Sara, a strong-willed, passionate girl.

Sonja Wende, who was good with animals and a little bit prescient, farseeing.

Willem, capable and decisive, who also had an easy hand with the farm animals.

And Neddy Wilfrid, the only one with dark hair, though his eyes were as blue as his brothers' and sisters'. Neddy had been Eugenia's easiest birth yet, and he was a dear, quiet babe, smiling far more than he cried, which was seldom.

Seven children in seven years. With a sigh of relief, Eugenia put away her supply of the herb feverfew (which eased morning sickness and the pains of childbirth), as well as her voluminous childbearing shift, which had seen her through the seven pregnancies.

But then Elise, who at eight was our second-eldest child, died suddenly.

Elise had never been a strong child, but Eugenia had had a special fondness for her, partly because she was an east-born like herself.

There is no pain deeper than that of a parent losing a child, but there were still six children who needed our care, and slowly, time healed the sharpest of our grief. Yet even as it did, the empty space at the east point of the compass began to gnaw at Eugenia.

Neddy

FATHER TOLD ME THAT he first began to design wind roses when he was engaged to Mother. As part of his apprenticeship, my grandfather gave him piles of maps to study. And he quickly noticed a symbol on almost every chart, usually in the bottom left corner.

Father told me that the symbol was called a wind rose because it bore a resemblance to a flower, with thirty-two petals, and it had long been used by mapmakers to indicate the direction of the winds. Some were simple and some elaborate, but all used a spear-point fleur-de-lis as the northern point of the rose. He also said that mapmakers would paint their wind roses in brilliant colors, not just because they were prettier that way but also because they were easier to read in the dim lamplight of a ship's deck at twilight.

I loved learning about the history of mapmaking. I dreamed that when I grew up, I would go to one of the big cities and study with distinguished scholars on a wide range of subjects, including maps and exploration. Or else I'd be a poet.

I wrote one of my first poems about a wind rose:

The spear points north, south, west, and east,
Wind always shifting, a wandering beast.
A beacon to sailors on the high seas,
Journeying afar on the wind's soft breeze.

The best that could be said of it was that it was short.

Father

ONE PROBLEM WITH MY being a mapmaker is that I hated to travel. ("A born southeast," Eugenia would say.) And I blamed myself when the mapmaking business failed. In fact, it had already been on shaky ground, but when Esbjorn and his wife died in an influenza epidemic and the business fell to me, it soon became clear that I couldn't make a go of it. It didn't help that two of Esbjorn's biggest customers had also died in the epidemic.

Eugenia had already worked her way through half of the compass points, so there were four children at home but not enough food to go around. When a distant cousin of Eugenia's offered us a small plot of land to farm, we seized the opportunity and moved the family to a remote pocket of northern Njord.

The cousin was generous, charging only a nominal rent, and all went well, for a time.

Until Elise died.

Rose

I CAN'T REMEMBER WHEN I first learned that I was born as a replacement for my dead sister, Elise. It was just one of the things I knew, the way I knew other things—like the story of the stormy circumstances of my own birth, the unending catalog of Mother's superstitions, and my father's skill at drawing wind roses.

Mother was always telling me about Elise—how good she was, how she always did as she was told, how she stayed close by, and what a great help she was to Mother in the kitchen.

I never could do any of that. It was partly that curious, exploring side of me—I just had to see or taste or hold whatever it was that had caught my eye. But it was also some crazy restlessness, like my legs *needed* to be moving. I could never keep still, except once in a while, when I was with Neddy.

It was during one of the rare moments when I was being still with Neddy that I first discovered sewing.

I was very young, maybe four years old. I was sitting on Neddy's lap and he was telling me a story about Bifrost, the rainbow bridge. In the old tales, Bifrost connected our world with Asgard, the home of the gods.

Mother was sitting across from us, by the hearth. And she was mending. I'd heard the word *mending* before but didn't really know what it meant, except that it had something to do with making clothing last longer, and that it was something I'd be expected to do someday—something that even at age eight Elise had done very neatly and always sat still for. So, whatever it was, mending had seemed a vaguely threatening thing, providing Mother with yet another reason to scold me.

But as I lay back in Neddy's lap, my eyes idly fell on some breeches of mine that Mother was just beginning to work on. There was a great ugly tear in the backside that I had gotten sliding down a small waterfall earlier in the day. My near drowning at the bottom of the waterfall had left me more subdued and tired than usual. I closed my eyes sleepily, drawn into Neddy's description of Thor swinging his mighty hammer as he crossed the rainbow bridge. When I opened my eyes again, I saw that the rip in my breeches had disappeared.

I sat up, wide awake. It was magic.

It might be thought odd that I had never noticed Mother sewing up a hole before, but usually she saved her mending for later in the evening, the peaceful time of day when I was asleep.

I was by her side in a flash, all trace of sleepiness gone, the Bifrost bridge forgotten.

"Do it again," I demanded.

"Do what?" she asked, bewildered.

"Make a hole go away."

She smiled and picked up another piece of mending. She showed me how she threaded the needle, then neatly stitched up a small tear in Sonja's smock.

I watched, avidly, and then said with conviction, "I want to."

Mother hesitated a moment, weighing her natural concern about little fingers and sharp objects against the desire to encourage this unexpected interest in mending. Realizing it was a way to keep me sitting still, she agreed, and though a few drops of blood were spilled, I stubbornly kept at it, determined to master this magical talent. As I poked and prodded the fabric, I badgered Mother with questions about the needle, the pins, and where the thread came from, amazed to learn it came from my own dear sheep Bessie and all her friends and relatives.

From that evening I was hooked, and I know both Neddy and Mother were pleased. Mending was one of the few things that kept me indoors where they could keep an eye on me.

Father

"YOU TELL ME ABOUT ELISE," Rose would say to me.

I suppose that was natural enough, though at the time I did worry that Eugenia spoke of Elise too much, setting her up as some sort of ideal that little Rose would never be able to measure up to. I needn't have worried. Rosie was her own person from the beginning. She never showed any signs of changing her nature to please her mother—or anybody else.

She did ask me once to draw her a picture of Elise. Her request took me by surprise, but the more I thought about it, her curiosity was understandable. I confess I spent far too much time on the little drawing, but I think the work did me good, and Eugenia, too. It brought back many good memories.

When I showed the drawing to Rose, I couldn't tell what she thought at first. She just studied it very carefully for a long while. I had used my small supply of paints to enhance the drawing with color, and the only question Rose asked was about Elise's hair: "Is that the right color, Father?" I said yes, it was a close match, and Rose leaned down and laid a small lock of her own chestnut hair next to the yellow.

"Neddy and I are the only ones who don't have yellow hair," she said matter-of-factly.

I nodded. "Your mother's father had your color hair. That's where you and Neddy get it."

"The one who sailed on ships?"

"Yes."

She smiled. Then she asked me, as she often did, if she could see her wind rose, the one I had designed for her. Shortly after the birth of our first child, Nils Erlend, I had drawn a wind rose especially for him. And though I did not believe in the birth-direction lore, I confess that I used images from it to design the wind rose. Nils Erlend's design contained, among other things, a soaring white tern (a bird indigenous to our most northerly lands), and a ledger and quill for toting up accounts.

I did the same for each child born. Rose, in particular, loved to pore over her drawing, tracing the lines with her fingers. I was always a trifle uneasy when she did, afraid that her keen little eyes might see the lie there. It was so glaring to my own eyes and it made me sad, for to me it marred the beauty of what was certainly the best of all the wind roses I had designed.

A few times late at night when the children were asleep and there was no danger of being overheard, I brought it up to Eugenia. The lie.

"Do you not think it would be best for Rose to know the truth of her birth? She is young yet, 'twould be less..." I paused. "... less harming, to learn it now."

"I do not know what you are talking about, Arne." And truly she didn't.

She no longer saw the truth. She had erased it from her mind completely. And I wondered then if she wasn't a little touched—*brann om hode,* as they say in the old language. Indeed, the serene sureness with which she said that Rose was an east-born made me doubt my own sanity. Maybe it *had* never occurred. But of course it had.

It had been a month before Eugenia's lying-in time when she and I went out to Askoy Forest to search for herbs. We tried to do this together every fortnight or so, a habit begun sometime after we moved to the farm. It was a way to spend a few quiet hours together, uninterrupted by a child's cries or questions. When the children were young, our neighbor Torsk's wife had volunteered to watch them while we were gone, but now we could leave Nils Erlend and Selme Eva, the eldest two, in charge.

Eugenia's pregnancy had been uneventful except for the extraordinary amount of movement from the baby. Eugenia swore to me that the baby had taken it upon itself to explore every last corner of her womb. One morning after a particularly sleepless night for Eugenia, I told her, "This child will be reaching for a map before her mother's milk."

I instantly regretted my words, because Eugenia pursed her lips and said, "East-borns are not explorers."

I had a little shiver of foreboding at her words. Eugenia was so set on this unborn child being an east-born, so sure. It was like she was tempting fate.

The day we went off herb hunting was cloudy. Eugenia was keen to find some burdock as well as more feverfew. She had just come across a lush stand of burdock, and was leaning over to pick some, when she staggered slightly. "Uumph."

"Baby kicking again?" I asked.

"Like he's trying to kick his way out," she complained, straightening slowly.

"*She* needs to learn some patience," I replied with a grin. "Another four weeks to go, at least."

The sky rumbled softly.

Looking up I said, "Best we be heading back. Those clouds to the north look black."

Eugenia nodded and moved toward her basket. But before she could reach it, she leaned way over, clutching her hands to her belly. Her protracted cry drowned out the rumblings of the sky. Eugenia lowered herself to the ground, her face twisted with pain.

I was at her side in a moment, trying to keep my voice steady. "We'll start back, soon as this pain passes."

Eugenia shook her head. "No," she whistled through her teeth. "It's coming. Fast."

"But I don't..."

"You'll birth him, Arne," she said.

I had helped with all the other births and was not frightened of it. But a storm was about to break overhead and I was worried. As I set about trying to make Eugenia more comfortable on the ground, I murmured a silent prayer.

She was deep into birthing pains now and her gusting screams echoed in the Askoy Forest.

At one point her eyes flicked open and she looked around, panic-taken. "The sun, where's the sun?" she muttered, then trailed into a drawn-out moan. It may have dimly registered on me that Eugenia was concerned about the birthing direction, but whatever I was thinking went straight out of my head when I realized that I was looking at the heel of a small foot.

The baby was facing the wrong way.

A hollow panic began to burn at the bottom of my belly. I closed my eyes and thought hard. What did the midwife do when the baby faced the wrong way? Some kind of herb, I guessed...I laid a hand on Eugenia's stomach and focused my thoughts onto this unborn child. "Turn yourself about, bairn," I whispered, willing the baby to listen. But nothing happened.

"Eugenia," I said softly into her ear, "the baby is facing the wrong way. I'll need to go for help."

"No!" Eugenia cried out. "He's coming now." Her eyes roamed the bit of darkened sky she could see through the trees, looking for the sun. "Where is it? . . . What direction, Arne?"

I felt a great weight of confused emotion. It was incomprehensible to me that with both her life and the life of our child in the gravest of danger, she could think only of her cursed superstition. Then I thought to myself that perhaps she did not truly understand the peril she and the baby lay in.

"I can't do it myself, Eugenia," I said. "We need . . ."

"The sun . . ." was all Eugenia said, only the whites of her eyes showing.

Suddenly there was a great heave under my hands.

Eugenia let out a scream and lifted her body, turning slightly to the right. Large raindrops began to pelt her upturned face.

I stared in amazement at the top of my child's head. Somehow the bairn had turned itself. It was truly miraculous.

I don't remember much about the next several minutes. Then, "Push now!" I shouted at Eugenia.

And suddenly I was cupping a squalling baby in my two hands. It was small and red and wrinkled, and had a mass of dark hair. A girl. Rain washed down the puckered face. Eugenia held her arms out to us and I quickly folded our bairn into them.

She murmured soft words of welcome over and over, and kissed the clenched eyes and fists.

As she did so a crack of light filtered in through the branches above and Eugenia glanced upward. And suddenly her damp, flushed face turned a shade paler and her smile vanished. I looked up to see what she had seen, and unexpectedly saw a rainbow with the watery sun behind it. It was beautiful, I thought, and to me was a good omen. The rain still fell, lightly.

"North," she gasped in disbelief.

Then I understood. And I almost laughed out loud in relief.

"She's a north-born then, is she? Oh well, it must have been destined..."

"No!" she screamed at me. "She is *not* a north-born. She will not be a north bairn."

"Eugenia, come. There is nothing wrong with a north child. High-spirited perhaps. Besides, it is naught but superstition."

"She is Ebba."

I nodded, puzzled. "'Tis a nice name, *Ebba*. Then you will part with the practice of naming with the direction?"

"I was facing east when the birthing began."

I thought back. The sky had been dark; there was no way to tell what direction Eugenia had been facing.

"She is an east bairn and her name is Ebba," Eugenia said defiantly.

I nodded slowly, though I felt a stirring of unease.

"I will not have her die," she whispered.

Die? I thought, then remembered the *skjebne-soke*'s prediction. Death by ice and snow.

"And, Arne, you will never tell a living soul."

"Tell what, Eugenia?"

"That she is anything but an east bairn. And she *is* an east bairn." Her eyes burned wildly in her pale, wet face.

I laid my hand on her tangled hair. "You want time to think on it, Eugenia," I said.

"No." Her voice was implacable. "She is Ebba Rose, for the compass rose, because she is my last," Eugenia said firmly, her eyes intent on mine. "Promise me, Arne. You will never tell another living soul."

I hesitated. Finally I said, "I promise," because I could not bear the unhappiness behind those eyes.

She smiled then and bent her face over the baby again, murmuring her love.

Later I took the baby from her so Eugenia could rest awhile before we began our walk back to the farmhold. I lightly ran my finger over the tips of the standing-up chestnut hair of my daughter. The hair was damp and cool, and as I looked into her wrinkled little face, a thought came, unbidden, unexpected. *Nyamh, born of the rainbow.* Had I heard it in a poem long ago? One of Neddy's poems? Whatever the case, from then on, though I honored my agreement to Eugenia, in my heart I called my daughter Nyamh.

When I wrote in the family birth book of the beginning day of my eighth child, I wrote *Ebba Rose*. And when I drew the wind rose, as I had for each of my eight children, hers was the most intricate and would easily have been the most beautiful had it not been for the lie. A strange thing came over me, however, as I drew, and almost without meaning to, the drawing I did also told the truth. But it was only there for one who wanted to see it.

It was a secret, and so it remained until that catastrophic night when the white bear came to our door.

Troll Queen

IT BEGAN DURING MY FIRST journey to the green lands. The joy that seemed to steal my breath forever. And the knowing-I-must-have or I would perish.

He was a boy then. Playing a game with other children. A round red ball they threw back and forth. Laughing. He and the other children left, then he came back to find the ball, alone. Sweet, fortuitous miracle. I could have willed it so, with my arts, but was too dazzled, unthinking.

His eyesight must have been better than most soft-skins', for he saw me. Or perhaps that *was* because of my arts, used even without my knowing. I wanted him to see me.

He ran up to me. His face was so strange, with its curling-up mouth showing white teeth, and his bright green-blue eyes. He held out the ball and said, "Would you like to play?"

That is when it began, the strange breath-losing feeling. The wanting.

And so I took him. Not then, that day. But later.

My father's rage was immense. He said I had broken all the laws of our people, the most ancient, the most binding of laws.

I tried to explain to him the way I had done it, so that none of his people knew I had taken him. It was very clever, ingenious. But it was not enough, and my father set up an enchantment. Binding. And with conditions.

I hated it but could not change it. My father was still more powerful than me then. It could not be undone. Even now it cannot.

The conditions were intended as punishment, for breaking the ancient laws, but my father also wove in the opportunity for me to have that which I desired. And once the conditions were met, then the softskin boy would be mine. Forever.

White Bear

Throwing a red, red ball.
A voice like gravel.
Lost.
Then...

Huge, lumbering body.
Four legs, not two. Wide silent feet.

Smells, overwhelming.
Hunger, all the time.
And hot. Prickling, stuffed-in heat.

Need to move, always move.
Find the cold lands.
Snow and ice
White, endless.

Alone.
Lost.

A red ball. Lost.
Lost.

Neddy

ROSE WAS DIFFERENT FROM the rest of us.

Her eyes were not blue like ours but a striking purple that looks black in some lights. She was small and stocky, with gleaming hair the color of chestnuts. My hair was brown as well, but the rest of our family had fair hair, and we were all long-limbed and tall—all except for Rose. Yet despite her short legs, she managed to move faster than any of us.

She was different in other ways, too. She was noisier, more independent.

"Rose knows her own mind," Father would say. He said she was a throwback to Mother's great-grandfather, the explorer. But Mother would disagree, saying Rose was just a bit wild starting out and would settle into her true east nature as she grew up. She always pointed to Rose's love of sewing and weaving as proof of her theory. "The interests of an east-born, if I've ever seen them," she'd say confidently. "She'll settle down. You'll see." I wasn't so sure.

It was because of Rose and her short, fast-moving legs that I first learned how quickly and how easily you can lose that which you love the most. The second poem I wrote was about losing Rose. It was a clumsy effort, heavily influenced by a legendary poet's version of Freya's lament when Odur was lost to her; I relied heavily on the phrase *cruel waters*. Rose was two years old at the time and I was only six.

Mother was baking and the rest of us were scattered about, doing chores around the farm. Rose was taking her morning nap, or at least that was what Mother thought. When she went to check on her, Mother discovered that Rose's small bed was empty. Calling Rose's name, she began searching the house. Not finding her, she went outside and her shouts grew louder and more frantic. Soon we were all caught up in the search.

We spread out, each heading away from the farmhouse in a different direction. Being the youngest, I was sent northeast, as it seemed the least likely direction she would go; there was an old stone wall there that no two-year-old could climb.

Or so we thought.

There was some snow on the ground, though the day was not bitter cold. When I reached the stone wall, I climbed up (with some difficulty) and sat atop it, peering around. Despite my parents' certainty that she would never have gone this way, I wasn't so sure. I knew my baby sister well enough to know that she always did what my parents least expected. The stone wall bordered a small meadow that gradually turned into a hill. Just beyond this hill lay a much bigger, rockier crag, and on the other side of that was a steep drop into a gorge with a pool of water at the bottom.

I saw no sign of Rose in the small meadow, nor on the hill. But suddenly uneasy, I ran across both, and then climbed the rocky crag. When I got to the top, I looked down. Standing beside the pool was a large white bear. Rose dangled limp from its mouth, and they were both dripping with water.

The creature swung its head to face me, then began moving up the rocks toward me. I stood still, frozen by fear. I could see that the white bear was carrying Rose by her clothing—a bunched-up wad at the back of her neck—like a mother cat carrying a kitten. The animal stopped a stone's throw from me and gently laid Rose down. Just before it turned to move away, I caught a glimpse of the bear's eyes. The expression there was like none I'd ever encountered in an animal before. It was a look of immense sadness.

I quickly knelt beside Rose. I listened to her chest and found she was breathing steadily, but she was pale and still, and there were vivid red scrapes on her cheek and knees. Then her eyes opened and she smiled. "Neddy," she said happily, putting her arms around my neck.

I picked her up and carried her home. I told my parents where I had found her but not about the bear. I don't know why not. Perhaps I thought that none of my family would believe me, that they'd think it was a story I'd made up. But that wasn't the reason. There was something about the bear that frightened me, something beyond its bigness and fierceness, and I didn't want to think about it, let alone talk about it.

Somehow Rose had climbed over the stone wall, made her way across the meadow, climbed up both the gentle hill and the rocky crag, then slipped and slid down the other side into the icy water of the gorge. Father thought Rose must have crawled out of the water herself. But I knew it was the bear that pulled her from the pool, and that it had probably saved her life. She would have drowned if the bear had not rescued her.

Rose had no memory of the bear. I'm quite sure she never actually saw it.

And I never told anyone.

White Bear

Warm place.
Skin itches, all the time.
Plunging into cool water, relief.

Purple eyes. A child.
Up above on the rocks.
Smiling down unafraid.

I remember.
Long ago.
A ball.
A red ball.
Then nothing.
Lost.

The girl above.
Falling.

Purple eyes shut. Her face.
Floating, bruised.

Lift her up, above water.

A boy. Pale eyes, frightened.
Thin arms. Raises her to him.
Takes her away.

Alone.

Rose

FATHER TOLD ME THAT my first gift was a pair of boots, made of the soft leather of reindeer hide. Which was very fitting, for I loved wearing boots.

I always wore my older brothers' and sisters' hand-me-downs, though that never bothered me. The boots had already been resoled many times by the time I got them, but I must have put more miles on those boots than all of my brothers and sisters together.

By the time I was five or six, I had already gone missing more times than my parents could count. One of my favorite games was to imagine myself a bold explorer, like my grandfather and great-grandfather. I had made it my goal to discover and claim every square inch of the land that lay within walking distance of our farm.

On the day I first saw a white bear, I had slipped out of the house when my sister Selme was distracted by a frog I had hidden in a pan in the kitchen cupboard. I climbed the stone wall that lay to the northeast of our farm and ran through the meadow, but instead of climbing the rocky crag (which I'm told I had fallen off of and then nearly drowned when I was two years old), I headed due north. I walked a very long way, finally coming upon a small grove of trees. There, standing among them, was a white bear. It stood very still, watching me.

I stopped, staring with delight at the snow-white fur. I wasn't close enough to see its eyes clearly and what expression they held, but I was too young to be afraid, so I smiled widely at the animal. It gazed at me for a short time, then turned and lumbered away. I tried following, but it had vanished. Soon I got hungry and turned toward home.

I didn't tell Mother and Father about seeing the white bear, especially Mother, because I knew she'd insist on keeping me even closer to home. "You see!" she'd say. "Dangerous wild animals are out there. It's not safe."

I told Neddy, though, and was disappointed at his reaction. He frowned and said in that superior, older brother tone I hated, "You mustn't go anywhere near a white bear, Rose. They are dangerous and fierce creatures, with long, sharp teeth that will gobble you up. They are always hungry and they move very fast." He acted like he was some kind of expert on white bears.

I didn't pay any attention to him. From then on the white bear was my imaginary companion on all my explorations. I would pretend that I was riding along on its white-fur back, the two of us a fierce duo conquering and claiming new lands by the score.

I spent much of my childhood longing, in vain, to see a white bear again. It was extremely rare to see white bears in our part of the country. They were ice bears, *isbjorn*, that usually made their home in the snowy north.

White Bear

Watching for the child.
The girl with purple eyes.
Purple eyes.
And her smiling mouth.

Standing in the trees, watching her.
The girl.
Taller.
Unafraid.

She moves toward me.
Purple eyes, trusting.
Cannot.
Not safe for her.
Hunger.
Hunger.
Hunger.

Must go.
Quickly.
To feed.
Now.

Then return.

Neddy

WHEN ROSE WAS FIVE, she began to weave. The first thing she made was a belt with a crude design of a white bear. Those were her two passions: weaving (or sewing) and exploring with her imaginary white bear.

Inside the house she could always be found weaving belts on her small, rigid heddle loom. When we had more belts than we could ever use (some of the farm animals even sported Rose's belts), Mother taught Rose to work the household loom. By age eight Rose was her older sisters' equal when it came to weaving.

Then one day, taking a basketful of eggs to Widow Hautzig, Rose laid eyes on the widow's loom. Widow Hautzig was a local craftswoman who had a small business weaving coats and rugs and various other items to sell both in nearby Andalsnes and to wandering merchants who would take them to fairs and markets farther afield. To Rose, who knew only our own rough one at home, the widow's loom was large and impressive. It was twice as tall as Rose, and the wood was polished and carved with simple designs.

Unfortunately, Widow Hautzig was a grouchy old woman with no patience at all for a small, wild girl desperate to learn all about her beautiful loom. More than anything in the world, Rose longed for a loom of her own, a fine big one like the widow's. But she knew that was impossible, that Father would never be able to afford it. Still, Rose was stubborn, and she would not rest until she had found a way to get the Widow Hautzig to let her use her loom.

When she was nine Rose found out that Widow Hautzig had a weakness for chanterelle mushrooms. So Rose trained her favorite dog, Snurri, to sniff out chanterelles in the forest. After much hard work she struck a deal: In exchange for a weekly basket of chanterelle mushrooms, Widow Hautzig would teach Rose how to work her loom. Though the lessons were short and very disagreeable (often Rose would come home in tears over some gibe of the widow's), still Rose was a determined pupil, and before long the baskets of chanterelles were being traded for a chance to actually do her own weaving on the loom.

She could only do this during the very short breaks between Widow Hautzig's own projects, some of which took a long time to complete. And Rose would have had no time at all on the loom were it not for Widow Hautzig's rheumatism. When her rheumatism was acting up, the widow would take a long rest, sometimes even as much as a fortnight if it was a particularly bad bout.

"Thank God for Widow Hautzig's rheumatism," Rose would say every night before bed. Mother once overheard her and scolded her, so Rose was careful to whisper those words to herself from then on.

Even with Widow Hautzig's rheumatism, Rose never could weave anything that required more than a few days' work. Then, one day, as she was trying to discourage Snurri from digging under Widow Hautzig's storage hut, Rose saw something through a crack in the woodwork of the hut. There were no windows in the hut, but it was not locked, and without asking permission, Rose entered the small building. The inside was cloaked with dust and cobwebs, but Rose barely noticed. Her eyes were riveted by a good-sized loom leaning against the far wall of the hut. The frame listed at a precarious angle; the warp beam and heddle rods were splintered; there appeared to be no crossbeam at all; and a tangle of decayed and unraveled warp thread sprouted from top and bottom, but Rose was not discouraged.

It took Rose a long time and many baskets of chanterelles to convince Widow Hautzig to let her try her hand at fixing up the broken-down loom, which had been the castoff of an old aunt of the widow's. In return the widow made Rose clean the filthy old storage hut until it was spotless.

Rose then cajoled Father and me, as well as Willem, to help her repair the loom. Widow Hautzig offered no assistance, and even insisted that it not be removed from her property. She also complained unceasingly of the small amount of noise we made, hammering and sanding and such.

I was appalled when Widow Hautzig did not give Rose the loom outright, since she had no use for it herself. What rankled even more was that the nasty woman even continued to demand chanterelle fees for the use of the loom we repaired, and made Rose work in that window-less, unheated hut.

Nevertheless, I'd never seen Rose so happy as when she could grab a few moments to go off and work on the loom.

I wrote a poem about Widow Hautzig. It began

Hautzig the weaver, queen of the dead.
The strands in her loom dripping with red.
Lips dry as bone, her hair made of snakes,
The souls of her victims to Hel she does take.

Well, maybe I exaggerated. But only a little.

Rose

THE FIRST THING I MADE on Widow Hautzig's loom was a table runner. It had a simple reindeer design in the weave, and I was absurdly proud of it. My next projects were a shawl for Mother and head scarves for my three sisters. Then I made a jacket for Neddy and a pair of breeches for Father.

The last thing I made on that loom was for me. A cloak. It took me nearly half a year to finish. It was during this time that things went so wrong with the farm.

Father told me the bad luck began the year I was born. The barley crop failed, and that setback was followed by an unusually harsh winter that killed off our largest sow. Since then there had been blight that killed our fruit trees, a sickness that went through our poultry, not to mention a heartbreaking series of crop failures. By the summer when I was working on my cloak, there was so little to go around that it didn't seem right to be hunting chanterelles for Widow Hautzig; nor was there much time for weaving, other than that which was strictly necessary. We were all working so hard just to keep from starving. And there was no extra wool for spinning.

For a long time I had been in the habit of scrounging for tufts of wool. I would find them stuck to fences and the bark of trees. But it really wasn't enough, and it was only thanks to Father that I was able to finish my cloak at all. He brought me wool, clumps that he had bargained for from neighbors, and he insisted that I take breaks from chores to go chanterelle hunting with Snurri.

Widow Hautzig's tongue grew sharper over the years. She was unsympathetic to our ill fortune, sometimes even openly cruel about it, making nasty remarks about my father's farming abilities. I would have stopped going altogether had I not been on the verge of finishing my cloak. It was the best piece I had ever made. As our life got worse and worse at the farm, I even thought I might sell it, to bring in badly needed money, but Father wouldn't hear of it. He said the cloak belonged to me. The next thing I made, he suggested, we would sell.

I showed the cloak to Neddy first. I met him coming home from Widow Hautzig's, the material folded in my arms. It was a sunny day, with a brisk autumn wind blowing, and I was feeling a little breathless, irrationally excited about the thing I was carrying.

He knew at once. And smiled his dear, slow smile. "Show me," he said simply.

I started to unfold the cloak, then, impatient, I shook it out. It caught the breeze, billowing up between us. Then it flapped into Neddy's face and we both laughed. He took hold of his end and I held tight to mine. We lowered the cloak and Neddy saw the pattern for the first time.

"A wind rose," he said, then realizing, "*your* wind rose."

I nodded. "Do you think Father will like it?"

"Of course. It is beautiful."

I laughed again. I couldn't help it, for I knew he was right.

"Look," I said, pulling the cloak downward and gesturing for Neddy to lay it on the grass. "Now I'll never be lost, no matter how far I travel." Glancing quickly up at the sun, I pulled off my boots and, in my stockinged feet, positioned myself at the center of the cloak. "See, I am the compass needle," I explained somewhat proudly.

"Put it on," Neddy urged. He took the cloak from me and fastened it at the neck.

The cloth felt warm and solid and good around me.

"Fit for a queen," Neddy said, holding up the ends and pretending to be my courtier. I laughed, remembering the games we'd played as children; I'd be Queen Rose and he would be my loyal wizard or squire or tutor, whatever role he felt like playing that day.

Then he let go of the cloak, and the wind grabbed it again. Neddy tried several times to catch hold of it, and we were both laughing until tears came into our eyes.

It was then I saw the bear. Neddy and I were standing near a thick cluster of whitebeam trees, and it was through the trees that I saw it. That is, I saw its eyes and could make out a faint blur of white fur through the branches. We looked full into each other's eyes for what seemed a long time. Neddy was still going on about Queen Rose, but his voice faded and I was aware of only those black eyes.

I should have been frightened, with a large wild animal not fifty feet away, but I was not.

White Bear

Unafraid.
Her mouth. A smile.

Piercing.
So long ago, so much lost.
Alone.
Always alone.

A cloak. Catching the wind.
Colors.
North.
South.
East.
West.

Purple eyes.
North south east west.
East.
Unafraid.

Neddy

ROSE WHISPERED SOMETHING, but I couldn't hear it. Her eyes were fixed on the trees that lay a stone's throw away.

"A white bear, Neddy," she said, louder.

But by the time I turned to look, there was nothing there.

Rose dragged me over to the whitebeams and the two of us examined the ground for markings of a large animal. "You believe me, don't you?" Rose asked. There was nothing to show a bear had been there.

And yet I believed her, though I did not say so.

"'Tis almost suppertime," I said abruptly, and began to lead the way back. Rose took off her cloak and, folding it as she walked, trotted along beside me.

"What is it, Neddy?" she said.

"Nothing," I replied, trying to keep my voice normal. "It's gotten late..."

But I was lying. I was frightened. Not of the white bear, at least not for myself.

"Are you sure?" she persisted.

"Yes."

Rose gave me one last sidelong glance.

"I wish you had seen it, Neddy. It was so large, and its eyes..." she said. "I get this feeling it wanted something. And that it was sad."

"Must be your imagination," I said, making my voice light and teasing. "This time of year it's still too warm for a white bear. And you know they don't come this far south, even in winter. Perhaps it was a white doe. Their eyes sometimes look sad."

But of course I was lying. For I had seen the eyes of a white bear, that time years before. And I felt sure it was the same one.

I knew about white bears. After that day when I had looked into the eyes of the white bear that saved Rose, I set out to become an expert on them. I would interview everyone I came into contact with, to see if they had ever seen a white bear or if they knew anything of white bears. Most knew nothing. My main source of information turned out to be a peddler who had traveled into the far north and had once even been on a Saami expedition of white-bear hunters.

"Before going out on the ice to hunt the white bear," the peddler told me, "the Saami taught me. They said I must know the *isbjorn* by heart if I was going to hunt him. They called him the Great Wanderer or Ghost Bear. Other names they used are: He Who Walks Without a Shadow. Ice Giant. Nanook. The Traveler. Great White. Sea Bear." The peddler paused, letting those names settle into my memory.

"The white bear is a solitary wanderer, never moving with a pack or even a mate. He walks on all fours, but when he stands he is nearly ten feet tall." The peddler raised one hand as far as he could above his head.

"He lives by his sense of smell," the peddler continued. "There is a Saami saying about white bears: 'A pine needle fell in the forest. The hawk saw it. The deer heard it. The white bear smelled it.'

"His eyes are black. His nose is black. His paws are black and the five claws on each of his paws are black. The rest of him is snow white."

I listened to the peddler, my eyes held by a scar carved into the skin just below his hairline. Maybe a white bear had given him that scar, with a thrust of black claw.

I learned more. I learned that the white bear's habitat lay well to the north of us, in the region where snow can remain on the ground for twelve months of the year. It is true that an occasional white bear had been known to travel as far south as our farmhold, but only very rarely and only during the deep winter months.

I learned that the white bear's eyesight is not as good as its sense of smell, but that it is still very strong. The bear has an extra eyelid to protect its eyes from snow glare, and it can see underwater and through a driving blizzard.

I learned that of all bears, the white bear is the most fur-clad, every inch of it covered except its nose and paw pads, and the fur is dense and soft. It has forty-two teeth, including long, sharp canines for piercing flesh. It eats meat but can also survive on berries and grasses if it has to. The white bear's strength is legend. It is said it can kill with one swipe of its paw.

I even wrote a white-bear poem. It began

Ghost bear wanders, always alone;
king of the north,
dispensing death from his traveling throne.

It was shortly after this effort that I decided I wouldn't be a poet after all.

Father

THE DAY ROSE CAME HOME with her finished cloak she seemed different, as though something had happened, something important. Neddy, too. They were both quiet, inside themselves. It didn't seem to be a quarrel between them. I asked Rose if Widow Hautzig had been unkind or hurtful that day, but she said, "No worse than usual," and then shook out her cloak to show me.

I stared at the cloth, amazed. I was hardly able to fathom that my own Nyamh, my Rose, had created such a thing. It had more color and inspiration than anything Widow Hautzig could even have dreamed.

"Your wind rose," I said.

"Yes, Father. I hope you do not mind that I copied it."

"Of course not. It is..." I faltered, suddenly realizing that the lie was there, too. Unknowing, Rose had woven the lie into her cloak.

I began speaking again, expressing my admiration for her artistry. I think Rose sensed something, though, for I felt her puzzled glance on me several times as everyone gathered around to exclaim over the cloak. Eugenia prepared a special meal that night, scraping together what she could from our sparse larder, in honor of Rose's accomplishment.

I think that day, the day Rose brought home the cloak, was the last our family knew of happiness. She was almost fifteen years old then, but we had been suffering ill luck for a long time, since the year she was born. Occasionally the thought would cross my mind that our "luck" had been affected by the lie of Rose's birth, but I would quickly berate myself for being as superstitious as Eugenia.

I was not cut out to be a farmer. When we first moved from Bergen to the farm, we were fortunate, but when things went poorly, my decisions made them go still worse. By the autumn when Rose finished her cloak, we were barely scraping by and my children knew more of hunger than I could sometimes endure.

One of the factors that had contributed mightily to our reversal of fortunes was the fact that Eugenia's cousin, who had fallen on hard times of his own, had been forced to sell all his landholdings. Our farm had been purchased by a prosperous merchant who lived a distance away, in the city of Oslo. It was more than a month's journey by horse to Oslo, and thus we never saw the merchant, nor even heard directly from him. All of our communications came by messenger from the merchant's deputy, a man called Mogens. Our rent did not go up right away, but slowly, over time, it did rise, and eventually the rent was nearly equal to what we could produce, with very little left for us. Over the years our two eldest children left the farm. Nils Erlend set out for Danemark, where he hoped to make his way, and Selme Eva married an ironworker and moved with him to a village in Njord far distant from us. We rarely heard from either of them.

The day after Rose brought home her cloak, we received a final blow. A letter arrived from Mogens saying that due to lack of payment of rent, we must vacate the farm in less than a month.

Except for the cousin who had originally owned the farm and Eugenia's sister, who had emigrated to Iseland after her husband deserted her, there was no one left alive in Eugenia's family. We would not have considered burdening our two eldest children with the dire news, especially since neither of them was doing much more than getting by. The only people we could turn to were my family.

With a heavy heart I composed a letter to my brother, who ran the family farm. I was not at all sure he would take us in, for we had fallen out of touch many years earlier. Even if he did take pity on us, it was a long journey to the place where I grew up in central Njord, and I worried that we would not even have the wherewithal to undertake it. We had already sold the wagon and all the remaining farm animals just to cover our debt to the man who owned the farm.

But as I looked upon the gaunt faces and worn, frayed clothing of my family, I knew there was no other choice.

There were moments during those dark days when I was lost in despair. I believed myself to be a failure as a husband and a father, and was submerged in the guilt of what I had brought my family to. I even thought of ending my own life.

Eugenia was my anchor then. Despite her superstitious notions, she was a strong and loyal woman, and it was she who kept us all together and alive in a way that was truly remarkable. Never did she blame or castigate me, or rail against her fate. Somehow she made every spoonful of food stretch to two, and found ways to make even the most threadbare of clothing serve.

It is also true that she was wont to come up with tortured reasons, based on superstition, for why our fortunes had turned so ill. Still, she stolidly shouldered the burden of our poverty and kept us going.

Then Sara, our third eldest, fell ill.

Neddy

WHEN SARA GOT SICK I saw the fear come into Mother. Up until then she had been calm and steady. But I knew that Sara's sickness brought back to her (and to Father) the memory of Elise's death.

There were five of us children living at home then. Myself, Rose, Sara, Sonja, and Willem.

We had been waiting to hear back from Father's brother, who was our only hope at the time. But it became clear that even if he agreed to take us in, we would not be able to make the journey, not with Sara so ill.

Thankfully, our neighbor Torsk offered us a temporary home so that we would not be without shelter when the landowner came to evict us. But Torsk had also been hard hit by the weather, though he at least owned his own farm. And we knew we could not strain his meager resources by staying too long.

I had made up my own mind that, like my oldest brother, Nils, I would leave home and seek a way to earn my living. I would then send all I earned back to my family. My long held dream of one day studying with scholars in one of the big cities was gone.

Mother was with Sara constantly, completely unmindful of her own comfort and health. Father wandered around the farmhold in a daze, looking as though he had aged twenty years. We had little more than a fortnight before we had to leave the farm.

The cold hit early that autumn. This was the last blow in a series of terrible setbacks. We had been slammed with an early blizzard before the last harvest (what there was of it) could be gathered. I think we were numb by then, lacking even the spirit to lament our misfortunes. It warmed enough several days later to melt the snow, but the damage had been done. What had followed then was our typical autumn weather—a succession of blustery, chilly rainstorms.

It was during just such a storm-drenched night, as we huddled around the hearth, that we heard a scratching sound coming from our front door. Mother was at the far end of the great room, sitting by Sara, who had just fallen into a fitful sleep.

The sound came again, and after exchanging a look with Father, I went to the door and cautiously opened it a crack, wondering who or what could be out on such a night.

All I saw was a white blur before the door was flung wide. I stepped back and something large and wet brushed by me.

I turned to stare at an enormous white bear standing in the middle of the great room.

The wind howled in, spewing cold rain, but we were unaware of it.

"Close the door." It was a massive, strange voice. And though it seemed impossible, I knew at once the voice was coming from the white bear.

My sister Sonja swayed and looked like she might faint. I moved to her quickly, putting an arm around her shoulders. She was trembling.

Rose went to the door and shut it.

It was like a dream, gazing at the immense animal that had entered our home. Standing erect on all four feet, he was as tall as me, and water dripped off him onto the wooden floor. And I remembered water dripping off white fur from long ago.

I guessed from the moment he brushed by me that this was the white bear I had seen as a child, the one that had saved my sister Rose. If I had had any doubts, they were dispelled when I looked into those black eyes. It was the same bear. And I was filled with a terrible foreboding.

He gazed around the room, from one to the other of us. His eyes stayed longest on Rose. Then he turned to Father.

"If you will give me your youngest daughter..." The eerie huge voice echoed in the room. He spoke slowly, pausing between each word, as if the act of speaking was difficult, almost painful for him. "Then the one who lies near death will be made well again. And you will be no longer poor but wealthy, and will live in comfort and ease."

The silence in the room was punctuated only by the sounds of the storm outside and an occasional crackle from the hearth fire.

The white bear spoke again. "If you will give me your youngest daughter, then the one who lies near death will be..." And he repeated the words he had said before, again with the same painful slowness.

Mother had risen from her place beside Sara's bed. "You would make our Sara well?" she said in a near whisper. Her eyes burned with a look of desperate hope.

"Yes." It was a growl.

"How?"

"If you will give me your youngest daughter, then the one who lies near death..." And he seemed on the verge of saying it all over again.

But Father stepped forward. He looked like someone who had just gathered his wits after a blow. "Enough," he said loudly. "You shall not have Rose. Or any one of us."

The white bear turned to look at Father, and then swung his head in Rose's direction. "Do not decide now," he said, and this time he was speaking directly to her. "I will return in seven days. I will hear your answer then."

He turned and made his way to the door. And though I had seen Rose shut it securely, the door seemed to open of its own volition and the bear went through, disappearing into the night.

Father quickly crossed to the door and shut it with a slam.

We were all stunned and quiet. Had it not been for the large puddle of water in the middle of the room where the bear had been standing, I think that, except for Rose and Mother, none of us would have believed the thing had happened at all.

"Arne," said Mother.

"Father," came Rose's voice.

They spoke at the same time, but Father shook his head.

"We will not talk further of this," he said, his voice deep, with a dangerous, implacable tone. "It is madness and sorcery and we will not be part of it. Not for any wild promises or guarantees of riches."

"But Arne," my mother said. "Think of our Sara ..."

"No!" he thundered. I couldn't recall ever hearing Father raise his voice to Mother before. It was almost as shocking as the talking white bear.

Mother, her face white and strained, said, "But we must honor his request. If we do not 'twould only bring the greatest ill fortune and calamity upon us all."

"Eugenia," Father said, and his face was taut with rage, "we will talk no further of this. Go to Sara. The cold air can have done her little good."

And Mother complied, but despite the frightening anger in Father, there was still that burning hopeful light in her eyes, and I knew she would not leave the matter as it stood.

I went for a shawl for Sonja, who was trembling, then I crossed to Rose. She had seated herself in a chair by the fire, and I sat beside her. She was not shivering, though her skin felt cold to the touch when I took her hand. And she, too, had an expression in her eyes that frightened me. It was not hope but excitement, mingled with traces of confusion and fear.

"What can it mean, Neddy?" she said in wonder.

I shook my head.

"When I was little, Mother told me stories about animals that could speak. I didn't believe her, not really, but now . . ."

I remained silent.

"Did you see how his fur glowed?"

"It was wet from the rain," I said abstractedly.

"A white bear," she breathed. "Just like the one I had as an imaginary companion when I was a child."

I leaned over to poke the fire.

"And did you see his eyes? Oh, Neddy, do you think he can be the same bear I saw the other day? I think it is."

I shook my head, for some reason wanting to discourage the idea. But then Father came up, interrupting us. "There are still dishes to be cleaned, and I think then we had all better go to bed."

We both stood up, obediently. Then Father caught

Rose's hand. "I will not let any wild beast take you, Rose," he said to her. "You know that. I will always keep you safe."

"But Father, what of Sara?"

"We will care for her. She will get better."

Rose shook her head. "We should at least have listened to . . ."

"No," Father broke in decisively.

Later, as we made our way to our beds, Rose whispered, "Why does the white bear want me, Neddy?"

I shook my head. I could not guess, except that somehow I felt sure it had something to do with the sadness in the animal's eyes. Some great need.

Rose

DURING THE DAYS THAT followed, I felt nervy, jangled. I jumped at the slightest noise and could not concentrate on anything for longer than a minute or two.

We were all on edge.

Father forbade any discussion of the white bear and his request. I could hear him quarreling about it at night with Mother. They tried to keep their voices low, but one night I could not help overhearing what they said.

"I will not sacrifice one daughter for another," Father said.

"'Tis not a matter of that," Mother replied. "And if we do nothing, Sara will surely die."

"What makes you so certain that this white bear will heal Sara?"

Mother spoke softly in reply and I could not make out the words.

But then Father cut into the low rumble of her voice. "Are you truly willing to put Rose's life in the hands of a wild creature of the north for a questionable promise of miracles? It is folly. If Rose goes with the white bear, we will surely never see her again. To barter her life for Sara's health—well, it is not even a matter for debate."

As the seven days passed, Sara got no worse, but neither did she get better. The local healer said there was nothing more we could do other than continue the herbal infusions we had been giving her. We went about the business of readying ourselves for the move to neighbor Torsk's farm until such time as we would hear from Father's family.

I thought mostly of the white bear; I could think of little else. And I had made up my mind that despite my father's objections, I must accept the bear's offer.

I tried speaking about it with Neddy one afternoon as we folded our meager supply of linens into a trunk.

"I will go with the white bear," I blurted out.

Neddy looked at me with horror.

"I cannot stand by and let Sara die," I continued, my words spilling over one another in my haste to make Neddy understand, "not when there is something I can do to prevent it."

"Rose," Neddy implored, "you must not even consider it!"

"And the bear has said that he will take away this poverty into which we have sunk," I said, ignoring him. "Just think, Neddy, Father could make maps again. And you, you could go to Bergen and study with scholars, the way you have always dreamed."

"No!" Neddy said forcefully. "Even if the creature could bring such a thing to be, it would not be worth the price you must pay."

I was silent. I could see that talking it out with Neddy would be fruitless. I must keep my thoughts and plans to myself.

Aside from the more logical reasons for going with the white bear, I had another reason. And that was simply that I *wanted* to go. It was madness, I knew, to consider going off into unknown lands with a wild beast that would most likely devour me at journey's end. I did not want to die. And yet, I wanted to go.

I knew Father would never agree to it.

As for Mother, it confused me to hear her arguing in favor of accepting the white bear's offer. Did she love me so little? If it were Elise the bear had asked for, would Mother have been so eager to hand her over?

On the sixth day after the visit of the white bear, I returned early from Widow Hautzig's. As I entered the outer room of the farmhouse, I chanced to hear Father and Mother talking loudly from inside the great room. I thought they were arguing again, and was on the verge of making my presence known to them when I heard Father say, his voice anguished, "It is nonsense, I know, but I keep thinking that it is the lie of Rose's birth that is behind this."

Lie? I felt the hairs on my neck rise.

Mother's voice came back, sharp. "There is no lie. She is Ebba Rose."

"Eugenia, she is no east child. You and I both know it."

"She is Ebba Rose." The words were said slowly, implacably, as if to a half-wit.

"No," and Father's voice was loud. "She is Nyamh."

"Nyamh?" There was a pause. "She is not Nyamh." Mother's voice was now cold. "I thought you did not even believe in birth direction. Superstition, you always say."

"Nor do I," Father answered. "At least I did not think I did. My mind is all turned around these days. But I will tell you, when I first held her I looked into her eyes and she was Nyamh. And I have always called her so, in my heart."

The tangled truth behind my father's words began to unravel itself inside me.

Nyamh begins with an *N*. *North*. I had been conceived to take Elise's place. But I was a north bairn. I had filled my own place on the compass rose. I felt a great excitement stir in my chest. And then, great anger. My breath grew short and my cheeks were flaming.

My father and mother had lied to me all those years. I moved toward them, without thinking, and in doing so my elbow caught a wooden bowl, which clattered to the floor.

"Who's that? Is someone there?" called Father.

Suddenly I did not want to see their faces. Not then. I needed to think. I bolted out of the house, refastening my cloak against the cold autumn day.

As I ran I became aware that, in addition to the anger, a sense of exhilaration was growing in me, the feeling of a puzzle piece falling into place. I was a north. It was obvious. No wonder Mother had tried so hard to keep me close, to mold me into another Elise.

Mother's feelings about north people were well known to us all. Every time she heard of some wild or destructive act by a stranger, she would inevitably shake her head with disapproval and say, "That's a north-born, mark my words."

I knew that my birth had come on suddenly on a stormy afternoon. Mother must have fabricated a truth she could live with. And Father had gone along with it. "The lie of Rose's birth...Nyamh."

I felt as though I no longer knew my parents. Or myself.

Then I thought of the wind rose Father had designed for me. It was a lie as well. I tore off the cloak I had made and spread it on the ground.

I knelt by the design. Yes, there was the sun rising. But the white form I had always thought to be a cloud was a bear. I could see it now, upside down. White bear, *isbjorn*, stood for north. Father had not been able to help himself. The truth was there, too. Truth and lie, side by side.

Nyamh. He called me Nyamh when first he held me as a babe. Ebba was a lie. I had never liked the name Ebba, I thought, smiling grimly to myself. Was Rose a lie, too? No, Rose was at the center of the wind rose. One need be no direction at all to be Rose.

And then it struck me. Did anyone else know? Was it just Mother and Father's secret, or...? Did Neddy know?

For some reason I had to find out.

Neddy was at our neighbor's, helping repair a fence. I picked up my cloak and draped it over my arm. I did not want to wear it anymore. Shivering, I began making my way in the direction of Torsk's farm.

Neddy

IT WAS NEARING TWILIGHT when we finished with the fence. I bade good evening to Torsk and watched for a moment as the big man shambled away. He was a good soul. I could not help but wonder what he would say if I told him that six days before a white bear had come into our great room and asked to take Rose away in exchange for Sara's restored health and a life of ease. I could picture Torsk's expression, a sort of gentle bewilderment; then he would smile and say, "One of your stories, is it, Master Ned?"

It sounded like a story, one murmured by the fireside to an audience of wide-eyed children on a winter night. One of the old tales, of Loki, shape-shifted into a white bear, demanding the life of one maiden to buy eternal happiness for Midgard, the land of the humans. It was not the kind of thing that truly happened in ordinary life.

For all that I loved the old tales of magic, I did not actually want there to be talking animals and mysterious requests on storm-tossed nights. Such things were for stories and ought to remain there.

During those six days I tried very hard to convince myself that it had not happened. That we had all had some sort of collective dream. It could have been that way. It was no stranger a notion than what had actually unfolded in our great room.

But I knew it had happened. And that the next day the white bear would return.

Though we had not spoken together alone since that night, I had been watching Rose and suspected that she was still planning to go with the bear. The thought of her leaving filled me with an overpowering ache, and I vowed to myself that I would not let her go—no matter what.

As I rounded the bend to our farmhold, I was surprised to see Rose coming toward me. The air was cold, and yet I noticed she was carrying her cloak instead of wearing it. I felt a tremor of alarm. As she drew nearer I could see she was very pale, and there was a wildness about her eyes. At first I thought she had been crying but could see no trace of tears.

"Rose, what is it? What has happened?" I queried, fearing that Sara might have gotten worse.

Rose was staring at me strangely, as if trying to read something in my face.

Abruptly she took her cloak in her hands, and as she had done on that day that now seemed so long ago, she shook it out, splaying it wide. The afternoon was still and cold, and the wind did not catch the cloak as before. Carefully she spread it out on the ground, then looked up at me again.

"Rose?"

Still she did not speak.

"You're shivering. Why do you not put the cloak on?"

"Did you know?" she asked, her voice higher than usual.

"Know what?"

"The lie? 'The lie of Rose's birth.' The lie in there." She jabbed a finger toward the cloak.

I stared back at her, bewildered.

"The lie, Neddy. I was born for Elise. East. But I am Nyamh." She said the name defiantly.

I still did not understand, although some glimmer of the truth was beginning to dawn on me.

"I am north, Neddy, not east. A true north." And she knelt and pointed to the white cloud at the north of the wind rose in her cloak. "A white bear for north," she said.

So she had learned the truth at last. A truth that I had guessed at a long time before.

She read it in my face. "You knew! Didn't you, Neddy?"

I was silent a moment. Then I nodded. I saw tears come into her eyes, though she blinked them away angrily.

"At least...I didn't *truly* know," I said quickly. "I guessed."

"Why did you say nothing?"

"Because . . . it was only a guess, and I . . ." How could I explain that I felt the same way as Mother? I did not want Rose to be a north if it meant she would always be going away.

Her eyes suddenly blazed. "I do not know you, any of you." And to my horror she grabbed up her cloak, and using her teeth to make the first tear, she savagely tore it in two. Then she took each of the two halves and ripped them again.

"North, south, east, west," she chanted, "who's the one you love the best? . . ." She tossed the ruined cloak at me and stalked away.

I picked up the torn pieces and followed after her.

"Rosie!" I called. "Please wait."

She slowed. I put a hand on her arm. "I'm sorry. I thought I must be wrong. I could not imagine Mother and Father lying about such a thing."

She turned and I pulled her to me, holding her close. She was trembling so violently that I took off my own coat and wrapped it around her. "It's all right," I murmured. Gradually her shaking lessened.

Then she looked up at me and said, "I mean to go with the white bear, Neddy."

"No," I said sharply. "You cannot."

"You won't change my mind," she said. "Perhaps it was always my destiny." She pointed to the topmost piece of torn cloak that I carried. It was the section with the design of the white bear.

86

I stared at the white shape. "You must not go," I said. "Father will not allow it," I added somewhat lamely.

"He cannot stop me."

"Please do not set your mind on it, Rose. Not yet. Maybe Sara will be better in the morning."

Rose was silent, then nodded. "I will think on it. But in exchange you must promise me, Neddy, that you will not tell Father that I have learned the truth. Nor tell him that I am thinking of going with the white bear."

Clutching at these small shreds of hope, I agreed.

When we returned it was almost suppertime and everyone was busy. No one noticed that Rose wore my coat and that I carried the four pieces of her cloak. Silently I offered Rose the pile of fabric, but she shook her head and, handing me my coat, went to help with the meal. Not certain what else to do, I stuffed the pieces into my coat pockets.

That evening Father broke his silence about the white bear.

"Tomorrow we will do as we always do," he said, "but in the evening only I will stay to give the bear his answer. The rest of you will go to neighbor Torsk's farmhold. We will think of some reason to tell Torsk, perhaps repair work that I must do on my own, work that would disturb Sara. And you will all stay with Torsk until I come for you."

Several voices spoke at once, objecting to this plan. Mother felt strongly that both she and Rose should be with Father when the bear came. And Willem and I both insisted that *we* should be there, in case the animal should attack.

Then Rose spoke out, her voice quiet and firm. "I must stay with you, Father."

"No," Father said, his own voice just as firm. "I will not allow it."

"The white bear may require an answer from me."

"She is right, Arne," Mother put in.

"No," he said again.

Rose took a breath, spots of color in her cheeks. "If I am not here when the white bear comes," she said calmly, "is it not possible that he may come to neighbor Torsk's, putting him in danger as well?"

Father shook his head, but I could see doubt come into his eyes. There was silence for a few moments and then finally he said, "Very well. You may stay."

"Let me stay, too, Father," I said quickly.

He nodded curtly. I wondered if he, too, feared what Rose might do and wanted two of us there to stop her should the worst occur.

"You must arm yourselves, at least," my brother Willem said.

Father nodded agreement. "Although, in truth, I do not believe the bear will harm us," he said. "Nor do I think he would take Rose by force. If that were his aim he would have done it when first he came."

I had been watching Rose closely, especially when she told Father that she must stay with him, to give the bear her answer. I had never known Rose to lie, especially to Father. It kindled in me the hope that she *had* reconsidered and would not go with the white bear. But then I remembered the lie Father told Rose, and her anger, and I was no longer sure of anything.

Father

WHEN MAPMAKERS OF OLD were faced with charting an unknown area, one that had proved unreachable, the temptation was to fabricate, to look into the imagination. They would depict the area as being inhabited by fearsome, man-devouring monsters, especially in the vast reaches of the sea. Master Esbjorn found the practice antiquated and unacceptable. He believed that if the truth was not known, the paper should be left blank.

I was like a long-ago mapmaker. When faced with uncharted territory—a talking beast in my home—I saw evil. And when my wife spoke of giving in to the request of an evil creature, I saw evil in her, too. To willingly sacrifice one daughter for another was an abomination. For the first time in our married life, I began to doubt my Eugenia.

We borrowed a small cart from Torsk to transport Sara. We told him that I needed to make repairs on the chimney before the landlord came to take over his property. It would be a sooty, messy job, and it would be safest to have at least part of the family move to Torsk's farmhold sooner rather than later. He was willing and so we bundled Sara into the cart. Fortunately, it was a fair day, though cold, and she was no worse for the trip.

Rose, Neddy, and I made our way back to the farm in silence. Eugenia had left a pot of soup on the hearth for us, along with a small loaf of brown bread. Rose deliberately laid out a tablecloth, one she had made herself, and Neddy set the table.

We ate the modest meal in silence. The minutes ticked by.

After we had finished eating, and had washed and put away the dishes, Rose took up some sewing while Neddy read. I aimlessly poked the fire, then sat down to look over our accounts, though my mind was not on my task.

It grew late—later, I thought, than when the white bear had come before. Hope began to flicker in me that he would not come after all. Perhaps a hunter had felled him. Or perhaps he had changed his mind. I was about to break the silence in the room to give voice to these thoughts, when there came a noise from the door.

This time no one opened the door. It swung open on its own. And standing there, the moon shining bright behind her, was Eugenia.

I let out a deep breath, then crossed to her.

"What are you doing here, wife?" I said, my voice ragged. "Is it Sara? . . ."

She stared at me, then shook her head sharply in the negative. She sidestepped away and went to Rose. "Daughter," she said, "I do not want to lose you. I have always tried to keep you close. But you must go with the white bear."

"Eugenia!" I shouted.

"You will use all your wits and your east practicality. And you will not be lost to us, not forever. I know it." She took Rose's hand as she spoke.

Rose was pale. She stood. Then she deliberately removed her hand from Eugenia's and stepped away from her.

"'East'?" Rose whispered. "'East'..." she said again, louder, shaking her head. "No, not 'east,' Mother. *North*." And her last word filled the room.

Then the white bear was at the door. And before any of us could move, Rose had crossed to him. She reached behind a large wooden trunk that stood by the door and drew out a small knapsack. She must have hidden it there earlier.

"I will go with you," Rose said to the bear, and I watched, unbelieving, as the animal's great paws flashed and Rose was suddenly astride the bear's back as if he were some enormous horse.

The white bear turned and disappeared through the doorway.

Neddy let out a cry and ran after them, grabbing his coat as he went.

I started after them as well, but Eugenia blocked my way.

"She must go. It is her direction. Her choice."

I looked back at Eugenia. Then looked from her to the empty doorway. I had lost everything I held dear. And there would be no reclaiming it.

Neddy

I COULD SEE A BLUR of white ahead of me.

"Rose!" I shouted. "Wait! Rose ..." I kept calling as I ran, till my throat ached. But somehow I kept the white blur in sight and they must have slowed, for I began to gain on them.

Then I realized the bear had stopped altogether.

The moon was very bright and I could see them clearly. Rose in a blue dress, sitting perched on the back of the massive beast. She looked unsure of herself, as though she wanted to find a way down but couldn't. It wouldn't be like dismounting from a horse. The bear abruptly kneeled and Rose managed to awkwardly slide off.

Rose tentatively moved toward me, looking over her shoulder several times. "I chose, Neddy," she said. "It is the right thing to do."

I wanted to grab her, to carry her back home to safety, but all I did was nod silently. I said, "Here," and held out the four pieces of her cloak. "I pinned it together. You can sew it whole later. Truth or lie, it may be cold where you journey."

She took the ragged cloak from me and fastened it around her shoulders. "Thank you, Neddy."

"One thing more," I said. And quickly I blurted out the tale of the white bear's rescuing her from the gorge when she was little. "If he did that," I ended lamely, "then surely he can mean you no ill." I believe I spoke these words as much to reassure myself as I did to reassure her.

She leaned over and hugged me. We held each other for a long moment. Then she broke away and lightly crossed to the white bear.

I watched as he once again lifted her to his back.

And they were gone.

BOOK TWO

South

They journeyed far and the white bear said,
"Are you afraid?"
"No," she replied. "I am not afraid."

Troll Queen

IT IS CLOSE NOW. Very close. And it shall unfold as I had planned from the beginning.

"Would you like to play?" he had said. A boy with a curling-up mouth and a voice soft as fresh-fallen snow. With those words came the wanting. And all was changed. Irrevocably.

I was Princess then, and The Book my father had given me was new. The Book had been a gift to me on the eve of my first journey to the green lands, to begin recording my royal days.

Today I travel to the green lands and I can hardly believe it. Ever since I was a baby, Urda, my old nurse, has told me stories of the softskin folk. Now at last I shall see them for myself.

When the king's eldest child reaches the age of knowing, it is the tradition to take him or her to see the green lands that lie outside Huldre. It is a strange world, my father says. He says it exists mainly for us to use—a place to get slaves and the raw materials for some of our food and clothing.

He says they are a very queer people, the softskin folk, not like us at all. They are backward and plain. Short lived. No arts like ours. Their jewels are pale, and except for a very few who are of royalty, most live in small drab huts, like our servants' quarters. It sounds very strange indeed.

But Urda told me more, told me about different things they have, amazing things. Something called music. And many, many kinds of animals. And bursts of fragrant color that grow out of the ground, called flowers. And their food is melting soft, too, exotic and all different flavors. My father calls it repulsive, says it would make me sick, but in spite of that I am curious.

The journey was long, but the sleigh was comfortable and there was plenty of hot slank to drink. In fact, it grew so warm after a time that we gradually had to peel away all our furs. How can the softskins stand this pressing warmth? It makes me feel choked and prickly.

We will stay for a week in the green lands. Our lodging is in a palace of rock, though my father says it is nothing like the Ice Palace of Huldre. He said it is not used often, only when we need to journey here to replace servants. And it is hidden from the soft-skins' sight.

Softskin folk do not live as long as we do and must be replenished. So we come every twenty or thirty years to take away more. My father says it is best to choose unwanted, unmarried people, not children, because less fuss is made when they disappear. Not that they could find us anyway. It is too long, arduous, and puzzling a journey for softskin folk. And it is too cold in our land for softskins; without slank they would die within a few hours, a day if they were well equipped. Father says there have been a handful of softskins called explorers who have journeyed to within a hundred miles of our land. We collected one or two of these, he says, and they made especially good servants because they were so hardy.

In appearance the softskins are very different from us, but we are able to move among them easily because of our arts, and they don't even know we are there.

Urda takes me tomorrow to see softskin folk. I can hardly wait!

I cannot sleep. The most amazing thing has happened. I actually met one of the softskin folk! A boy. I touched his skin and it was as soft as they say—softer! And his voice...it was like a...I don't know. Like the song of the creatures they call birds that we heard on our journey south, yet odder and more beautiful.

In Huldre I have seen the softskin servants only from a distance, for they do the most menial work in the kitchen and stables. (Troll servants wait on the royal family.) And our softskins are dull and broken from living long in Huldre. So I had not known what they are truly like. Urda had told me they are ugly and their voices sound awful—thin and watery— but she was wrong.

Urda fell asleep; because she is old she is always sleepy, and she drank plenty of slank with the picnic lunch we had. So I wandered off by myself. I moved through the grass, which was green and soft when I bent down and ran my fingers across the tops of the thin stalks. I felt almost dizzy from all the smells that filled my nose. Sweet and thrilling they were. And the changeable feel of the gentle wind on my skin. So different from the hard and constant wind in Huldre.

Then I saw some children playing in the distance and thought I would use my arts to get closer without being seen, but abruptly their game ended and they all went away.

Except there was one boy who came back.

"Would you like to play?" he said, holding up a round red object.

Because of my arts, I could understand his words, but still I could only stare. What had happened to my breathing, I wondered. Then the round thing came flying at me and I ducked.

His mouth curled up, showing even more teeth,

and he ran to get it. "It is a ball," he said. "I'll teach you how to catch it."

And his words and the curling-up mouth made me feel strange inside, warm and melty, like taking a gulp of slank on an empty stomach. "Show me," I said eagerly in his language.

And there came a surprised look on his face. "Have you been ill? Your voice is ..." he started but stopped.

After that I didn't speak again, but I began to understand about throwing and catching the thing he called a ball.

"I hope you didn't think I was teasing you," he said. I didn't understand the word teasing, but he went on. "Your voice is fine," he said. Still I kept silent, and we continued to throw the ball, back and forth.

Then I heard the sound of someone calling, and he said he had to go, that his servants were looking for him but perhaps we could play again another time.

I watched him run down the mountain toward a large building. He moved quickly, with grace.

When I went back Urda was searching for me, still groggy from her nap. I told her I had taken a walk. I decided I wouldn't tell her about the boy. The next day I would make her take me there again. And I would make sure she drank even more.

Rose

THE WHITE BEAR HEADED due south of the farm, keeping to the woods and away from the places where people lived.

It was a frosty, clear night, and the stars shimmered against a black sky. Usually, looking up at the stars on such a clear night filled me with a breathless pleasure, no matter how often I gazed at them. But that night I was hardly aware that there *was* a sky.

Riding a bear was nothing like riding a horse. First of all, the bear was far larger, and I could not ride with both legs straddling his back, the way one does with a horse. At first I didn't move at all but stayed frozen in the position I had been in when I had landed on the broad back—sort of a crouch, my legs tucked under me. When he first began to move, I instinctively grabbed hold of the great ruff of fur at the back of his neck to keep from sliding off.

But after a few hours I grew stiff. I had the feeling we would be traveling for a long time, so I got bolder and began to shift my body, trying to find a comfortable position. I finally settled with one leg dangling down and the other bent under me. I didn't need to use my legs to hold on. Despite his enormous speed, the white bear's gait was surprisingly smooth and his back so broad that as long as I kept a firm hold on his thick fur, I was in no danger of falling off.

The white bear's fur was extraordinary. It was as soft as rabbit's fur, yet much thicker and longer. When I burrowed my hands into it—which I only worked up the courage to do after we had been riding a long time and my fingers were numb with cold—my hands and forearms disappeared up to my elbows. And the fur was so warm. It took only moments for my fingers to thaw. My legs, too, stayed warm, nestled in the deep fur.

But the rest of me—my face and upper body—was cold, and I was very glad of my cloak. I thought of Neddy finding pins and carefully lining up the torn edges, and my eyes blurred with tears. Better not to think about Neddy.

I thought instead of the beast upon which I was riding. I remembered the imaginary companion of my childhood. How many times had I imagined myself riding a magnificent white bear through the night?

He moved faster than I would have thought possible for such a large animal, and by daybreak we had journeyed far, into country I had never seen before. The land was heavily forested; there were fewer and fewer evergreens, more broad-leaved trees. We were still heading south.

Though the journey lasted seven days, the white bear stopped only once.

During that time I must have been in some kind of trance—or maybe it was an enchantment or spell. For those seven days I neither ate nor drank, nor slept. The strangest thing was that I didn't feel any different, except extremely aware and alert. It all seemed very natural; I was drinking it all in—the vivid greens of unfamiliar plants, the distant call of a strange bird, even the approaching smell of the sea.

When the white bear did stop, it took me by surprise, and I found myself slipping off his back and landing quite hard on sand. Catching my breath, I sat up and gazed around me. We were on a remote stretch of brown sand and waves were breaking not twenty feet away. It was dawn, and over my right shoulder the sun was just beginning to rise. Considering the direction we had been traveling, I guessed that this must be the southern reaches of Njordsjoen, the North Sea. And even though there was an enormous white bear not two feet from me, I felt a thrill of wonder. My grandfather had sailed this sea, and my great-grandfather before him. I had always promised myself that one day I would come to Njordsjoen, although I never could have imagined it happening quite like this.

Out of the corner of one eye, I saw the bear fiddling

with something small and dark, and then he pulled at it with his great paws. Like taffy, whatever it was began to lengthen and grow.

I watched, dazed and fascinated, and then suddenly he came toward me, and before I knew what was happening, I was being encased from head to toe in some kind of soft, pliable covering. It was brown and smelled of fish and musk, and I thought maybe it was a sealskin. Then he pulled it up over my eyes and I felt myself being patted all over, as if I were a bairn being checked to see that my blankets were snug on a cold night. Suddenly I felt a pressure on the back of my neck and shoulders, a clamping down. I was being lifted and we were moving forward. Then the light and sound changed, became dimmer and muffled, distant.

Though I could see nothing, I knew we were then underwater.

I panicked for a moment, wondering how I was going to breathe, but I quickly discovered that I could breathe quite normally and gave myself over to the sensations of traveling under the sea, swaddled in sealskin and being carried, I suspected, in the jaws of a great white bear.

We were not long in the sea. If anything, the white bear swam faster than he ran. A strange regret overcame me when I felt myself being carried out of the water and laid upon the ground. The bear made quick work of removing me from my cocoon, and soon I was again on his back and we were speeding through a completely foreign country.

Only once did the white bear speak. It was soon after our sea crossing. We were moving through a lush, rocky valley crowded with rushing streams and slippery boulders.

"Are you afraid?" came the words from deep inside the bear's massive chest.

"No," I answered, and it was true. I had been too busy watching and listening; absorbing all the sensations, from the wind on my face, to the rhythmic rocking of the sightless underwater world, to the rich, flowery smells of the air as we moved southward. I had been caught up in the easy grace of the bear's motion and had given little thought to where we were going or to what would happen once we got there.

But later, during the fifth or sixth night, I did begin to think of those things. I must have sensed that we were nearing the end of our journey.

The moon had waned since that first night we set out, but it was still bright and I could clearly see the landscape around me. The land was mountainous in places, though the mountains were small and green rather than towering and jagged as in Njord. There were no pines at all; instead there were lush, broad-leaved trees, some with splashes of bright-colored blossoms. The smell was different, too—a thicker, richer smell of earth and flower and ripe fruit.

I was suddenly very hungry and thirsty, and found myself wondering if the white bear was hungry, too. The thought crossed my mind that *I* was to be the beast's meal, at the end of a long journey. I shivered, though the air was warm.

We were moving along the base of a small mountain, through a thick forest of some kind of pungent, wide-spreading tree I had never seen before. Though I could not make out any sign of a path, the white bear was sure-footed. I had the feeling he had gone this way many times.

Without warning he stopped, and after seven days and nights of constant motion, I felt dizzy at the lack of it. There was a ringing in my ears. My stomach growled and my throat was dry.

The white bear knelt as he had when I'd said good-bye to Neddy, and I sensed he wanted me to dismount (if indeed that is what you call getting off a bear's back). I was even more awkward than before; going seven days with no food or sleep had left me weak. And though I didn't exactly fall off as I had on the sandy shore, I still wound up on my backside.

The bear stepped away. I heard a low rumbling from his throat, and even some faint words, but I couldn't make them out. And then there was a soft whooshing, and a piece of the mountain suddenly swung aside, as if it were a great earthen doorway. An entryway into the mountain lay open, and inside, a muted light flickered.

"Come," said the white bear.

I gingerly got to my feet, swayed a moment, then stumbled forward, my eyes fastened on the warm light within.

The bear let me go first, walking just behind me. If I hadn't been concentrating on putting one foot before the other without collapsing entirely, I might have been very frightened. As it was, I made it through the entryway and the next thing I was aware of was a delicious aroma, as of a great stewpot of juicy meat and vegetables simmering on a fire. My mouth watered; I let out a groan and forgot entirely about being afraid.

"This way," the bear said, and I followed, my nose telling me that he was leading us to the source of the smell.

We traveled down a long hall, past several rooms, and I got a fleeting impression of browns and golds, antlers on the wall and fur rugs on the floor. It reminded me of descriptions I had heard of a wealthy person's hunting lodge. Except it was bigger, as big as I imagined a castle would be.

At last we came to a room with a large fireplace and a great long table, which was laid out with various shapes and sizes of dishes, some covered with cloths. And in the fireplace was hanging a large black stewpot, the source of the wondrous aroma.

I stood still, swaying slightly as I stared at the pot, when I heard the white bear's voice. "Eat," he said, and then he left the room.

I made my way as fast as my limbs would carry me to the fireplace, took up a bowl, and ladled steaming stew into it. I crouched there by the hearth and spooned the tender chunks of meat and vegetables into my mouth.

When the bowl was empty, I filled it again and then staggered over to the table and fell into a chair.

I emptied that bowl, too, with the aid of a great hunk of melting-soft bread I had found in a cloth-covered basket. I peeked under a few more of the crisp white cloths and found baked apples in pastry, and strawberries, and rich, thick cream, and all sorts of delicious cakes. Tempting though it was, I was suddenly exhausted and could barely keep my eyes open. I ate a few bites of a small piece of yellow butter-cake with blackberry preserves in the center, and drank half a cup of fresh frothy milk. There was a large dark-red velvet couch not too far from the hearth, and I sank down upon it, my stomach uncomfortably full. I thought about the white bear, wondering uneasily where he was at that moment, and then I fell asleep.

Troll Queen

EVEN THOUGH I WAS little more than a child when I wrote in my Book about the green lands and about the softskin boy, I could see ahead to what I had to do.

> *I am very angry at Father. We are leaving tomorrow and he will not let me take the boy with me as my servant. He says we cannot take children. And especially not this boy, because of who he is—he is important to the people in the green lands, Father says, like I am in the Huldre land.*
>
> *Father is king and must be obeyed. For now. But already my arts are close to being the equal of his, and soon I will have my way. I will come back to this place and find the boy, and then he will be mine.*

White Bear

Here.
After so long waiting.
Her purple eyes.
Torn cloak.
Skin pale, sheer as ice.
Exhausted.
But unafraid.

Must remember.
Conditions, rules.

So long ago.
Playing.
A ball.
A voice like rocks.
Then...

Body split, stretched.
Pain. And ...
All changed, in a moment.
Lost.

But now ...
Hope.

Rose

WHEN I AWOKE, my head was heavy. But I knew where I was right away. At home, even in summer, there would be a cold tang to the air in the morning, and the mattress I slept on with my sister was not covered in velvet and overstuffed with down.

I sat up, stretching, and saw that the table had been cleared while I slept, except for a covered basket, a crock of butter beside it, and a large white teapot. Steam was rising from the pot's spout. My stomach growled and I realized I was ravenous again.

I stood and made my way to the table. I lifted the white cloth and breathed in the aroma of cinnamon and hot dough. Breaking off a piece of bread, I slathered it with butter and shoved it into my mouth. We hadn't been able to afford butter in a very long time, and I closed my eyes in sheer delight. I then drank a cup of what turned out to be a sweet, fragrant tea, exotic and fruity, like none I'd had before.

As I stuffed myself with bread and butter, I wondered where the food had come from. Was there a kitchen with a bustling staff of servants? Or was the food the result of an enchantment?

My stomach full, I got up from the table and set off to explore.

I thought of the white bear and felt uneasy, fearing that he might spring out at me from inside a room or around a corner. But there was no sign of him.

I started down a hall with a vaulted ceiling. The walls were a light polished stone, and sconces holding oil lamps were placed at regular intervals. In between the lamps were large paintings and tapestries. The tapestries in particular drew my eyes; they were done in vivid hues of reds and blues, and depicted lords and ladies in old-fashioned courtly garb. The handiwork was exquisite.

I came to an open doorway and peered in. It was a drawing room, and it, too, was filled with paintings and tapestries. There was a lush deep-green carpet and various pieces of overstuffed furniture. As in the hallway, light was provided by oil lamps, both on the walls and set on tables. I picked up one of the handheld lamps and took it with me in case there were places not so well lit.

I continued my exploration. The next room I came to was also furnished with tapestries, rugs, and overstuffed furniture, as well as shelves of books lining the walls. The library, I thought. But I was wrong. Many of the rooms turned out to have books. Finally I came to one that could not be mistaken for anything but a library. No tapestries there—every inch of the walls was covered with shelving, from floor to ceiling. It took my breath away. In Njord the only places I knew to have so many books were the monasteries. If only Neddy could see this, I thought, but I quickly brushed the thought away. I wouldn't think about Neddy now.

In addition to the many books I found in the rooms I explored, I also noticed something else that was plentiful. Whoever had decorated this place clearly had a love of music. There was a musical instrument in almost every room.

Then I came to a large room that was devoted entirely to music, as the library was devoted to books. It was breathtaking. In the center of the room stood an enormous grand piano, beautifully painted and carved. And in a large ornate cabinet was an astonishing collection of pipes and flautos that appeared to have come from all over the world. There was a lacquered bamboo flauto in the shape of a dragon that looked to be from the Far East, and there were pipes made of ivory, reed, and soapstone. Some were elaborately carved, some had double pipes, but there was one flauto that was clearly favored. Displayed in a beautiful box lined with blue velvet, it wasn't fancy like some of the others but had a simple, classic beauty.

There were sheaves of sheet music tied up with ribbon, and there were chairs lining the sides of the room that looked as if they could be pulled out to form rows for an audience. If I closed my eyes, I could imagine a gathering of finely dressed ladies and gentlemen seated there on a Sunday afternoon, applauding enthusiastically for the performance of a musician. I liked the room very much, although there hung an air of sadness about it, perhaps because it was empty of people.

I went into room after room. I was going to count them but quickly gave up. The place was enormous, and because of its size I began to think of it as a castle.

I got the feeling that the castle was carved right into the mountain, which was impossible, yet by then I had become accustomed to impossible things. There were no windows or doors that I could see, save for the large door we had entered. Most of the rooms looked as though they had not been used in a long time. It was not because they were stuffy or dusty (in fact, they were neat as a pin), but there was a general sense of emptiness, even loneliness, about each room.

I became more and more intrigued as I explored, forgetting completely my uneasiness about the white bear.

I began to weave a picture in my mind of whoever it was who lived there (other than a white bear). It became a sort of game to piece together the clues that revealed him. . . . Well, that was the first thing I figured out—that it was a man who lived there. There was little of a feminine touch in most of the rooms I had seen.

He loved music. And books. I thought again of the library. *Neddy.*

I was suddenly hit with a pang of homesickness so severe that I sank down on the thick blue carpet of the room in which I stood. I had been so swept up in the wild ride getting there and then exploring the castle that I had barely thought of my family at all. There I was, thousands of miles from those I loved most in the world, in a strange deserted castle, no doubt with an enormous white bear prowling somewhere nearby.

A chill went through me and I wrapped my pieced-together cloak tighter around my shoulders. *Oh, Neddy...*

I am not one who cries easily, but at that moment tears spilled from my eyes. I don't know how long I sat there, huddled into my cloak, feeling miserable.

It was hunger that finally got me to my feet and moving again. It had likely been hours since the hot bread and tea. But I wasn't sure how to find my way back to the room where I had eaten. So I decided to go forward, and rushed down the corridor, ignoring the rooms to either side of me, thinking I might find a stairway that would take me back down to the floor where I had begun.

I had just glimpsed a flight of stairs and was heading toward it when something caught my eye—a door was slightly ajar and I could see lamps lit inside the room. The merest hint of color and light flashed out at me. I pushed the door open and then caught my breath in amazement.

A loom. It was the most beautiful loom I had ever seen, more beautiful than I could ever have imagined. It was made of a rich chestnut-colored wood that was polished so that it gleamed, and the posts were carved with intricate designs, as were the crossbeams. The warp threads had been set up with an astonishing palette of wool in such rich colors as the pale green of early spring grass and the purple of fleur-de-lis.

I ran my fingers reverently along the threads. In a sort of trance I sank down on the small stool that was perched in front of the loom, as if it had been waiting for me. I felt like I was in a dream, watching myself, but I took up the shuttle and beater and began to weave. Though it was a completely unfamiliar loom, with a different feel to the shuttle and the tension in the warp threads, it took only a few passes before I understood it, and then I was gone, lost in the world of texture, color, and movement that I loved so well. I could feel the grass brushing against my bare feet, and the violet smell of the fleur-de-lis was thick in my nostrils.

The loom was like a Thoroughbred compared to the worn, stumbling workhorse of a loom I had used in Widow Hautzig's shed. And working on it was as different as the looms themselves. It was the difference between walking with a stranger and walking with your heartmate. It was the difference between working for duty and working for love.

I have no idea how long I wove.

With no window to the outside world, I could not keep time. I might have been an entire day at the loom, or even longer. What finally brought me to my senses was hunger. My head was light and there was a faint buzzing in my ears. But still I could not stop. My fingers slowly moving, I gazed around the room.

There wasn't just the one loom but several others—small hand looms, a weighted loom similar to the one at home, and an upright loom that I guessed to be a tapestry loom, though I had never seen one before, only heard Widow Hautzig describe them. In addition to the looms, there were several spinning wheels (which I would have gone to examine more closely if my knees had not been so weak) as well as shelves filled to overflowing with everything that one could possibly want for creating cloth and sewing it together.

There was a whole section of shelving devoted entirely to thread. A rainbow of colors and textures. Some spools even looked to have silk thread on them, with colors that included shimmery golds, silvers, and bronzes.

There were bins of carded wool, baskets of raw fluffy wool awaiting carding, and skeins of finished wool, ready for weaving. There were bottles of liquid color for dyeing and bowls of powdered pigment in every color ever seen in nature and some I had never seen before. There were sharp, glittery scissors, needles for knitting, and sewing needles of every thickness and length. I was dumbstruck.

But finally, I knew I must find something to eat or I would become ill. I lurched to the door and out into the hall. My head swimming, I made my way to the stairs.

Just looking along the curving staircase made my ears ring and my legs shake, but I started down anyway. I finished my descent sitting, dragging my rear down each step like a very young child.

At the bottom I pulled myself upright using the banister and began to walk forward. I sniffed the air for the smell of stew, but there was no scent. I began to worry that I was far from that room where I had eaten. Or that the food was in a different room.

Or worse, that there would be no food at all.

At the end of the hall I rounded the corner, and standing there was the white bear. He was somehow larger and whiter than I remembered. I let out a small scream and fell clumsily to the ground. I felt close to fainting but took several deep, gasping breaths and the feeling passed.

The white bear watched me with his sad black eyes. Then he said in that hollow deep voice that always seemed like it was wrenched from him, "There is food. Come."

I got up shakily and followed.

After a while he stopped, and I stopped, too, stumbling a little.

"If you need … grab … my fur."

"Thank you," I replied, my voice thin. I was too addled by hunger to be afraid. I reached up and set my hand on his back.

He started walking again, and I followed along to the room he had led me to before, when we had first arrived.

I did stumble once along the way, and kept myself from falling by grabbing a handful of white fur. He didn't pause or flinch.

Once again there was a stewpot on the hearth, with a thick soup of lentils and ham bubbling inside. The white bear stood in the doorway, watching me for a moment, then he turned and disappeared.

As I ate, my mind whirled with thoughts about this extraordinary place and all the things in it—the loom, the delicious food that appeared out of nowhere, and most of all, the white bear.

Troll Queen

BEFORE I TOOK THE softskin boy, I went back several times to the green lands. I traveled in my own sleigh, taking only Urda, and I did not try to talk to the boy but only watched, learning of his life. I wrote in my Book:

It seems these softskins die with great frequency; their lives are shortened by a wide variety of illnesses and accidents. The boy I watch is a fifth-born child, but two older than he have already died. It shall be no surprise then if he, too, shall seem to perish.

It was simple, the plan I came up with. I chose an ill-favored troll to sacrifice, one who would be little missed in Huldre, and then with my arts summoned up a very simple act of shape-changing.

If only my father had not been so angry.

Neddy

IT IS ODD, THE TWISTS that life will sometimes take. The ewe that you think will give birth with ease dies bringing forth a two-headed lamb. Or the ski trail that you have been told is treacherous, you navigate easily.

The days that followed Rose's departure were dark and more painful than anything I could have imagined. Father was a ghost of a man, pale and hollow-eyed, moving about the farm clumsily, as if he didn't belong there. He avoided all of us, especially Mother. She spent her time with Sara. It was as if she believed that by nursing Sara and restoring her health, she could justify Rose's sacrifice. But of course nothing could. Not ever, not even if Sara were to suddenly leap from her bed, fully recovered. As it was, there was no change in her condition.

I spent my time in a dazed sort of twilight world, going about my chores, but my mind was always on

Rose, imagining her in every possible situation except the one that ended with her gone forever.

Outwardly we busied ourselves with getting ready to leave the farm. Neighbor Torsk was kind and helpful; I think even in his simple way he was aware that something was very wrong with our family. Mother told him that Rose had gone to live with relatives in the southeast for a time, and that the rest of us were hoping to follow her as soon as Sara's health improved.

At first, because Father was so lost in grief, my brother Willem and I did all the heavy work about the farm—repairing and cleaning and sorting. But after several days Father set aside his lost look and threw himself into the labor with a frightening intensity, as though work was the only thing that kept him from madness. By the end of the week our farmhouse looked as good as it possibly could have, given our reduced circumstances.

The day before the landholder was due to take possession of his property, we had nearly finished with the packing; there was so little worth taking away with us. I was out by the henhouse, feeding the few scrawny chickens we had left, when I heard the sound of wagon wheels. Soon a handsome wagon pulled by two gleaming horses came into view. I called out to Father, who was nearby. Mother was at neighbor Torsk's with Sara.

The wagon came to a stop and a tall, well-dressed gentleman alighted and stood for a moment gazing at the farm. He had a look of ownership about him, and I knew at once that the landholder had come a day early.

My heart sank a little. Though I had been expecting that moment for a long time, it still pained me. Then the man strode toward Father and me, a pleasant expression on his face. "You must be Arne," he said to Father, extending his hand.

"Master Mogens?" my father said hesitantly, taking the proffered hand.

"No, Mogens works for me, watching over my holdings. I am Harald Soren, the owner of this property."

"Well met, Master Soren. This is my son Neddy."

I shook the man's hand, impressed in spite of myself at the kindness and intelligence I saw in his eyes. I had spent much of the past months disliking—even despising—the man, but now that he was in front of me and the day had arrived for him to take away the only home I had ever known, I could not help but think he looked a good and decent fellow.

"I hope you will find everything in order," my father said stiffly.

"Oh, I am sure..." Master Soren began. "But first, let me apologize for arriving a day early. The journey took less time than I had thought it would. The map I used was poor," he said with a frown. "It is difficult to find maps of decent quality." His eyes held an exasperated look, then he gave a shrug. "At any rate, I have taken lodgings in Andalsnes. And I can come back tomorrow if that suits you better."

"Oh no, today is just as good as tomorrow," Father replied with courtesy. "May I show you around the farm?"

"That would be most kind of you."

I wondered what must have been going through Father's mind as we took Master Soren through the farmhouse. For myself, I found it hard to hate the man, with his shiny boots and kind eyes, looking over my home as if he were assessing a mare he had just acquired.

Then we came to the storage room. Father still had not taken down the few maps he had hung, maps of his own design, made back when he was apprentice to my grandfather. I also saw that all of our wind rose designs lay scattered over the worktable, with Rose's on top.

I heard Master Soren give a sudden intake of breath. He quickly strode over to the nearest map pinned to the wall and studied it closely, his concentration focused and intent.

I saw him trace Father's signature with his finger, then he turned, his eyes bright, and said, "Am I to understand that you made this map?"

"Yes, though it is many years old..."

"Did you, by chance, apprentice with Esbjorn Lavrans?"

"Yes," Father answered, and smiled for the first time in many days. "Esbjorn was my wife's father. He died some years ago."

"Well I know. A great loss, it was." Soren paused. "I had heard there was an apprentice, but no one knew anything about him, after Esbjorn's death. And since then I have had to get my maps from Danemark, at great cost and much difficulty. Even then, they are either out of date or incomplete. And the maps of Njord..." He gave a snort to indicate his contempt.

Then his eyes fell on the wind roses. Again he moved forward, his eyes alight.

"May I?" he asked. Father dumbly nodded, and we both watched as the man slowly and reverently looked at each design.

"But these are superb!" he exclaimed, lowering the last into the box. "How is it that I have never seen or heard of your work before?"

"Because I have done none," Father replied. "Except for my own pleasure, when time allowed. I am a farmer now."

Harald Soren gazed at Father and a silence grew in the small room. When Soren spoke at last he sounded angry. "It is a waste then, a shameful waste."

Father's mouth opened, and I thought he looked angry as well, but he said nothing.

Then Soren smiled and spoke, his voice warm. "Such a talent as you possess! It is a damnable waste for one such as you to be spending your time mucking about with pigs and plow horses. Not that farming isn't a noble calling... But mapmaking! Come, let us find a place to sit. I would talk with you further about your maps. And I could do with a cup of grog or whatever you have on hand."

Father looked stunned. "Of course," he said. "I should have offered sooner..."

"I'll go," I said to Father.

"Thank you, lad," said Soren. "Now, Arne, show me all your maps and charts and wind roses. I must see everything."

And so it happened that while I served them cups of watery ale and some stale bread and cheese, the two men put their heads together over Father's precious pile of maps. And they were like two children with a game of *hneftafl*. I had not seen Father so happy in a very long time.

Soren *was* a good man. It had been his assistant, Mogens, who'd made the decision to evict us. Soren was an ardent voyager and left most of his affairs in Mogens's hands. But being between journeys, he had a mind to come himself to see the farm, which had been so long in the hands of one family, with the thought that he would like to know more of that family's circumstances before he turned them off the lands.

"Mogens means well," Soren explained, "but he can be a bit rigid in following the dictates of business."

Soren asked Father many questions, and by the time twilight came he knew more about our family than most of our neighbors. When he learned of my sister Sara's illness, he expressed the sincerest of concern and sympathy. The only thing Father did not tell Soren about was Rose and the white bear. Instead he told the same lie that Mother had told our neighbors—that his youngest daughter, Rose, whose wind rose design Soren had particularly admired, was visiting relatives in the south. Father's face was so stiff and white when he said the words that I was sure Soren sensed something amiss; but if he did, he chose not to question further.

When Soren left that evening for his lodgings in Andalsnes, he said, "I will return tomorrow to talk with you further, Arne. But there will be no more mention of leaving your farm."

Father and I stood watching as Soren's carriage rattled down the road and out of sight. We then turned and stared at each other with the stupefied expressions of men just awoken from a dream.

Soren did not return the next morning.

I began to think that the whole encounter *was* a dream, or some sort of cruel trick. But later in the afternoon Soren came riding up in his wagon, bringing with him the doctor from Andalsnes. It was I who brought the doctor to Sara at Torsk's farm, while Father stayed behind to talk with Soren.

Dr. Trinde bade us leave the room while he examined Sara. As we waited I told Mother, Willem, and Sonja all that had happened with Soren.

When I had finished, Mother said to me, "Is this true, Neddy? We don't have to leave the farm?"

I nodded. Mother closed her eyes. Clasping her hands together tightly, she was silent, her face pale. Then her eyes opened, and leaning close, she stared at me, a strange smile on her face.

"This happened because of the white bear," she said in a low voice, her eyes fixed on mine. I looked back at her in astonishment, which quickly turned to anger. That she should use the fortunate turn of events to justify Rose's sacrifice ... I shuddered with revulsion and pulled away from her.

"Mother ..." I began, my voice raw, when suddenly the doctor appeared.

"I have here a list of herbs that I will need for Sara's treatment," he said, unaware of the tension in the room. I tried to focus on his words. "You should know," Dr. Trinde went on gravely, "that it will be touch-and-go for a few days, but," and he paused for a moment, "I think there is every reason to believe that Sara will pull through."

Mother's eyes filled with tears, and she reached out and hugged me tightly to her.

"You see?" she whispered. "It was all for the best."

I pulled away sharply. Then, grabbing the doctor's list of herbs, I slammed out of Torsk's farmhouse.

Rose

I FELL ASLEEP AGAIN on the red couch by the hearth. I must have been still tired from the long journey, as well as from the many hours I had spent at the magnificent loom.

When I awoke, my mouth felt sticky. Actually, I felt sticky all over; suddenly I could even smell the odor of seal on my skin. More than anything else in the world, I wanted a bath.

But I had no idea how to go about finding a place to bathe.

I didn't know where the food came from or who kept the lamps lit and the hearth fire going. Was it all magic? Or were there servants who disappeared when I came into sight?

The first thing to do was to find the kitchen. There *had* to be a kitchen. And where there was a kitchen, there would be water, and maybe even a large tub for bathing.

I once more set out to explore, this time with a purpose. As I roamed I began to form a map in my head. And what had appeared to be a confused labyrinth to me the day before began to take on a pattern. It took some time, but I finally figured out that there was a block of rooms on the second floor that did not seem to have corresponding rooms on the floor below. It might just have been the way the building had been cut into the mountain, but I decided to investigate further. Then I discovered a large heavy tapestry that covered one end of a first-floor hall. It depicted a nobleman in a red cloak offering a small red heart to a lady in a blue gown, with a crown of pearls on her head. I lifted up the heavy cloth and found a door. I tried the handle, expecting it to be locked, but it turned easily. Then I slipped through the doorway, finding myself in a spacious kitchen.

Standing at a worktable in the center of the kitchen, her hands covered with flour, was a woman. She was a head taller than me and wore a plain black dress, covered by a black apron with flour all over it. She had the whitest skin I had ever seen, almost as white as the flour. Her hair was the same bright white as her skin, and she wore it in a long braid down the back of her dress. She was not a young woman, yet she was quite beautiful. Her features were perfect, her eyes large and black and staring at me.

"Hello," I said.

She said something in response, but I couldn't understand her. She was speaking another language and her voice was rough and gravelly.

I must have looked startled, for she clamped her lips shut. Then I noticed what looked like a boy hiding behind her. He had the same kind of white-skinned beauty as the woman, though his hair was dark brown rather than white.

The woman said something to the boy in a whispering voice that sounded like chicken claws scratching over a rough surface. He crossed to a basket nearby and pulled out a pastry of some kind. Then he hesitantly came over and offered it to me.

"Thank you," I said, taking it. He was not a boy at all, I realized. He was only a little shorter than me and his features were those of an adult, and like the white-haired woman, he had a perfect nose and wide black eyes. He was staring at me even more intently than the woman had.

"My name is Rose," I said to the small man. He did not respond, nor did he take his eyes off me. Suddenly he reached out and touched the back of my hand. As he drew his hand back, with a sideways glance at the woman, his eyes grew even wider, if that was possible, and he rubbed the finger that had touched me, his expression filled with awe.

The woman glided over to us and gently slapped the man's hand, shaking her head and making more guttural sounds.

He sheepishly backed away.

"It's all right," I said. "He didn't hurt me."

The woman just shook her head at me. Then she picked up a glass and pointed to it.

"No, thank you," I said. "I'm not thirsty. What I would really like is a bath."

She just looked at me blankly.

I tried to pantomime washing myself but couldn't seem to get the idea across. The small man let out a grating noise that sounded like it may have been a giggle.

But finally something dawned in the woman's eyes and she purposefully strode over to me, took me by the wrist, and led me out through the door covered by the tapestry. The feel of her skin on my wrist startled me. It was rough, as gravelly and coarse as her voice had been. I glanced down at her hand; the texture of her skin was like the bark of a tree, whorled with ridges, fissured. I could make out traces of the flour lodged in the crevices of the white skin. Her touch repelled me, but I didn't let my feelings show.

To my relief she dropped my wrist when we were in the hallway. I understood I was to follow her.

She led me up the stairs and along the hall I had explored the day before. Stopping in front of a door not far from the weaving room, she turned the handle and we entered. It was a lovely room, not fancy but warm and comfortable. A fire burned in a large fireplace and there were several overstuffed chairs in front of it, but the first thing I noticed was the large, lovely bed made of dark polished wood. It was piled high with puffy quilts and pillows. And sitting beside the bed was the small pack I had brought with me from home.

I turned toward the white-skinned woman only to find she was gone.

I quickly explored the room, discovering a large jug of water, a bar of white soap, and a basin large enough for bathing. Using a large kettle I warmed the water over the fire and had the most wonderful bath I could ever remember having.

I dressed in a clean shift and tunic, and then sat in one of the chairs by the fire. I wanted to head directly back to the loom, but instead I made myself sit still and think.

I reviewed it all in my mind. The white bear appearing in our house. His request. The discovery of my parents' lie. The anger in me that drove me to go with the white bear. The journey. And this castle with its comforts, the fires lit all the time, the delicious food, the white-skinned woman and man. But mostly I thought about the white bear.

It was the white bear who had brought me. And I had no idea why, or what I was to do.

Perhaps I had been brought here to be a servant, to help the white lady and her companion. But the room she had led me to, where my things were, was hardly the room of a servant. I thought of the loom. Perhaps I had been brought here to weave, to make something for the white bear. Something in particular. Clearly, no expense had been spared outfitting that room. But why me? Surely there were weavers of far superior skill in the world.

The loom. I wanted to see it again. But I continued to hold myself still. I needed to keep thinking.

Maybe the white bear had tried other weavers, but none had families so willing to part with them.

I suddenly felt impatient, and stood up. It was useless trying to sort out the inexplicable. Only the white bear knew the answers to these questions and it was to him I must go.

I exited the room, then hesitated. Where would I seek him? The only places I had seen him so far were the room with the food, the front entrance, and the hallway between the two.

I found my way to the front door. There was no one to be seen in any direction. Perhaps, I thought, I should try the door. It would undoubtedly be shut fast. It was.

My hand was still on the doorknob when I heard a noise, like a sigh or a puff of wind. I whirled around, but there was nothing, or no one, in sight.

He must be here somewhere.

And so I began an exhaustive search of the castle, room by room, hall by hall. I thought I had been over every inch of it but still discovered parts I had not seen before. When I came to the weaving room, I resisted the urge to stop my search, though the loom was as beautiful as I had remembered it.

I tried the door behind the tapestry, the one leading to the kitchen, but this time it was locked. I halfheartedly pounded on the door, but no one came. It seemed unlikely the white bear was in the kitchen, nor did I believe that I would get any help from the two white-skinned folk, so I resumed my search.

Finally, when it seemed I had been over the whole castle twice, I gave up. Nowhere was there a large white bear.

I was angry. What right had he to be wandering around the world outside while I was a prisoner? I realized I was being ridiculous, and it was lucky that I hadn't been able to find the white bear, for I could easily have said something stupid and gotten myself eaten.

I returned to the entrance, and though it was late, well past time for the midday meal, my stomach felt tight and I was not hungry for any of the good food that would surely be waiting for me in that room with the dark red couch. Then I thought of the loom, and this time I did not hesitate.

Once again my hands became a part of the warp and weft, and my body again found the rhythm of the picture I'd begun. It was a meadow not far from our farmhold; the spring-green grass was dotted with purple fleur-de-lis, and an impatient brook cut through the foreground. I believed it was the best work I had ever done. Then I heard a noise. This time when I turned, the white bear was lying on the rug not four feet from me, his black eyes watching.

Troll Queen

ON THE DAY I BROUGHT the softskin boy to Huldre I wrote in my Book:

> It is done. He is here at last and my joy is un-bounded.
>
> But my father rages at me. It must be undone, he says.
>
> I point out to him that it cannot be undone. Death is death in the green lands as well as in Huldre.
>
> "Then there will be punishment," he says. "You cannot keep what you stole, unless conditions that I set down are met."
>
> I have never seen my father so angry. But I am not worried. I shall meet his conditions. And it shall be as I have willed it to be.

Neddy

THINGS HAPPENED very quickly after Harald Soren arrived.

Sara's health began to improve. She grew a little stronger each day, and before long she was joining us at table, her appetite restored. The doctor said she might always be more prone to catching cold but otherwise should live a healthy life. Mother was overjoyed, but she never said anything more to me about owing Sara's recovery to the white bear.

Father and Soren spent all their time together, poring over maps and charts.

One evening, after a long day spent shut up in the storeroom that served as Father's work area, they came into the great room, and I could tell at once from the expression on both their faces that something important had happened.

Father cleared his throat. "It has been decided . . . that is . . . Well, you ought to tell them, Harald."

"Of course. The long and short of it is that I am setting Arne up in his own business. The business of making maps," he said grandly.

Mother let out a glad cry, and Sonja and Sara went to Father, hugging and kissing him. I stayed where I was but gave Father a happy grin.

Soren laughed and barreled on. "I have spent much of the day trying to convince Arne that you should all move to Trondheim; I own a splendid house there that would be perfect for you, quite close to my own home . . . But your father would not hear of leaving this farmhold, though I can't for the life of me figure out why."

I knew why. It was because of Rose. Father wanted to keep everything just as it was before she had left us.

"I will be honest in saying that I would much prefer the work to be centered in Trondheim," Soren continued, "but for the time being I have deferred to Arne. We have begun making plans for the storage room to be enlarged so that Arne will have an adequate workshop. And as soon as I return to Trondheim, I will order all the supplies Arne will need and have them transported by wagon."

Over dinner that night Father and Soren went on to tell us the rest of what they had planned for the mapmaking business.

"You know that ingenious little device that your father invented, the one he calls a strip map? Well, I want your father to make more of them, many more. Unless I am much mistaken, there is remarkable potential in those strip maps."

We were all well familiar with Father's strip maps, as were most of our neighbors. Each map was carved onto a narrow strip of wood and was thus far easier to consult than a large piece of vellum, as well as being considerably more durable. It showed landmarks, bends in the road, crossroads, and the like, and as such a strip map was ideal for short journeys, for well-traveled and possibly confusing routes between villages. Over the years Father had made many strip maps of the lands radiating out from our farmhold.

"I have even drawn up a contract." Soren held up a sheet of parchment. "It gives Arne a generous share of any profit that might accrue from those strip maps of his."

"Will you have to travel a good deal?" I asked Father, knowing how little he liked this aspect of the mapmaking business.

Father nodded.

"Oh yes, he will have to do a great deal of journeying," put in Soren. "I must insist on that. In truth it is my goal to eventually map all of Njord." He laughed. "I know, I know. Never let it be said that I lack for ambition."

I was surprised at Father's easy acceptance of this condition, given his strong dislike of travel, but he explained it to me later.

"I mean to search for Rose," he said.

"Then I will go with you," I said at once.

"No," he replied firmly. "You must stay here and watch over the family. You and Willem will run the farm. Soren has come up with a simplified plan of fewer crops that will mean less work. He has also promised new seed and a new, healthy plow horse."

And so, before we knew it, building had begun on Father's workshop, and Father himself had departed with Soren on the first of what was to be many journeys.

Several weeks later a whole wagonload of crates arrived with all the supplies Father required to start his mapmaking business. To my surprise and joy I found that tucked in among the inks and vellum and tools were some books for me. Apparently Father had told Soren of my interest in scholarly pursuits, and I marveled all over again at the kindness and generosity of this man who had become our guardian angel. We were indeed very fortunate.

Our neighbors must have been astonished at our sudden reversal of fortune, but they were happy for us. To thank neighbor Torsk for his previous generosity, Mother invited him to dinner when Father returned from his first trip, a journey that had been extremely productive mapwise but had yielded no clues as to where Rose had been taken by the white bear.

As Mother served a thick potato soup, Torsk earnestly congratulated us on our good fortune.

"You'll be able to send for Miss Rose now that things are going so well for you," he said with a large smile.

Father stood up suddenly and left the table, his face pale.

Mother tried to smooth things over, offering Torsk some bread. "Rose will indeed be returning to us soon," she said. "You know, I was just speaking with Widow Hautzig, who heard from a *skjebne-soke* down near Andalsnes that the winter will be a mild one..."

Father, who wasn't to have departed for a fortnight on his next exploratory journey, left the next morning. He assigned me the task of setting up his workshop and said he hoped to return with good news.

Rose

IN A DIM CORNER of my mind, while I was still caught in the spell of weaving, I'd been vaguely aware of something moving into the room and settling itself near me. But I was oblivious to anything but the loom, and if I had any thought at all, it was that my dog, Snurri, had come to keep me company. Snurri was getting on in years and loved to lie beside me while I sewed or worked the household loom.

When I discovered that what I thought was Snurri was really the white bear, I jumped up from my stool, dropping the shuttle. It went skittering across the floor, unspooling the deep garnet-red yarn I had been using to create a sunset. The shuttle came to rest beside the bear, the yarn looking like a trail of blood from the loom to his gleaming white fur.

My fear turned quickly to anger, and foolishly forgetting the bear's enormous size and strength, I strode over to him and grabbed up the shuttle, my eyes blazing.

"How dare you sneak in here!" I said. "I have looked everywhere, through every corner of this place, and now you turn up and just sit there, as if...as if..." I trailed off, not able to find the words. Then I began again, my voice shrill with frustration. "Where am I? Why have you brought me here?!"

The white bear rose slowly, almost apologetically, as if he did not want to remind me just how very big he was.

He was so overwhelming, so white and so large, that the room seemed to shrink. Whatever other words I had been about to say died on my lips.

"Come," the bear's voice rumbled.

And quietly I followed him back to the room where I had my meals; in my mind I called it the red-couch room. Another pot was bubbling on the fire, but I barely noticed. I sat on the couch. The white bear took a place by the hearth. He remained standing on his four paws.

"To talk...is hard...I can only do...little." He paused, took a breath. "Your questions...I cannot... answer."

I sat still, mesmerized by his hollow voice and the blurred edges of the words. The sound came from deep down in his chest. His mouth moved but not the way people's lips move when they talk. I could see glimpses of his black tongue, rippling.

"Anything you need...wool, color." He stopped again and breathed heavily. "Ask."

I nodded. "How long am I to stay here?" I could not help myself; I had to know.

"Cannot...answer" was all he said. Then, "Stay... with me."

"I cannot leave?"

"Stay...no harm." It seemed to be getting more difficult for him, as though finding words was almost an impossible strain.

"But the woman in the kitchen, who is she? May I speak to her?"

The bear had begun to lumber toward the door. His steps were unsteady, his eyes clouded.

"Was there something you wanted me to make on the loom?" I asked.

The white bear kept moving, though just before going through the door, he turned his head sideways and the words *"no harm"* came again.

I sat for a moment, watching the now empty doorway.

I found myself wondering why he had brought me to this room to speak to me. Then my stomach rumbled and I realized I was starving.

I grinned. The white bear was making sure I ate.

It is difficult to explain, but after that interaction with the bear, I felt more at peace.

Nothing had changed, I didn't understand any more than I had before, and I was still a prisoner. And yet for some reason the words *"no harm"* comforted me and stayed in my head. For some reason I believed them.

I ate a nourishing meal from the stewpot, accompanied by dark bread and a cup of goat's milk. Then I returned to the loom and worked until I was sleepy. I had no idea whether it was day or night. I would have to make more of a routine for myself so that I would know when the day was done, although when I exited the weaving room, most of the lamps in the hall had been extinguished.

So it was nighttime—at least in the castle carved into the mountain.

A small lamp had been lit and left for me by the door. I picked it up and made my way down the darkened corridor. It was eerie, walking through the echoing halls of the castle, but I firmly repeated to myself the words *"no harm."*

I went to the room where my knapsack had been placed and unpacked the little I had brought with me. The bed looked a lot more comfortable than the red couch. And it was, far beyond anything I had ever slept on. It was large, so large I felt that my whole family might easily have fit in it.

Several oil lamps set in wall sconces lit the room. The oil in the lamps was different from any I had known in Njord. It smelled sweeter and burned cleaner and more slowly. But I had been unable to discover how to light the oil lamps myself. I looked for flints or some kind of striker but found none. In the castle there was no need to light a lamp myself, for each time I entered a room, lamps and candles were already burning.

When I was ready to sleep, I blew out all the lamps and candles but one, so the room wouldn't be completely dark.

As I lay there nestled in the softness of the mattress and comforters, I thought of my family. At home I was used to sleeping with at least my two sisters, and I felt lonely and strange, lying by myself in that large bed.

I slept. Sometime later I awoke, softly. My sister Sara had just climbed into bed and I pulled a little away, because her feet were always chilly and I was so warm and drowsily content in the soft...

Suddenly I came wide awake. I was not at home and it was not my sister who had climbed into bed beside me.

Troll Queen

I STILL HAVE MY father's decree in my Book:

My daughter, the princess, has defied me and taken a high-born softskin. As punishment she shall forthwith be bound by my edict in this matter.

The boy stolen from the green lands shall be transformed into a white bear. He will reside in the castle carved into a mountain in the softskin land we call Suudella, and he will be given enough arts so that he may survive. A Huldre servant will also be supplied to serve him in the castle in the mountain.

Further, no request that he shall make of one of Huldre shall be denied. Except the request to be released from his enchantment. To be released from the enchantment, the white bear that was a softskin must abide by and satisfy a set of inviolable conditions.

These conditions shall be made known to him in their entirety.

So it has been decreed, and let this stand as an example to those who would defy their king.

Rose

IT WAS PITCH-BLACK in the room. I lay there in the darkness, my heart pounding and my limbs stiff, thinking desperately of what I could use as a weapon to protect myself. But the figure beside me in the bed stayed well away; there were at least two arm-lengths between us, so large was the bed. It briefly adjusted the covers and then lay still.

Of all the things that had happened to me during the past days, this was surely the strangest, the most confusing. At first I wondered if the white bear himself had climbed into bed with me. But though it was a large bed, it was not so large as to fit both a huge bear and myself, with two arm-lengths between. And as my pounding heart slowed, I reasoned that, based on the tilt of the mattress, the weight of whatever was beside me was not much heavier than my sister, although it was difficult to judge because of the distance between us and the soft-ness of the mattress.

The minutes went by and there was no movement at all from the figure. At first my mind whirled frantically, trying to fathom who or what it was. The white lady or man from the kitchen? Or another such person of the castle whom I had yet to meet? Was it indeed human? Or beast? Perhaps an enchanted king or some kind of ghost or spirit. But gradually my thoughts ran out and my fear and confusion seemed to drain away. Amazingly, I slept.

When I awoke there was a dim light in the room. The door was partially open and the light was coming from the lamps lining the hall. I could see that there was no one in the bed next to me, and for a moment I wondered if the whole thing was a dream. But the bed linens on that side of the bed were rumpled, and I knew it wasn't.

There was food waiting for me when I went down to the red-couch room, but I was distracted as I ate the porridge and fruit. I could not stop thinking about the strange episode of the night before. I thought about it continually through the day, as I sat at the loom. I kept having the nagging feeling that, despite the evidence of my own senses, it *had* been the white bear that had lain beside me. I alternately dreaded and looked forward to going to bed that night. I dreaded it because the whole thing might happen again, and I looked forward to it also because it might indeed happen again and maybe this time would be explained. I resolved to keep the oil lamps in the bedroom lit.

The white bear did not visit while I wove, which, oddly enough, disappointed me. Though I doubted I would get an answer, I still yearned to ask him for an explanation of my night visitor.

When I was done weaving for the day, I ate a meal of meat stew and bread, and, taking the oil lamp with me, went up to bed. The lamps in the hall were no longer burning.

I washed, then put on my nightdress from home. I left one wall lamp lit as well as the handheld lamp, which I put on the table by the bed. I slipped under the covers and waited. I was determined to stay awake so that if the visitor came again I would be able to see its face.

I don't know how long I lay there, eyes wide open, waiting, but suddenly the lamps went out. I started to sit up; I was sure there had been oil enough in those lamps to last the night through. But I froze when moments later I felt something climb into the bed and pull up the covers. I briefly cursed the lack of a flint to relight the lamp, vowing to search for one in the morning.

But this time I had been fully awake when my visitor settled onto the bed, and I was better able to gauge the give in the mattress. It confirmed my initial feeling that this was a being somewhat larger than my sister but certainly not as huge as a bear. It could not be the white bear.

I thought for a moment of trying to speak to the figure but had a strong sense that I should not. Something mysterious was happening, and I felt that the sound of my voice would be jarring and wrong.

Again, the visitor did not move and stayed well away from me. And again I felt my tension drain. As I was drifting toward sleep, I even had the sensation of comfort, almost like I was at home sleeping beside my sister.

And once again the next morning, my visitor was gone.

Father

FOR MY THIRD JOURNEY I headed due south. My previous two had been north and northwest. Soren was eager for me to explore to the south, as there were so many areas there that remained uncharted.

In the course of mapping the lands I traveled through, I spoke to many local inhabitants, asking them about towns, rivers, and lakes, and the best routes between this point and that. Always at the end of our conversations, I would throw in a casual question about white bears, saying I had heard they were occasionally seen about and had any passed through of late. I dared not ask whether anyone had seen a white bear and a young girl traveling together, for I would surely be thought mad. Even my innocent question about white bears raised eyebrows, especially the farther south I went. *A white bear? This far south?* their faces would seem to say.

Though I had my work to occupy me, I was still beside myself with worry about Rose. Every dead end, and every blank look at my queries, sent me deeper into despair.

But in a small town not far from the seacoast, I finally had luck.

I came across a gentleman leading two heifers along a country road. We bade each other good day, he gazing with curiosity at the pad of paper and other tools I had been using to mark the road. We conversed for a moment, as I explained that I was a mapmaker, then casually I trotted out my usual query about whether he or anyone he knew had ever seen a white bear in the vicinity.

"Only the likes of Sig Everhart has ever claimed to see bears, and that's only when he's paid one too many visits to the wine barrel," the man responded with a laugh.

"Ah yes, wine can make us all see things." I laughed with him, but my interest quickened. "And where might I find this Master Everhart?"

"Lives in town," the man replied, cocking an eyebrow at me.

"I'd be obliged if you could direct me," I said.

And the man did, saying, "Sig's a good fellow, except for his weakness for wine."

But I was already hastening along the road to town. I quickly tracked down the man in his barn, where he was halfheartedly grooming a scrawny horse. He was clearly nursing a painful hangover.

I was not in the mood for tackling the subject sideways, so I just came right out and asked, "Have you seen a white bear in the past month or so?"

He frowned, and said suspiciously, "Ah, after a bit of fun, are you, stranger? Who put you up to it? Asa? Or Jonah?"

Impatient, I told him that no one had sent me and that I just needed to know the answer to my question.

Sig Everhart looked at me, then turned aside and spat into the hay. "Saw a white bear—last full moon, I think it was. Past midnight. I had lost my way in the woods outside town. Mind you, I was drunk as a horned owl. But I saw it, I swear. And it had summat riding on its back."

My heart felt like it would pound its way out of my chest. I grabbed the man's arms with my hands. "Which way was it going? How fast did it travel? Could you see what was on its back?"

He pulled away from me, looking wary. "Probably naught more than a ... What do you call them? ... Hallucination. Brought on by the drink. Haven't been that soused since. Although last night I came close ..."

"Please," I said, my voice cracking. "Just tell me."

The man must have sensed my desperation, for he held up a placating hand. "Sure, sure. Well, whatever it was, hallucination or not, it was moving fast. But it had slowed down, to pick its way over Rilling Creek. And it was heading south. Could see naught of what rode its back. Could have been dirt even, or leaves. Or the wine..." he added with a grimace, putting his hand to his temple.

That was all I could get from the hungover Sig Everhart, but it was enough to give me my first spark of hope in a long while.

In my own mind I had no doubt that what the man had seen was my Rose riding on the back of the white bear. And so I found my way to Rilling Creek and from there headed south.

But days turned to weeks, and I could find no other trace of Rose and the white bear. I combed each village, asking everyone I saw. I roamed the woods, the meadows.

Finally I came to the sea, the farthest south I could go. I had combed the coastland, east and west, asking everyone I met, knocking at the doors to hundreds of strangers' homes. And so I stood by the water's edge and stared over the waves. It had been more than two months since I had left home, and the only clue to Rose's whereabouts had been from a drunken sot. But it was a slender thread of hope and I clung to it like a drowning man.

Rose

I LOOKED IN VAIN for a striker; I could not find even a
flint or a bit of iron. I tried fashioning something for myself. But nothing worked. When nighttime came (or at
least what could be considered nighttime in the castle), I
could find no way to illuminate the utter blackness of my
bedroom, no matter what I tried. Candles, oil lamps—
all were extinguished the moment before my visitor arrived. Night after night it happened, the unlightable
darkness followed by the give in the mattress, and the
odd thing was, I grew used to it.

I decided it was an enchantment. And that I wasn't
meant to see who, or what, my visitor was.

One night I did try speaking out loud to my visitor,
but my tongue felt overlarge in my mouth and my voice
came out hoarse and unintelligible. And what was there
to say, really? There was such an air of wrongness about
it, as if I were violating some sacred code or rule, that I

did not try again. At any rate, there was no response to my croaking, not even a rustle of a sheet.

One or two times I was overtaken by the strong desire to reach over across the bed and touch whatever it was, to see if my fingers would encounter skin or fur or... But that, too, felt strictly forbidden, even more than talking, and somehow I knew I must not risk it.

Yet I never stopped trying to guess who my visitor was. I came to believe that it *was* the white bear. His smaller size was due to the fact that he had shed his fur for the night, which would also explain the lack of bulk. From riding on his back, I knew just how deep and heavy the bear's coat was. And this theory fit with something I had noticed—that the figure next to me often shivered, pulling the covers up close and tight as if to warm himself. I couldn't imagine just what the bear would look like without fur, but the idea didn't repulse me. Instead it made me feel sympathy for him.

With time, life at the castle took on a routine. I measured my hours by the number of feet of weaving I had accomplished and by the grumblings of my stomach, and I measured my days with a calendar of sorts I made from a piece of fabric. Each day I put one stitch in the fabric. I changed the color of thread when I had counted thirty stitches. For exercise I walked the halls of the castle. I grew to know by heart every doorway, every painting on the wall, every inch of every rug. And one day I discovered something that made my imprisonment in the castle easier to endure.

Behind a dark-hued tapestry at the end of a dimly lit hall on the top floor, I found a door. The door opened onto a small, winding staircase, which was not lit. I went and got a candle, and climbed the stairs. At the top, which must have been the highest point of the castle, I found a tiny window. I could see little through it—just the sky and a lone tree branch—and could open the thick glass pane only about an inch. But the opening gave me the faintest taste of fresh air, as well as a sense of night and day beyond that which was provided by the lamps and candles of the castle. I visited that window nearly every day.

Another place I went each day (other than the weaving room) was the room I called the library. Most of the books were in Fransk, a language I knew because my mother had taught it to me as a child, though I was not fluent.

There were also books in Latin, which I knew very slightly from our family bible, and I even found two books written in Njorden. One of them, to my delight, was a book of the old stories like the ones Neddy used to tell me, the ones with Freya and Thor and Odin and Loki.

The white woman and man kept things in the castle running smoothly. They provided me with delicious, nourishing meals. They kept lamps and fires lit in the rooms I used, and tidied up after me and the white bear (whose only bad quality I could see was his shedding; I'd occasionally come across tufts of white fur stuck to the edges of furniture). They did all this without my seeing them, except for now and then, and those times they would always hurry away. The door to the kitchen was kept locked, and the few times we came face-to-face, the language difference made it impossible to understand each other.

The white bear visited me daily as I worked the loom. Usually it was in the afternoon and he would lie on the rug near me. I took to talking to him, though he rarely responded. I would tell him of my family, of life on our farmhold, and of the places I had explored beyond the farm. I would also tell him stories, both from my memory of the ones Neddy had told me and those from the Njorden book I had found.

I didn't know what he thought of my chatter, but I came to believe he liked the sound of my voice. If I was in a quiet mood, he would raise his head expectantly, as if waiting for me to start talking.

I grew used to his presence, and his sheer immensity no longer distracted me. A wordless communication developed between us. I could read his mood by the way he held his head, the small sounds he made, and even the way his fur lay on his body. Much of what I understood about him I saw in his eyes, those deep, expressive black eyes. I sensed something almost human in him, a thin, wavering strain of thought and feeling that was decidedly nonanimal. I believed it was where his limited ability to speak came from.

I wondered if at one time he had been either all animal or all human, and then those two elements of him were mingled, though clearly the animal in him had become the stronger and that was why words were so difficult.

There were times I sensed he hated that nonanimal flicker inside him, wished he could obliterate it altogether. And there were times I felt he clung to it for dear life. There were also a few times that I felt that this barely perceptible flicker was the only thing that kept him from ripping me to shreds or devouring me whole.

On one occasion I was coming out of my room on my way to the loom. I had just bathed and my face was flushed from the heat of the water I had bathed in. The white bear was standing just outside the door, and I nearly ran into him.

I heard a low growl coming from deep in his throat, and I glanced up into his eyes. To my horror they were blank, almost unrecognizable, with a terrible hunger in them. I stepped back, my heart thudding in my chest. He bared his teeth, something he'd never done before, and the growl grew louder. He took a step forward.

Without thinking I darted backward into the room, slamming the door behind me.

Desperately my hand scrabbled for a key or lock, but there was none. I pressed my back against the door, knowing how futile the effort was, given the enormous strength of the white bear. Batting down a door would be child's play to him. I heard a scratching sound on the door, then a sudden unearthly roar, like that of a creature in indescribable torment.

The roar echoed for a moment, then all was still. I waited a very long time before venturing out of my room again.

After I finished the weaving of the meadow from home, I moved on to a design from one of the stories I'd read in the Njorden book. It was a harsh tale about the trick Loki played on Idun, the guardian of the golden apples that ensured immortality to the gods. My weaving depicted Idun in the place the terrible giant Thiassi had taken her—a cavernous hall lit by columns of fire that burst from the earth.

When I was finished I was well pleased. I had intended both pieces as wall hangings, inspired by the tapestries on the walls of the castle. But though there was no fault or mistake in either, when I gazed at them side by side I began to feel dissatisfied with both. The first was lovely to look at, but it had no feeling to it. It was a pretty scene, remote and at a distance. The second piece had an anger to it that made me feel unsettled and unhappy.

I decided to take a rest from weaving to work on another kind of project instead. So I set about repairing my torn cloak. It was the last thing Neddy had given me, and if I was ever allowed to return home, I would need my "compass." Strangely, I gave no thought to making a new cloak. The old one was a link to my life back home, and I didn't want to break that link despite the lie that was woven into it.

Using the castle's good, strong thread and sharp needles, I quickly mended the cloak. And the white bear watched me, as he always did. When I came to the part of the wind rose where Father had hidden the truth, I felt tears prick my eyes. I thought of my father, of the pain I must have caused him with my anger. He may have been wrong to go along with Mother's lie, but he had done so reluctantly. I remembered the name that Father had called me in his heart. *Nyamh*. And more tears fell.

"You are sad," came the deep hollow voice.

I jumped a little, because the bear had not spoken to me in a week or more. But then I nodded, wiping my face with the edge of the cloak.

"Why?"

And the words came tumbling out as I told the white bear the whole tale of the birth-direction lie. When I was done, we were both silent. Then he said, "Rose . . . Nyamh . . . East . . . North . . . West . . . South . . . You are . . ."

I laughed a little. "I am *all* of the directions?"

He nodded.

"Are you saying you think the whole birth-direction superstition is nonsense?"

"No." He sounded definite, but when I asked him to explain what he meant, he did not answer but lay with his eyes shut, as though the small amount of speaking he had done had worn him out.

I sat watching him, confused but no longer sad. Again, despite his size and despite the fact that he had taken me from my family and home, I felt stirrings of sympathy for him.

"Is Sara well?" I blurted out.

He opened his eyes halfway. "Yes." The word was expelled from his chest like an arrow pulled from a wound. And then he left the room.

I thought of Sara as I finished mending and cleaning the cloak. I was relieved to hear that she had recovered. And I believed it to be true; for some reason I could not imagine the white bear lying.

I took my mended cloak to my room, folded it neatly, and stored it in my pack from home. Then I returned to the weaving room and began to think about what I wanted to make next on the loom.

My eye had been caught by spools of gold, silver, and pearly moon-colored threads, and I suddenly decided to make a gown for myself. It was a ridiculous decision. I had never made any clothing that did not have some practical use, and there was certainly no call for ball gowns on a remote, impoverished farmhold. Nevertheless, I decided to do it. After all, there was nothing I *needed*. Everything—my lodging, food, drink—was being taken care of for me. So why not go ahead and make something thoroughly impractical?

At first I could not decide which of the shining

threads to use. I was drawn most to the pearly moon-thread, as I called it, but the others were so lovely, too. Then I made an even more ridiculous decision. I would make three gowns. "Well, why not?" I said to myself. I had all the time in the world, and each color would make a beautiful gown.

I would start with the silver, then gold, leaving the moon-thread for last.

I felt a thrill of excitement as I cast the delicate yet amazingly strong silver thread onto the loom. It should have been difficult to work with, so fine were the strands, but because of the exquisite craftsmanship of the loom, it was not.

I would make the fabric first, I decided, then design a pattern later.

As I wove, my mind twirled pleasurably through dozens of possible dress designs. I knew little about the latest fashions, but there were pictures in the book of Njorden tales, and the gowns worn by Freya, Idun, and Sif were lovely.

The shimmering fabric took shape under my fingers and I was in awe of its beauty. The further I got, the more I began to have doubts about using it to make a dress for myself. It really was fitting only for a princess or some other grand lady, not the daughter of a poor farmer. If (no, *when,* I told myself firmly) I ever left the castle, there would be no place in my life for a gown made of silver fabric.

I decided I would sell it. Such a sumptuous gown

would fetch a small fortune, and that kind of money would help pay back all our debts on the farm, or it could enable Neddy to go to Bergen or Oslo to do the scholarly work he had always yearned to do. It could even help set Father up in a mapmaking business of his own.

So I kept weaving and planning the design of the dress. And if I occasionally imagined myself wearing it... Well, there was no harm in that.

When I had woven enough of the glittering silver fabric, I began work on the dress. I went slowly and carefully, unaccustomed as I was to handling such exquisite fabric, and I did not want to make any mistakes.

Because I had to concentrate while I was creating the gown, I did not talk as much to the white bear. As a result he seemed more restless and would not stay with me but would pad in and out of the room with a put-upon expression in his black eyes.

At last I finished. Shaking it out, I held the dress up. It was a simple design, falling to the floor in silvery folds from a high waistline. I decided I must try the gown on, telling myself I just needed to see that it hung right. Remembering the long mirror in my room, I hurried there, carrying the dress. A little nervously I slipped the gown on, my back to the mirror. When I turned around I barely recognized myself. I stared for a moment, then let out a laugh.

I looked ridiculous, like an awkward little girl trying on her mother's wedding dress. I made a face at myself in the mirror, then grinned, saying, "That's what comes of putting a fancy dress on a girl who belongs in muddy boots and torn cloaks."

I had enjoyed making the dress, anyway, and believed it would fetch a high price, so I launched right into the making of the next, this time using the gold thread. This thread, too, was extraordinary, no thicker than the filament of a spider's web, yet it was just as strong as the silver. I felt like I was working with the spun gold from fairy tales. The dress turned out to be more elaborate than the silver one, and just as lovely.

And so I came to the moon-thread. While I was making the fabric, I told the white bear the tale of the Maid of the North and of how Vaina the song maker tricked Seppo the sky maker into going to the frozen land by singing into creation a giant pine tree with a moon and stars in its branches. By the way the white bear held his head, and the expression in his eyes, I could see that he was listening intently.

I marveled as the fabric took shape on my loom. The gold and silver had been beautiful, but this was something extraordinary. It seemed from another world entirely, a world you might glimpse on a frozen, misty winter day with the northern lights blazing above. I remembered the first time I had seen the northern lights as a child. I was breathless with excitement, convinced I was seeing the way into a whole new land, or into Asgard itself, where Freya and Idun and the thunder god Thor lived.

I hadn't understood Father's logical explanation about the phenomenon of the aurora. To me it was sheer magic.

And the fabric I had made looked almost as much like the northern lights as it did the moon. At once moon white, the cloth would come startlingly alive with pearly, rippling color when the light caught it in a certain way.

When the time came to design the gown, I didn't look at any books but let the fabric itself guide me.

I cut and stitched and pieced the gown with the greatest concentration. Then I found a spool of pearly moon-ribbon and a small bowl of pearly buttons I had not noticed before, and used them for the finishing touches. I barely noticed if the white bear was there in the room with me.

The moment I was done, and had sewed on the last pearly ribbon and button, I ran to my room so fast I was out of breath when I got there. And in my haste I forgot to shut the door behind me.

When I stood before the mirror in this dress, I did not laugh. For just a moment I saw myself as beautiful. And I smiled at my reflection. Dreamily I thought how I might put my hair up and wind a length of moon-ribbon through it.

Then I heard a noise. A gusty, sighing sound like I had heard once before, when I first came to the castle. I spun around and saw the white bear standing in the doorway.

I froze. I was afraid for the first time in a long while. We stared at each other. For what felt like an eternity, all I was aware of were those black eyes, fierce and sad, fixed on mine. Finally the white bear lowered his head.

He kept it low for several moments. Then he raised it again, turned, and walked away and out of sight.

My cheeks were flushed and my heart beat fast. I crossed to the door and shut it. I noticed that my hands were shaking.

Quickly I took off the dress, my fingers trembling. I donned my old clothing. Next to the glory of the moon gown, my worn woolen dress looked particularly shabby. Instead of wasting time on impractical ball gowns, I should have been making sturdy new clothing for myself.

"Enough of fairy-tale moon dresses," I told myself firmly. But my face was still hot and I didn't know why.

White Bear

Glowing.
The moon through a doorway.

Breath hard in my throat.
Heart full to burst.

The moon through a doorway.
And in its light...
Hope.

Neddy

WHEN FATHER RETURNED from his journey, he told me of his exhausting, disappointing search, and also of the one little glimmer of hope. A sighting by a drunken fool was too pitiful to pin one's hopes to, but we both did anyway.

In the meantime, we were just beginning to experience the fruits of our newfound good fortune. The "journey maps" that Soren had thought so promising turned out to be vastly successful, exceeding even his expectations. Demand for more, with increased routings, came pouring in. My brother and sister and I were put in charge of drafting new maps based on the new charts Father had brought back. Father supervised us, until it was time for him to leave again. Between that work and watching over the farm, I barely had time to look at the books Soren had so kindly sent to me.

I noticed that in Father's absence Mother was becoming even more superstitious than before. In part this was because Father wasn't there to temper her, but I also believe that because in some way—either small or large, depending on your point of view—it was Mother's superstition that had caused us to lose Rose, she had to justify herself. If it was superstition that lost Rose, then superstition would also bring her back. At least that was my best guess as to why Mother was behaving the way she did.

I also noticed, as we all did, that Mother had suddenly gotten quite chummy with Widow Hautzig. The unpleasant woman had come nosing around when she got wind of our reversal in fortune, and we were all mystified at first by the burgeoning friendship until we discovered that Widow Hautzig was also very superstitious. Rose had commented on this to me once or twice, but I had paid little attention. Also, Mother had found an herbal remedy for rheumatism that Widow Hautzig swore by, and this, too, tightened their bond.

I overheard them one day going on about some charm worn around the ankle that would direct a person to that which was lost. I thought I heard the old widow whisper Rose's name, and I saw Mother shake her head with a sidelong glance at me. I wondered then just how much Mother may have confided in Widow Hautzig, and the thought made me uncomfortable.

Father returned from his most recent journey, but this time he had not even a kernel of hope to offer. He seemed tired and out of sorts. And not long after his arrival home, I came across Mother and Father quarreling. She was urging him to tie the herbal charm around his ankle when he set off on his next journey to seek Rose. Father's face was pale and his tone was tight, as if from the strain of holding in a great rage. "I want none of your charms, Eugenia. It was your foolish superstition that led us down this road and I'll have none of it. Not ever again, do you hear!" And he stalked away.

The look on Mother's face at first made me want to comfort her, for she seemed confused and unhappy, even a little lost. But then I saw her give a shrug, and her features resolved into a placid, comfortable expression. And instead of comforting her, I, too, walked away.

There was money by then to make improvements to the farmhouse, and Mother enjoyed the choosing and spending, though she tried not to show it too much. We were all aware, every minute of every day, of that which was lost to us, and no amount of comfort or wealth would make up for that.

One of the first purchases Mother made was the loom owned by Widow Hautzig, the one that we had repaired. (It seemed to me that the least the widow could have done was to give that loom as a gift to us, especially because we had been the ones to restore it to working order, but despite her close friendship with Mother, the widow was as grasping as ever.) Mother cleaned and polished the loom, and set it in a place of honor in our great room, where it awaited Rose's return.

Widow Hautzig took to accompanying Mother on her occasional shopping trips into Andalsnes. They spent much of their time at a shop run by Sikram Ralatt, a traveling merchant who had recently come to Andalsnes. He sold various concoctions and herbal remedies, as well as a whole line of charms promising one outcome or another. As I said, Father was either traveling or working in his new workshop, and paid little heed to what Mother was doing. But I saw and was uneasy.

Rose

I SET TO WORK ON a dress of plain gray wool, and the feel of the coarse thread settled me. I had hung the dresses of silver, gold, and moon in a large cupboard in my room, where I kept my own few items of clothing. But every night before bed, I would see those extravagant gowns lined up in a row and I would flush with embarrassment. I kept reminding myself I had made them to sell but didn't really believe it.

One evening I could no longer stand looking at them and decided to pack the dresses away, ready for taking with me if I—no, *when* I—left there. Though I wouldn't have dreamed of taking anything else from the castle, like a book or a fine bowl, for some reason I didn't think twice about taking the gowns away with me. The way I looked at it was, taking something that already had been there when I arrived was the same as stealing, but I had created the dresses myself, and the materials I used . . . Well, those were little enough payment for my lost freedom.

Taking the silver gown over to the bed, I carefully began folding it. The gowns were not small, with their large floor-length skirts. I would need something much bigger than my little knapsack from home to carry the dresses in. But a curious thing happened while I folded. The gossamer fabric compacted, even seemed to shrink in on itself, and with each fold it got smaller and smaller. I kept folding, amazed by the strange properties of the fabric, until I was left with a small square that fit into the palm of my hand. I stared at the small silver packet, unbelieving. And yet there it was.

I became suddenly worried that something had happened to the dress, that it had been crushed and compacted beyond wearing, so I unfolded it. And the reverse occurred. When I was done the dress shook out beautifully, unwrinkled and intact. So I folded it all over again, and did the same with the golden gown. It, too, folded neatly into a small square. As did the moon dress.

I looked at the three small packets lying on the bed, wondering if they would fit into the leather wallet I had brought with me. Neddy had made it, and because I had no money, it held a small sewing kit with needles, pins, and several kinds of thread.

I retrieved the wallet from my bag and, taking out the sewing kit, slipped the folded dresses into it. They fit perfectly, as if the wallet had been designed for storing them. I stowed the full wallet in my bag, which I placed back in the cupboard.

The gray dress was quickly finished, although working on it was quite boring in contrast to creating the three gowns. Then, in quick succession, I produced thick woolen stockings, woolen mittens, and a hat and scarf, all out of the same gray wool. Making those sturdy garments was like returning to a diet of hard bread and water after overindulging in the likes of champagne and cream-filled cakes. Bland and dull that "diet" may have been, but it steadied me and I was pleased with the fruits of my labor.

One night as I lay in bed, I noticed that my visitor was shivering more than usual. I almost spoke, thinking to offer an extra blanket, but bit the words back. And in that moment I lit on what my next project on the loom would be.

I would make a soft flannel nightshirt for my visitor, for the furless white bear, as I had come to think of him. And I would use his own fur to make the flannel even warmer. Whenever I had come across a tuft of white fur in the castle, fur the white bear had shed, I would collect it. It had been sheer instinct, a throwback to the lean days when I had saved every bit of sheep's wool I found on bushes, fences, and the like. And the bear fur was so luxuriant, so soft, I hadn't been able to curb my thriftiness and so had accumulated a large basketful.

I had never spun bear fur into thread, but with the marvelous spinning wheels in the castle, I thought I'd be able to manage it. I mingled the bear's fur with some soft (and very white) sheep's wool I had found in a bin, and soon I had spun enough yarn for my purpose. I cast the silky thread onto the loom and began to weave.

The white bear was absent during much of this time. It was nearly spring, according to my crude fabric-calendar, though I could not tell if the tree branch I saw through my window had any buds on it.

It was while working on the nightshirt that I set myself the project of learning more of the Fransk language. Mother had claimed I had a talent for learning languages but had wasted it because I would not sit still long enough to be taught. The only reason I let her teach me Fransk at all was because I was certain I would be traveling the entire world on the back of my imaginary white bear and would need to know as many languages as possible. Fransk was the only language my mother knew with any fluency, but she also had taught me what she knew of the Tysk and Gronlander dialects. And I was always eager to pick up any foreign words from strangers who passed through our part of the world.

I was close to finishing the nightshirt when I was hit by a terrible feeling of homesickness. It was the first time since those early weeks of living in the castle that I had felt it so strongly. It may have been the thought of spring, or maybe just that I had been in the castle for so long, but whatever the reason, the feeling was over-whelming. I tried to ignore it and concentrated on the soft white cloth.

I was fashioning it into a long, generously sized shirt. I decided against buttons or ties, thinking that if I was correct, paws would not do well with them. I made it so it could be pulled on over the head. If I was wrong, and my night visitor was not a bear but a person, then a small brooch could be used for fastening at the neck. In fact, I found such a brooch in the music room. It was fashioned in the shape of a silver flauto, very similar to the one that held the position of honor in the box with the blue-velvet cloth.

On the night I finished the shirt, I laid it carefully on the far side of the bed and placed the brooch beside it. I was intensely curious about what my visitor would do. Would it alter at all its nightly routine? Would it put on the shirt? Finally speak to me? Or would it not even notice the white shirt in the complete blackness of the room?

I lay waiting, tense with anticipation. Then there came the barely perceptible sighing sound of the door opening and shutting. No light ever spilled into the room, for at this time of night the hallway was pitch-black as well. There was the usual silence as my visitor crossed the room. Typically then I would feel the give in the mattress, followed by the adjustment of the covers. But this time the silence lasted longer. I strained my ears, all my senses. What was he doing? . . . Was he . . . ? And then, yes, I felt sure the nightshirt was being lifted off the bed. A sound of rustling fabric, as though it was being slipped over a head, arms pushing through the sleeves. There came a very faint clicking sound, of metal against metal, as of a brooch being fastened.

Soon there was the familiar give in the mattress, the covers pulled up, and then, nothing. I had not expected words, a conventional thank-you, so was not disappointed in the silence.

In the morning the nightshirt was neatly folded at the foot of the bed, the visitor's side, with the brooch attached at the neck. This pleased me very much. It was a sign the shirt had been worn and appreciated. And I had noticed no shivering at all during the night.

While I was dressing I kept looking at the folded bundle at the foot of the bed. Finally I could contain myself no longer and crossed to it, unfolding and pressing the nightshirt to my face. I breathed in.

I'm not sure what I was seeking, possibly the smell of the white bear. There was a trace of that smell, but it could easily have been because of the bear fur I'd used in weaving the shirt. But there was another very faint smell that I could not identify, nor put words to—a good smell.

Then I folded the shirt up again and placed it on the bed.

Each night I laid the shirt out on the side of the bed and every morning it would be folded at the foot. And my visitor never again showed any signs of shivering.

Every seven days I washed the shirt, along with my own clothing. It was one chore that from the beginning I had insisted on doing myself. In those first weeks I had set up a room especially for washing. It was one of the plainer rooms in the castle and had a generous hearth fire for heating water and the stones I used for ironing. The white woman and man caught on right away and made sure the fire was always lit on washing day. The nightshirt never got dirty or smelled any different from the first time I had put it to my nose, but I wanted to keep it fresh.

One washing day I had just given a final rinse to the nightshirt and was holding it up over the hot water. With steam rolling off its surface, I was thinking how the whiteness of the fabric had a ghostly sort of glow. Then I heard a sound. It was that sighing sound I had heard before, when I was trying on the moon dress and saw the bear through the doorway. And there he was again, standing in the doorway watching me, his eyes avid, almost hungry. Startled, I dropped the nightshirt back into the bucket and hot water splashed up on me. I let out a little cry and the white bear took a few steps toward me. Unhurt, I brushed at the water on my clothing, but my eyes locked with those of the white bear. He gave a low growl, like he was in pain, then he swung his head around and padded quickly away, down the hall.

The homesickness that had begun while I was finishing the nightshirt grew worse. It was intensified, I believe, because I had nothing more I wanted to make on the loom. Or it may have been my homesickness that made me lose interest in weaving, sewing, and spinning. Sitting there at the loom suddenly felt dull and tiresome.

I thought constantly of my family, trying to picture them as spring came to the farm. I did not know for sure that they were still there; in fact, they probably were not, in that they had been on the verge of moving away, but I stubbornly kept imagining them there, in all the familiar places.

I thought about the land around our farm, of my favorite rambles, of the snowdrops that would be coming up beside the creek, and the carpet of spring heather that would blanket the hills to the west. I would sit on the red couch by the hour, gazing vacantly into the hearth fire, thinking of the way the wind had felt on my skin. And the sun hot on my hair.

When I wasn't in the red-couch room, I would sit beside the small window at the top of the castle. I could then clearly see that the lone tree branch had sprouted the beginnings of leaves. I tried jamming my hand through the tiny opening in a ridiculous attempt to reach the leaves, but the branch was much too far away and all I got were scraped knuckles. Some days it was too painful to see the blue of the sky and the green of the new leaves, and I would retreat to the red couch.

The white bear would find me there and I could tell he was uneasy. His eyes watched me with a sad, unsettled look and his skin twitched, as if he was reflecting the restlessness and unhappiness he saw in my face.

I no longer spoke to him or told him stories. I was angry. After all, he was the reason I was not out walking my own familiar trails; it was he who had brought me to this prison. When those feelings grew strong, I would stalk out of the room and restlessly roam the corridors and rooms of the castle. The white bear did not follow me.

My unhappiness began to affect my sleep. I tossed and turned, uncaring whether or not I disturbed my unseen companion. Still, despite my unhappy state I did not violate the unspoken rules about trying to touch or speak to the visitor. Something kept me, just barely, from straying over that line. I still laid out the nightshirt but only out of habit.

I ate little and could tell that I was getting thin and unhealthy, yet I did not care. I had no will for anything except either sitting and staring or incessantly roaming the castle. I had lost interest in my makeshift calendar and no longer knew the day or even the month. Gradually my little spurts of anger at the white bear became the only moments I felt much of anything at all, and after a while even my anger grew dull.

One day I was sitting on the red couch, staring at nothing, when the white bear came into the room. He did not lie in his usual spot but stood facing me and spoke. I had not heard his voice in a long time.

"You . . . are ill?"

"No," I said apathetically.

"No food . . . pale."

"I'm not hungry."

"Then unhappy . . ." he intoned mournfully. ". . . lonely?"

I looked up at him. "I need to go home," I said simply, "or I think I might die."

I thought I heard a groan escape from deep in the bear's chest.

I felt a stirring of the old me. "You must let me go. For a visit only. Please."

He lowered his head in that nodding gesture I had come to know.

My heart started pounding. *Home. Fresh air. The wind.* I thought I might faint.

"When?" I asked, barely able to hide my excitement.

"Tomorrow." His voice filled the room, though faintly, like the knell of a far-off bell.

Neddy

IT WAS ONE OF THE fairest springs we'd ever had on the farm. Each day dawned clear and fresh, with a bright blue sky. And somehow the very beauty of the days sharpened my feelings of missing Rose.

Early in lambing season I began to notice that Mother and Widow Hautzig were up to something. They were always whispering together or spending hours in the woods collecting things they kept hidden. My guess was that they were concocting some sort of charm, either a finding charm to bring Rose back or a love charm to heal the rift between Mother and Father. If Father had been at home, I would have talked to him about it, but he was gone again.

Soren had told me about a scholar in Trondheim who was eager for an apprentice or assistant. After hearing about me, the scholar suggested that we meet. I knew Soren was longing for Father to move the mapmaking business to Trondheim, and that he was trying to enlist me in his efforts. Though I was sorely tempted to meet the scholar, I felt as Father did. Because of Rose I did not want to leave the farm. So I put Soren off, saying I was not ready yet, and thanked him for his generous efforts on my behalf.

One day I was walking from Father's workshop up to the house for the midday meal. Willem, Sonja, and I had completed the most recent order from Soren, and I was eagerly looking forward to spending the afternoon poring over the new books he had sent. I saw a figure dressed in gray standing in front of the farmhouse. She was facing away from me, but I knew at once who it was.

"Rose!" I cried out, unbelieving.

She turned to face me. I ran to her, folding her in my arms, my eyes blinded by tears. Then I held her away from me, drinking in the sight of her standing there, solid and real. She looked thinner, but her face glowed with happiness.

"Rose, are you truly back? I can't believe it," I said.

The smile on her face wavered. "'Tis only a visit, Neddy," she said in a quiet voice.

"Why?"

"I promised."

"The white bear?"

"Yes."

"Where is he?"

"He is gone but will return for me."

"How long?"

"One month."

"That is too short! Surely . . ." I stopped when I saw her expression.

Hearing our voices, Willem and Sonja came out of the farmhouse. There were cries of joy and many hugs, and shortly thereafter Mother and Sara came walking up the road, in company with Widow Hautzig.

"Rose? Is it Rose?" Sara cried, and soon Sara, Rose, and Mother were embracing one another all at once while Widow Hautzig looked on.

"Sara, you look well! You are fully recovered?" Rose asked.

Sara smiled and nodded.

"Oh, Sara, I am so happy to see you." And Rose embraced Sara all over again.

"But Rose, you are so thin!" Mother said, tears in her eyes, as she tightly clasped Rose to her. "Come inside," she said, pulling Rose into the farmhouse. "There is soup on the hearth. And then you must tell us everything!"

Rose was so busy gazing around the farmhouse that she seemed barely to hear Mother's words. "Everything is different," she said. "The new furniture. Fresh paint. What has happened while I was gone?"

"Ah, it is a long tale," Mother replied. "Sit down, and I'll fetch you a bowl of soup. Sara, get Rose a cup of apple mead."

Rose obediently sat. Then her eyes lit on the loom.

"Oh, it's Widow Hautzig's loom. How kind of you to give it to us," she said to the widow.

Widow Hautzig had the grace to look a little embarrassed, but Mother rescued her. "It is yours now, Rose. I knew you would be back." She and Widow Hautzig exchanged a look as Mother placed the bowl of soup in front of Rose.

"I . . . I'm sorry, Mother, but I'm not really hungry. Where is Father?"

"Your father is not here, Rose," Mother replied. "He is a mapmaker now. Off on an exploring journey."

"And searching for you," I added.

"A mapmaker! Oh, I am so glad," Rose said happily. "When will he be back?"

"We don't know," I responded. "Last time he was gone nearly two months."

"Oh no!" Rose said, obviously distressed. "I haven't much time . . ."

"What do you mean?" Mother asked sharply. "You are back to stay, aren't you, Rose?"

Rose shook her head. I could see her hands were tightly clenched in her lap.

"Rose is only visiting," I said. "She can stay for one month, no more. Come, Rose, let me show you Father's new workshop."

Rose quickly got to her feet, giving me a grateful look. "I'll eat later, Mother," she said as we went out the door.

"Is Father really a mapmaker, Neddy?" she asked. "Tell me everything!"

While we walked I told her the whole story, of all that

had happened since she had left us. I didn't show her Father's workshop after all, not then, for we decided to keep walking until we got to our favorite spot, the hillside where Rose had first showed me the wind-rose cloak.

Rose listened in amazement. When I was done, I leaned over and took her hand. "Now it is your turn," I said. "Tell me where you have been and all that has happened to you."

She was silent. "I cannot, Neddy," she finally said.

She loosened her hand from mine and, standing up, threw her arms out and put her face toward the sun. "It is so good to be home!" she said, joy radiating from her.

I smiled. Then Rose leaned down and, grabbing up a fistful of heather, put it to her nose, breathing in deeply. I remembered how Rose always loved to smell things. I used to call her an elkhound; her favorite dog, Snurri, was an elkhound, and like all of that breed, he had a remarkable sense of smell.

"Oh, it's wonderful, Neddy. You don't know how wonderful." She went darting about, touching things, smelling them.

Finally she sank down beside me again. "I'm sorry, Neddy. I would like to tell you everything, but I cannot, not very much anyway. There were parts that were very, very nice. And there were some parts that were hard. Like not being able to do this..." She buried her nose in heather again. "And the loneliness. The being shut inside..." She shivered a little, then brightened. "But it is fine, Neddy. I don't mind going back, as long as I can have a little time like this."

"But why must you go back? You do not owe the white bear anything."

"Sara is well now," Rose replied. "And Father's workshop...the good fortune that came to our family because I..."

"You sound like Mother! Rose, those things had nothing to do with the bear. It was coincidence, nothing more. Harald Soren, a flesh-and-blood man, brought about our good fortune, not the bear."

Rose looked at me. There was a yearning in her face, as if she wanted very much to believe what I said. "You can't know that, not for sure, Neddy," she said slowly. "And besides, I made a promise."

"To the bear."

She nodded, her eyes bright. I thought she might weep, but she didn't. "Don't let's talk about this anymore, Neddy."

"I won't press you," I said. "But if you do wish to talk about anything at all, I am here."

"Thank you," she replied softly. And we began making our way back to the farmhouse.

"What is that nasty Widow Hautzig doing here anyway?" Rose asked in a low voice as we saw Mother and the widow coming out of the front door.

"She and Mother have grown thick as thieves," I replied.

"What does Father think of it?"

"He barely notices, he's gone so much. And..." I paused. "Well, there is ill feeling between Mother and Father."

"Because of me?" Rose said quickly.

"It began then," I answered, somewhat unwillingly.

"I am sorry to hear it," Rose said. "Oh, how I wish Father would return!"

"So do I," I replied fervently. "What joy it would give him to see you back home."

Rose

I HAVE ALWAYS THOUGHT time to be a very fickle thing. When you are unhappy, doing something you'd rather not do, time crawls at the slowest, cruelest pace. But when you're happy, it speeds up faster than a skier racing down an icy mountain.

The moments at home seemed to fly by.

How I wanted Father to return! So he'd know I was well and safe, and so I could make up for the anger I'd shown him before I had left. The thought of him wandering the land, looking for me, maybe even putting himself in danger, was almost enough to dampen the joy I felt being home.

The journey from the castle with the white bear had been much like the one before, but the white bear wasn't in such a hurry and I was not so confused and apprehensive. That first moment when I stepped out the doors of the castle in the mountain, I thought I might burst into tears or faint or have some sort of hysterical outburst, but I did nothing except stand there, breathing in my first draught of fresh air in more than six months. The air was fragrant with spring flowers. It was sheer bliss.

The white bear had watched me, letting me get my fill, then he had said, "Come," and I climbed onto his back. I was awkward again after so long. And it felt strange to me, riding on his back as if he were my pet horse, especially because I knew him so well. It was almost like climbing onto Neddy's back. But I was quickly distracted by the immediate need of finding my balance as the white bear began to run.

We stopped occasionally to eat and rest, though always well away from any town or people. He was very good at finding berries and other fruit, and even brought me fresh meat (seal, when we were by the sea, and badger or stoat inland), which I cooked over a fire. My appetite had returned.

Because I was not in such a daze that time, I was even able to enjoy the travel. I marveled all over again at the underwater sensations in my sealskin apparatus. It was the most extraordinary thing, to blindly float through water, carried like a tiny child.

He spoke to me several times during the journey, which may have been part of the reason we went slower. The talking always wore him out and he did not move as swiftly afterward.

During our first stop after crossing the sea, he said to me, "Only a visit … If you do not return … great harm."

The word *"harm"* was said forcefully, yet he did not seem to be threatening me, only telling me a fact; as if the possibility of harm was something he had no control over.

"A month...one cycle of moon...no longer," he said.

"I understand," I said.

"They...family...will want you to stay...will do anything."

"I give you my word," I said a little shortly, annoyed by the suggestion that my family might behave less than honorably or trick me into staying.

He plowed on, with great effort. "Do not tell... They will ask...not tell." He was agitated, more upset than I'd ever seen him. His eyes were fixed on me, entreating.

"I promise," I said.

"Your mother...Be most careful...Do not tell... about white bear." His humanness was wearing thin, I could see; he was struggling to form the words. "Do not...alone with mother...not listen." He gave a low growl, almost of pain, and turned, padding slowly away from me until he disappeared from view among a large cluster of trees.

He returned a short time later with two dead hares. We did not talk while I prepared and cooked them.

He left me several furlongs from the farm, by a brook with a willow tree bowed over it. "I...go no farther...In a month . . . here . . . I will wait." Again those eyes were fastened on me, devouring, as if the sight of me had to last him a very long time.

For some reason I wanted to reassure him. "I will be here. One month." Then I looked up at the blue sky and could just make out the sliver of the new moon. "When the moon is new again."

He lowered his head, then turned and bounded away. I watched him a moment, marveling as I had before at his grace, the enormous strength in that massive body. At that moment it was impossible to believe that such a great beast had anything to do with the invisible figure who had slept beside me every night. But then I remembered that the last night before we had left the castle, my visitor had shivered for the first time since I'd made the nightshirt.

"Rose?"

It was Mother. I had been home a little less than a fortnight and that afternoon had taken a walk by myself, saying I wanted to collect flowers for the dinner table. I was lost in thought when Mother found me by the creek we used to call Rosie's Creek. I started a little, dropping a few stems of oleander. She bent over to retrieve them.

"I'm sorry I startled you," Mother said, "but I wanted to see you, alone. We have barely had any time together since your return."

I took the flowers from her, saying, "It's nearly suppertime, isn't it? We'd better be getting back," and I began to walk briskly in the direction of the farmhouse.

Mother laid a hand on my arm and I was forced to slow my pace. "There is no hurry, Rose. I must talk with you. It is important."

Her voice was trembling a little and I looked at her sideways, surprised.

"Oh, Rose, I have been wanting to explain, about your birth."

I became alert.

"You left so suddenly, there was no chance..." Her voice was choked with emotion and she coughed to clear her throat. "I know that you were very angry. That you felt we had hidden the truth from you. I realize now it was I who had hidden the truth from myself. That was the real lie. I was so set on what I believed to be the truth, I could accept no other. Your father tried to reason with me, but I would not listen. I still do not understand, but I must acknowledge now that you have a streak of northernness in you."

I opened my mouth to speak, but she stopped me. "Very well, perhaps you are even *all* north. I don't know—the circumstances of your birth were so muddled. But I will tell you that there were reasons, good reasons, other than the empty space on the compass rose, why I did not want you a north. Reasons that spring from love, not stubbornness. And I do love you, Rose, no matter what point of the compass you are."

Tears stung my eyes. I did not realize until that moment that those were words I had never thought to hear from my mother. And had longed for.

She saw the tears standing in my eyes and pulled me to her, stroking my hair gently. I felt like a small child again, being comforted for my freshest hurt.

"What reasons, Mother?" I said finally.

She hesitated before speaking. "The words of a *skjebne-soke*. She prophesied that..."

"That what?" I pressed, pulling away from her.

"That any north child I had would die." She finished reluctantly, her words coming fast, "Crushed by an avalanche of snow and ice."

"I see."

"No, it is I who sees what utter foolishness it was to believe her words. Why, only last week I heard that Agneta Guthbjorg had a baby girl instead of the boy that same *skjebne-soke* foretold."

"Well, I'm certainly glad to hear it," I said dryly. We exchanged smiles.

We resumed our walk to the farmhouse. "I wish your father would return," Mother said wistfully. "Neddy may have told you that there is a distance between us of late. I think that seeing you home and safe would help heal that distance."

"I would like to see it healed," I said.

We walked for a few moments in silence.

"May I..." She paused. "...ask about your life these past months? Are you comfortable? Do you get enough to eat? You look so thin."

"Only because I grew homesick. But it is not so bad there, Mother. I do have plenty to eat."

"And the white bear? Does he live with you, where you are?"

"He does. Mother, I cannot talk about this. I made a promise."

She gazed at me closely, as if trying to read how safe I really was.

"The white bear is good to me," I said.

"What manner of place do you live in?"

"It is a comfortable place. I call it a castle, but it reminds me more of a large hunting lodge, like the ones the wealthy people in Andalsnes keep in the mountains."

"Are there servants?"

"Yes, of a sort. I rarely see them."

"How do you spend your time?"

"I weave. And sew. There is a loom there, a very nice one." The words were completely inadequate when I thought of that magnificent loom. "I made this dress," I added, gesturing at the gray dress I wore but thinking of the three gowns that were folded in the leather wallet, which I had left at the castle.

"It is very fine, Rose. I'm glad you have a loom," Mother said. "And the white bear, do you see him every day?"

"Usually," I said shortly. I tried to quicken my pace a little, but Mother's arm linked in mine made it difficult; she would not be hurried.

"What are your sleeping arrangements? Do you have a comfortable bed?"

I stiffened, hoping Mother had not noticed. "Very comfortable" was all I said.

I spotted Neddy coming from Father's new workshop and breathed a great sigh of relief. Pulling my arm from Mother's, I energetically waved at Neddy, calling out to him.

I thought I detected a little frown on my mother's face as Neddy joined us. *She wants to know more,* I thought. *The white bear was right.*

And the white bear was right about something else as well. At dinner that night each member of the family, except Mother and Neddy, said a little piece about how my leaving with the white bear had had nothing to do with Sara's getting well and the reversal of the family's fortunes. It was Harald Soren who was responsible—as well as Father and his talent at mapmaking. The appearance of the white bear, his request and my departure with him, were nothing more than a coincidence. Even Sara said she thought it was nonsense that a white bear, albeit a talking one, could have cured her. It was the doctor and the medicine that had cured her. And therefore, they said unanimously, I must not think of going back. I must stay home, where I belonged.

I turned to Mother. "What do you think? Was it a coincidence?"

Mother set a pitcher of sweet cream on the table, for pouring over our bowls of fresh strawberries, then sat down. She looked me in the eye. "No, I for one do not believe it was a coincidence. I think our good fortune was in part because we granted the white bear's request. But, Rose, I also believe that by having done so, you may consider your obligation fulfilled."

"The white bear asked me to return. And I gave my promise."

"I don't understand... Sikram Ralatt expressly said..." Mother looked puzzled. "In that case, though it pains me beyond words to say so, I believe you must return."

"Oh, Mother!" cried Sara.

"How could you, Mother?!" Sonja said.

I listened to the chorus of protest and disappointment from my family, then said, as brightly as I could, "There's still heaps of time. Let's not worry about partings now. Are there any more strawberries, Mother?"

Neddy

I SENSED THAT MOTHER'S words caused Rose pain. Or maybe it was that they caused me pain. I could not believe that once again Mother was choosing superstition over her daughter. Ironically, Rose and Mother were of the same opinion—that she must return with the white bear—but they came to it from very different directions. For Rose it was a matter of keeping a promise. For Mother . . . Well, she did not want to transgress on any of her foolish superstitions. If only Father had been there. . . .

Every day we watched for him and every day he did not return. We tried to excuse Rose from doing any chores around the farm, but she insisted on doing her share. In private she told me that she actually missed doing chores, and described her makeshift laundry room as providing the only chance she had to do her own work. She actually let slip many little details of this nature, and gradually I felt I'd gained a piecemeal, sketchy picture of her life at the castle.

"You sound almost as if you are fond of the bear," I said one day, after Rose had described a typical afternoon spent weaving and telling stories.

She looked a little startled. "I don't know. Yes, I guess I am, in a way. Sometimes I feel sorry for him. Not pity—he would hate that—but when I see in his eyes the nonanimal part of him trying so hard to hang on, to keep a tiny grasp... Oh, it probably doesn't make any sense to you."

"You feel compassion for him."

"Yes." She got a faraway look in her eyes. "Like when he shivers—" She stopped with a guilty look.

"Shivers?"

"At night. You see—" She stopped again. "You must promise to tell no one," she said, very serious. "Especially Mother."

I promised.

"I have this feeling I should not speak of what happens in the castle at night, though he never told me not to, not specifically... But I find it so confusing, and strange. Talking it over with you might help me." And then she told me of her nightly visitor, of the darkness that couldn't be lit. Of the nightshirt she had made for him. And lastly of her suspicions that it was actually the white bear that slept beside her.

"Sometimes I can hardly stand not knowing. I want to reach over and feel his face. Or *its* face. But I daren't.

I tried different lamps, even making my own flint. But nothing worked. I think it must be an enchantment of some kind, Neddy. What do you think?"

I didn't know what to say. Her tale sounded fantastic, like one of the stories I used to tell Rose when she was little. I shook my head. Then I was struck by a thought.

"Is that why you're going back, Rose? To break the spell?" I asked.

Rose laughed. "It sounds so ridiculous when you say it like that. Anyway, it's not that. It's more like I feel there's something I ought to be doing that I'm not. And if I did whatever it is, I could help the white bear."

"Perhaps just being there is enough. Maybe he is lonely. And having you there keeps that little spark of humanness alive in him."

Rose smiled at me. "You are so wise, Neddy. Well, I'd better get these in some water." She stooped to gather up an armful of oxeye daisies she had picked earlier.

Just then, out of the corner of one eye, I glimpsed a flicker of green, the same color green as Mother's cloak. I instantly guessed that Mother had been eavesdropping on our conversation and wondered uneasily how much she had overheard. I decided not to mention it to Rose, not wanting her to be angry with Mother.

It was a foolish, foolish decision.

Troll Queen

IT IS WELL TO BE prepared, to look ahead and set events in motion that will bring about the desired result at the desired time. If there are to be conditions—and what a confounded waste of time that there should be—then you use your wits and your arts to ensure the outcome is as you will it to be.

It was no difficult matter to set up a potion maker in a softskin village—to disguise a young troll, with a desire to please his queen. And then to give him the words and goods to entice a pair of foolish softskin women.

Even if she defies her own nature and returns with him, I will prevail. As I must.

It will soon be over.

And I will have my husband.

Rose

ONLY ONE DAY BEFORE my departure, and Father still had not returned. Already my family was begging me to stay longer, at least until Father came back. For a moment I imagined doing as they asked and pictured myself going to the white bear and saying, "Just a bit longer. Just until Father comes home." And then I would remember that look in his eyes.

The harm he had spoke of—I wondered to whom it would happen. To me? Or to him?

The thought of those doors to the castle in the mountain shutting behind me made my breath go short and my heart pound in my chest. Remembering the despair I'd felt, the indifference to the days passing, frightened me. Maybe this time I *would* die.

I told myself that month of freedom would last me for a long time. And perhaps he would allow me to visit again, even longer the next time. But I didn't believe it.

Anyway, it didn't matter. I had made a promise.

I was in the room I shared with my sisters, doing the scant packing I needed to do, when Mother entered. I had successfully avoided being alone with her after our one encounter, and I felt guilty, though I was always kind and attentive to her when we were with others. My heart sank a little when she appeared then, but I smiled at her.

"I won't disturb you long," she said. "I have brought a few things for you to take back." She laid a small bundle on the bed next to me. Opening it she handed me a jar. "Some of neighbor Torsk's sweet honey. And look, a vest made for you by Widow Hautzig."

"Oh, how nice," I said, admiring the soft heathery wool, though I knew full well that Mother had surely paid the widow generously for her work.

"And here is some of that toffee candy you like so well. And a new handkerchief. And some hair ribbons from Sara . . . Your hair is getting so long, my dear, and quite lovely. Oh, and a candle, and flint. 'Tis a special flint, the latest thing. And the candle is also quite nice, slow burning, and I am told it will stay lit even in a strong wind. Whether or not that is so, I can't say, but it may come in handy during your journey back to the castle."

I gazed at the candle, which was a creamy ivory color, then up at Mother's face. Had Neddy told her of the unlightable darkness in my bedchamber? I did not believe it of him. Yet a candle, a candle that stayed lit... Her face was calm, placid. There was no hint of deception there.

"Just a few things from home, dear, that may bring you comfort until you can return to us for good."

"Thank you, Mother." I leaned over and hugged her. Then I took the things she had given me and stowed them in my pack.

I didn't know how I would get through the good-byes. I had thought of slipping away during the night to avoid them altogether, but that would have been cowardly, and I didn't want to miss even one moment with my family.

The night before the moon had been new, the same silver eyelash I had pointed to when I had parted from the white bear. I had counted the days carefully.

When the time came for me to leave, we were all subdued. I gave each of them a quick hug, swallowing my tears.

"Let me walk with you, partway at least, to where you will meet..." Neddy said.

I nodded and was grateful for his arm around my shoulders as we left the farmhouse. And the tears I had held back overflowed down my cheeks.

Fishing in my pocket for the handkerchief Mother had given me, I said, "Neddy, please, when you see Father, tell him that... that I love him and that I am sorry for the angry words I said when I saw him last." I paused. "And tell him to forgive Mother, if he can. She needs him, I think "

"I will tell him," Neddy responded.

"And keep an eye on Widow Hautzig, Neddy. I don't trust her."

"Nor do I."

"I'm sorry that I didn't get to meet your Master Soren. Thank him for me, for all he's done for us. And Neddy..." I turned and looked him in the eye. "Go to Trondheim, study with the scholar there. Do not wait for me to return. I will know how to find you if you are not here."

Neddy was silent.

"Promise me."

"I don't know..."

"Neddy."

"I will think about what you said," he replied reluctantly. "But you will be back soon," he added with conviction. "And you can come to Trondheim as well." There was a pause. "Rose, if...if anything should happen, if you need me for anything, promise me you'll get word to me. I will come to you, *no matter where you are.*"

"Thank you, Neddy. I will be fine."

It was time to part. I clung to him a moment, then hurried away.

The white bear was where I had left him a moon cycle ago, standing beside the brook and weeping willow. He looked as if he had not moved from the spot.

I didn't know how to greet him, so said nothing. He gazed at me for a long time, and I read something approaching joy in those bottomless eyes. I felt guilty at the traces of tears on my face.

Then he said, "Come," and I had to find my balance on his broad white back all over again.

White Bear

Waiting.
Curling slice of moon.
One month.
Hungry, pacing.
Frozen inside.
Will she ... ?

Then she comes, through the trees.
A great easing,
melting,
unbinding.
Hope.

Feel her above,
legs against my skin.
Moving through meadows,

undersea.
When we stop,
drinking in her voice.
Her purple eyes.

She came back.

Rose

IT WAS AFTER MIDNIGHT when he spoke again. We were moving through a gorge and I had been half asleep. "What did you say?" I mumbled groggily.

"Did they ... your family ... ask you ... do anything?"

I thought a moment, then said honestly, "They asked me to stay with them."

"Nothing else?"

"No."

"You ... are sure?"

"Yes, I am sure." I wondered what lay behind the question, what it was he feared.

"Your mother ... did she not ... ask you ... give advice?"

"I told my mother only a little. Enough to reassure her that I am safe. I am safe, aren't I?" I asked boldly.

The white bear made a sound that could have been

a chuckle. "You are ... safe," he replied after a few moments.

I didn't know how I was going to feel when the doors of the castle shut behind me, but as with leaving my family, it wasn't as hard as I had feared. The memory of moonlight and cool night air was still fresh, and perhaps it would last me a long time.

I climbed off his back and stood before him in the front entryway of the castle. There was an awkward moment, as though neither of us knew what to say or what to do next.

Then the white bear said, "Thank you ... for coming back," and turned to walk away.

"Wait," I said. "Can you not ... ?" I groped for the words. "Please ... tell me why I am here, and what it is I can do to ... help you?"

He turned and looked at me. " ... Cannot."

Then I couldn't help myself. I was already feeling the walls close in on me. "Am I to be allowed to visit my family again?" I blurted out.

I thought his head drooped a little at that, but he lifted it and said, " ... not talk of that ... now." He disappeared down the hall, his massive feet making no noise on the thick carpet.

Well, at least he hadn't said no, I told myself, and made my way to the room with the red couch.

———

I was happy to see the loom again and had many ideas for clothing I wanted to make for my family. But I set them aside for the moment. I was much more focused on a new thought: During the journey back to the castle, I had vowed to get to the bottom of the mystery surrounding the white bear.

The obvious source to learn more about him was the two servants.

I began to spy on them, being careful so they wouldn't guess what I was up to. I would go to my loom dutifully as they expected me to, then would sneak out into the halls of the castle to see where the two of them were. As time went on I observed a pattern to their daily schedule and began work on a map of their movements. First I came up with a list of their duties, the jobs they did to keep the castle running—at least those things that were visible to me: starting and tending the various hearth fires; lighting, filling, and putting out the oil lamps; providing me, and themselves, with meals (I suspected the white bear did his own hunting outside the castle); general cleaning, dusting, and so forth. I had no idea where they got the raw materials for making meals, but having seen no sign of chickens or cows or vegetables growing in the castle, I determined they must have such things delivered. If that was the case, the deliveries had to be made infrequently and at odd hours, because I had never seen any sign of the front door opening.

Unless it was all done by magic. Yet even though I was living with a talking white bear in a castle inside a mountain, my mind still rebelled at the whole idea of magic. After all, I hadn't seen any mystifying transformations, things flying through the air or anything like that. The unlightable darkness of my bedroom and the lamp that went out for no reason were the only real signs that anything supernatural was going on.

I made it a point to wander along the hallway with the tapestry-covered kitchen door, and whenever I saw the two servants, I tried to be friendly. I would smile and speak a few words, offering by pantomime to help them carry things.

The woman would smile back blandly but remained aloof, resisting my efforts. I could see, however, that the little man was interested. He would nod and smile back, and once he let me carry wood for him. The woman was with him then and she frowned, saying something in their language that prompted him to take the wood back from me.

Clearly, if I was to have any luck at all communicating with the man, I needed to catch him alone.

According to my map the woman servant laid the fires in the rooms I used most—the one with the red couch, my bedchamber, the laundry room, and the weaving room. While she was attending to those, she sent the little man to check whether I'd used any of the other fireplaces during the previous day. If I had, which was rare, he was in charge of laying them afresh, after reporting to her.

So one afternoon I used a candle to light a fire in a small room on the second floor, as far away as possible from the kitchen or any of the other rooms the woman would be working in. It was a library of sorts, though it had fewer books than the big library on the first floor.

The next morning I got up early and hid myself in the second-floor room. I watched as the little man entered and inspected the fireplace, which had ash and burnt kindling in it. He lit the lamps in the room and then left, so I settled myself with a book in a large, comfortable chair. A little while later the man opened the door. Seeing me sitting there, he began to back out of the room, but I hopped up and, smiling warmly, beckoned him in. With a quick backward glance out into the hall, he slowly entered, carrying his bundle of wood and kindling.

"Hello," I said brightly.

He just stared at me.

Then I said, "Rose," and pointed to myself.

Again he looked at me dumbly.

I did it again. "Rose."

Something lit in his eyes. "Tuki," he said, and pointed to himself. I couldn't be sure if Tuki was his name, or nationality, or even species, but I nodded enthusiastically and pointed to him, saying, "Tuki."

And to my pleasure he responded by pointing to me and saying, "Rose."

I clapped my hands with delight. And then I pointed to the book I was holding and said, "Book."

He looked a little puzzled but then pointed to the book and said, *"Kirja,"* which I hoped meant "book" in his language.

After that he set down the wood he was carrying, and we went around the room pointing to things, each giving our own name for it. He seemed to enjoy this greatly, as if it were a splendid game, and I wondered if, despite the fact that his features looked adult to me, he might not actually be a child.

As we moved around the room, he would deliberately brush against my arm or hand, and I remembered the first time we had met and how he had appeared to be fascinated by my skin. And for myself, I was struck again by the white-ridged roughness of his.

When we came near the fireplace, he suddenly remembered his reason for coming to the room and quickly retrieved the wood. While he hurriedly laid the fire, I sat in a chair and watched him. He finished, then gazed at me, a questioning look on his face.

I nodded, and only a moment after he had bent over the wood, flames sprung up. I hadn't seen a striker or a candle and wondered if he had used some kind of magic spell to light the fire.

I pointed at the flames licking the logs and said, "Fire."

He looked at me, grinned, and said, *"Palo."* Then he left the room.

"Good-bye, Tuki!" I called to him.

I was pleased. This was a good beginning.

One of my favorite rooms in the castle was the music chamber, even though I didn't know how to play any of the instruments. Occasionally I would sit at the piano-forte and play on the ivory keys, but I could not make a melody out of the sounds.

The instruments that I liked the most were the flautos and recorders, especially the lovely flauto in the box with blue velvet. It was so beautiful I had been shy about even touching it, but one day I worked up my courage and took it out of the cabinet. I placed the mouthpiece to my lips and blew. A loud ringing note came out, startling me so that I almost dropped the instrument. But I held on and tried again. As that second note died away, the white bear entered the room. I fought down the instinct to hide the flauto behind my back as though I were a naughty child caught playing with grown-up things. As he came closer I could read a sort of yearning in his eyes. He lay down on the rug near the cabinet and looked up expectantly, as he did in the weaving room when he was ready to hear a story.

I shook my head. "I don't know how to play," I explained, my cheeks a little red.

"Play," he said.

"I can't." But he just stared at me with those yearning eyes. So I tried.

And though the tone of the instrument was lovely, my playing sounded like two birds of different pitch scolding each other.

The white bear closed his eyes and flattened his ears against the sound.

"Well, I warned you," I said.

Then he got up and crossed to a polished wooden chest and, using a large paw, pushed the top up. I could see bundles of paper inside, some bound, some tied with ribbon. I knew what the papers were.

"I cannot read music," I said.

The white bear sighed. Then he turned and left the room.

After he'd gone I went to the chest and sat down beside it, taking out a bundle of the papers with music written on them.

It became my new project, learning to read music. I was lucky to find a book in the chest that showed which note corresponded to which hole on the flauto.

Occasionally the white bear would come into the music room and sit and listen while I practiced, which made me self-conscious. But he never stayed long. It was as if he could only take it so long, hearing the music he knew mangled beyond all recognizable shape.

Meanwhile, the nighttime routine had taken up where it had left off. My first night back I saw that the white nightshirt was neatly folded at the foot of the bed. I picked it up, shook it out, and then carefully laid it on the side of the bed.

When the lights went out (and I still stubbornly kept at least one lamp or candle lit each night, just in case the enchantment might fail), I felt my visitor climb into bed and pull up the covers. I thought I heard a sigh, the kind of sigh a child would give after a thunderstorm is over, a sound that said that everything was once again all right. My throat grew tight with sympathy, and I felt pangs of guilt thinking of how cold and lonely the bed must have felt in my absence. I wondered if he had worn the nightshirt.

I began to have dreams about my nightly visitor. The first was actually a pleasant dream in which I awoke in the morning to find the white bear by the side of the bed, wearing the nightshirt (which had magically expanded to fit his large frame), and he was telling me he would take me home. So I climbed onto his back and we floated up into the air and flew above the land until I could spy my family's farmhouse below. We began to descend, too fast I thought, but the white bear said, "You are safe," and we landed softly in a field of snowdrops.

When I actually awoke in the morning after that dream, I half expected to see the white bear standing by the bed, but in the dim light from the lamps in the hall, I saw only the empty space beside me.

Sometime later I had another dream that was very different. In the dream I had managed to light one of the oil lamps. When I brought the lamp close to the stranger, I saw that its face was green and scaly and had a long, thin tongue that slithered in and out of its mouth while it breathed. I let out a cry and the monster awoke, opening a pair of hideous yellow eyes. Its tongue then brushed across my face and I woke up screaming, this time for real.

Again it was morning and I could see in the dim light that my visitor was gone, but I shuddered. What if it *was* a monster that lay beside me every night?

Tuki must not have said anything to the woman about our first encounter, for the next morning he appeared in the room where I sat waiting for him.

We went through much the same routine as before, teaching each other new words. I wasn't at all sure we would ever get to a point where we could actually converse and I could ask him questions about the white bear, but I felt I must try. And I believed the most important thing about my getting to know Tuki was the feeling I was finally doing something.

This went on for several weeks, though I was constantly worried that one day the woman would figure out what was going on and put a stop to it. Tuki seemed to trust me, even like me, and I was growing fond of him. He was so like a child—eager to please, sometimes impatient, and always wishing to be praised and petted.

We ran out of things to point to, and not wanting to upset our routine by shifting to another room, I began to use books, pointing to illustrations in them to continue our makeshift language lessons. Tuki was not a quick learner, but his eagerness to please kept him trying, and he was starting to remember some of the words I was teaching him, like *Rose* and *hello* and *good-bye*.

I found his language difficult but was beginning to

understand parts of it. I made a little dictionary, to which I added new words every evening before bed. I kept it hidden in the closet, in my pack from home.

Finally I decided the time was right to introduce the subject of the white bear, and in preparation I went through practically every book in both libraries until I came across a book on animals that had a small picture of a white bear. I took it with me to the room on the second floor.

When we began our game that morning, I casually picked up the book about animals and began to leaf through it. I pointed to pictures of a wolf (*"susi"*), a beaver (*"majava"*), a rabbit (*"kaniini"*), and then finally came to the page with the white bear on it.

"White bear," I said.

"Lumi karhu," he said, then added, *"vaeltaa."* Then he looked at me a little uneasily. I cast about in my mind for words he might recognize that would help me ask him about the white bear. But I realized that nearly all the words I had learned were objects, not verbs. Annoyed with myself for not being better prepared, I decided I would have to settle for knowing the name for white bear in Tuki's language. It was a start.

"*'Lumi karhu'?*" I repeated. "Or is it *'vaeltaa'*?" He nodded at both, and I got the impression that they were two separate names for white bear. I wished I could press him, but I could tell he was uneasy. To distract him I pointed to more animals and we resumed our game.

The next time I brought a book of maps I'd found in the library. It was a beautiful volume entitled *Ptolemy's Geographica,* and in addition to the maps, which had been wrought in vivid colors and gold leaf, there were detailed drawings depicting the various regions of the world. I had heard of Ptolemy from my father; he was a Greek who had lived centuries before and was one of the first mapmakers. I thought of Father with a pang. How he would have treasured such a book.

I opened to a map of Njord and pointed to the spot where the village of Andalsnes would be found. "Rose from here," I said.

He stared down at it, shaking his head, mystified.

"Tuki from where?" I asked, riffling through the pages of the atlas, a questioning look on my face.

He smiled to see the pages fluttering and reached over to take the book, wanting to do it himself. Gleefully he thumbed the pages, causing them to cascade down. He did it over and over—fast, then slow. Suddenly something caught his eye, and he stopped and paged back to what he had seen.

With a smile he pointed to a small drawing that lay next to the map of the far northern land of ever winter that lay within the Arktik Circle. In this book the land was called Glacialis. In my country we called it Arktisk. The illustration Tuki was pointing to depicted high ice cliffs amid a frozen landscape of snow.

"Tuki is from Arktisk?" I asked.

He shook his head, not understanding.

"Tuki from a land of snow?" I hugged myself, as if cold.

He nodded enthusiastically, hugging himself and pretending to shiver. "Tuki," he said, pointing again to the picture of ice cliffs.

Then I pointed to the wind rose at the corner of the page. "North?" I asked, pointing to the *N* at the top.

He shook his head, again not understanding. I sighed.

That day I learned the words for snow (*"lumi,"* which explained the first word Tuki had used for white bear) and ice (*"jaassa"*), and then he came out with the word *"Huldre."* I wasn't sure, but I thought maybe it was the name of the land he was from. And I got the impression that Tuki was homesick for his icy home; his face had taken on a sad, faraway look.

Several days later we were looking through some other books I had brought from the library. We came to a picture of quite a grand palace in a book of old tales.

"Jaassa," he said excitedly, jabbing his finger at the drawing. I was puzzled, wondering if the same word was used for *ice* and *palace* in his language.

"Ice?" I said.

"Ice," he repeated, nodding and pantomiming cold.

Was he trying to tell me he lived in a palace in his icy land? I was becoming frustrated. If only I could ask him straight out what I wanted to know: *Where are you from? Who do you serve? Who sleeps in the bed with me at night?*

Suddenly I got an idea. I took up a book and skipped

to the end, where I found several blank pages. Heedlessly I tore them out, and while Tuki looked on with interest, I found a burnt stick in the fireplace. Using the charred end, I drew three stick figures, two female and a male. I pointed to one and said, "Rose," then to the male figure, saying, "Tuki." Finally I pointed to the third figure, on which I had drawn an apron, and turned to Tuki with a questioning look.

"Urda," he said after a moment, a delighted look on his face because he understood the new game I was playing.

"'Urda,'" I repeated with a smile. Then I turned the paper over and drew, as best I could, a bed. On one side of the bed I drew the stick figure that represented me. I pointed to it, saying, "Rose." I pantomimed sleeping. Then I pointed to the empty space beside me on the bed.

"Tuki?" I asked, though I knew he could not be my visitor, who was at least my size, probably larger.

He shook his head, mystified.

Then I said, "Urda?" My heart was beating fast. I felt I was on the verge of learning something important.

Again he shook his head.

My finger shaking slightly, I once more pointed at the empty space beside me. *Lumi karhu?* I said. "White bear?"

He looked wary, the way he had the first time I had brought up the white bear.

"White bear sleep with me?" I said, my voice cracking a little.

Suddenly the door swung open and there stood the woman called Urda. She looked at us. Then she quickly crossed the room and took Tuki by the wrist. She pulled him from the room, speaking sharply as she did. She did not give me so much as a backward glance.

Troll Queen

SHE IS CLEVER, more so than I gave her credit for. But her efforts to know the truth are fruitless. And I am pleased rather than disturbed by her actions, for they mean that, very soon, her curiosity will overmaster all else and then it shall be over.

He will be mine. Forever.

But she has raised his hopes. Too high. And I cannot help feeling sad for the disappointment he will soon know. (How strange to have such a feeling! If he were still alive, Father would say that is what comes of consorting with softskins.)

But the disappointment will fade; indeed, it will be only a short time before he has no memory at all of the softskin girl he set his heart on.

Neddy

FATHER RETURNED home a week after Rose left.

"How is it that you, all of you, allowed her to return to the white bear?" he asked in disbelief.

"She said she must," I told him. "We could not change her mind. You know Rose when she is set on a thing."

"Was she bewitched, do you think?"

I shook my head. "She seemed herself, Father."

"She was well?"

"Yes. A little thin when she first arrived. But Mother fattened her with all manner of good soups and meat pies."

"Then she is not well fed at this—what did you call it? ..."

"Castle in the mountain," I replied. "She said her meals are more than ample. It was homesickness that caused her to lose her appetite."

"Then will she not be homesick again? Oh, would that I had been here!"

We were having this conversation in Father's workshop, just the two of us. Suddenly the door flew open and there stood Mother, pale and breathing hard.

"I have done something...Oh, Arne..." And she sank to her knees, weeping.

I stared at her in confusion while Father crossed the room and bent over her. "What is it, Eugenia? What has happened?" His tone with her was gentler than I had heard in a long time.

"You will never forgive me. I will never forgive myself," she gasped between sobs.

Father pulled her up and led her to a chair, where she slumped, clutching at the handkerchief Father gave her.

"Oh," she moaned, "why did I not give her only a handkerchief, and a bit of toffee candy? Fool that I was..."

"Stop this, Eugenia." Father's voice was still kind, but it held authority. "Tell us about it. From the beginning."

And she embarked on her tale.

As I knew, Mother and Widow Hautzig were regular visitors to Sikram Ralatt, the new shopkeeper in town who sold potions and charms in addition to his regular merchandise of soap and herbal infusions. Mother had purchased a handful of charms from him, such as the one she'd wanted Father to tie around his ankle before one of his journeys.

"When Rose was home, Neddy," Mother said, wiping her eyes, "I happened to overhear the two of you talking.

It was about her sleeping arrangements at the castle. When Rose said she was sleeping next to some unknown creature night after night, I became frightened for her. I was afraid it might be some hideous monster, or a wicked sorcerer, or...a troll..." She looked at both of us beseechingly.

Father opened his mouth to speak, a confused look on his face, but Mother plunged on.

"I knew that if I spoke to Rose about it, she would brush me off, saying there was nothing to worry about. I was so upset that I confided my concern to my good friend Widow Hautzig, and she advised me to go straight to Sikram Ralatt, to see if he had some charm that would protect and help my dear Rose. So I did—I told Sikram Ralatt about someone close to me who was in danger, who slept in a room that because of some spell or another was impossible to light. I asked him what could be done. And it was then he sold me the flint and the candle."

We stared at her, Father in complete bafflement and I in horror.

"I...I gave them to Rose," Mother went on. "I said nothing to her, leaving it to her own inclination whether or not to use them. But I confess that I hoped she would. That her curiosity would lead her to light the candle and look at who was beside her."

"Well, Eugenia," Father said, still perplexed, "perhaps it was not well to meddle, but I do not see..."

"You haven't heard the worst of it, not yet," Mother interrupted, tears spilling down her cheeks. "I...I went into the village today and found that Sikram Ralatt is gone, disappeared without a trace, his shop cleared out, empty. As I went about, inquiring after him, I learned that he vanished the very day after Rose left. And what's more, there are all sorts of terrible rumors flying about the village. That he was ... he was ..." Fresh sobs shook her shoulders. "Oh, what have I done, what have I done?!"

Rose

AFTER THE WOMAN called Urda snatched Tuki away that morning, I rarely saw him. When I did it was only in glimpses, and despite my friendly greetings, he kept his eyes averted. The only indication that he heard me at all was that his white skin turned a pinkish color, especially around the ears. Urda acted the same as always, not angry or hostile, just blandly indifferent.

To make matters worse, I had had a new nightmare. In it I was able to light the lamp, and when I brought it close to the face of my visitor, I saw that his head was turned, facing away from me. His hair was a rich gold, and I tapped him on the shoulder, to awaken him. The head turned to face me, and when it did I saw there was no face at all, just a great gaping hollow. I screamed.

This time when I awoke, the scream raw in my throat, it was still pitch-dark in the room. I heard a rustling and then some hurried footfalls. I didn't dare reach over to see if my visitor was gone but tiptoed across the room, feeling my way in the darkness, and found the door ajar.

White Bear

She dreams.
Cries out.
In fear.

I dream.
Of peace.
An end.
Finally.
To tell her.

Soon it will be over.
Freedom.

Rose

BECAUSE OF THE nightmares I dreaded the time when the lamps in the halls were extinguished. But in contrast with the nights, my days with the white bear were happy ones. There was an ease between us, like that of close friends who could read each other's moods in an instant. And the humanness in his eyes seemed to be almost always there now. I looked forward to his arrival in the room with the red couch. I would sit on the rug before the fire, a book in hand, and he would come and settle beside me. While I read aloud he would rest his head on his massive paws. Oftentimes he would close his eyes while he listened; I could tell he was not asleep because when we came to a twist in the story or a climactic moment, his eyes would open. He also made small noises that told me he was alert to every word—a rumbling, purrlike sound when the story was particularly satisfying, or a grunting when the tale took a more unbelievable turn.

The stories I read to him were good (some were wonderful), but at times they were almost beside the point. It was the companionship that mattered, especially when we would laugh together at something funny. (Although the sound of an enormous white bear laughing out loud is not for the faint of heart; the first time I heard it, I had to fight back a strong urge to flee the room.)

There was one story in particular that made us both laugh. It was an old Njorden tale about a crotchety husband who always complained about how easy his wife had it, how he had to go off every day to the fields while all she did was sit around the house. The wife grew tired of his complaints and one day said to him, "Do you think you could do the work at home better?"

"Of course," the husband replied. "Any man could."

"Then why do we not switch tasks? Tomorrow I will mow the hay, and you will stay here and do the housework."

The husband agreed to the plan.

Needless to say, while the wife busily mowed row after row of hay, the hapless husband wound up accidentally killing the pig, spilling cream all over the kitchen floor, and letting every last drop of ale run out of the barrel. The part of the story that amused the white bear most was when the husband dropped all the freshly washed clothes in the mud, having gotten tangled up in the washing line.

"I suppose you think you could do better?" I laughed, forgetting that I was speaking not to a person but to a large white bear. He stopped laughing, and I looked up in time to see the unhappiness in his eyes before he left the room.

I thought then of his sigh as he had watched me rinsing the white nightshirt.

I grew better at playing the flauto. I had taken to performing for the white bear, sifting through the sheet music to find the simplest piece for a beginner. I would sit on a small velvet chair and he would lie on the rug at my feet and listen, again with his eyes closed. There was one melody in particular, I could tell, he liked more than any other. It bore the title "Estivale," which I figured out meant "of the summer." I rarely could play it straight through without some kind of mistake, but he didn't seem to care. It didn't matter that my playing was less than impressive; for him it was just that I did it at all. And what mattered to me was the stillness when I was done, and the pleasure in his eyes.

One afternoon, many months after my visit to my family, I played "Estivale" better than I ever had, and the white bear let out a deep sigh of pleasure. Looking into his eyes, which seemed more human than before, I suddenly blurted out, "Who are you?"

Before he could react I continued, unable to stop myself. "Where are you from?" I asked. "How long have you lived here in this mountain? Are you under an enchantment? If you are, how can it be broken?"

Even before the last word died on my lips, I regretted my rashness. The ease between us vanished at once; his eyes clouded over, the animal blankness came back. Then he got up and left the room.

The next day he did not come to the room at the usual time. After waiting for a long while, I realized he was not coming at all. I cursed my impulsive tongue and felt lonely and sorry for myself the rest of the day. I tried working at the loom, but it held no appeal for me and I soon gave up. Later I saw Tuki scurrying along behind the woman Urda, and I loudly called out to him by name, but he stuck close to her and they soon disappeared into the kitchen. The door, I discovered, was locked behind them. I went up to my peephole to the sky and sat there at the window, numb, staring at the branch. It was bare. Winter was not far off. Except for the month spent at home, I had been at the castle in the mountain for almost a full year.

That evening my nightmare was particularly intense. My scream still burning my throat, I lay there, shivering, torn between fear and anger. My visitor had scurried away, scared off again by my scream. How long was I supposed to live like this? How was I going to stand it? I thought I would surely go mad if I could not learn who slept beside me night after night. Was it a monster, or a hollow-faced nothing, or the white bear himself? I felt that if I only knew the answer, I could go on, I could endure my life there in the castle.

Suddenly I thought of the candle and flint Mother had given me. What had she said? That the candle would stay lit even in a stiff wind and that the flint would spark a light every time. I wondered uneasily if the candle and flint could possibly light the unlightable darkness. *Dare I try?*

All the next day I wrestled with the question. The white bear did reappear briefly for our afternoon reading, but I was distracted and he was remote, restless, more animal than human. I tried to play "Estivale," but my fingers felt leaden and my breath short. When I finished we just sat there, still and unhappy, a strained silence between us. Suddenly the white bear got up and exited the room, giving me an unreadable look over his shoulder as he went.

I wandered the castle restlessly, my thoughts jumbled and my head aching. Again I had no will for weaving. Nor did I have any appetite for my evening meal, and leaving the food on the table barely touched, I sat for a time on the red couch, gazing into the fire. I was still undecided. I told myself the candle wouldn't work, then countered by saying that it was still worth trying. I told myself what a horrible mistake I would be making, how trying to light the darkness might upset the balance, possibly even bring harm. But then I reasoned it was a simple enough thing, lighting a candle. No one would even know; I could light the candle, have a quick peek, and that would be that, no one the wiser.

I went to bed as usual, and soon after, the lights were extinguished. I still did not know what I was going to do.

I had not actually gotten out the candle and flint but had left them at the top of my pack so I could get at them easily.

I was wide awake when my visitor climbed into bed next to me. I listened closely to the rhythm of his breathing, and after what felt like hours, it seemed to be regular and deep and I was sure he was asleep.

Quietly I slipped out of bed and crossed to the cupboard. I had left the door partway open because it had a slight squeak to it and I didn't want to risk making noise. My hand shaking slightly, I felt in my pack for the candle and flint. They were where I had left them. I took them in hand and slowly crossed to the bed.

I felt my way carefully to the other side of the bed and stood there for several long moments, trembling, listening to him breathe.

I fought against feelings of panic that shuddered through me. *I should not do this.* But I had to know.

I turned my back to the bed. Then, taking a firm grip on the candle in my left hand, I squeezed hard on the mechanism of the flint. A bright spark flared, but I had misjudged the placing of the candlewick in the dark. Moving the wick closer, I tried again. This time it worked. The candle lit and slowly, silently, I turned toward the bed, holding the candle aloft.

Troll Queen

FOR ONE HUNDRED AND FIFTY softskin years (a period of time in Huldre called an *alkakausi*), my softskin boy was to be a white bear. And at the end of those hundred and fifty years, if the conditions were not met, he would be mine.

The conditions were meant to punish me but also to challenge me. It was the sort of intricate, elaborate contest my father enjoyed setting in motion and then watching unfold.

It was unfortunate my father died before seeing this particular challenge wind down to its conclusion.

But I have watched. And waited, patiently I think.

There were a few halfhearted attempts along the way. It was always tricky for him, balancing the bear and the man inside him. Mostly the bear won.

As the hundred and fifty years draw to a close, this last

one, this softskin girl with the sturdy body and violet eyes, has come very close. She has nearly fulfilled one of the conditions.

But not the most difficult. I always knew her curiosity would be her undoing.

Rose

IT WAS NOT A MONSTER that lay sleeping on the white sheets. Nor a faceless horror. Nor even the white bear.

It was a man.

His hair was golden, glowing bright as a bonfire in the light of the candle. And his features were fair, I suppose, but he was a stranger and that somehow was the greatest shock of all—that I had been lying all these months beside a complete stranger. I had to hold the candle steady against the violent shudder that shook my body. Then I noticed the stranger was wearing the white nightshirt, the one I had woven. It fit him well, not too wide nor too narrow across the shoulders; the sleeves falling to his wrists, neither too long nor too short. I thought how lucky I had been in estimating the size, with only the feeling of his weight on the mattress to go by, then realized how absurd I was to be standing there thinking about how well the nightshirt fit.

He lay on his side. I stared down at his hand, which curled gently on the white sheet in front of him. There was a silver ring on his smallest finger. I could see sparse golden hairs on the back of his hand, and the curved fingers seemed vulnerable to me. I suddenly felt ashamed, staring down at this sleeping stranger in a pool of candlelight. I felt myself blush, my skin hot and uncomfortable. I raised the candle, thinking to blow it out at once but hesitating briefly for a last look at his face.

And then his eyes opened.

I let out a cry, my breath going short. They were his eyes, the white bear's eyes. My body jerked with the shock of seeing familiar, even well-loved, eyes inside a stranger's face.

In that moment the candle tipped and hot wax spilled onto the stranger, onto the shoulder of the white nightshirt.

He let out a cry of his own, and the sound of it shall remain seared in my heart forever, so horrible was it to my ears. It had nothing to do with the pain of hot wax burning the skin but instead held an enormous aching grief; it was a keening of loss and death and betrayal.

"What have you done?" were the words wrung out of him. It was a stranger's voice yet held dim echoes of the white bear.

But even worse than that cry, and what pierced me even deeper, was the look in his eyes. The utter hopelessness.

"No!" I cried out, and I became aware that something

247

was happening around me. There was an immense roaring in my ears that obliterated all sound. Shards of light and color exploded against my eyes so that I had to close them, and my feet were standing on nothing. I had a sensation of falling yet not moving at all. Flinging my arms out, I reached for the stranger with the golden hair, but my fingers touched nothing. And there *was* nothing, except sound and color and a terrifying spinning sensation.

Suddenly I felt cold air on my skin, and my feet were on solid ground. Opening my eyes I saw that I was no longer in my room in the castle. There was no castle. I was outside in the night, standing beside the mountain, which loomed above me in the darkness of night.

The stranger with the hopeless eyes was standing in front of me. He was tall and I had to tilt my head back to look up at him. Just behind his head was the moon, gibbous and bright, with a cloud floating past it.

"What have you done?" he said again, this time in a whisper.

"I'm sorry," I answered, my own voice breaking, the words pathetic and flimsy in my ears. I wanted to avert my eyes from his, from the pain, but I could not.

"If you had only held on one last cycle of the moon..." He trailed off, though his eyes remained on mine.

"What..." I began urgently, not wanting to know but needing to, "what would have happened then?"

"I would have been freed. After so long..." He hesitated. "I do not know anymore how long. It feels like several lifetimes..."

"You were under a spell?"

"Yes. White bear by day; boy...then man...by night. I could not speak of it. The only way I could be released was for a maiden to live with me, of her own free will, for one year. And during that time she was not to gaze upon my human face."

I heard a faint jingle of bells, though they registered only dimly, so lost was I in the damning words. "And now?" I asked, dreading the answer.

"I go with her. Forever."

"Who? Who do you go with?"

He shook his head, hopelessness flooding his whole body.

"Can't you tell me?"

"It does not matter. I know her only as Queen, and her land is far."

"Where is it?" I asked, willing him to tell me.

He laughed suddenly, and I could hear the full-throated, grating sound of the white bear's laughter in it. "East of the sun and west of the moon," he said.

I stared at him stupidly. "What do you mean?"

"Just as I said—east of the sun and west of the moon is where her land lies." Again he laughed, bitterly.

The bells I had heard earlier were louder now.

"She comes," the stranger said. Then he grabbed my hand and pressed something into it. "Her power is...

strong," he said, his mouth twisting as though the last word did not do justice to the truth. "I would not have her harm you."

A sleigh was approaching, pulled by four magnificent white reindeer. The sleigh was a silvery white color and the reins were lined with silver bells. I caught a glimpse of a pale face, cold and beautiful, and behind it, Tuki and the woman Urda. And then before I could move, the stranger with the white bear's eyes was gone, and the sleigh with him.

I could no longer hear the bells. I was alone.

Troll Queen

I COULD HAVE HAD a servant drive the sleigh. But I have always loved the reins in my own hands. The reindeer are superb, the best of the herd. The snow took great care and effort to bring, but I am pleased with my handiwork. It is the finest way to begin the journey to his new home.

I made sure that Urda and Tuki wrapped him well in furs and gave him frequent draughts of slank. The cold will be an adjustment for him, but soon enough he will grow used to it.

His lovely face is pale and pinched with unhappiness, but it does not disturb me, for in time that will fade. There is *rauha* in the slank and this will help ease his pain, and blur his memories as well.

She was a flawed, unfinished child, unworthy of him.

I flick the whip ever so slightly, and the reindeer soar

across the sky. My arts keep the softskins below from seeing us.

I look back at him, bundled in his furs. His eyes are
closed, the lashes dark against his white cheeks; perhaps
he sleeps. The breath-stopping joy fills me until I feel I
shall burst apart.

Rose

WHAT HAVE I DONE? I thought, and sank to my knees, weeping.

It was the cold that brought me out of my grief. I discovered with a shock that I was lying in my nightdress in several inches of snow.

The cold had seeped into my whole body, and I began trembling violently. Then I remembered the stranger pressing something into my hand and I uncurled my frozen fingers to find his silver ring. I could see it only faintly by the moonlight. The ring was plain—a polished, gleaming silver—but there was a word etched inside of the band: *VALOIS*. *Fransk,* I thought, but I didn't know what the word meant. Another sob rose in my throat, but I swallowed it. Slipping the ring onto my thumb (the only finger it fit), I told myself I must do something, beginning with getting out of the cold.

I stood, gazing around me. The mountain before me was covered in snow, and there was no sign on its surface of a door or entrance to the castle. I wondered if the castle was even still there, or if my actions had caused it to disappear altogether, along with the white bear. But there was no white bear anymore. A stranger had stood in his place. A stranger whose life I had destroyed with one reckless choice.

Shivering violently I suddenly noticed that my pack from home was sitting nearby in the snow. I ran to it, and inside I found all the things I had originally brought with me from home. There were also a few items I had added since, including the dictionary of words from Tuki's language I had made. My leather wallet was there, too, and despite my frozen hands, I couldn't help opening it. Glimmers of gold, silver, and pearly moon shone out at me. Breathing hard I shut it again. This then was all that was left of the castle in the mountain.

I dug deeper, found the wool vest made by Widow Hautzig, which I pulled over my nightdress, and then some wool socks, dragging them hurriedly onto my frozen feet, followed by my old boots. Finally I wrapped myself in a woolen sweater from home and then my mended compass-cloak.

It was as I was fastening my cloak that I saw the candle and flint lying in the snow. My cheeks flamed and I crossed to where they lay. I was tempted to grab them up and hurl them away from me as far as I could. But instead I deliberately picked them up, dusted off the snow, and thrust them into my bag.

I was shivering so hard I could barely breathe. If I didn't find shelter soon, I would lose my wits. I began to move around the base of the mountain and after a short time found a small, low cave. I wedged myself into it, wrapping my cloak tightly around me. Searching the back of the cave, I found a handful of dry kindling, and though I loathed the sight of it, I used the flint my mother had given me and managed to get a small blaze going.

As I sat there before the tiny fire, my shivering subsided somewhat. My thoughts had been as jangled and shivery as my body, but they, too, quieted.

What did it mean? *"East of the sun and west of the moon."* Was it a clue, directions of some kind to the far-away land where the pale woman he called Queen was taking him?

But how could that be? Neither the sun, nor even less the moon, provided any sort of fixed point from which to take that kind of bearing. They were always moving across the sky. What was east of the moon at midnight would be entirely another direction by dawn. It made no sense.

Maybe if I could figure out the positions of the sun and moon at the very moment when he had spoken those words, then I could at least chart the right direction.

I remembered looking up at him, the moon almost

directly above his head. My back had been to the mountain then. So I had a good idea of the moon's position at least.

But what of the sun? Could I make any sort of calculation as to its position? I didn't know how soon it was until sunrise. And even if I did know that the sun was an hour or two below the horizon, what did that gain me? How could there be a reachable destination lying east of the sun and west of the moon when the two directions were opposite? My father had taught me that the earth was a round ball, and so, I reasoned, there would be a point, on the far side of the globe, where the two directions would meet. . . . My head began to ache.

"East of the sun and west of the moon." As unfathomable as the words were, I realized I must figure them out, reason it through. For I would go to this impossible land that lay east of the sun and west of the moon. From the moment the sleigh had vanished from sight and I could no longer hear the silver bells, I knew that I would go after the stranger that had been the white bear to make right the terrible wrong I had done him.

It didn't occur to me to do anything else.

I could just as easily have looked around and thought, *At last, I am free to return to my home and family!* I could have put it all behind me and briskly turned my steps toward home. But I did not. Instead I was busily mapping out a journey to an unreachable place.

In the meager light of the small fire, I gathered my things together. When weaving a cloth, you must always know where you are in the design. So it was with me. Before I could begin to chart my course, I had to first find out where I was.

All that mattered was to make things right. And I would do whatever it took, journey to wherever I must, to reach that goal.

BOOK THREE

West

*She would search for him. In the land that lay
east of the sun and west of the moon.
But there was no way there.*

Rose

THOSE FIRST FEW DAYS were as grim as any I can remember. I had no idea where I was, much less where I was going, and I could not stop thinking about the candle wax dripping onto his skin, the cry of despair, and the sleigh disappearing from my sight. I rewove the scene over and over in my head until I thought I would lose my reason.

I had caught a chill, no doubt from lying weeping in the snow, and was plagued by a nasty cough and a nose that wouldn't stop leaking.

I walked for three straight days without finding any sign of a town or farm. I chose my direction by instinct, thinking that I would follow in the general direction the sleigh had been heading—north. I still wore my night-dress under the vest, sweater, and cloak. But the weather was gradually warming, and most of the snow had melted by twilight of the third day.

The fourth day I came across a large farm. My spirits rose. I was hoping desperately for some kind of assistance—food, directions, anything. I had eaten nothing aside from what remained of Torsk's honey and the toffee Mother had given me many months before. But the closer I came to the first building, a pale blue barn of medium size, the clearer it became that the farm was abandoned. There was no sign of a living creature, human or animal. However, it did not look as though it had lain deserted long, for all the buildings were well maintained, and as I searched the grounds, I even found feed in the troughs, and heaps of dung that didn't look much older than several days. Suddenly it occurred to me that the farm may have supplied the raw material for all the fine food I had eaten at the castle, and I wondered if those who ran the farm had disappeared, as well as the animals, along with the man who had been a white bear.

Anything that I could have eaten had vanished as well, and I found only some dried-up carrots and beans at the bottom of a few pails in one of the barns. I stuffed those in my pocket and resumed my journey. There was a dense forest surrounding the farm and the traveling was difficult. It took at least a day and a half to get through the forest.

Finally I stumbled out of the tangle of the trees, onto a stretch of meadowland. I was weak, my stomach tight with hunger, and my cough had worsened. But much worse than either my hunger or the cough that tormented me was the sound that kept ringing in my ears, the cry of despair from the man who had been a white bear. I heard it as I walked through dull-green grass and knee-high shrubs. I heard it when I dozed fitfully at night. I heard it when I awoke to a pale wintry sun. But I continued to struggle forward, telling myself that somehow I would make things right again.

Though I did not see any specific places I recognized, the gently rolling hills and the shapes of the trees were familiar to me from my journeys with the white bear. I knew it was winter, but clearly the winters in this land were much milder than in Njord, and some of the time it was warm enough for me to take off my cloak.

On the seventh day it began to rain. That night I made myself a bed of leaves in a small grove of some kind of broad-leaved tree I did not recognize. After eating the last of the shriveled carrots, I slept restlessly and awoke feeling feverish. When I got unsteadily to my feet, I was wracked by a cough that doubled me over. I sank to my knees, feeling lightheaded and dizzy. All I had eaten for the past seven days were toffees and the few shriveled carrots and beans. I thought ruefully of the last meal I had had in the castle. Melting-soft bread and creamy butter and herb-crusted meat with tender chunks of vegetables...

I groaned.

I was able to travel only a short distance that day, too weak to stay upright for long. That night I huddled under some bushes, feeling damp and chilled, though my face felt hot with fever. When I awoke I could barely move. Every time I lifted my head, the world around me spun crazily, and deep, hacking coughs felt like they would split my chest apart. I forced myself to my hands and knees and crawled forward but was stopped by another spasm of coughing.

I lifted my blurred eyes to look at the sky. *I'm not going to make it,* I thought. *But I have to.* Then I saw something that made me blink. A thin curve of woodsmoke against the gray sky.

I staggered to my feet and took several steps forward. But then I tripped over a low-lying shrub and fell to the ground. I began coughing and could not stop. Finally it subsided and I lay there, wrung out, my eyes closed.

I thought I might just go to sleep for a while, and then the cry of despair from the man who had been a white bear rang again in my ears. "I have to get up," I croaked. I struggled to raise myself, but a mist of gray veiled my eyes and I sank back to the ground, resigned. So weary. I heard footsteps in the grass, but it did not matter. "I'm sorry," I murmured, then slipped into unconsciousness.

White Bear

I CANNOT THINK CLEARLY. I am human again, but I am lost. There is something in the drink they give me, and I want to refuse it, but I am cold, chilled through to my soul, and the drink warms me. I cannot remember. Except, just barely... her. Her face, all white and pinched and filled with despair, and guilt. Her name...

Rose.

Must remember.

The beautiful pale queen drives the sleigh. She looks back at me frequently. We rise high, moving quickly through the sky, but I see glimpses of the lands I once roamed as a white bear. Rolling hills laced with white. A boundless gray sea. And then jagged peaks crowned in glaring ice.

I am wrapped in fur. But it is not *my* fur. My limbs feel strange, thin and wavery and weak. My face is bare, strangely bare, I can't get used to it, and the cold wind rips at my naked skin. I dip my head under the furs, but the heavy warmth makes me feel sleepy and muddled. I raise my head up again, trying to remember. I want to remember.

Rose.

Tears come and they freeze on my face.

Rose

PEERING DOWN AT ME, a young face framed by dark braids. Her eyes widened. *"Maman, Maman!"* she called out.

I could smell food cooking. I was inside a home of some kind.

A woman's voice answered the child, but I could not make out the words she said. Another face loomed beside the face with braids. It was a kind-looking woman, with auburn hair and a broad, friendly mouth.

"Comment allez-vous?" she said.

She was speaking Fransk, I suddenly realized. It had been long since I had heard it spoken. When I read to the white bear from the Fransk books in the castle, I had always translated the words to Njorden. I closed my eyes at the memory but opened them again when I started coughing.

"Estelle," I heard the kind lady say, followed by more words. The girl with the braids disappeared.

My chest ached, but I could not stop coughing. The woman put a cool cloth on my head, and then the girl handed her a cup that the woman put to my lips. Between coughs I managed to drink something warm and fragrant. Some kind of tea, I thought, with honey in it. My coughing finally subsided and I slept.

When I awoke again the light was dim. I could hear the woman's voice, singing softly. I turned my head and saw her sitting by the hearth, sewing. I was lying on a mattress stuffed with straw, with a warm woolen blanket pulled over me.

The woman noticed that I was awake and, setting aside her mending, came to my side.

"Comment allez-vous?" she said again.

I thought she was asking how I was feeling but was unsure.

The woman must have seen the dim light of recognition in my eyes, for she nodded encouragingly and repeated the question.

"...*regretter*..." I stammered, "but I do not...*parler* Fransk." My accent was probably unrecognizable, for she looked puzzled for a moment but then understood, I think.

"Njorden," I said.

Again she nodded. *"Oui, Njord."* The girl with the braids appeared beside her mother.

"Maman?"

"Estelle, elle est Njorden," the mother said to the girl, gesturing to me.

I started to cough again. The mother bustled into the kitchen, bringing a cup that she filled from the kettle resting on the hearth fire. Again I drank some of the sweet honeyed tea.

"Thank you," I said. *"Merci."*

After several days of tea, and soup, and the kind attentions of the woman, whose name was Sofi, along with her daughter, Estelle, I regained some semblance of strength. At least I was able to sit up on the third day. I was still plagued by coughing, but each bout got a little shorter.

My knowledge of Fransk from childhood and the time I had spent in the castle teaching myself made it possible for me to communicate with Sofi and Estelle, if they spoke slowly. I learned that mother and daughter lived by themselves in the fairly remote part of Fransk, Sofi's husband having died several years before. Sofi had thought about moving to a coastal village where her brother lived, but she loved the countryside too well, as did Estelle.

I was vague about my own circumstances. I did not want the nice woman to think I was a lunatic by speaking of castles in mountains and enchanted bears. Instead I said I had become lost while traveling to visit relatives. I don't know what she made of me, with my tattered nightdress and small knapsack, but she did not press me with questions.

The girl Estelle was very friendly. She loved to listen to the way I mangled Fransk words and would laugh delightedly before correcting me. On the fourth day Estelle suddenly asked if I came from the forest *"hanté par les fantômes."* I asked her what that meant. Estelle rose to her feet and put her arms above her head, scrunching her face into a grotesque mask. She stalked about the room, moaning and crying. I stared at her in complete bewilderment. Sofi joined us, laughing.

She tried to explain, saying that Estelle was acting the part of a *fantôme*.

I was still baffled. I asked if *fantôme* meant "monster," or "troll."

Sofi shook her head. I realized Estelle thought I had come from a haunted forest, and I asked them to tell me more. Sofi described a very dense wood several days' distance from their cottage. The forest had the reputation of being haunted, she said, because of the unexplained disappearances over the years of several people who had last been seen near there. It was in a very remote part of the country and not many lived in close proximity, but the few who did gave the forest a wide berth.

I honestly don't know what got into me at that moment, but I blurted out that yes, I had come through the forest *"hanté,"* and that I had come there after having lived for nearly a year with an enchanted white bear in a castle in the mountain beyond the forest.

The two of them stared at me without speaking. Uneasily I wondered if Sofi was regretting having taken in a madwoman and was trying to figure out how soon she could send me packing.

Then Estelle burst out, *"Maman, c'est l'ours blanc!"*

"Oui, oui," Sofi responded distractedly. Sofi then told me that Estelle had come to her a handful of times over the past two or three years, claiming to have seen a white bear loping through a nearby meadow. Sofi had not believed her, thinking Estelle was making it up.

"It is true," I said earnestly. Sofi shook her head in amazement, and I spent the next hour or so telling her what had happened in the castle and of my plan to go in search of the land that lay east of the sun and west of the moon.

"Fantastique," Sofi finally said in a soft voice, but then she added firmly that before I could even think of embarking on any kind of journey, I must first regain my strength and get rid of my cough. And though I was impatient to resume my travels, I knew she was right.

There was a fine, sturdy loom in a corner of the room, with the beginnings of some woven cloth at the bottom, and the next day, because I had no money to repay Sofi for her kindness, I offered to help with their weaving. Sofi said I did not need to repay her at all, but I insisted. So I made my way over to the loom, sat on the small stool, and began to weave.

It felt good to be at a loom again, though at first it brought up memories of the castle. But the loom was much more like the one at home, and so I thought of Neddy and Snurri, and as usual I got lost in the work. When I came to myself I discovered that I had completed a very long length of cloth. Both Sofi and Estelle were beside me, looking at me as if I were a troll with seven heads.

"Magnifique!" Sofi cried. Holding the cloth bunched in her hands, she asked where I had learned to weave. And Estelle piped in that my hands moved so fast, she could barely see them.

I was embarrassed, saying my skill wasn't really anything; it was just that I had begun young. Sofi again shook her head in amazement.

That afternoon Sofi went off to collect kindling and fetch water from the well. She declined my offer to help, saying she'd rather I stay behind and help Estelle prepare the evening meal. We were done quickly, a meat-and-vegetable stew we left simmering in the pot on the hearth fire, and Estelle suggested we play her favorite game. She brought out a wooden board with squares painted on it and a small box of playing pieces. It looked something like *hnefatafl*, a game I had played back home, although there were more pieces for Estelle's game. The little figures were skillfully carved out of wood, with small pieces of amber for the eyes.

Estelle enthusiastically described the rules of the game, which she called *echecs*. Having done this, however, she quickly lost interest in the actual game and began making up rules of her own and stories about the small figures.

"Father carved the pieces," she said in Fransk, "and I have given each one a name."

She held up one intricate piece, saying, *"C'est la grande dame, Queen Maraboo!"*

According to Estelle, Queen Maraboo was a very brave young woman who met with many heart-stopping adventures, including vanquishing an impressive array of hideous creatures, among them a troll-witch with twelve heads, a slithery creature called Boneless that stole your bones because he didn't have any, and a ghost-wolf that breathed fire and could only be controlled by singing. My knowledge of Fransk was sorely tested by the tales, but I managed to follow along fairly well and my vocabulary grew.

Estelle played the part of Queen Maraboo, while I was assigned roles that corresponded to the other pieces of the board, either those who served Queen Maraboo or those who were her inept enemies. But when I was assigned the role of the ghost-wolf and my howl fell short of her expectations, Estelle decided that she was tired of playing *echecs*.

She then began to teach me a clapping game. It was similar to games I had played with my sisters, when they could get me to sit still long enough, but the rhyming song was unfamiliar and difficult for me. This is how it went:

"The old woman must stand at the tub, tub, tub,
  The dirty clothes to rub, rub, rub;
  But when they are clean, and fit to be seen,
  She'll dress like a lady and dance on the green."

Estelle recited the words as we alternated slapping to-gether our right hands and then left hands, clapping in between. I found my thoughts drifting to my makeshift washing room at the castle, and to all the times I had carefully washed that white nightshirt. I blinked back tears and lost the beat of the clapping.

Estelle scolded me.

"Teach me another," I said, swallowing hard.

Estelle happily launched into another rhyme, with an-other whole set of handclaps and rhythms. Then we did another, and another. At one point Estelle asked me about the silver ring I wore on my thumb. I said that the man who had been a white bear had given it to me before he disappeared. And I took it off my thumb and showed her the word *VALOIS* inscribed on it. Estelle did not know what it meant (nor did her mother when I asked her later). Putting the ring back on my thumb, I returned to the hand-clapping game with Estelle.

The last rhyme Estelle taught me went like this:

"The sun shines east, the moon shines west,
  and pigs turn somersaults in a bobolink's nest.
  The sheep jumps the sun, the cat chases the moon,
  and they eat strawberry jam from a gold-plated spoon."

She repeated it over and over, and it seemed as if she could go on forever, but finally on the tenth chorus of the cat chasing the moon, Sofi returned and it was time for supper.

When I lay on my straw-filled mattress that night, Estelle's rhymes echoed in my ears. Sheep jumping over the sun and cats chasing the moon... *I might as well chase the moon myself*, I thought, *as find my way to a land that lies east of the sun and west of the moon*.

And then it struck me, like a great, ringing kick to the head. And I sat up.

"East of the sun and west of the moon" meant nothing. It was nonsense, like one of Estelle's rhymes. Neddy would have called it a *conundrum*, his fancy word for riddle. But it was a riddle with no solution. When the stranger with the white bear's eyes told me he was going to the place that lay "east of the sun and west of the moon," he was telling me he was going nowhere, to a place I could not follow him to. Why he chose those words, I did not know. Perhaps it was all he had been allowed to say. Or perhaps it was all he had been told.

Well, it didn't matter. Whether or not the words were a fraud, he was *somewhere*. And I would find him. I decided I must leave the next day.

"It is too soon," Sofi protested. "You need more time to get better."

"I have to go," I said.

"Then Estelle and I will go with you," Sofi replied, her tone as definite as mine had been.

I stared at her. "I don't even know where I am going."

"I will start you on your journey then. Surely you know which direction you will begin with?"

"North," I replied. "The sleigh was going north. And the man Tuki spoke of a land of snow and ice. I think the pale queen took him to her home in that land."

Sofi nodded, then said, "I have something that might help you." She left the room.

She returned bearing a rolled-up sheet of parchment. I guessed immediately what it was. A map. It had been her husband's, brought back from a sea voyage. He had been a sailor; it was at sea that he had died.

It was a good map, made by a Portuguese mapmaker.

"It is yours now," Sofi said with a smile.

"Oh no, I cannot take it."

"Yes," she replied, and would not let me refuse.

She unrolled the map, flattening it on the table in the kitchen, and pointed to a spot in the southwest of Fransk. "This is where we are," she said.

I found Njord on the map and couldn't believe my eyes. The distance the white bear had traveled was fantastic. In seven days he had journeyed through most of Fransk, at least half of Njord, the countries of Tyskland, Holland, and Danemark, as well as the sea that lay between Njord and Danemark. Such a journey, on foot, would take me a year or more, and that did not take into account getting across the waters of Njordsjoen.

Sofi was watching my face, seeing the wonder and then the dismay there, and she put a comforting hand on mine.

"Courage," she said.

I studied the map for some time and decided that I would travel to the port town of La Rochelle, where I hoped to find a ship to take me north. I had no idea how I was going to pay for such a journey but thought maybe I could work for my passage. It would be much faster to travel by ship than to make the long trek north on foot. It turned out that Sofi's brother lived in La Rochelle and knew the harbor well. She thought he might be able to help me. And Sofi and Estelle were going to take me all the way to La Rochelle. Sofi had not seen her brother for a long time, she said, and accompanying me was the perfect opportunity for her and Estelle to visit.

We set off the next morning.

Troll Queen

OUR ARRIVAL AT THE PALACE was all I could have desired. There was a large assemblage to greet us, everyone brilliantly attired. And I was told that Simka had
been working night and day on the sumptuous feast that
we will enjoy this evening. (Simka's prowess in the
kitchen more than makes up for her foul disposition.)
The only thing that marred the homecoming was a trace
of unease I could read in the eyes of my closest advisers.
No one dared to say anything out loud when I said that
the softskin man would be given the suite of rooms beside my own, but I sensed their displeasure.

Urda—sour, complaining Urda—is the only one
who would ever dare to say that I am making a mistake
in bringing the softskin here. All the way home in the
sleigh she griped at me, saying that my people will never
accept a softskin in the palace. I finally had to stop her
tongue with my arts. (How she loathes it when I do that!)

Urda is wrong. I have always been able to bend my people to my will.

I will present him to the entire court at the feast this evening. But I will not tell them that the softskin man is to be their king. Better to wait, give them time to grow used to his presence here, before I tell them to prepare for a wedding.

As for me, to see him walk through the gates of my palace is the culmination of all my dreams, my plans. The joy I feel is immense; it burns inside me as though I have swallowed a piece of the sun.

Rose

THE JOURNEY TO La Rochelle took less than a fortnight. I was glad of the company of Sofi and Estelle, though I worried about taking so much from them and giving so little in return. Sofi brushed aside my concerns, but I vowed I would find some way to repay her.

At one point during the trip, Estelle said to me, "Are you not afraid to go to *la terre congelée?*"

La terre congelée was what Estelle called the Arktisk region. I thought for a moment and then said, "No."

"Ah," Estelle said with a broad smile, "you are just like Queen Maraboo!"

I laughed. "I'm not too handy when it comes to ghost-wolves and creatures with no bones."

Estelle laughed, too, and our talk turned to La Rochelle and her uncle Serge. But it was true what I had said to Estelle. I was not afraid. I had always had a secret desire to someday go to the lands of the far north. When I was little Father had explained to me that the world was round, and he described the lands of ice and snow at the farthest points to the north and south of our world. He even demonstrated this for me on a small leather ball, painting two splotches of white at opposite ends. It was amazing to me that there were places in the world where for part of the year the sun never shone at all, and for the other part it shone all the time. And where the snow never melted away. And where there were more white bears and snow owls than people. Knowing that I was a north-born, it made sense that I should be so fascinated by the Arktisk region; it was in my nature, the direction I naturally gravitated toward.

When I was a child one of my favorites of Neddy's old stories was of the goddess Freya, and how she journeyed through the world, looking for her lost husband, Odur.

"Odur is in every place where the searcher has not come. Odur is in every place that the searcher has left."

It was one of the stories I had told the white bear in the castle, and I knew it was one of his favorites as well. He would hold his head up, eyes alert, especially when I came to the part about how Freya searched everywhere, even going to the frozen land of the far north, the land called Niflheim, where she came upon a grand ice palace. Freya was imprisoned there, in that palace, and had she not been one of the immortals, she would have been frozen alive. But she escaped, using her cloak of swan feathers, which carried her swiftly through the air whenever she put it on, and she soared along the northern lights until she was safely home in Asgard. She never did find her husband, Odur. And I remember thinking as a child that she gave up way too easily. He was somewhere, I had thought, and she ought to have found him.

I made Neddy tell me that story so many times that he finally got tired of it and refused to tell it ever again. But I continued to dream of frozen wondrous Niflheim and pictured myself traveling there on my white bear. How strange life was, I thought, that it should turn out that I would go to the frozen lands not *with* my white bear but in search of him.

Sofi's brother, Serge, was happy to see his sister and niece. He and his wife were very generous, giving me food and lodging. Serge said he would find out about ships traveling north, though he warned me that passage would not be cheap. When I suggested I might work for my passage, he was polite enough not to laugh outright, but he did say that there wasn't much call for young girls as shipmates.

I was silent a moment, thinking, then asked, "Is there by chance a shop in La Rochelle that might be in the market for fine dresses?"

Both Serge and Sofi looked at me in surprise. I repeated the question.

"There is a haberdasher in the center of town," Serge responded with a sideways glance at his sister. "But I don't know..."

"Please tell me how to get there," I said firmly.

Serge gave me directions, and Sofi and Estelle insisted on accompanying me.

We entered the shop. It was a tidy, well-kept establishment, and the dark wooden shelves that lined the walls were crammed with bolts of fabric in every imaginable hue. There were also gowns displayed but not many. I approached the proprietor of the shop, a stout woman with a lace cap. "I have a gown to sell," I said.

She studied my travel-worn clothing with a skeptical eye. "I do not trade in farm-made clothing," she said frostily.

When I fished the leather wallet out of my pack, she looked even more scornful. But as I pulled out the square of silver fabric and began unfolding it, her eyes opened wide.

I smoothed and shook out the silver dress, which was just as shimmering and beautiful as I remembered it, and Estelle cried out, *"C'est magnifique, Rose!"*

"I did not realize...I am very sorry if...It is very nice indeed," the proprietor stammered, her manner suddenly fawning. "I should be very glad to buy it from you."

Sofi helped me bargain with the woman, for I was unsure of the value of the Fransk coins that she offered. And I came away feeling very rich, although Sofi claimed that the woman should have paid even more.

We returned to Serge's house, and Estelle told him all about the *"magnifique"* dress.

"What have you learned about ships traveling north?" I asked Serge.

"There are only two," he said. "One is a run-down vessel with a poor excuse for a captain. Not something for you even to consider," he said with a frown. "The other, however, is a Portuguese caravel helmed by a captain named Contarini. Captain Contarini has a very fine reputation. He is said to be a bit on the stern side but an excellent seaman. And Contarini is willing to take you to Tonsberg, although the cost will be high."

I was disappointed; Tonsberg was a port town at the southern end of Njord. I had hoped to find a ship going farther north.

"What about the other vessel you mentioned? Where is it going?" I asked.

"I doubt old Thor even knows."

"What do you mean?"

"Thor is a notorious drunkard. He got his nickname because he claims to be descended from some notorious Viking, and he acts and dresses like one himself. Thor's ship is a *knorr* and it has seen better days."

"A *knorr*?"

"One of those old-fashioned longships built in Viking manner. Thor's is the only one I've ever seen in this harbor. The only advantage of booking passage with Thor," added Serge, "is that he'll only charge the price of a barrel of ale. But it's out of the question. Pay Contarini's fee, and at least you know you'll arrive in Njord in one piece. You should be able to find another ship in Tonsberg, heading farther north."

I agreed and the next morning Serge took me to the caravel. Before leaving, though, I said my good-byes to Sofi and Estelle. At first Sofi refused to take any of the money I had gotten for my dress, saying that the weaving I had done at her cottage was payment enough, but I made her take a few coins—to pay for the map, I argued.

Estelle gave me a big hug, then handed me something small. It was the Queen Maraboo playing piece. I told her she shouldn't break up the set, but she said that her uncle Serge could carve her another and that I must carry it with me on my journey, for good luck. "To help you find *l'ours blanc*," she said. Thanking Sofi and Estelle one last time, I headed off with Serge to the docks.

Captain Contarini was a small, hard-eyed man who grudgingly agreed to take me on board as long as I paid the full price up front and vowed to stay out of sight.

"It is bad luck," he said, "to have a woman on board. You will stay confined to your quarters until the ship docks in Tonsberg." Meals would be brought to me, and that was all the contact I would be allowed with the crew. Serge supervised the payment of the fee, making sure I was not cheated; as it was, I paid Captain Contarini almost all I had gotten for my silver gown.

I bade Serge farewell and the captain hustled me on board, taking me quickly belowdecks. We wound through some narrow passageways until coming to a small storage room. Captain Contarini handed me a bucket, a skin-bag of water, and a thin wadding of cloth for a mattress. "Do not leave this room," he said with a frown, and slammed the door shut behind him.

I looked around my cramped quarters with misgiving. It was a gray, windowless closet of a room. I could feel the ship rocking gently on the water, and that, combined with the stuffiness of the room, already made me feel queasy. Serge had said the journey should take no more than five days. Surely I could stand anything for only five days, I thought. But I felt choked and stifled. The thought of not being able to breathe fresh air . . . Only five days . . . But my feeling of uneasiness grew. This was far worse than the castle, I thought. I did not think I could stand being locked up in that room for five days.

I went to open the door. It was locked from the outside. Captain Contarini was taking no chances.

I felt a surge of anger. I had had enough of locked doors. Using a needle from my sewing kit, I managed to pop the lock. I picked up my pack and, finding my way with difficulty, went to the deck of the ship.

Captain Contarini was furious when he saw me. While the sailors watched with interest, the captain grabbed my arm and hustled me off onto the dock.

"I will not be locked belowdecks," I said before he could speak.

"Then you will not travel on my ship."

"Very well. Give back my money."

"Certainly not. We struck a bargain. Just because you

choose not to keep your end of it, it is no concern of mine." He turned and began to head back up the gangplank. Suddenly he swung around to face me. "And do not think of getting your man Serge to intercede. I am a good friend to the authorities here and no one will listen to the claims of an unescorted ————." The word was Portuguese, but his glance was so scathing I knew it was something insulting.

I stood there on the dock, enraged at the captain and even more annoyed with myself for my rash decision. I did not like the idea of going back to Serge and Sofi.

Impulsively I decided I would find the other ship, the one with the disreputable Viking captain.

I found the longship after some hunting. It was off in a little-used part of the harbor, but I knew it at once. There was no other ship like it. It was long and slender, with a single mast, and it sat low in the water. The curving bow and stern posts were indistinguishable from each other, except that there was a steering oar at the rear, and when I got closer, I could see that the bow had a carved figurehead. Because the figure was so weatherbeaten, I had trouble making out what kind of beast it was, with its staring eyes and fierce, bared teeth, but I thought it was a bear. Which could be a good omen, I told myself.

There seemed to be no one about, so I stood, gazing at the ship. Despite the longship's peeling paint and worn appearance, I liked its lines. I noticed there was cargo on board, lashed down and covered with animal skins.

"You there!" came a harsh voice from behind me. He was speaking in Njorden. "What do you want?"

I turned to face an enormous man with a long, bushy beard and a pair of fierce blue eyes. He had long, bushy hair as well, and both beard and hair were butter yellow, though streaked with gray. Over his broad shoulders he wore a cloak that was fastened by an intricately wrought brooch, the metal tarnished. A long knife in a leather sheath lay against one hip, and around his neck was a necklace from which dangled what I recognized to be the silver hammer of Thor; it, too, was tarnished.

"Pardon me," I replied quickly. "I was admiring your ship."

"Njorden, are you?"

I nodded.

"Then get along to your mother. The harbor is no fit place for a maid," he said dismissively, and he boarded the slender ship with an easy grace despite his size.

"I am looking for passage to Njord," I called to him.

"You'll find none here," he said without glancing in my direction.

"I understand you journey north."

"I carry only cargo, not passengers."

"Please, sir. I will work. I must get to . . ."

"No!" he thundered, this time glaring at me with those fierce eyes.

"Forgive Thor's ill manners, miss," said a voice behind me, also in Njorden. "He is short on ale."

I turned to see two men. They were rough-looking in

garb and hygiene, but there was a twinkle in the eye of the smaller of the two, the one who had spoken. He was slight in build, though he looked agile and his thin arms were roped with muscle. His skin was deeply browned by the sun. He moved quickly as he boarded the *knorr* and went to a sea chest, on which he settled himself comfortably, leaning up against the side of the boat, his hands behind his head.

The other man was fair haired, tall and slow moving, with a broad, ugly face. He said nothing, though he looked calm and not unkind. He nodded at me as he, too, climbed on board.

"Ask if she cooks, Thor," said the small man. "I don't think I can abide another sea journey eating your cooking."

"I can cook," I said quickly. "And I'll pay for my passage besides."

"Listen to that, she cooks and has a dowry." The small man grinned. "Tell me, are you betrothed, maid, for if not, I would make a fine husband for any..."

"I'll snatch out that flapping tongue of yours, Gest, if you don't get to work!" Thor bellowed.

The small man rose quickly and began to do something with the rigging.

"Please," I said to the man called Thor. Though he was intimidating, I managed to look him straight in the eye. "I haven't any money..." I began.

He snorted. "Be off with you. You've wasted enough of my time."

"But I do have this…" I continued, undeterred. I took out my leather wallet. I hated to give up another of my beautiful dresses, and so soon after the first. But I had to travel north.

As I shook out the gold dress, all three men stared. But then Thor growled, "What do I want with a lady's gown?" He pointedly turned his back on me and returned to his work.

The one called Gest said, "Don't be a fool, Thor. Why, you could buy a brand-new *knorr* with what you'd get in Paris for a dress like that. And you could fill its hold with enough ale to last a year, to boot."

Thor slowly turned back, his face showing a flicker of interest. "Give it here," he said, stepping back onto the dock. He ran the glittering fabric through his dirty calloused fingers. "Very well. I'll take you north," he stated gruffly.

"Oh, thank you," I said.

"I'll have this now," he said, taking the gown from me. "We leave at sundown." Roughly he folded up the golden fabric, and tucking it under his arm, he set off for town.

"You won't get nearly as much as it's worth, here in La Rochelle," Gest called after him. But Thor ignored him.

Gest shrugged. "The man's got a mighty thirst on him." He turned his attention to me. "Well, welcome aboard the good ship *Sif*," he said. "What's your name, lass?"

"Rose," I replied.

"Rose, is it? I am Gest, at your service, and this is my mate, Goran." The fair-haired man nodded at me. "I don't suppose, Miss Rose, you know how to make raspberry cake out of salt pork and hard bread?"

"Perhaps not, but I can manage *rommegrot*, if you have a measure of wheat flour," I said.

A wide smile creased his face. "Ah, bless you, child," he said.

"May I ask," I said, "where exactly this ship is headed?"

"You may well ask. The destination is upward of Suroy, but with old Thor at the steering oar, you never can tell. If he's full of ale, which is what that golden dress is headed for, he's likely to steer us into a storm cloud thinking he's found Valhalla."

I felt giddy with excitement. Suroy was near the top of Njord and this was just what I'd hoped for, though I was also a little uneasy at Gest's words. I could only pray that he was exaggerating.

I decided to use the time until sundown to write a letter to my family. When I was done I went back to the caravel and, keeping out of sight of Captain Contarini, managed to find a friendly sailor who was willing to take my letter—along with the last of my coins—across to Tonsberg, and then make sure it got from there to Andalsnes. Of course, I had no guarantee he would do as he said, but I sensed an honesty in him, as well as a dislike for the way his captain had treated me.

It was approaching twilight when I found my way back to the *knorr*. But before I even saw the ship, I could hear Thor singing at the top of his voice.

"Reach for your mead horn and raise it high.
Odin the great! Thunder god Thor!
Balder the mild, and Freya sweet.
We toast until Valhalla is reeling!"

As I came up to the *knorr*, I smelled a strong stink of ale.

Thor was sprawled at the rear of the ship, his hand gripping the steering oar. Gest greeted me cheerfully, helped me aboard, and gestured to me to take a seat. "Could be a rocky departure," he warned.

"Ready to cast off?" he called to Thor.

Thor kept singing.

Gest nimbly unfastened all the ropes binding the boat to the dock, and he and Goran pushed off. The sail filled and the ship lurched forward. "That old souse won't give up the steering oar for the life of him," Gest muttered as he passed me, grabbing at a rope that was whipping around the deck.

Anxiously I gazed ahead at the seawalls protecting the entrance to the harbor. We looked to be heading straight toward the starboard one, but eventually Thor heaved the steering oar and we just cleared it. He laughed loudly and then resumed his song. We were out on the open sea.

"We are lucky," Gest said. "We have a southeast

wind." It served us well for the first two days of the journey.

I had never been on anything larger than a rowboat, much less a ship such as this. It was clinker-built, Gest told me, which was a style of boat building that involved overlapping the planks in a fashion that made it shimmy through the waves like a sea-dwelling snake.

Surprisingly, I took to life aboard the *knorr* without difficulty. Gest had predicted I would get seasick, being such a landlubber, but I did not. I loved the sea wind on my face and the feeling of skimming the waves.

On the second day of the journey, we spied the brooding white cliffs of the land called Anglia to the northwest. If I had not known better, I would have thought the cliffs were snow-covered, but Gest told me they were white because of limestone, a chalky rock.

Soon we came out on Njordsjoen, the sea I had traveled through in a sealskin, borne by the white bear.

The journey was uneventful for the next five days. I learned how to cook on a *knorr* when the water wasn't too choppy, using a small cauldron hung on a tripod. My cooking was only just adequate, given what I had to work with, but Gest praised me lavishly—mostly, I think, to annoy Thor. Gest was an extremely amiable, entertaining traveling companion, while Goran remained silent, and Thor spoke only to the two men, ignoring me almost completely.

Eventually Thor sobered up, at least for a time, and it became clear that he knew his boat and the seas—and that he would have been a very good captain, were it not for his weakness for ale. Gest had been right; most of what Thor got for the golden dress had gone to buying casks of ale. They were stowed in the sturdiest part of the storage area belowdecks, and Thor visited there frequently, refilling a smaller cask that he would keep at his side.

There was one time when Thor lay passed out at the rudder as we hit a patch of choppy seas. Goran took over the steering oar and held us fairly steady, although when Thor had finished sleeping it off, he groused that Goran had put us off course. Goran and Gest seemed to be used to Thor's unreliable behavior, however, and took it all in stride.

For navigating, Thor used a *leidarstein*, an ugly brown stone he always carried with him in a small leather pouch. My mother had a *leidarstein* that had been handed down to her from her mother, so I had seen how one worked. But it never failed to amaze me, watching the needle slowly swing toward the polestar in the north.

On the sixth day we came into sight of the Shetland Islands, and Gest told me that the southern region of Njord lay directly east, though we were too far away to see it. If we continued at our current rate of travel, he said, we should reach Suroy in eight or nine days.

But the next day the wind deserted us. After several hours becalmed, Thor suddenly shouted at me to take over the steering oar. Until then my jobs had been confined to cooking and bailing out water (which, because of the low sides of the *knorr*, was an ongoing and crucial job). Gest and Goran lowered the sail, while Thor gruffly instructed me on how to hold the tiller steady. Then, because he was the largest of the three men, Thor took an oar on one side of the ship while Gest and Goran manned two oars on the other side.

It did not take me too long to get the feel for holding the ship steady, especially with Thor barking out instructions. The rowing was hot, backbreaking work, and I felt sympathy for the three men, their muscles straining and sweat rolling down their faces. At midday Thor came back to the steering oar while I prepared a meal of smoked fish and hard bread. He took many breaks from steering to refill his mug of ale, and I could see that Gest was watching him closely.

The sky began to cloud over, and naively I thought this a good thing because the rowing wouldn't be so hot for the men. But the air felt strange, making my skin prickle. When the wind began to blow again, whitecaps appeared on the waves. It was coming too quickly. And the sky kept getting blacker.

Thor jumped up, draining his mug. "Raise the sail!" he shouted.

Gest frowned. "Looks a big one, Thor. Best we not risk the sail."

"Let it blow!" Thor threw back. "We'll ride her out. And make good time, too."

"But the wind has shifted all around the compass these past few minutes," Gest responded, "from south to east to west. You know that portends..."

"We'll raise the sail!" Thor thundered. "'Rather founder than furl,'" he said, sounding as if he was quoting something.

Reluctantly Gest and Goran went to unfurl the sail. The wind tore at them, and the fabric snapped as they struggled to raise it. But finally the sail was aloft, and as the wind filled it, we shot forward through the roiling sea.

Thor had grabbed the steering oar from me. I could smell the ale on him and felt suddenly afraid. Gest and Goran were moving around the boat, checking on ropes and making sure everything was tightly lashed down. I picked up a bailing bucket without being told.

Rain sheeted down from the sky, mingling with the surging spray from the sea. In short order I was soaked through but was too busy bailing to care. Gest and Goran soon joined me.

The waves were getting higher, and it seemed for every bucket of water I tossed overboard, three bucketfuls came sloshing over the sides of the *knorr*.

But it was a wonder to me how that ship rode the waves. Every time I saw a huge wave looming toward us, I was sure it would be the end—that the ship would be swamped and we would capsize. But every time, the *knorr* slid up and over the wave.

The wind was shrieking and the sail was stiff and distended, as though a giant fist were thrust in it at the bottom, hurling the *knorr* along with a violence unlike anything I had ever seen. The ropes holding the sails were taut, stretched to their limit, and I imagined that at any moment they would snap.

At the steering oar, Thor concentrated his whole body on wrestling the wind and enormous waves for control of the *knorr*. His eyes burned and his face was lit with some primitive emotion; it almost looked like joy.

Then Gest shouted to Goran. They threw aside their bailing buckets and made their way to the sail, untying ropes as they went. They were lowering the sail. I looked over at Thor and saw that his face was suffused with rage.

"Cowards!" he shouted. I was afraid he was going to lunge at them, but he kept still, just barely.

The wind was lashing the sail, which snapped and bucked like a living thing at the two men as they wrestled it down. They secured the sail as best they could, then returned to bailing. The *knorr* steadied with the sail down. I could hear Thor still shouting curses at his crew.

As we crested one very large wave, I saw a mountain of water bearing down on us. I let out a cry of fear and Gest muttered a prayer. Then I turned to see Thor charging toward me, the tiller swaying crazily behind him. No more was there rage in his face, just a fanatical sort of determination. The wind blew back his mane of hair, and he looked like some crazed sea-god. Grabbing hold of me with his thick arms, as if I were no heavier than a child's cloth doll, he carried me across to the prow of the ship and then thrust me under the deck boards, wedging me in tightly. My cheek scraped against a barrel and my shoulder struck my own pack from home, which had been stored down there with other cargo. I inched forward, clutching my pack to my chest. I dimly heard shouts and the wind screaming, and then there was a great violent crashing sound as a giant wave slammed down on the *knorr*.

When I came to, I could still hear the wind, but it was no longer screaming. Miraculously the ship was still afloat. I lay in a chilly pool of water and wine, which had spilled from the cask on which I had scraped my cheek. I could hear no other sounds but the creaking of the ship, the sloshing of water around me, and the diminishing fury of the wind.

Gingerly, my head pounding, I wriggled my body backward, then slowly pulled myself out from under the deck boards. I sat up, waist-deep in water, and the ship seemed to spin dizzily for a few moments. I closed my eyes, then opened them.

I could see no one.

Troll Queen

HE CANNOT GET USED to being without fur. I see him rub at his skin, and he remains quiet most of the time.

I call him Myk now, and he seems to understand it is his new name. Beyond the sadness, the quiet, I see the softskin boy that I first met in the green lands. He is all I ever wanted. His voice; his soft, warm skin; even the smile, which it is true I do not often see now. Two days ago was the first time, some caper of Tuki's. But it was as I remembered it, like sunlight on the snow, melting, good.

I continue with my arts, trying to soften my own skin so that he will feel more as if he is with his own people. So far the change is only temporary, which is frustrating, but I will keep experimenting.

Tuki is acting strangely with me. He scurries away when I come near. I can see Urda is worried; she knows what I will do if he gives trouble. Perhaps it was a mistake sending him south with Urda, to be so long gone from here, but Urda would have been too lonely without her son there. It is her own fault anyway; she admits she should have kept a closer eye on him and not let him spend time alone with the softskin girl.

The changes to Myk's quarters are almost complete. He has books and musical instruments. It may have been a mistake to make the flauto just the same as his favorite one in the castle. I saw a look in his eye the first time he held it, as though some small memory was pricking at him. But it passed. And the thanks he gave me were deeply felt.

I am pleased to be home, and to have him here with me at last. Now there is only the wedding to prepare for. So much to be done, but such delicious planning. Much as I want him to be my husband at once, now that he is here I can take the time to make the wedding feast as it should be. But not too much time.

It will be the grandest and finest celebration ever in Huldre. Perfect. Lavish. All the most important of our race, from all corners of the earth, shall be here.

An event to do us both honor. The queen and her king.

Rose

I COULD NOT at first take it in.

I was alone, completely alone on the vast sea, in a battered, broken, waterlogged *knorr*. The mast was gone; all that remained was a jagged stub little taller than I. The sail had come loose from its lashing, and part of it lay draped across the deck while more than half of it hung overboard, dragging in the sea. And there was a large tear through it. The steering oar was gone, and it looked as though much of the cargo had been swept overboard as well.

I began to shake.

The wind had subsided to a stiff breeze and the *knorr* rode the waves, oblivious that its sole occupant was a disheveled, terrified girl. My trembling grew worse. Then, telling myself I must not give in to panic, I stood up. I needed to find a bucket. The *knorr* had taken on a great

deal of water during the storm and was riding dangerously low.

But I could see no buckets for bailing. What if they
had all been washed overboard? Perhaps one had gotten
lodged under the sail. With difficulty I lifted one side of
the wet, heavy sail. Gazing down I let out a gasp.

At first I thought the thing was a dead sea creature,
then realized with horror it was a bloody leg. It lay
oddly, looking as if it were disconnected from a body.
My heart beating fast, I heaved up more of the sail.

There was Thor. The leg stuck out at a strange angle
from his body. As I pushed the wet sailcloth off him, I
saw that his eyes were closed and his face, too, was covered with blood from a jagged gash on the forehead. He
looked dead—his skin was gray and there was so much
blood—but then his body twitched and he let out a soft
moan.

One arm, too, was bent at an awkward angle, and the
hand was clutching the broken-off tiller. I leaned over
him, feeling for his pulse. It beat under my fingers but
was slow and irregular. Thor moaned again.

It took all my strength to wrestle the huge sail completely off him. Breathing hard from the exertion, I
searched for something to stanch the flow of blood from
his forehead and his leg. I found several cargo boxes
lodged underneath the deck boards, and inside one was a
large bolt of linen. I went back above and got the knife
that Thor wore at his side; his eyes barely flickered as I removed it from its sheath. Returning belowdecks I used the

knife to cut and tear off a length of the fabric. I took it back up to Thor and swabbed at the cut on his face. The cut was deep, with jagged edges, and I could see the whiteness of bone underneath. It needed stitching, I thought, reminded of injuries I had seen back on the farm. For the time being I tied a makeshift bandage tightly around his head, then turned my attention to his leg. The gash there wasn't as deep, I was glad to see. But his leg definitely looked as though it was broken. His arm, too.

Thor's eyes flickered again as I worked over him, but then he lapsed back into unconsciousness. After wrapping his arm and leg to keep them steady, I covered him up to his chin with dry cloth, making him as comfortable as I could.

I rested a moment, then shakily got to my feet. I searched the ship from fore to aft, assessing the damage and confirming the grim truth that both Gest and Goran were nowhere to be found. They had been swept overboard. Anxiously, but with a sense of futility, I scanned the sea around me. Nothing but water. No sign of man or cargo, or even land.

My head pounded from the blow that had knocked me out. I sat there for a long time, staring at the water. I wanted to cry for the two men who had been swept into the sea, but I could not.

I remembered Gest, his courtly, laughing jests, as well as the musty, fishy smell of him. And Goran's slow movements and calm manner. How could they be gone, just like that?

As for Thor... He was lying there, not very far from death himself. It was a miracle that I had survived the monstrous wave. And it was because of Thor that I had. I laid my head on my knees and closed my eyes. I listened to the water sloshing over the sides of the boat. I ran a finger across the smooth silver of the ring on my thumb.

Then I felt a warmth on the back of my head and raised my eyes to see the sun piercing the gray mantle of clouds above. Somehow the sight brought me out of my own private grayness.

I glanced over at Thor. If I was going to survive, I needed him. And I had to survive, because of the thing I had set myself to do. Gazing up at the sun's position in the sky, I guessed that there were several hours before nightfall.

I retrieved my pack from under the deck boards and crossed to Thor. He was still unconscious, his pulse the same. I unwrapped the bandage on his head, which had soaked through with blood, and using a needle and a length of flaxen thread, I stitched up the gash. I had a fair amount of experience with such needlework; early on, Father had put me in charge of stitching up the wounds of the animals on our farm. Using a couple of broken planks and more cloth, I also did the best I could to set his broken leg and arm. Thor came to as I worked over him. An agonized scream burst out of him as I forced his leg bone into place. And another one, less intense, when I set the bone in his arm, pain shuddering through his body. By the time I had finished, he was unconscious again.

I made him as comfortable as I could, laying him on his side and covering him with dry cloth. Then, taking the piece of steering oar from Thor's hand, I went to inspect the tiller, wondering if there was some way I could repair it. It looked bad but not impossible, I thought.

First, though, the sail. It took some time to drag up the portion that hung over the side, but finally I had it all in, stretched out on the deck to dry in the sun. There was a jagged tear across much of the bottom of it. In the process of moving the sail, I found one of the buckets and bailed until well after sunset.

I thought the ship might be headed west, because the sun had set directly in front of us. But east or west . . . in truth it mattered little in which direction we were heading because I had no idea where we *were*.

It grew cold without the sun. I searched but could not find any of the skin-sacks we had slept in on the ship. Exhausted, I crawled under the cloth I had used to cover Thor and lay beside him, thinking to keep us both warm. I must have dozed, for I suddenly came awake, uneasily, with the feeling that I was being watched. Disoriented, I thought for a moment that I was back in the castle and had just awakened beside my visitor.

But it was Thor's blue eyes that were gazing on me. They were unfocused and unreadable, but they were open.

The night was surprisingly bright; the moon was half full and the stars were like a million cold-flamed flickering candles spread across the sky. I could see Thor's face clearly. I sat up.

"Thor?" I said. He did not reply; nor did his gaze waver from my face.

"You were injured," I explained.

He blinked and tried to move his injured arm toward his face. Then he let out a groan and stopped moving. "Gest, Goran..."

I could just barely make out the mumbled words. "They are gone," I said simply.

He closed his eyes then and kept them closed.

"Thor?" I whispered, feeling for his pulse.

His lids twitched.

"Rest now," I said, and I settled back down beside him. I listened intently to his breathing, which was ragged for a while but finally became more regular. Then I, too, slept.

When I awoke again it was dawn. The wind had freshened and the sun shone in a cloudless sky. Thor still slept.

I rose and stretched. If only I could repair the sail enough so that I could use it, maybe I could sail the *knorr* on my own. But even as I thought that, I knew it would be impossible. I hadn't the strength or the skill. I cursed myself for not paying closer attention to the men as they worked the sail. What would I do if Thor did not recover?

Luckily, there was food as well as water. I had found both when I searched the ship. Secure in a spot under the deck boards of the stern had been a crate of hard bread as well as a barrel of smoked and dried fish. I had also been quite excited to find a small box filled with pears from Fransk, which Gest had told me Thor planned to sell to the Njordens for a profit. But most important of all, I found two large casks of freshwater, along with four of ale and several of wine. I should have known that Thor's precious ale would survive—he stored it in the most protected spot on the ship.

I moved toward the center of the ship to see if there was any way I could light a cooking fire. I had found the cauldron and tripod the day before, also lodged under the sail, but there was nothing dry enough to use for kindling. I hurriedly ate a small meal of bread and smoked fish, then went to Thor.

He was awake, staring up at the sky. I filled a cup with water and sat beside him.

"Thor, drink this."

He glanced at me, then turned his gaze upward again. "Leave me be," he muttered.

"Just a little water," I coaxed.

He ignored me.

His manner frightened me. There was a blankness in his face, and it seemed as if he had made a choice to die rather than fight.

I sat still, uncertain of what to do.

"Thor..." I said. "You need water."

He did not respond.

I held the cup to his lips. "Please..."

He reached up with his left hand and, with a jerking motion, swatted the cup. The water spilled out, soaking the front of his clothing. "Leave me be," he repeated.

I felt a stirring of anger. He had wasted a cupful of precious water.

I left him. The sail was almost dry and I set about mending the tear in it. The cloth was thick, and it was difficult working a needle through it. It took most of the day to complete the mending. I checked on Thor frequently, each time offering food or water. But he continued to ignore me. I had seen his look before, in the eyes of a mother cow that had lost too much blood in a difficult birth and in those of a lamb whose neck had been broken in a fall.

I felt grief for the man, but also fear for myself. And I felt occasional surges of careless anger as I sat, thrusting my needle through the heavy cloth of the sail. *Let him die if he chooses. I will manage.*

But then I would look at the broken mast, the endless sea around me, and knew I could not.

I made the final knot and gazed at my handiwork with a sense of futility. I would never be able to raise the cursed thing. With an oath that would have done Thor proud, I stood and crossed to the dying man.

Standing over him I said loudly, "All right, go ahead and die! You called Gest and Goran cowards for lowering the sail, but it is you who is the coward."

His eyes flicked over at me and I thought I saw a spark of something in them.

"I did not think 'twas the way of a Viking to slink into death like a wounded lamb," I went on recklessly.

Then Thor muttered something I could not hear, but it sounded like he was cursing me.

"You may curse me all you like, but I am not the one who has given up," I said.

He raised his head and said, his teeth bared, "I am no coward."

"Then drink this," I challenged, holding the cup of water up to his face.

"To Niflheim with your blasted water," Thor rasped. "Bring me ale."

Without hesitating I quickly went to the casks of ale and drew him a brimming cupful. I held it to his lips, but he brought up his left hand and roughly took the cup from me. While he drank I got some hard bread and smoked fish. The ale was gone when I returned, and he snatched the food from me, crumbling it into pieces that he stuffed in his mouth.

"More ale," he muttered between bites.

Neddy

THE LETTER FROM ROSE arrived just after the fall harvest.

Dear Neddy,

I am writing to tell you that I am safe and well and no longer living at the castle with the white bear. It is a long story and one I hope to tell you at the end of my journey. But I made a wrong choice, one that hurt someone very badly, so I must now undertake a journey to a far distant land—one that lies east of the sun and west of the moon.

Because you are cleverer than me, you will have already figured out that there is no such land. Nevertheless, I go there. It seems right somehow that I should journey to a place that does not exist; it is where Mother always feared I would end up.

And please tell Mother the candle worked all too well. But tell her, too, that the choice to use it was mine and I do not blame her.

Just as the blame is mine, the journey, too, is mine, and I must undertake it alone. So do not try to come to me. I need to set right the wrong I have done, and when I have I will return home. Trust me, Neddy, and try not to worry.

Tell Father I love him. And tell Mother and Sonja and Willem and Sara that I miss them and hope that we will all be reunited before too long.

My love to you, Neddy.

Your sister, Rose

Rose

DURING THE NEXT FEW days the weather stayed fair. Thor continued to lie where he was while I brought him food and ale—mostly ale. He finally had me roll the cask over and set it beside him so that he could refill his own cup.

I had my doubts that ale, especially in the amounts he was consuming, was a particularly healing drink. But at least he had decided to live, and he had the constitution of an ox. Each day he gained in strength. The gray pallor was gone and the wound on his forehead was healing.

Thor was soon sitting up and, on the second day, even stood for a few minutes, leaning on a makeshift crutch I had fashioned from a splintered deck board.

As he lowered himself back into a sitting position, I asked, "Do you think it possible that Gest and Goran could have survived?"

Thor snorted, then took a long draught of ale.

"But they might have gotten hold of something to float on. They were good swimmers, and perhaps there was land..." I gazed out over the endless expanse of water. "Well, isn't it possible?"

"Anything's possible," Thor said. After refilling his cup he leaned back, eyes closed.

"I had a son once," I heard him say.

"You did?" I said stupidly. I had never pictured Thor as having any kind of life outside the ship, especially not a family.

"Egil was his name. Died at the hands of a band of thieves and murderers. Along with his mother. My wife." His voice had softened slightly as he said *wife*.

When he opened his eyes, they were laced with bitterness. "It is *possible* they would have lived if I had been there to protect them. But they died. Like Gest and Goran. And like I would have if you'd left me alone."

"Well, I couldn't leave you alone. And you saved my life, sticking me under the deck boards the way you did. 'Twas only common courtesy to return the favor."

Thor suddenly threw his head back and laughed. It was a full-throated reckless sound, and I liked the sound of it, even though I knew he was drunk.

"May I commend you on your manners?" he said.

I laughed, too, and there was some sort of softening between us. After that, if we were not exactly friends, at least Thor did not act as though I were not there.

Later that day I asked Thor if he had any idea where we were.

He finished the ale at the bottom of his cup, then looked up at me with something like a smile on his face. I thought he might even laugh again. *"Hafvilla,"* he said.

"Where?"

"Hafvilla. 'Tis a word in the old language," he explained. "The Vikings used it when they found they were hopelessly lost."

"I think we have been heading mostly west, since the storm," I said, attempting to be helpful.

With a shrug he refilled his cup.

"Is there any way we can rig up a new mast?" I asked, trying a different tack. "I mended the sail."

"Well, aren't you the clever seamstress?" he responded unpleasantly.

"Thor..."

He shrugged again, gazing critically around the *knorr.* "We might fix something up—not as tall, of course, but enough to catch a little wind."

"If you tell me what to do...I am stronger than I look."

"Are you indeed?" Thor replied with a trace of skepticism, looking me up and down.

"And I want to learn, all that you know—about sailing the *knorr,* how to navigate, everything..." I said in a rush.

He was silent for a time, then he turned and stared at me, as though considering me in a new light. "You don't fancy floating around on the sea forever with a drunken old sot, eh? Well, maybe I will teach you. I'm not much good as a captain, am I?" he said, gesturing at his bound-up leg and arm. "And my ale supply will run out sooner or later."

"Sooner, I should think," I retorted.

"You'll need to pay close attention. I'll not say things twice. And I am not a patient man."

That was an understatement. Thor was ill mannered and ill tempered, and how much of either depended on where he was in his drinking. If he'd had too little, he was impossible; if too much, he was careless *and* impossible.

Still, he managed to cram a great deal of information into a short span of time. His knowledge of the ship and of the sea was impressive, and it was obvious how much he loved it all, which made up for his gruffness. He instructed me as I repaired the steering oar and then rigged up a short mast from deck boards. He taught me about the rigging, and even explained to me the smallest details of how the *knorr* had been built.

Finally he launched into the subject of navigation.

"There are as many ways to find your way as there are sailors. Smell the different flavors of a stretch of coast, listen for the curve of the shore, taste the air," he said to me.

He explained how to read the stars, the sun and moon, the tides, the weather, fish and bird life, and even water temperature, color, and texture. And then with great solemnity, he showed me how to use his highly prized *leidarstein*.

Much of what he taught me had a practical simplicity

to it, but taken altogether it was overwhelming, and there were times that I despaired of remembering it all.

By the end of the first two days of Thor's instruction, my hands were raw from handling the rigging, my back was sore, and my head ached from all I'd been trying to absorb. I recalled my previous ocean crossing—the simple, dreamlike trip through the sea, wrapped in a sealskin and carried like a baby in the mouth of a white bear. And I realized how much more complicated life is without the benefit of magic. Rubbing linseed oil into my blistered hands, I thought wistfully of how magic lets you skip over the steps of things. That is what makes it so appealing.

But, I thought, the steps of things are where life is truly found, in doing the day-to-day tasks. Caught up in the world of enchantment as I had been at the castle, it had been the routine things I had missed most, which was why I had set up that laundry room and insisted on doing my own washing. But I had missed so much. Sitting at the table back home and peeling potatoes with my mother and sisters in a companionable silence. Feeding the chickens, their urgent feathery bodies crowding my legs, and looking up to see Neddy coming back from the fields. Going on one of my long exploring walks, having a blister come up on my heel but at the same time stumbling upon a fox den and catching a brief glimpse of a mother fox nursing a brand-new litter of kits. And though I might have wished away the blister, slowing down to favor the pain in my heel was part of how I came to see the kits.

And I knew, without ever having been told, that the white bear would have gladly traded the comfortable magic life in the castle in exchange for a whole horde of blisters on his feet.

Finished with the linseed oil, I took up some rigging that needed repair, and I had a memory, clear as day, of the face of the stranger who had been the white bear— and of the hopelessness in his eyes. I could not help the hot tears that smeared my vision.

"Work too much for you, eh?" I heard Thor say.

I quickly blinked away the tears and looked over at him, a cup of ale in his hand and a sneering look on his face. "Of course not," I retorted.

"A little too much sun in the eyes then?" he asked sarcastically.

"I was remembering something," I replied stiffly, and focused on the length of rope in my hand. "Someone."

There was a silence. Then, "Forgive me. 'Twas ill spoken," came the unexpected words from Thor.

I looked at him, amazed.

"Why do you go to Suroy?" he suddenly asked. It was the first time he had ever asked me a question about myself.

I looked at him and for some reason I told him the truth. I think it was because of his eyes. They reminded me, for just a moment, of Neddy's.

I spoke for a long, long time, telling the whole story. I expected at any moment he would interrupt me with a shout of laughter or disbelief. But he did not.

When I came to the end, I took a deep breath, my fingers unknowingly twisting the ring on my thumb.

Thor was silent. Then he said, "'Tis a strange tale."

There was a pause. "And so you go north, to make things right with this white bear. Or the man that was the white bear."

I nodded.

"My grandfather said once that a white wolf spoke to him. But then, he was overfond of mead." Thor grinned. "An appetite that runs in the family." I did not return his smile, and his faded, too.

"I have traveled north," Thor said, a far look in his eyes. "Well beyond Njord. Saw a white land way off in the distance, but I had to turn back because of the ice. If something remains of magic in the world, I believe it would lie in the far north, in the places where people cannot go."

We fell silent.

Thor broke the silence at last, and it was the first time he called me by name. "Well, Rose," he said, "once we get that sail raised, the *knorr* shall take you north. After all, you did save my life. And 'tis only common courtesy to take you where I said I would."

We both laughed then.

Neddy

IN HER LETTER ROSE had sounded different. Older, I guess, her tone more serious. And it wasn't the words of the letter but the new voice that made me feel sad, as though I'd lost the old Rose forever.

After Mother confessed her folly that day, she and Father had come back together. Widow Hautzig had been banished from the household, and Father set out on no more journeys.

Once we received Rose's letter, Father and I spent many evenings talking about what to do. Despite the few clues Rose had let fall during our conversations while she was at home, we were still no closer to knowing where the castle was, except that it lay across a body of water. Finally we decided that for the time being we would do nothing; we would trust Rose and rely on her to find her way back home to us.

Although Mother agreed with that, she believed she must do more than just sit and wait. It was she who made the effort to find out all she could about the disappearing merchant, the one who had sold her the candle and flint. There wasn't very much to learn, though there were rumors aplenty. There was one story going around that he had been spotted late one night by the Romsdal Fjord and, when he turned around, was seen to have no back at all, only a big hollow space where his back should have been.

The only facts that could be pinned down were that the merchant said he came from Finnland and that he had an aversion to very warm weather, although even on the hottest days he wore long sleeves and long pants, as well as gloves made of soft leather. He made no friends and kept very much to himself. The other interesting facts that Mother told us were that the skin on his face was odd, scarred and ridged, and that he had an unusual voice, rough and deep, as though he had a perpetual sore throat or cough.

One happy event that occurred at about the same time was that my sister Sara and Harald Soren became engaged to be married.

Sara told me that at first it was her gratitude to Soren that made her like him so well. But as her health improved and they spent more time together, the gratitude ripened into love, and though he was a good deal older, it became clear they cared very much for each other.

Sara didn't want to set a date for the marriage until Rose returned—which we all understood—but we also felt that Rose would want her to go ahead with her life.

"She'd hate to think that you are delaying your happiness on her account," I said to Sara.

Sara nodded, then replied, "What of you, Neddy? Harald has said that you only have to say the word and he will get you a position with one of the leading scholars in Bergen, or even Trondheim, which is not so very far away. What you have said about me is just as true for you."

Sara was right. I had put off deciding to go, because of Rose. What if she came to visit and I was not at the farm? But receiving her letter had changed things. I gave serious thought to taking Soren up on his offer.

The matter was settled when Soren convinced Father to move the mapmaking business to Trondheim. Though not as large as Bergen or Oslo, Trondheim would afford a larger market for the maps Father made as well as more people he could hire to do the work. In addition, Father and Soren had discussed building a printing press in Trondheim. Printing presses had come only very recently to Oslo and Bergen, and were thriving. Soren felt the time was ripe for the business.

I still had my doubts. A part of me felt that if we moved on, it was as if we were accepting that Rose was gone forever. But a bigger part of me knew that she was not. Rose was alive somewhere and traveling the path she must, the way she always had.

Rose

A WEEK AND A HALF after telling Thor of the white bear, I spotted a seabird. At first I did not take in its significance. I was at the steering oar and, despite the chill in the air, feeling drowsy. It had gotten bitter cold in the past few days, and I was wearing all the clothing I owned. Thor had been sleeping for a long time, the result of his latest round of drinking. It was just after dawn and I watched the bird soar, its whiteness vivid against the blue sky. It dipped low, almost to the surface of the water, then rose again. The white bird had come from the west and, wheeling around, eventually headed back in that direction.

Then I remembered: A bird means land! How many times had Thor made that point? Even as recently as the day before, he had told me a story about a Viking explorer who had been lost at sea for weeks, near starvation, and the sight of a gull had caused him to convert to Christianity on the spot.

I let out a shout. "Thor!"

There was no response, so I left the steering oar and went to shake him awake.

"A bird, Thor," I said. "I saw a seabird."

He came awake and, though groggy, raised himself to a sitting position.

"A bird, eh? Where?"

I explained that it had flown away in a westerly direction.

"Is it possible?" he muttered to himself. "Could it be? ..." A strange look of pain passed over his face.

Grabbing his crutch he hobbled over to the steering oar, ordering me to adjust the rigging while he changed course. He set the nose of the *knorr* due west, then ordered me to bring him a new cask of ale. I hesitated. "Get it for me now, you lunkheaded laggard, or I'll throw you overboard!" he roared with such force that I decided it was best to do as he said.

I scanned the western horizon eagerly, but by midmorning there was still no sign of land. Sunset would come in only a few hours. The sun was then setting in the early afternoon, which meant either that we had traveled quite far north or that it was almost winter solstice—or both.

We sailed through the long, frosty night. I slept fitfully, keeping watch over Thor, who was helping himself to frequent draughts of ale.

At dawn I offered to take over the steering oar, but Thor refused, though he reeked of drink and his movements were clumsy. I was the first to spy what looked to be a thin white finger of land. I pointed it out to Thor. He grunted and poured more ale.

The wind had weakened and shifted to the south, so it took a long time to tack toward land. To make matters worse, an icy sleet had begun to fall.

By the time I could make out features of the land, Thor was roaring drunk. He was zigzagging sloppily through the water and finally stopped steering altogether, slumping sideways on the bench, singing under his breath a song about "journeying on to Vinland." I suddenly saw that we were bearing down on a snow-covered headland, and I hastily squeezed in next to Thor and took the steering oar in hand.

I managed to avoid the boulders sticking up out of the water, but with a sinking feeling I saw that there were many of them. It did not look like a promising spot for me to try to land the *knorr*, inexperienced as I was. Because the wind was coming from the south, I steered a northerly course, hoping to find a better landing place.

With no one to secure the rigging, the sail flapped. I silently cursed Thor. Why had he chosen this of all times to drink himself into a stupor? And just what was that land? I bound the steering oar in place with a strap of leather and went to find my pack, pulling out the map that Sofi had given me.

I scrutinized it. Based on the shortening days, Thor had said he believed we were at least as far north as Suroy, perhaps farther, but he had no idea how far west we had been driven by the storm. Then the land could be Iseland, or . . . it could even be the desolate land called Gronland.

And then I remembered.

Not long before I'd spotted the white bird, and during one of Thor's rare sober spells, he had told me about the death of his wife and son. Thor had been working for a prosperous merchant seaman but had hopes of one day owning his own ship. Then he was offered a place on a vessel that was going to Gronland, a place the Vikings had first settled but long ago abandoned. There was said to be good whale hunting off the coast of Gronland. Because the profits promised were large, and because of his great admiration for his Viking forebears, Thor leaped at the opportunity.

The voyage had not been a success, due to bad weather and an outbreak of sickness. In fact, the ship did not even reach Gronland before it had to turn back. Thor returned home to find that in his absence his wife and son had been killed by thieves. The next few years he was lost in barrels of ale, followed by several more years spent in gaol for killing a man he had mistakenly thought to be one of the killers.

After he got out of gaol, Thor worked a series of odd jobs, eventually scraping together enough money to buy himself a very old, decrepit Viking *knorr*, which he rebuilt. He set himself up in business as a merchant seaman and, for the past dozen years, had been able to make a living.

As I remembered all of this, I realized that the prospect of our coming to Gronland had brought back memories of Thor's failed voyage—and of all he had lost.

I felt pity for him then, but I was angry as well. I would never be able to land the *knorr* on my own; certainly not along such a rocky coast. My only hope lay in finding some kind of natural harbor.

The sun had set by then and I managed to steer the ship through the night. The moon shone inconstantly, moving in and out of cloud cover, and I could only occasionally make out a dim outline of the land we glided past. Finally I decided to drop anchor, thinking to wait until morning to try to find a place to land. Shivering, I covered the snoring Thor, noting that he had almost completely emptied an entire barrel. I burrowed under my own layers of cloth and quickly fell into a deep sleep.

I awoke to find snow falling, and a good two inches of it already accumulated on the cloths covering me. There was a trace of light from the predawn sun.

Dusting the snow off, I got up and stretched. Thor was still passed out, his mouth hanging open and his breathing loud. I gazed toward land and in the gray light could just make out what looked to be a slim outcropping a little to the north. I wondered if there might be a harbor of sorts within it.

After attempting in vain to awaken Thor, I raised the sail and steered the *knorr* toward land. As I went closer I saw that the arm of land did provide protection for a cove of sorts. Suddenly all I wanted was the feel of land under my feet, and I recklessly pointed the bow toward shore. The light was so dim that I could barely tell where the sea ended and the shore began, but I didn't care.

The water was fairly calm in this natural harbor, and the *knorr* glided through the gray waves, snow still lightly falling. My eyes straining, I thought I saw a cluster of shapes on the beach ahead that from such a distance looked like standing stones.

All was silent; even the slapping of water against the hull seemed muffled by the falling snow. Somehow I managed to avoid the rocks. There was a grinding sound as the prow of the *knorr* slid up onto the snowy beach and came to a stop.

I sat for a moment, unnerved by the lack of motion. Thor let out a grunt and shifted on the bench, still passed out. I stood and made my way forward to the prow. The sun had not yet risen and the light was the same dim gray. Despite my many layers of clothing, I was shivering again. I lowered a plank from the side of the *knorr*. Using it as a bridge I descended to the beach.

I stood by the hull for a moment, swaying dizzily after such a long time at sea. But then I heard a noise coming from the beach. I turned and saw the strange shapes I had thought to be stones moving across the beach toward me, their feet making quiet crunching sounds in the snow. The one closest to me raised a hand and all the others stopped, but the small figure with the raised hand kept moving toward me. I stayed very still, my heart beating fast.

It was a woman with dark, creased skin and narrow bright-black eyes. She was dressed from head to toe in various animal skins. She wore a hood with silver-gray fur around her face. The fur obscured her features, save for those penetrating black eyes.

She stepped forward until our noses were almost touching, and stared directly into my eyes. I stared back, which turned out to be the right thing to do, for I found out later that she was the local shaman and was then reading my soul with her eyes. Had I looked down or away from her, the shaman would have deemed that I had things to hide—and I most likely would have been killed.

As it was, the shaman apparently found my soul to be satisfactory, or at least harmless, for she smiled at me and then spoke. I didn't understand her, though the language was vaguely familiar to me, with a faint echo of Njorden.

I said, "I am from Njord."

"Ah, Njord." She nodded, then gestured at the *knorr*, taking several steps toward it.

Assuming that meant she wished to board the ship, I led her to the makeshift gangplank. She followed me aboard and slowly made her way from fore to aft, her eyes sweeping the battered *knorr*. She came to a stop in front of Thor, who was still sprawled in a drunken stupor. Leaning over his prostrate body, she reached out and held up the tarnished hammer necklace he wore, inspecting it closely. Then she took her thumb and raised his eyelid, revealing the bloodshot white of one eye.

Looking at me she said something that sounded like the Njorden word for *illness*. I shook my head and pantomimed drinking a mug of ale.

A slow smile creased her face and she nodded in understanding. Then she crossed to the prow and called out to the figures standing on the shore.

They responded by gathering around the *knorr* and pulling the vessel far up onto the beach. I clung to the mast to keep my footing.

The woman gestured for me to follow her as she disembarked. "I am Malmo," she said as she stood facing me on the beach.

"My name is Rose," I replied, wondering if we should shake hands. But she did not offer her hand.

Instead she said, "You will come with Malmo." She then set out across the beach, away from the *knorr*.

"But my friend..."

"We bring him, too," Malmo said.

And I followed her. For some reason I trusted Malmo. Perhaps I had inadvertently looked into her soul as she was inspecting mine; I sensed that she meant me no harm.

She led me away from the water until we came to a cluster of stone buildings. Malmo directed me to one of the larger buildings and opened the flap of animal skin that served as a door, gesturing for me to enter.

"Malmo home," the shaman said by way of explanation. The building was a small structure made of stone, clay, and dried grass. It had two rooms, both small; one was for cooking and eating, the other for sleeping.

Malmo gestured for me to sit, handing me a fur-skin for warmth. Then she went outside again, leaving me alone briefly. She soon reappeared with several of her people, who were carrying Thor. He was still unconscious and they laid him on a raised sleeping platform, then covered him with fur-skins.

Two women entered the home, bearing bowls of stew and steaming cups of mead. Malmo smiled at me, saying, "Eat, rest." And once again she departed.

Hungrily I ate, then bundled myself into the furs. I sat there, Thor snoring softly nearby, and thought about all that had happened since I'd left the castle. And for the first time I found I could think about the white bear with some kind of hope. I was getting close to where he was. Warmed by those thoughts, and by the stew and hot mead in my belly, I drifted into sleep.

BOOK FOUR

North

*She traveled on the back of the North Wind
to the very end of the world.*

Rose

WE HAD COME TO the village of Neyak on the northeast-
ern coast of Gronland. Malmo showed it to me on the
map. She and her people were Inuit and had lived on that
land since Sedna, the Mother of Sea Beasts, came to guard
the oceans. Malmo knew the Njorden language because
whale hunters from Njord had come to their land before.
She had nothing good to say about them, though. Her
opinion of the Vikings was even lower. They had been
the first to come in their longboats—with their hammers
of the thunder god Thor around their necks—bringing
devastation and fear to the Inuit, whom the Vikings called
Skraelings, or "the ugly ones." It had taken the Inuit
years to get rid of the marauding invaders, and there remained a distrust that had been passed down through the
generations. Still, it was clear that my particular "Viking,"
with his broken limbs and giant hangover, did not exactly
inspire fear.

Thor remained in his ale-induced sleep while Malmo and I talked. She knew enough Njorden that we were able to understand each other fairly well. I told her of the deadly storm we had encountered and of the loss of Gest and Goran. She asked where I was bound.

"North," I said. "Can you tell me about the lands that lie north of here?"

Malmo nodded gravely. "There is a land north of Gronland that forms the ice sky of the earth. There are tales from Inuit who lived long ago about an ice bridge that connects Gronland to the ice sky, but there is no one living now who has found the ice bridge—or at least who has returned to tell the tale."

"I will find it," I said.

"You? Find the ice bridge?" She chuckled, eyeing my clothing.

Pulling my cloak tighter around me, for I was cold even inside Malmo's home, I replied with a rueful look, "I know. But I am set on traveling north. I will do whatever I must."

"Why?" Malmo asked.

And I told her the entire story, just as I had told it to Thor—and to Sofi and Estelle before him.

She listened closely, her bright eyes intent on my face.

"*Seku nanoa,*" she said, with a note of reverence in her voice. She took a stick from the fire and, using only a few strokes, deftly drew the exact likeness of a white bear.

Then she looked at Thor in his near comatose state. "What will you do with the Viking?"

I was silent. I was ashamed to realize I hadn't thought about Thor at all, not when it came to my journey north. I gazed sideways at him, his beard and hair matted and wild, an arm and leg still wrapped in cloth that was stained with seawater, blood, and ale. And his ship was in little better shape than he.

The shaman looked from one to the other of us, then she leaned forward, gazing into my eyes.

"You journey on," she said, "and the old Viking will stay. There is healing here, if he will be healed. If not, he will find his own journey."

"Thank you," I replied.

Thor awoke soon after, groggy and ill tempered. Malmo arranged for food to be brought to him, ignoring his request for ale. Then she gestured to me, saying, "You eat later. Now, you need much."

Thereupon we embarked upon a most extraordinary "shopping" expedition. In the first place we entered, Malmo held a lengthy conversation with the man who lived there, gesturing at me several times, saying *"seku nanoa"* ("white bear"). The visit wound up with the man bustling around his home, collecting a variety of things that he then gave to me. Malmo said the name of each thing in Inuit, but I had no idea what most of them were.

We then went to another Gronlander home, where I was given even more gear. Then another and another, until I was laden down with such a dizzying array of objects that Malmo had to help me carry them.

When we finally returned to Malmo's house, we found Thor asleep again. I wondered if he had gotten his hands on more ale, but Malmo said no, he had been given a healing drink that brings sleep.

She set about explaining to me each item I had been given.

There was an *ulu*, the most important of the various knifelike objects I had received. It consisted of a sharp slate blade embedded in a bone handle. Then there was a snow knife made of narwhal ivory, which was used for making snowhouses; and a snow beater, a larger blunt-edged blade, also of ivory, which a person used outdoors to knock snow off clothing.

Among the other things were: a long, thin tube of ivory used for drinking meltwater off the surface of ice; a needlelike probe for locating the breathing holes of seals; a pair of ivory snow goggles, to protect the eyes from the brutal glare of sun on ice and snow; a bola, a contraption made of ivory balls attached to a length of sinew that was thrown up into the air to snare birds; several small, thick pins made of bone, to plug the wounds of seals so their blood wouldn't leak out (apparently Inuit cooking used seal blood, a delicacy I was not all that eager to try); something called a *kitchoa*, or ice scratcher, made of seal claws and used by hunters to simulate the sound of seals moving across the ice, so that while at their breathing holes they would not be frightened away by approaching hunters; and a pair of short skis made of whalebone, with a strip of reindeer fur on the underside, hairs pointing backward. (Apparently the backward-facing hairs allowed for greater speed for a skier going downhill while acting as a brake against slipping backward when going uphill.)

And then there was clothing. For my outer layer I was supplied with a knee-length parka of reindeer hide, the fur turned outward. Beneath that I wore another layer of reindeer hide—trousers and an undercoat—the fur turned inward. My long underwear was made of feathered duck skins, the feathers turned inward. (That would take some getting used to, I thought.) Then there was a pair of two-layered boots; the outer layer lined with fur, the inner with duck feathers, again turned in. There was also a pair of mittens made of the hide of a white bear. Of course, putting my fingers into them reminded me of my white bear, although when I put my nose to them, they did not have the same scent at all.

I looked at the large pile of items in some dismay. How would I carry them all on my journey north? I asked Malmo. In reply she handed me a large knapsack made of reindeer hide. She said that what I wasn't wearing on my body would fit into the pack, including my tattered pack from home. I was skeptical, but she turned out to be right.

I was also concerned about paying Malmo and her people for all they had given me. I offered Malmo my moon dress, but although she gazed at it with polite admiration, she had no interest in owning it. Certainly there was no use for a ball gown in the village of Neyak.

Malmo was more interested when I told her about the crate of pears from Fransk. Thor and I had eaten many, but plenty still remained.

In the morning when I awoke, I discovered that neither Thor nor Malmo was in the house. I ate a bowl of porridge that had been left on the hearth and then put on some of my new clothing. (I wasn't yet ready to try the feather underwear.) When I stepped outside into the chill air, I felt snug and warm. I made my way to shore.

I ascended the makeshift gangplank of the *knorr*, then stopped abruptly when I saw Thor. He was seated in his old place by the steering oar, with a barrel of ale beside him.

"Is that your breakfast?" I asked somewhat severely.

"Drink of the gods," Thor said with a grin, and took a long gulp. He gazed at my new garb with amusement. "Gone native, I see."

"Thor, I mean to journey north," I said, going to sit beside him. He took another long drink. Then he raised his mug.

"'North, north, north, she sailed to Asgard and on to the north, north, north,'" he sang lustily.

"The people here are good," I went on, ignoring his song. "I am sure they will help you repair your boat. And you might find some who wish to journey to a new land. Or you could stay here with them. I believe they will make you welcome."

"'Welcome, ho, to the halls of Valhalla, where the ale flows and the boar's head roasts.'"

"Thor," I said with some urgency, standing and moving in front of him so he could not avoid my eyes, "the ale will be gone soon. You cannot bury yourself in it always. You must go on. Find a new life, or a new journey. It can be done."

His blurred eyes focused for a moment, then slid away again. "'North, north, north...to Asgard,'" he sang.

I got to my feet. "If I am able, I will come back here when I am done with my own journey. To see what you chose."

"Chose, Rose," Thor said in a singsong voice. "Rose chose to journey north, north, north..."

I moved to the hold, where the crate of pears was stored. "I am giving these to Malmo and her people. To repay their kindness."

"What, no more golden gowns?" Thor said with a trace of his old sneer. Then he refilled his mug.

"Good-bye, Thor," I said.

Neddy

THE MOVE TO TRONDHEIM went smoothly. Only Willem stayed behind. Neighbor Torsk had agreed to buy half the farm, and so he and Willem would work the land together.

In Trondheim, Mother and my sisters devoted their time to outfitting and decorating the new house, a handsome dwelling near the center of town. It had all the latest conveniences and Mother was delighted. Father and Soren spent every waking moment on the new printing press, which they fussed over like a pair of doting parents. As for myself, I had become assistant to a Master Eckstrom, the esteemed author of many well-regarded books of scholarship. The king himself, in Danemark, had commissioned Master Eckstrom to write an exhaustive history of the combined kingdoms of Njord and Danemark, and I was one of several assistants hired to help in that massive endeavor. Master Eckstrom was a

kindly if very busy man, and he was not often in Trondheim, his duties to the king requiring him to be in Danemark much of the time.

I did my work in what used to be a monastery, which
Master Eckstrom had converted to a private library for
the use of scholars to pursue religious and historical research. Presiding over the library was a cheerful soul by
the name of Havamal, who had previously been a monk.
He was the caretaker of Master Eckstrom's valuable collection of books. Havamal was extraordinarily helpful.
He knew the location of every volume in his library, and
sometimes even the page number of the bit of information I sought. He also became a friend. I felt very fortunate in my new life.

Soren was too busy with his printing press to pay
much heed to wedding plans, but Sara, with the enthusi-
astic help of Sonja and Mother, was beginning to make
preparations for a spring ceremony. We all fervently
hoped Rose would return to us by then. And Willem had
made a solemn promise that if Rose should indeed come
home to the farm, he would send word without delay.

Not a day went by that I did not return to our fine
new home in town hoping for such a message. And each
day I was disappointed.

Rose

MALMO APPEARED ON the morning I was to depart. I had packed my gear and was eating a bowl of thick porridge. She entered the house and came directly to me.

"If you will have me as guide, I will go with you north," she said without preamble.

I was speechless for a moment, not sure I had understood her. "You mean you would go with me, travel north with me, to find the ice bridge?"

Malmo nodded. "As shaman I have always wished to see the ice bridge. But I did not care to leave my people."

"And now?"

"Now there is an ice bear in peril, and my animal is *seku nanoa*, white bear."

"What do you mean 'my animal'?" I asked.

"Each shaman has her own animal. It is *tornaq*, the source of power." She paused. "Before you came here, I dreamed of bear. When you told me of your journey, I believed it was *ooblako,* a portent. In my dream last night I traveled to the ice field." She gestured in a northward direction. "And there I saw *seku nanoa* again. He spoke to my soul, and so I go with you.

"I cannot be long gone from my people," she went on. "Should Sedna grant us the way to the ice bridge, I will leave you there."

Dismissing Sofi's map as inaccurate (at least when it came to Gronland), Malmo brought out a long, thin carved piece of wood that showed the coastline of the northern half of Gronland. She followed the curve of the intricate carving of inlets and headlands with her finger, showing how we would travel by water along the coastline up to the Tatke Fjord. We would then paddle inland, north along the fjord a short distance. When the fjord ended we would travel northward by foot and ski.

Grateful, I thanked Malmo. I felt lucky that she would journey with me, not only for her knowledge and experience of the land but also for her companionship.

The boat we would use for the sea portion of our journey was called a *kyak,* a small two-person craft propelled by paddle. Our gear would be stowed under a stiff waterproof cover with two openings for Malmo and me.

Malmo and I finished loading the *kyak* at midday. I was just settling myself into it when she grabbed my arm and pointed to something behind me.

I turned to see Thor heading toward us from the direction of the village. He was hobbling, still leaning on his crutch. I stepped out of the boat and went to meet him. He looked slightly better than the last time I had seen him, though the stench coming from him brought tears to my eyes. I saw at once that he was sober.

"Came to say a proper good-bye," he said roughly. "I won't have it said old Thor has forgotten his manners."

I smiled.

"I wanted to give you this, for your journey," and he thrust at me the leather pouch containing his prized *leidarstein.*

"Oh no, I—" I protested.

"Take it," he said almost threateningly. "It's not much good in this godforsaken place where the water freezes before you can blink, but have it anyway. I've been thinking I might try one of these newfangled compasses. That is, if the old *knorr* is ever fit for sailing again."

"She will be. You'll see to her," I said.

He nodded absently. Then leaning toward me, he took my hand. "I hope you find the white bear. And set things right with him."

"Thank you, Thor."

"Well, it's back to the *knorr* for me. Have just a little bit left at the bottom of that cask," he said with a grin.

"And what will you do when it's empty?"

"Ah, I hear they have a concoction here, fermented reindeer milk or summat. Might give it a try. Or might not." He winked at me.

I stretched up on my tiptoes and gave Thor a kiss on his matted beard. "Good-bye."

Right before we were to depart, I slipped the small Queen Maraboo game piece into the pocket of my parka. I figured I was going to need all of Queen Maraboo's courage for the journey ahead, and I wanted her close at hand.

Malmo and I set off in the *kyak*. She set me in front and patiently taught me how to paddle. I realized, as we made our way against the waves out of the harbor and into the deep water, that this was the third vessel in which I had traveled the sea since leaving home—sealskin (carried in a white bear's mouth), *knorr,* and now *kyak.* I found the *kyak* the most frightening. I was so close to the frigid water, with only the stiffened hide of a reindeer between me and it, and the paddling was awkward and tiring. But gradually I grew used to the sensation and the rhythm of the paddling, and I came to love traveling by *kyak.* I felt part of the sea, moving through the water, using its power and motion to propel our craft.

We traveled north, along the coastline, and the farther north we went, the more ice there was in the water, sometimes big chunks of it. It took all our concentration to maneuver around the ice; one stretch was particularly deadly, and we had to paddle our way through it, twisting and swerving until I thought my arms would fall off from the exertion. Not long after, we encountered a large iceberg that looked like a ghostly white castle as we glided past, its top a battlement of jagged spires. Malmo told me that in the far north the sea was impassable for ships because of the ice.

For nine days we paddled north. Malmo knew the places to land for rest and food. If there was no shelter to be found, such as an ice cave, we used a small tent of animal skin that Malmo had brought along.

On the tenth day we came to Tatke Fjord. The massive ice-scabbed cliffs were a breath-stopping sight, immense and overwhelming. They made the Romsdal Fjord near my home, which I had found awe inspiring as a child, look like a creek with knee-high riverbanks.

That was where we would leave the sea, turning the nose of the *kyak* into Tatke Fjord. As we followed the curve of the river, which was also choked with ice, I felt the weight of the snow-white spires towering above on either side of us. Without speaking we paddled the *kyak* through the water. I have never known a silence as complete as it was in that fjord.

After almost a day and a half of travel, ice made it impossible to go any farther into Tatke Fjord. We pulled the *kyak* up onto land and took out all our gear. Anchoring the small boat in the snow, Malmo said, "I will come back for it on my return journey."

And so we set off on foot, carrying our gear in packs on our backs, the skis lashed to them. At first I felt unbalanced and top heavy, as if the smallest puff of wind would knock me over. But as I walked I grew used to the load and gradually felt steadier.

Slowly we ascended to the top of an ice cliff, following a trail that hugged the side. It was a hard climb, the pack heavier than a dead sheep on my back, and my breath came out in great puffs of silver smoke as I trudged upward. In all that whiteness I never would have seen a path, but Malmo followed it unerringly. When we reached the top, we donned our skis.

The farther north we went, the colder it got. Before then I had thought I knew about cold. But the winters in Njord were springlike compared to the bitter, lancing cold of that frozen land. It was like a predatory, hovering beast, bent on sucking every bit of heat and life out of a body.

I am certain that had I not had Malmo as guide and companion, I would have died.

"It is a good thing you are shaped the way you are, you know," Malmo said. "Good for the cold."

According to Malmo my short, sturdy body was Inuit-like, well designed for enduring very cold temperatures, its compactness conserving heat. Even my dark eyes, though not as dark as an Inuit's, gave more protection from the glare on the snow than lighter eyes. It seemed ironic to me that if I had had the willowy form and sky blue eyes of my sisters, features I had always deeply envied, I may well have been doomed in the unforgiving land.

The surface stayed relatively smooth and we made good progress on skis. We spoke little, concentrating all our energies on moving forward. The ivory goggles I wore were continually iced up, but I grew used to that, as well as to looking out at the world through the row of miniature icicles that had formed on my eyelashes. I tried rubbing them away but found that in doing so I had broken off some lashes. Having once been told that my eyelashes were one of my best features, I stopped trying to get rid of the icicles, though I laughed at myself for such vanity. I would be lucky to survive at all, much less with my eyelashes intact.

One morning when we emerged from our tent, we found the land covered in a dense white mist. As we set out, Malmo warned me that things were not always as they appeared in a snow fog.

It was a completely white world, with no edges or contrast by which to measure things. At one point I saw a huge iceberg looming toward us and I cried out to Malmo, who looked as if she was about to ski right into it. It turned out to be a small hillock of snow that Malmo guessed to be several leagues ahead.

That night, as we huddled in our tent, Malmo told me stories of hunters in a snow fog stalking what they took to be a huge animal and finding it to be merely a small white hare. "And once," she said, "there was a hunter, one of my people, who came upon a small white bear cub. He reached out his hand to touch its fur and

348

discovered that it was a full-grown white bear, ready to attack."

I gaped at her, unbelieving.

"It is true," she responded serenely.

The snow fog stayed with us for several days. And then, on its heels, came the blizzard.

Troll Queen

THE PREPARATIONS FOR the wedding banquet have been going well, but I grow impatient. I had not realized how elaborate and complicated the many traditions of a Huldre royal wedding are. I am considering doing away with all of it and performing a simple ceremony of my own creation. That way Myk and I can be joined together when I wish. Tomorrow perhaps.

It is vexing that there are other matters to be taken into account. For example, if I move up the ceremony, then the southern trolls will not arrive in time. The wedding is to symbolize a historic meeting of our two lands, and to change the plan now would mean a loss of prestige—and could possibly cause a diplomatic rupture between us.

Furthermore, my people would wonder why I am not following Huldre tradition. Not that that matters.

Fah. I shall do as I please.

Rose

MALMO HAD READ THE blizzard's approach in the clouds and wind, and with a calm sort of urgency that was typical of her, she began to direct me on the making of a snowhouse. Using the snow knife I had gotten back in Neyak, I followed Malmo's lead in fashioning blocks of snow that we then piled on top of one another in a set pattern. Malmo's snow blocks were perfectly shaped into solid rectangles, while mine looked like messy blobs, but by the time we heaved the last block into place, mine were at least recognizable as a squarish shape. Malmo made about four blocks to every one I came up with, though with experience I got a little faster.

By the time the storm hit full force, we had fashioned a sturdy, fairly large snowhouse. We were just putting on the finishing touches when I saw the wall of blowing snow coming at us. Before I could move, it knocked me to my knees, and barely able to breathe, I tried crawling toward the snowhouse. But I could not see it. Panic rising, I flailed about, stretching out my mittened hands to feel my way to it. Then Malmo's hand locked around my arm and she dragged me inside. I lay there on my back, breathing hard.

I had no idea just how long I would have to remain in that hut made of snow.

Malmo knew. She told me that this was Negea, the wind that began at the very top of the world, from even beyond Niflheim, and Negea could flay the skin off a human in just a few seconds. She said Negea had been known to blow for weeks at a time. I thought she was exaggerating.

The days crawled along in that small white world, with the sound of howling wind forever in my ears. I could see how people lose their wits. Luckily, Malmo was wise in the ways of surviving such long spells of confinement.

Our second night in the snowhouse Malmo brought out her story knife. At first I didn't know what it was, thinking it another snow knife. It was also made of ivory but was smaller, with a different shape. And unlike the snow knife, the story knife had beautiful carvings on the blade, decorative pictures of fish and seals and sea and sun.

She gestured for me to sit beside her, and using the blunt side of the blade to smooth the snow in front of us, she then used the tip to sketch a picture into the smooth surface.

The designs were simple—stick figures to represent people and crude symbols for other elements, such as the sun, a tree, and a river. But oddly, I could recognize each thing she drew right away. She spoke as she drew, identifying and naming the figures and their surroundings.

The first tale she told was about a mother seal that cared for an Inuit girl after the girl's parents were lost at sea in a hunting accident. Malmo was a gifted storyteller and I sat enthralled, watching the knife deftly etch out the pictures that told the story. The characters she drew came alive like performers on a stage.

As the days passed, the story knife made the boredom bearable. Malmo even taught me how to use the story knife myself. I used it to memorize her stories, telling them back to her, as well as to tell her stories of Njord— the old stories of Freya and Thor and Odin. Some were the same stories that I had told the white bear back in the castle, and the memory of that time came rushing back. At such moments I would hand the story knife to Malmo, unable to continue. She understood.

Day followed day in the snowhouse, the storm howling around us. Even telling tales with the story knife began to seem tedious. But finally, just as we were reaching the end of our food supply (and I, the end of my wits), the blizzard ceased. I was lying on my back, staring listlessly up at the white ceiling, when I suddenly realized that the sound of the wind had stopped. I looked over at Malmo. She nodded at me. "Negea is done," she said simply.

The snowhouse had gotten buried under several feet of snow during the storm, so we had to dig our way out. Putting on our skis, we resumed our journey.

After several more weeks we came to the end of Gronland and the beginning of a large expanse of frozen sea. Malmo removed her skis and calmly explained that we would cross the sea of ice. The shoreline was too rough for skis, she said, adding that we should be able to use them again farther out. Looking at the broken, jumbled mass of ice lining the shore, I could see that what she said was true, and I bent to remove my own skis.

"The sea ice is thick?" I asked a little nervously.

"It will hold us," she answered with a smile.

Following Malmo I gingerly stepped from land to sea. I could hear the ice groaning and creaking under my feet as swift currents moved beneath it.

I grew used to that sound and eventually stopped worrying about the ice cracking or giving way beneath me. We threaded our way through the jagged ice of the shoreline, and as Malmo had predicted, the ice smoothed out, with only small ridges that our skis could navigate.

It took us more than a week to cross the frozen sea. One afternoon we stopped to hunt seal. Malmo found a breathing hole in the ice, and pitching our tent we began a patient vigil. She had set on the surface of the water a thin rod made of antler, which she told me would bob up and down at the slightest disturbance. We were stationed downwind of the breathing hole so our scent wouldn't reach the sensitive noses of any seals nearby. Hours passed. Then the antler rod gently bobbed on the surface of the water. Malmo moved with a calm but amazing speed, grabbing her harpoon and striking down into the breathing hole with all her force. She held fast until the seal grew tired, its struggle lessening. Handing me a knife she told me to enlarge the hole so we could bring the seal up. I worked as quickly as I could, and finally Malmo was able to drag the seal up onto the ice. It was still alive, barely, and she used a club to finish it off.

I had had plenty of experience butchering animals on the farm, but killing the seal was eerie to me, with the vivid red of its blood against the sheer white ice.

By the time the moon was directly overhead, we had fresh seal meat. Before eating, Malmo sang. She did this every time she was about to eat what had been caught in a hunt, and that night, out on the frozen sea, I asked her why she sang.

"It is the way we live in peace with the animals in our world. We are not separate from the animals or the sea or the ice but part of the whole. And so we must treat the animals, the sea, the ice with respect."

"But is it not disrespectful to kill?" I asked hesitantly, not wishing to offend Malmo.

She smiled as if at a child. "No. Because it is part of the cycle. We must hunt to survive. Disrespect would be to hunt when you are not hungry and then to treat the dead in a wasteful, unclean way. The words I sing are to ask forgiveness for taking the seal's life, and to send its soul safely to the spirit world."

As we reached the other side of the frozen sea, the surface became rough again and we had to take off our skis. The ice looked like it had exploded upward, making a towering forest of white. It was extraordinary. The glassy pinnacles rose as high as ten feet above us, and there were long, deep cracks in the surface. And the groaning, creaking sound was louder as the edges of the ice pack pushed more aggressively against each other. Occasionally there would be a loud cracking sound, like that of an enormous whip, and I would jump, my heart racing. Adding to my nerves was Malmo's warning that she smelled white bear around us and that we should be wary.

"I thought the white bear was *your* animal," I said uneasily.

"That will not protect us from a white bear that has not eaten in several weeks. Or a mother bear with hungry cubs."

We carefully made our way through the mazelike ice forest. My whole body was stiff with tension, my icicle-rimmed eyes darting from side to side as I watched for a white bear around every jutting spire of ice. And the cracks in the ice were widening; I could see black freezing water through some of them. The harsh cracking sounds grew more frequent.

It seemed to go on and on, the ice forest. I got occasional glimpses of what I took to be a shoreline, but it never got any closer.

As I rounded a particularly large tower of ice, my senses numb from constantly being on edge, there was a sudden blur of motion, white on white, and a snarling. I felt a burning line of pain along my jaw and was knocked to the ground, unable to breathe. I saw a spreading pool of red on the snow and realized it was blood—blood leaking from the throbbing on my face. But something was over me, blocking out the light, and I looked up into the face of a white bear, standing on its hind legs, teeth bared.

My breath came back then, ragged and gasping, and the strangest thing of all was that it wasn't the thought that I was going to be killed that frightened me the most but the primitive animal ferocity I saw in those small black eyes. They were nothing like the eyes of my white bear. In fact, there was nothing recognizable there at all, just the staring, voracious eyes of a predator that had found its next meal.

Neddy

My FAVORITE PLACE in the old monastery was the reading room. It was located in what had once been the chapel, and tall arched windows of stained glass lined the walls. There were ornate bookcases filled with handsome gilt-titled volumes, though the majority of books and manuscripts were housed in other rooms of the building. In the center of the room were several long tables at which one or two people usually were seated on wooden chairs.

Hours passed by like minutes in the reading room. Blurred shapes of ruby red, emerald green, and rich sapphire blue from the stained glass would dapple the pages as I read the old manuscripts. And I feasted on the words handwritten by men who had lived hundreds of years before me.

It was on a sunlit morning in late winter when a curious thing happened. I had already finished my assigned work for the day and, for pleasure, was reading an account of a sea voyage undertaken by a Viking called Orm. This Orm was an explorer of sorts, and he had told his tales of discovery to a monk back in the days when the old Viking ways were beginning to fade and the church was becoming more and more the center of life in Njord. The monk had written down the Viking's stories, apparently just as Orm had told them, and I read the stories with deep interest.

Perhaps because of my ancestors, I had always been drawn to accounts of journeys of exploration. Unlike my grandfather and great-grandfather, however, my interest had never been in the actual exploring, and unlike my father, I had only a passing interest in charting the world. Instead I was interested in the history of exploration—who went where, when they went, and why they had gone at all. And I had always been particularly intrigued by tales of northern exploration, because of that time in my life when I had taken it upon myself to learn all I could of white bears.

As I sat in the reading room that morning, poring over the long-ago Viking foray into the frozen waters well beyond the northern tip of Njord, I turned a page to find a drawing that made me catch my breath. It was a simple line drawing, apparently done by the monk from a description by Orm the Viking. The drawing depicted a large white bear standing on its four paws facing a man (or I suppose it could have been a woman—the figure was too swathed in fur-skins to tell anything about it but that it was human). The two figures were virtually nose-to-nose, with only a hand's length between them, and they looked, for all the world, as if they were conversing.

My eyes eagerly sought the text that explained the drawing:

Driven off course, in a northwesterly direction methinks, we are pressed on all sides by ice. My men clamor to turn south. They fear being trapped in ice for the long winter. Nevertheless, I press onward.

The ice comes and we are hemmed in. My men are afraid. It is the full moon and one night, unable to sleep, I wake and walk the deck. The moon is bright and there before me, on the land, is an extraordinary sight. As clear as if it were day, I see them. A small man in fur and a white bear. They stand on the ice facing each other. I felt a thrill of terror; the bear was surely about to devour the man. I have hunted white bear and there is no fiercer foe. But, most strange and awesome, the white bear did not eat the man. Indeed, they seemed to be gazing into each other's eyes, with the look of blood brothers, or father and child. The hair on my neck stood up and I called to my men so that I should not be the only one to see such a sight. But the sound of my voice must have carried over the sea and ice, for bear and man turned toward me, as one, and then they turned back, as though annoyed at the interruption, and moved

*quickly away over the ice, side by side. By the time
any of my men were awake enough to heed my words,
the man and bear were lost to sight.*

The narrative ended abruptly, with a sentence stating
that only Orm and two of his men survived the voyage.

I stared down at a band of blue across the parchment,
caused by the sun shining through the stained glass. My
heart thudded in my chest, and I was suddenly aware of
someone standing beside me. Except that when I turned
my head to see who it was, there was no one there. And
yet there was. *Rose.* I felt as sure of this as of my own
name. I could smell her. And I could even feel the soft
touch of her hand on my arm. She was wearing fur
mittens.

I closed my eyes.

"Rose?" I whispered.

And, clearly, I heard Rose say, "Neddy."

I was not sure of her tone. It might have held fear, but
I did not know. And then I could "see" her, with my eyes
closed, though her features were indistinct and blurred.

"Rose?" I said again. I wanted her to tell me where
she was, that she was safe and had done as she wanted,
but most of all, when she was coming home. I closed my
eyes, concentrating all my thoughts on the soft feel of
her hand on my arm, willing her to speak.

"Neddy," she said again, and that time I was sure
there was fear in her voice. And then I felt the touch of
her hand leave me.

"Rose!" I shouted, leaping to my feet. The few other people in the room looked up, startled. They must have thought me mad, watching as I groped like a blind man at the space beside me.

But it was no use. She was gone.

Rose

EVERYTHING WENT VERY still as I lay there, staring up at the animal. I thought of Neddy. I thought of my white bear.

Then I heard Malmo's voice. She was singing, and I sensed rather than saw her step around my prone body until she was behind me, facing the bear.

Distracted, the white bear looked up, and Malmo's eyes caught his and held them. Still murmuring her song, she began moving sideways, away from me. The bear dropped to all fours and, eyes fixed on Malmo, followed her.

I watched them, too dazed to move. When they were a stone's throw from me, Malmo stopped and the pair stood quite still, facing each other, continuing to look into each other's eyes. If their mouths had been moving, I would have thought them to be conversing.

Finally Malmo gave a nod and the white bear turned and padded away, going in the direction from which we had just come.

Malmo crossed to me then and knelt beside me. She reached into her pack and pulled out something that she pressed against the pain in the side of my face.

I looked again at the splash of red, so vivid on the ice. I saw that the blood was already starting to freeze.

"There may be a small scar. Hold this," she said calmly, indicating the cloth. She drew an ivory box from her pack and, taking off her mittens, dipped a finger in the cream inside. She rubbed the cream across the wound. It hurt, but then a warmth spread and the pain eased somewhat. "Can you travel?" asked Malmo.

"Yes," I said, sitting up, though a wave of dizziness passed through me.

Malmo sat beside me. "Let us wait a few moments," she said.

"How . . ." I began. "I mean, what did you do?"

"The white bear was hungry," Malmo said. "I told him about the seal's breathing hole we found. Perhaps he will be lucky."

"You spoke to him?" I asked in wonder.

"We do not use words," she replied. "I asked if he knew anything about your white bear."

My heart thudded unevenly. "And did he?"

Malmo nodded. "He knew of the man-bear. That is what they call him."

"Did . . . did he know where the 'man-bear' is?"

Malmo shook her head. "But he told me that he has heard that the man-bear came from the land across the ice bridge. That at some time the man-bear has traveled over the ice bridge from Toakoro. He did not know in which direction or when. *Toakoro* is their word for Niflheim. They do not go there. No animals do."

"Why not?"

"They consider it unsafe." Then Malmo stood, breathing in and testing the wind. "We must travel on. It is still a long way to the ice bridge and I must return to my people soon."

Shakily I got to my feet. The bleeding had lessened, and Malmo fashioned a bandage out of the clump of cloth she had pressed to my face. And then we resumed our journey.

We came to the end of the ice forest, and I stepped onto the shore with an immense sense of relief.

We donned our skis, and after that our journey took on a wearying sameness. Day followed day, although you could not call it day at all. It had been a long time since we had seen the sun in the land of endless night. There was no way of keeping track of time passing, though Malmo had an innate sense of when it was time to eat and sleep.

But the endless night in the frozen land at the top of the world wasn't like night back in Njord. Because of the unending whiteness that surrounded us, there was not the same kind of darkness. There was always a dim gray light; the closest thing I could compare it to was twilight back home—the twilight just a few moments before the complete black of night takes over. Yet you could still see a billion dazzling specks of light in the night sky. And when the moon shone, especially the full moon, an eerie pearly-blue light washed the white landscape.

We fell into a rhythm, Malmo and I, working together almost as a husband and wife who had been together for many years. I became nearly as adept as Malmo at skinning a seal, making a snowhouse, telling tales with the story knife. There was an immense satisfaction in doing the jobs well, although satisfaction was beside the point in a place where doing the job well meant surviving another day.

Living in the frozen world became second nature, and I grew to love the breathtaking beauty of the vast white landscape. And yet a part of me longed for the sight of a green blade of grass, or the smell of rain and wet earth. The only colors in the land were white, gray, and pale blue, with the occasional burst of red from the spilled blood of a seal, and even then there was no smell at all.

We traveled a long time, long enough for the sun to make an appearance in the form of a thin band of light on the horizon. And each day I could see Malmo becoming more restless. Finally, as we crested an icy summit, she said, "I need to return to my people. If we do not reach the ice bridge soon, I will have to turn back."

I began to worry that there was no ice bridge at all, that it would turn out to be nothing but a fragment of an old myth. But, I reminded myself, the white bear we had met up with "spoke" of the ice bridge.

It was during this time that I began to think about the man-bear I was seeking. The man, not the white bear, kept entering my thoughts. I had seen his face only briefly, and sometimes I could not remember it, but once in a while it would come clear in my mind, complete with that expression of desolation that ate at my insides. Even when his face was a blur to me, the one thing I never forgot about the man was the color of his hair in the candlelight as I had leaned over him.

I realized I knew nothing about him. Not even his name. To me he was "white bear" or "the white bear who had been a man." But the man with the golden hair had had a name—as well as a life—before the pale queen took it from him. A father, a mother, brothers and sisters perhaps. Friends.

Was he a craftsman? A farmer? A prince? How long ago had the pale queen taken him from his life? If by some miracle he got free of her, would his old life still be there? Would his family be long dead and buried? It seemed likely, from the few words he had spoken of his long captivity. Would there be even a building that once had been home waiting for him, or would it be occupied by strangers? My stomach twisted. And I felt a white-hot surge of anger at the pale queen. Her cruelty.

Why had she done it? He was a handsome man—I had seen that as he slept and when he gazed at me with such anguish. Perhaps that comeliness had been the beginning of her wish to possess him. But the source of her obsession would have to be more than that, to account for such a monstrous act of thievery.

I thought then of the castle. Had that been his home once, transported into the mountain? Parts of it had certainly had the feel of a young man's quarters. Or had the pale queen merely furnished and decorated it in the manner she thought he would prefer?

Then I remembered the room with the musical instruments, and the flauto that I had learned to play. And the sheets of music. I felt sure that those were from the life the white bear, the man, had once known.

That was one thing I knew about him at least. His love of music.

Troll Queen

I AM GLAD I DECIDED not to hurry the ceremony after all. I have had the inspired notion that Myk shall play his flauto at the wedding feast. This will please him. It will slow even further my preparations, for it will take time to get the instrument made and time for Myk to choose and practice what he will perform. But it will be well worth the extra time.

My people know little of music. I have tried to introduce it to them, but when they attempt to play, it does not sound as it does in the green lands. I believe that when they hear music as it should be played, their hearts will be won.

Myk is feeling more and more at home. His memories of a life before this have faded away to almost nothing. I relaxed the rule about not having softskins wait on the royal court, thinking that it would make him less homesick to have those of his kind around him. But it may have been a mistake. Occasionally one of the softskin servants will say something that seems to trigger some dim memory—I have come to recognize that puzzled, wistful look in his eyes—but then it passes. And I make sure that the softskin is taken away to *kentta murha*. Myk has asked where they go. I tell him they were moved to another position in the palace. He looks uneasy for just a moment, then that passes, too.

I have sometimes thought about doing away with the tradition of softskin slaves altogether, for then there would be nothing to trigger his memories, and it gets more and more difficult every year, the expeditions into the green lands. But I think my people would be unhappy. Who will do the work then? they would say. And if I replaced the softskin servants with trolls, there would be resistance. It could easily be done—my power is absolute—but it would be a difficult transition, messy. No, too much change is not prudent. Perhaps one day in the future, after they have gotten used to having a softskin king.

Rose

AT LAST WE CAME to the ice bridge.

We first spied it as we ascended a high snowy peak. The sun was peering over the line of the horizon and its light caused the ice bridge to glitter, hurting our eyes, even with snow goggles. We stood still, staring down at the bridge. Through my icicle-rimmed eyelashes, with the light dancing on it, I thought I could see all the colors of the rainbow. And it was a perfect arc, like a rainbow of molten light. The bridge was long, very long, but I could dimly see where it ended. The white icy land on the other side of the river looked much like the land we stood on.

I heard Malmo say something in Inuit under her breath.

As we skied down the slope toward the bridge, I thought of Bifrost, the rainbow bridge that connected the world of man to Asgard, the home of the gods.

At the bottom of the slope, we took off our skis and Malmo led me to the edge of the river that the bridge spanned. She held up one hand, indicating I should approach with caution.

"This river is Tawktoak Imuk," she said. A silvery gray, almost black, ribbon of water moved restlessly below us.

"Why is it not frozen?" I asked in wonder.

"It is not water as in our lands. Tawktoak Imuk is the black water that kills. To fall into the black water is to die; it makes the flesh fall away from the bone. Here I must leave you, Rose," she said. "I have been too long away from my people." She unstrapped her pack and the tent from her back and placed them on the ground in front of me. Then she donned her skis and said in her calm voice, "You will find the man-bear." She leaned forward and touched her forehead to mine.

"For you," she said, thrusting something into my hands. And then she turned and skied away, back toward the slope we had just descended.

"Wait, Malmo!" I called. "You forgot your gear..."

She turned and waved but did not turn back.

"Malmo!" I called again. "Thank you," I said under my breath.

I watched as she deftly maneuvered the slope and kept my eyes on her until she reached the top. When she got there, I saw Malmo lift her arms to the sky, and then she was gone. There was a white petrel riding the wind directly above the place she had been. I blinked. Was it possible that Malmo had turned herself into a petrel, or had she merely skied down the other side of the slope? I didn't know.

It was only then that I looked down at what I held in my hands. Malmo's story knife.

I turned to look at the ice bridge. All alone. Malmo was gone and I was by myself in a place where most living creatures would not survive more than a day. And I was proposing to enter an even deadlier place, one no animal would enter.

Fighting off the feeling of panic that flickered at the edges of my mind, I put my hand into the pocket of my parka and clutched Queen Maraboo. I said to myself, "I will cross this ice bridge and go into Niflheim and find the white bear and rescue him." After all, I was by then more than half Inuit. I had learned from Malmo how to survive in the frozen world.

I strode over to the ice bridge and placed a foot on it. At once my foot slid wildly, skidding off to the side. I had been wise enough not to put my whole weight on it, or I would surely have fallen, possibly even into the killing river itself. I tried again, even more tentatively. And then again. There was no possible way to get a foothold on the surface of the ice bridge. It was slicker than oil.

When the full impact of the situation hit me, I sank down onto the ground in front of the bridge. I felt tears rise but quickly fought them back, remembering they would only freeze on my face.

"There must be a way across," I muttered to myself. The white bear had crossed the bridge. He might have been on the Troll Queen's sleigh, but maybe not. . . . And I thought then of the white bear's long, sharp black claws.

What if I were to fashion claws for myself, I thought slowly. And I remembered the *kitchoa,* the tool made of ivory that the Inuit used to simulate the sound of a seal's claws scraping across the ice.

If I could somehow attach the *kitchoa* to the bottom of one foot . . . And make something similar for my other foot.

So I set to work. In Malmo's pack I found ivory fishing lures with curved hooks, and I thrust them through some strips of sealskin, which I then tied around my boots so that the hooks poked from the bottom. Attaching the ice scratcher to my other boot was somewhat more difficult, but I managed, using sealskin I had cut into thongs. The scratcher was bulkier and so my gait was lopsided, but I thought I could manage.

I sorted through Malmo's gear and my own, and discovered that she had left me all of her food as well. Gratefully I stowed it, and other bits of her gear that I thought would prove useful, in my own pack. I hoisted the bulging pack—with the tent lashed to it—onto my back and hobbled to the foot of the ice bridge. My uneven gait and the heavy pack made me feel clumsy, but the weight on my back, I thought, might give me more traction.

And so I began my slow, tortuous way across that bridge. Each step was a desperate and heart-stopping act: lifting and then carefully placing each foot, then digging it into the ice and holding my balance. At first everything in me was focused on my feet—lifting, planting, lifting again. As I developed a rhythm, I became more and more aware of that evil restless ribbon of black water below. My heart pounded and I grew lightheaded. I blinked rapidly, trying to clear the dizzy feeling, and endeavored not to look at the river at all. But I had to look down to know where to place my feet. The ice was translucent in places, so I could even see the river through the bridge. Worse, though, was the sound of the moving water. It didn't sound like the rivers back home, which made a soft gurgling, slapping sound as they lapped at the bank. Instead there was an insidious whispering noise, as if the river were saying something to me, beckoning me in an evil sort of way. It was far, far worse than the groaning ice back in the ice forest.

I was only a third of the way across, and my nerves were strung so tight I thought I would break apart. I began to sweat heavily and could feel a thin sheet of ice forming on my face.

Desperate, I willed myself forward, lifting one foot, then the other, and then quickly planting each one again.

It was at about the halfway point when a sharp, biting wind suddenly kicked up, and startled, I lost my concentration. My left foot slid forward and went over the side. I fell, trying desperately to grab hold of something, but my hands slid, my torso slid. And I could feel my whole body sliding inexorably toward the edge. Frantic, I dug into my pocket and grabbed the handle of what I thought to be my small sharp knife, the *ulu*. With all my strength, I stabbed it into the surface of the ice. Then I saw that it was Malmo's story knife. Miraculously it held, and I in turn held on to it, tightly. Slowly I dragged my dangling foot back onto the bridge, and digging the *kitchoa* into the ice, I pulled myself up until I was in a crouching position.

I made it the rest of the way across the bridge in this same crouched-over position, using the *ulu* (after carefully putting away the story knife) and my two clawed feet. When I finally reached the far end I tumbled off onto the snow-covered ground and just lay there, breathing heavily. From the position of the moon I guessed that the journey across the bridge had taken most of the day.

I sat up and looked around. I realized at once that the land was very different from the one I had left behind on the other side of the bridge. First, there was the wind. It was constant, sharp, and insistent. Everything about the place was sharp and biting and bright and hostile. The snow on the ground had the texture of broken glass, brittle and sharp edged. It had been blown by the wind into shallow, undulating ridges that reminded me of Tuki's skin. There were occasional formations of ice that resembled smaller versions of the pinnacles in the ice forest Malmo and I had traveled through, but these looked like actual daggers piercing up from the ground, as though they would cut you if you brushed against them.

I took off my makeshift claws and strapped on my skis. The hard, ridged snow was slick, and I was able to travel swiftly over it. The ice daggers broke under my skis, though I took care to avoid the larger ones. I headed directly north.

As Malmo had told me, there were no animals at all in this land, so I had to carefully conserve my remaining seal meat.

The journey was grueling—the constant knifelike wind nearly drove me mad. My senses went numb. I moved my legs forward and kept my eyes trained on the horizon. After seven days I got my first glimpse of the ice palace. I first spotted it as a piercing glimmer. The late-winter sun had just dawned for its fleeting daily visit, and sent light reflecting off the palace's sheer ice walls and slender glassy towers.

The palace lay directly north of me, and I was still a long, long distance from it, but as I slogged forward, and day followed day, I began to see how vast and splendid it truly was. It stood so tall and shimmering on the snowy plain that it could be seen for miles and miles. One morning, I emerged from my tent after a fitful night's sleep. The glare of the sunlight off the palace was so intense that I only just turned my eyes away in time to avoid doing them damage. From then on I had to be vigilant about averting my eyes, even with my ivory goggles on.

It took many more days to reach the palace. There were few places to hide on the icy plain, but I used all available ridges and hillocks, and the occasional snow cave, to try to keep out of sight of any who might be keeping watch.

When I had come within a quarter mile of my destination, I found a small icy cave, barely as tall as me, in the side of a hill. I dug out the snow inside so I could get deeper into the cave. It faced south, away from the ice palace, and I made myself a snug little camp, sheltered from the relentless wind.

In the cave I thought about how I was going to get inside the glittering palace. Being fairly close, I saw how enormous it was, perhaps three times the size of the tallest church in Andalsnes.

I was down to my last packet of smoked seal meat. I made a small fire, ate a little of the meat, and soon after slept, no closer to a plan than before.

I awoke to the sound of bells.

Neddy

I HAD ONCE TOLD ROSE that if she needed me I would go to her, no matter where she was. She needed me, I was sure of it. So I left the reading room and ran all the way to the printing press to find Father. But when I arrived Father was not there, having just left on an errand.

"I must have a ship," I blurted out to Soren.

He could see that I was half out of my mind with worry. He pulled up a chair and calmly beckoned for me to sit. "What has happened, Neddy?"

I poured out the whole tale, of Rose and the white bear and how I felt she was in danger and that I must go to her right away. My sister Sara had told Soren about Rose sometime before, and he was immediately sympathetic.

"Where do you think to go, to find your sister?" he asked, not unreasonably.

"North," I replied without hesitation. Though I had not had a clear view of Rose, I had had a sense of her as being dressed for cold weather in furs and mittens. I knew that feeling may have been just the power of association, given what I had been reading at the time, but nevertheless I was sure she was somewhere in the north.

"North, eh? That covers a lot of territory," Soren said. "Let me make enquiries," he went on. "Your father and I have long thought we ought to do so, but I confess we have both been so wrapped up in this new printing press. At any rate, I understand that the letter you received from Rose came originally from Tonsberg, via La Rochelle in Fransk. It seems to me that Tonsberg is where we should begin our search, and then move on to La Rochelle."

"That will take too much time," I said impatiently. "I must not delay."

"I understand," replied Soren. "It will only take several days, and that is what we shall need anyway to get a ship outfitted and ready to go."

"Thank you, Soren," I said, clasping his hand in a warm handshake.

Soren waved away my gratitude. "I am tired of being cooped up with this splendid but maddening contraption," he said, gesturing at the printing press. "And I have always wanted an excuse to journey north. It has been little charted and 'twould be a great feather in our cap to do so. Of course, I must be sure to be back in time for my wedding day," he added with a grin.

"Of course," I replied, grinning back.

———

Soren's inquiries proved to be very fruitful, as well as somewhat worrying. We learned that Rose had gone north in a ship—an old *knorr*—headed for Suroy at the top of Njord, but that the *knorr* had not reached its destination. And then Soren's enquiry agent made an extremely lucky discovery in Tonsberg. He found a sailor who had actually been on board Rose's ship headed for Suroy.

The sailor's name was Gest, and he said that the *knorr* had been hit by a mighty storm. He himself had been swept overboard but had managed to survive by grabbing hold of an empty ale cask. He was then rescued by a passing ship that took him back to Tonsberg. He said that his mate, a man named Goran, had drowned but that he did not know what had happened to the captain of the ship and the girl who had been a passenger aboard the *knorr*. His best guess, as it was of those who knew of the storm in question and which way it had blown, was that if the ship had survived the storm, it was likely to have been driven far west and north, maybe as far as Gronland.

I tendered my resignation to Master Eckstrom, telling him that a family emergency had arisen, and said a fond good-bye to Havamal. As a parting gift, my new friend gave me a manuscript, which he had hand copied, with extensive information about Gronland and the people who lived there, as well as some practical details about traveling by ship into frozen waters.

Father, Soren, and I departed two days later on a ship we had renamed *Rose*.

Rose

THE BELLS I HEARD sounded just like the bells on the sleigh of the pale queen. My heart pounding, I quickly got up and moved to the entrance of the cave, cautiously peering out. The sun had not yet risen and the light was murky, but by moonlight I could make out three sleighs. They were stopped about halfway between my cave and the ice palace. The sleighs were crowded with fur-clad figures. I could hear harsh voices—voices like Tuki's and Urda's—raised in what sounded like anger. Then I noticed a figure bundled in fur moving away from the sleighs, running raggedly in an eastern direction. And several larger figures had jumped out of the sleighs and were in pursuit, shouting. The largest of the pursuers had what looked to be a long whip, and he flicked it at the moving figure. The figure jerked violently backward. The wielder of the whip then reeled in the helpless person, clearly a woman from her screams, dragging her along the ground—the whip wrapped around her waist, her arms pinned to her sides.

Noise began to swell from the sleighs and several other figures jumped out.

Impulsively I ducked back into my cave, then quickly made sure all my gear was safely stowed and left it there. I stealthily began to make my way toward the sleighs. The scene was a chaotic one, with lots of shouting and figures running around in confusion, and the light was still dim. I slipped into the fray, joining a small knot of fur-clad figures who were huddled beside one of the sleighs. I could not see anyone's face, so bundled were they all in fur-lined hoods and scarves. With my own Inuit fur-skins, I blended in easily. A larger figure came striding toward us, speaking in a harsh, guttural voice, and I recognized the language as Tuki's. The figure's face was not covered, and I could see handsome features and ridged, white skin. I kept my eyes down and let myself be herded into the sleigh with the rest of them. The large one with the ridged skin jumped up into the driver's seat, then turned and glared at us menacingly, continuing to speak. A few words sounded faintly familiar, but the voice was so rough that I could not be sure. I thought then of the little dictionary I had made of Tuki's words and regretted that I had not thought to grab it out of my pack before leaving the cave.

The one with the whip came toward us, dragging the captive behind him. He shouted out something to our driver, and this time I clearly recognized one of the words he said. The word for "dead." It was a word Tuki had taught me back in the castle, when we came across a large fly, its legs sticking up in the air.

I shuddered. The figure roughly unspooled his whip from the body and left the inert form lying on the hard snow. By then order had been restored and everyone was seated in the sleighs. Using their whips on the reindeer, the drivers guided the sleighs toward the ice palace.

Someone near me was sobbing quietly, but the rest were silent. I wished I could see the faces of the forms clustered around me in the sleigh.

I gazed back at the huddled figure lying on the ground. And then I realized that these creatures, with their harsh voices and ridged skin, driving the sleighs were trolls. Tuki and Urda were trolls. And the pale queen who had taken the white bear was a troll. The Troll Queen.

I felt foolish that I hadn't figured it out before. How often had I heard stories about trolls, or Huldre folk, when I was young? They were described in many ways—hairy, enormous, three- to twelve-headed, drooling, hideously ugly—none of which seemed to describe Tuki or that pale beautiful queen. And yet there were a few things that did fit—the voice like rocks and the craggy skin—and I did dimly remember the few tales of Huldre folk, a more obscure kind of troll, describing them as beautiful.

We came up to the palace, and as we began to circle it, I saw that it was even larger than it had appeared from afar. In fact, it was more of a town. The ice palace itself towered above, and in front of, an extensive sprawl of smaller buildings. These were made of ice as well but not the same finely polished glittering ice of the palace; they were more opaque and coarsely hewn. A high wall made of blocks of ice circled the compound, with various gates and doors granting entrance. We passed through an imposing back gate made of black iron that stood open.

There were several trolls waiting to greet the sleighs. Some stepped forward and took charge of the reindeer, while others roughly steered the occupants of the sleighs toward a low-lying building. I heard the drivers of the sleighs speaking to the palace trolls, and recognized the words *"servants"* and *"dead."* There was another word I recognized. It was the word *"slank,"* which was a favorite beverage of Tuki's, although there was a particular kind of slank he hated. Urda gave it to him when he had been bad; it made him sleepy and forgetful. I resolved not to drink any slank until I knew what kind it was.

If it was not exactly warm inside the ice building we were herded into, at least it was not as cold as it was outside, and some of my fellow sleigh travelers began pushing off their hoods and unwrapping their scarves. I saw they were humans like me, and though their features and hair color varied widely, the expressions on most faces were similar—a dull, blank look, with their mouths hanging slightly open. The few who did not wear this slack-jawed expression looked frightened and confused. I tried to make my own face as blank as those around me, but I watched and listened closely to what was going on.

I understood the words *"rooms"* and, again, *"servants"* and *"slank."*

As we were led down a long hallway, I realized that the humans around me had been brought to the Troll Queen's palace to be servants. And that slank was what had put those dazed, blank expressions on their faces. It also, I guessed, kept them obedient. I wondered about the one who had tried to escape and was killed by the troll with the whip. Had the slank not worked on her, or had it worn off?

Then I was thrust into a small room, and the door was pushed shut behind me. I saw there was no handle at all on the inside of the thick ice door. Because of the diffused light that came in through the icy walls, the room was dimly lit, and I noticed a platform with a pile of fur-skins on it. And a bucket. That was all the room contained.

As I stared numbly at my new quarters, the door opened and a large troll appeared. He pushed a cart filled with steaming earthenware cups. Taking one off the cart, he thrust it at me, then quickly departed. I had made my face empty and slack, but he hadn't even looked at me.

Luckily he had not stayed to see whether I drank the beverage. I put it up to my nose, which was a mistake— for it smelled incredibly delicious, and hungry as I was, I had to struggle to keep from drinking it. But even smelling the slank made me feel woozy and stupid, so I began hunting around for a way to get rid of it. I discovered that the platform on which my bed of furs was piled was made of wood. It was also movable, so I pulled it away from the ice wall and poured my slank onto the ice floor, in a spot in the middle. Its heat ate a shallow hole in the ice. Then I pushed the bed back into place and sat on it, wrapping myself in a fur-skin.

So, I had done it. I had found the place that could not be found—the land that lay "east of the sun and west of the moon." And somewhere within the icy walls of the troll palace, I was convinced, was the man who had been the white bear.

White Bear

MY QUEEN IS VERY GOOD. She watches over me, ever thoughtful of my needs. I feel very fortunate to be valued so highly by my queen.

She is beautiful, too—the whiteness of her skin and her strong green eyes, her tall proud form, the richness of her clothing. She tells me that I once found her skin odd, its roughness and texture, but I do not remember this. In truth, I believe it is my queen herself who dislikes her skin, for she is always trying to change it using different creams she concocts with her arts. Some of the concoctions make my eyes burn or tickle my nose when I come close to her, but she will not give up the effort. I know she keeps trying partly because she so admires my soft skin.

I remember nothing of the time when we first met, my queen and I. She tells me it was in the green lands, and that I was never a servant like the other softskins.

She tells me that I was a prince in the green lands, but I remember nothing of this. Sometimes I am curious, but mostly it does not matter to me, what came before.

I do, however, remember little bits from when I was a white bear. When I put on my white furs to go outside with my queen, it feels strange, like I am putting on what should already be there. And I remember that it was an unhappy time for me, though I do not recall why.

It is to my queen that I owe my freedom from my long enchantment as a white bear. A sorceress from the green lands cast a spell on me, and when my queen discovered my plight, she used her arts to release me. Then she brought me here to her northern kingdom of Huldre. This is just one of the many things for which I am grateful to my queen.

I am very well content in my life here. If it were not for the nightmares, there would be nothing to complain of at all. And my queen is most generous when the nightmares come. If I cry out, which I often do, she will come to me at once and bring me a cup of warm slank. She sits with me until my shaking abates.

Another proof of my queen's kindness toward me is the high regard in which she holds my music. She had her craftsmen make me a flauto. It is a very fine instrument, and she loves to hear me play it. And recently she told me I am to play for our wedding feast. It is a great honor, and once again I am filled with gratitude to her.

I hope I shall make my queen proud.

Rose

AND SO DID MY LIFE as a servant in the ice palace begin.

At first I was given the grueling, filthy routine of emptying the buckets of waste from the servants' quarters. There were many buildings of servants, I discovered, and the waste ditch was a long walk, some distance outside the palace gates. I worked from the moment I was awakened by the troll with the slank cart (he carried a whip, as if the slank were not sufficient incentive to rise; he only had to use it on me once) until I fell into my bed of fur-skins at night. Food was meager, and I began to suspect that the slank, which I continued to pour away under my bed, contained most of the nutrients that kept the servants going, as well as provided warmth in the frozen environment. The other softskins, though still slack jawed and dazed in expression, looked reasonably healthy and well fed, while I grew thinner each day.

I was always cold, too. The trolls clearly had a much higher tolerance for cold, for they walked around with only a single layer of clothing while we softskins attired ourselves from the pile of fur-skins in our rooms. I had my parka and long underwear from Malmo, which helped enormously, especially on my treks out to the waste ditch.

After several weeks I was moved to the kitchen, which was a definite improvement because there were ovens that warmed me and I could snatch an occasional scrap of food. Trolls, I discovered, were fairly shortsighted, which made stealing food without being caught easier than I would have thought. The kitchen was the domain of a large, loud female troll named Simka. She, along with the rest of the trolls, clearly considered the softskin servants to be little better than animals and treated us accordingly. Kicking was her favorite form of communication and she had a powerful foot. Despite the padding of my animal-skin clothing, I was soon covered with black-and-blue marks.

As I have said, my fellow softskins were kept sedated and dazed by the slank. They made little effort to interact with one another, and when I did hear them speak, I discovered that they spoke in a wide range of languages. The trolls must have gone in their sleighs to many different parts of the world to collect their servants, and I wondered how they went about it.

There were several trolls in charge of the servants, and they had at least a rudimentary grasp of the array of languages spoken by the softskins. But most of the communicating was done by pantomime—which was sufficient for the menial jobs the softskins were assigned. In the few cases when more complicated instructions were necessary, higher-level trolls were brought in to make explanations.

As for myself, I made a few attempts to speak to my fellow servants but was always met by the same blank look. Whether that was because they did not understand Njorden, or because of the slank, I couldn't be sure.

Slowly I learned about the workings of the palace, and by keeping my eyes and ears open, I picked up more and more of the troll language. Frequently I wished that I had my dictionary as well as some of my other belongings, which were stowed back in the ice cave.

I discovered early on that the softskins were not closely guarded. I think that was because of the drugged slank we were given, and also because of the frozen, deadly land surrounding the palace. In addition, we were not viewed as individuals at all but more as a herd of cattle or sheep. We went where we were told, did as we were bid, and found our way back to our "stalls" at the end of the day.

There were no locks on our rooms. None were needed. I experimented one night and discovered that although the door was very heavy, I could push it open with great effort. And there was no one patrolling the halls at night.

I suppose it would have been noticed if a softskin was

missing when the morning slank was delivered, but it never happened. Occasionally a softskin would become confused and then be found wandering in a part of the palace it wasn't supposed to be in, but this did not cause undue alarm. The softskin was merely given a beating and led back to its room.

The troll language was very difficult to learn, bearing no relation to Njorden or any other language I had heard. It was lucky that I had made that beginning with Tuki, or I don't think I would have been able to penetrate it at all. As I learned more and more, I was reminded of times I'd had to pick out the stitches of a particularly complicated piece of sewing. One word might unravel a whole set of words, and then I'd come to a knot and have to begin all over again. Frequently I wished for something with which to write down the words I was learning, as I had with Tuki, but at least the lack of writing materials forced me to memorize. And learning the language gave me something to think about as I shivered in my pile of fur-skins every night.

I remember well the day I first figured out that *juhvihkia* meant "wedding feast." Simka had just given a solid kick to my knee, and I was hobbling over to place a tray of newly cooked nut cakes on a table. She said a sentence that made it clear to me that the nut cakes, along with the many savory items the kitchen had been producing recently, were for a wedding to be held in the palace. Then she said "Katal" and "Myk," with a knowing sort of leer on her face. I had already figured out that

Katal was what they called their queen, and I had frequently heard the name Myk as well as the word *softskin* spoken in conjunction with Katal. I had assumed that Myk was some special softskin servant to the queen. But, if my understanding was correct, this Myk was actually marrying the queen—a softskin and a troll. And suddenly I knew who Myk was. I felt as though I'd been kicked in the stomach, and I dropped the tray of nut cakes with a clatter. Simka exploded with rage, bearing down on me. She slapped me across the face repeatedly until my ears rang and my lip split open. Then she kicked me out of the kitchen with a powerful boot, and I fled to my little room. Pressing a cloth against my bleeding lip, I collapsed onto my pile of skins.

I lay there, desolate, staring at the icy walls. I'm not sure why it came as such a shock. What had his words been? *"I go with her. Forever."* The Troll Queen hadn't gone to all that trouble to possess the man who had been a white bear (I could not think of him as Myk...) because she needed a servant, or to acquire a new friend. He was to be her mate. And all this time I had been actually helping to prepare the very food that would be eaten at the wedding feast of my white bear. The thought of it made me sick to my stomach.

Since arriving at the palace, I had been looking for the man who had been the white bear. I had acted the part of a slack-jawed softskin, being careful not to draw any attention to myself but keeping my ears open, hoping for some mention of the words *lumi karhu* or *vaeltaa,* for "white bear." But of course there had been none. The white bear was now a softskin named Myk who was going to marry the Troll Queen. *How soon?* I wondered, and vowed to listen more closely than ever to the kitchen trolls' conversations.

But I was not able to act on this, for the next day I was moved to a job in the stables. My punishment for ruining a tray of nut cakes, no doubt. The work was cold and hard; I no longer could supplement my meager meals with kitchen scraps, and the troll who then oversaw me was just as unpleasant as Simka, if not so fond of kicking, which was small comfort. The one consolation of my new position was the reindeer. They were extraordinary, beautiful, with their soft, pristine white fur and their enormous black eyes. Mostly my job was to clean out their stalls, but occasionally I got to feed them as well and, even more rarely, curry them, brushing out their silky manes.

The best thing about being assigned to the stables, it turned out, was that it gave me, eventually, the opportunity to retrieve my gear from the cave.

I must have showed some skill at my duties—the reindeer liked me, I believe—and I was gradually promoted to a more responsible position in the stables. My job involved readying the reindeer when they were to be hitched up to their sleighs and even, happily for me, to take them outside the palace gates for exercise.

Initially I did this in company with a troll overseer, who watched me closely to see if I showed any sign of wanting to run away. I kept an obedient, subservient look on my face, attentive only to the animals and showing no interest in my surroundings. I must have convinced him, for I was then sent out by myself to exercise two of the reindeer. I rode one, holding the other's lead. The troll overseer clearly had decided there was little risk in my trying to escape, a softskin's chances of survival in that frozen landscape being nil, and presumably the slank was eliminating any such thoughts.

The first two times on my own I did not attempt to locate the cave, in case I was being watched. But the third time I casually made my way in the direction of the cave. It had snowed during the time I had been at the palace, and I began to despair of ever finding it beneath the snowfall. But then my eye fell on a familiar-looking hump, and as I circled it, I recognized the contours of the cave. I dismounted and, holding the reindeer leads with one hand, dug out the snow-covered opening with the other. Everything was just as I had left it. I had prepared a mental list of the items I wanted from my pack, and I quickly began digging them out.

It was freezing work, opening up my coat and placing those icy packets close to my skin. When I was done I fastened my coat and mounted one of the reindeer, pressing my body against the animal for warmth.

I was punished for being gone too long, for straying too far, with a boxing of the ears and no dinner. But no one noticed my bulging coat, and later I greedily ate a small packet of frozen smoked seal meat I had thawed using heat from the slank I was given. Despite my punishment, they wouldn't dare skip giving me that. I stowed all my things in the hole made large by the hot slank I poured away every day, and went to sleep that night with, for the first time in a long while, a full stomach.

One day while I worked, I heard the stable trolls say that the queen and Myk were to have a sleigh ride, but when they arrived I was hustled out of sight into one of the back stables. Apparently only a few softskins were allowed anywhere near the queen. But to think that the man who had been a white bear was only a short distance from me made my breath go short and my heart feel like it would slam out of my chest. If only I could have darted out, grabbed him by the hand, and fled from the frozen place. But I could not. I had to be patient.

The next day my job was changed again. At first I thought I was being punished for having strayed too far on the day I had sneaked to the cave. But I later realized the change was most likely due to some mending I had done on the harness for the reindeer, for I was moved to a position that involved mending and sewing, and my new troll overseers were well pleased to discover my ability in this area.

They started me on easy tasks, but it was not long before I found myself being set before a small loom. And when they saw what I could do on that loom, I was soon moved to a larger one. It was nearly as splendid as the one in the castle had been. I was presented with a fine array of materials—thread and yarn of the most delicate and richest texture, in colors that dazzled the eye. Apparently, perhaps because of all the white that surrounded them, the trolls had a fondness for bright colors, at least when it came to dressing up. And there were many orders for fine gowns and vestments. Because of the wedding feast.

Although I hated the creatures who had ruined the lives of their countless human slaves, it did not cross my mind to do anything but my best work for the trolls. I had no plan yet, but I felt that doing good work might somehow help me rescue the white bear.

It was not until I learned that the wedding feast was only a fortnight away that I began to make plans. And by then I had found Tuki.

Troll Queen

URDA HAS BECOME troublesome. She blames me for Tuki's odd behavior of late. To me his actions seem harmless; nevertheless, it worries her. He has taken to shunning all company, preferring to be by himself, playing with his little toys. Or else he is to be found hanging about the softskin servants. I do not know why he does this, for they cannot talk to him, but apparently he is content merely to watch them. It is clear he was contaminated by associating with the softskin girl at the castle in the green lands. I may have to eliminate him. In the meantime I need to find a way to mollify Urda.

Though it is of little matter to me whether or not Urda is happy, she has many friends, and I prefer allies at this time rather than enemies. The wedding feast is very soon now, and there is still much to be done. Nothing must go wrong.

Rose

TUKI AND I FIRST encountered each other in a remote hallway in one of the outer buildings, not far from the weaving room. I was very lucky that there was no one nearby when we met, otherwise I would certainly have been exposed and all would have been lost.

When he saw me for the first time, Tuki gave a shrill, keening cry, and then a great toothy smile spread over his face. "Rose," he said happily.

"Tuki," I responded softly, and, looking around uneasily, placed a finger to my lips. He understood, mimicking me with a finger to his own lips, and we had a hurried, whispered exchange there in the hallway. My knowledge of the troll language was severely put to the test, but somehow, with a combination of pantomime and words, I was able to arrange a meeting with Tuki late the next evening in the weaving room. I was fairly confident that I would be alone then but impressed on Tuki that he must come into the room only if he saw I was the only one there.

I had become a favorite of sorts with the trolls who oversaw the weaving and sewing, a pet among the rest of the dumb animals. I was a hard worker, and though I still acted slack jawed and compliant, I was a little quicker to understand what was expected of me than the rest. Because of this, and because of the pressing need for wedding clothing, I had been given greater freedom than the other softskins. I was also working longer hours.

I had tried my hardest to impress upon Tuki that our meeting was a secret but was not sure I had succeeded. All the next day I was on tenterhooks, waiting for a troll to appear and drag me off to an icy dungeon.

But Tuki came alone to the weaving room at the arranged time. I was alone, working on an elaborate crimson-and-orange gown. There was joy in his eyes, and he reached over and touched the skin on my face, with the same pleased wonderment he had always shown. Then he took my hand and led me around the room, pointing to things and proclaiming the troll name for each. Realizing at once he wanted to play our old game, I quickly responded with the Njorden word. By then I already knew many of the troll words he "taught" me but did learn several that I had been puzzled by.

As we began to run out of objects to name, I pulled Tuki over to a stool and had him sit beside me.

"Is Tuki happy?" I asked. I thought he might remember the word, which I had taught him back at the castle. But he did not, so I pantomimed *happy* as best I could.

He suddenly began nodding emphatically and pointed to me. "Happy."

I thought I understood him to say he was happy to be with me, although he could have meant he thought I was happy. And I remembered the frustration I had felt in trying to communicate with Tuki in the castle. Suddenly I thought of Malmo's story knife.

Again using pantomime and words, I told him that I must get back to work and that he should leave. But I asked him to come back the next night, and eagerly he agreed.

I worked quickly, to make up for the time I'd spent with Tuki. I fell asleep that night trying to figure out what I could use with the story knife instead of snow.

The next night I was ready for Tuki. I had managed to sneak a small sack of white sugar out of the kitchen, right under the nose of the terrible Simka, though she did manage to land a sharp kick to my shin as I ran out. Before Tuki arrived I spread the sugar evenly on the floor in a corner of the room.

When he came in I promptly led him to the sugar-covered floor and bade him sit beside me. I took out the story knife. He jumped up, thinking it a weapon, but I smiled reassuringly and urged him to sit down again. Warily he did, and I started sketching.

I began with a short, simple tale, the one Malmo had

first told me about the girl adopted by seals. I think Tuki understood most of it, and when I had finished, he clapped his hands enthusiastically.

"More!" he said, in Njorden.

I told him another story, then another. Finally, I again had to tell him to go so I could catch up on my work. I said there would be more stories the next night. He went, even more reluctantly than he had the night before. I swept up the sugar and hid the bag of it under some fabric.

I did not get much sleep that night, for I had to work very late to get the allotted amount of work done.

The next night I told Tuki one brief tale to start out with. Then I turned to him and said that I had an important story to tell him. It was about me, I said, and why I had come to the ice palace. I don't know if he understood, but he nodded very solemnly and made ready to watch the figures I would draw.

I took a deep breath, and using the story knife, I told Tuki my story from the very beginning, when the white bear first came to our door, to the time I spent in the castle with the white bear–man lying beside me in the bed; from the candle wax dripping on his shirt to my long and perilous search for him. I did not go into detail about my journey, just showed myself crossing land, sea, and snow to reach the ice palace. I then drew the Troll Queen and the white bear–man hand in hand, as though being wed, and myself bending over, weeping.

I looked up at Tuki, who had been silent throughout

the entire tale, his eyes round and intent, and saw that there were tears streaming down his ridged cheeks.

"The softskin man who was a white bear must not marry the Troll Queen," I said, my voice hoarse from the telling of the tale. "Will you help me, Tuki?"

He stared at me, tears still wet on his skin.

"Will Tuki help Rose?" I said again, my own eyes bright.

Slowly he nodded.

Troll Queen

URDA HAS ASKED a favor of me.

I am inclined to grant it. It is easy enough to do, and on the whole I believe the benefit outweighs any small risk.

She says that her son, Tuki, has come to admire my Myk and is eager to serve him.

I see no harm in allowing Tuki to be an aide or companion to Myk. Myk will be agreeable, I am sure, for he has a soft nature and will be patient with Tuki's childish ways. And Urda will be less inclined to complain about those long years of exile and the damage she feels it did to Tuki.

The only concern I feel is the possibility that Tuki was contaminated by his exposure to the girl in the castle, the one who raised Myk's hopes and then betrayed him. If Tuki became attached to her in some way, he might speak of her to Myk. I do not think there is anything now that would stir Myk's memory—the *rauha* slank is too powerful for that to happen—but such a slipup may trigger a nightmare. (I still do not know why the slank does not eliminate those occasional nightmares. It is irksome.)

I have therefore mandated that Tuki may serve Myk, but only if he agrees never to speak to Myk of the castle or of what transpired there. Urda has been told that if Tuki disobeys this order, he will immediately be put to death.

I will inform Myk of the new arrangements this evening.

Rose

MY PLAN WAS WORKING—so far anyway.

Thanks to his mother, Urda, Tuki had been appointed as a sort of companion to "Myk." When the Troll Queen was a child, Urda was her nursemaid—and since then the older woman had continued to hold a position of trust to the queen.

Tuki learned that Myk had a large cup of slank each night before bedtime. For a week Tuki had managed to substitute plain slank for the kind with the powder. I have some idea he switched his own slank, unpowdered, for Myk's, which he poured away. Tuki had also contrived to smuggle in several bundles of clothing that were crucial to my plan. And in between orders for dresses, I sneaked in time to do my own sewing.

There were only a handful of days until the wedding.

White Bear

I AM GLAD MY QUEEN assigned the troll Tuki as companion to me during these days before the wedding. I like him very much. He listens while I practice my flauto, and I see tears come into his bright, eager eyes when I play. And he nearly falls off his chair clapping when I finish. If the other trolls like my music even half as much, I shall consider my performance a great success.

He is good company, too. He likes to play games, especially a game in which I teach him words of my old language by pointing to things and saying the word, and then he tells me the troll word for each. I have learned much of the troll language from my queen, but Tuki has helped me learn even more. I want to assist my queen in any way I can when I rule at her side, and she is well pleased at my interest in the language of her people.

I have been feeling somewhat odd of late. Not ill or unhappy. Just a little different, like my sight is clearer, or my thoughts. Or perhaps it is that I feel more awake; I certainly rise in the morning feeling more alert. I can't quite figure it out, but I am glad of it.

I have even had brief memories of the time before I came to the ice palace. Even before I became a white bear. They are fleeting but pleasant.

Just today I recalled being a child and playing on a field of the greenest grass, with many bright yellow flowers poking through the green. There were other children and we were all laughing together at something. It was very enjoyable, the memory.

I have not told my queen because she does not care for mention of the past. And I do not wish to upset her, especially when she is so busy preparing for our future happiness.

Rose

TUKI MANAGED TO smuggle some of the plain slank to me, which was wonderful. Despite my increased status as seamstress and weaver, I still received only the most meager of meals, presumably because most of my nutrition should have come from the doctored slank, which I continued to pour away. (The hole under my bed had grown quite large.) I was becoming painfully thin and worried the trolls would notice. They never did, though. Softskins were viewed as a herd, not worth taking note of individually. Our function was to provide service to the trolls until our bodies wore out. Then we were replaced.

It was Tuki who told me that when that happened, when softskins became too old or too ill to work, they were taken to something called *kentta murha*. When I asked what *kentta murha* was, Tuki turned very white and silent. I could not get any words of sense from him after that, and finally he left me, still upset.

I continued with my tasks. The wedding feast would be the day after next, and there were still several gowns to be completed. I barely slept at all, so hard was I being worked. I felt fortunate that Tuki had gotten me the unpowdered slank, or I might well have collapsed from the lack of sleep and food. But the slank gave me energy and strength. And I needed all my wits about me for what lay ahead.

Troll Queen

FINALLY THE DAY HAS ARRIVED. I am extremely pleased to see that all my preparations are coming together, just as I had planned. The feast tonight will be the largest and grandest gathering in the history of our people. For the very first time the trolls from the bottom of the world have journeyed north to my kingdom. Even my father, in his prime, created nothing of this magnitude. It is extraordinary.

With my arts I myself made the gown I will wear. I will outshine the northern sun in radiance, which is not surprising in that I borrowed some of the sun's brilliance to create the fabric.

Simka has surpassed herself in the kitchen. And I am even pleased with Urda. Tuki has, somewhat to my surprise, been a great success as a companion to Myk. Myk has asked me to allow Tuki to attend him during the ceremony, and I have agreed. Urda is terribly pleased and has been bragging about it all over the palace. I hope the little fool does not make any stupid mistakes that will mar the splendor of the proceedings.

Last night Myk had one of his nightmares, the first in some time. I attribute it to wedding-night jitters and am not unduly concerned. He was very agitated, though, and I had to give him double the portion of the powdered slank. It was very peaceful, holding him in my arms as he settled down to sleep, his golden head resting on my shoulder. How I love him. It is why I have done all that I have done.

The guests for the feast will begin to arrive this afternoon, and the rooms have been made ready. Every room in the palace will be full. Most of the guests will be fatigued when they arrive, having traveled great distances, but there will be little rest for them tonight.

We will begin with the feast. Twenty courses of the greatest delicacies in Huldre. And then will come the dancing, which will last well into the night. And then tomorrow at midday, after Myk plays his flauto, we will be joined together ... forever.

Rose

I WAS KEPT BUSY until the very last minute, putting final touches on the troll ladies' gowns—letting out a seam here, adding a silk rose there. The noise was horrible, each troll lady stridently demanding something in a rasping voice. At times I felt I was attending a flock of cawing, brightly colored crows. My head ached and my fingers were numb.

And then finally I was left alone. I was instructed to clean up the mess of the sewing room and then return to my quarters. As had become usual, no one stayed to supervise me. Every available serving troll was needed in the kitchen, banquet hall, or stables. I breathed a great sigh of relief, for this was one element in my plan that I had no control over. Though it seemed likely the trolls would treat me as they had for the past several weeks, leaving me alone to clean up, still there had been no guarantee.

I had brought all I needed with me to the sewing room. And when the last troll had gone and I had given my dull-eyed acceptance to their final orders, I set to work.

First I pulled out my leather wallet from where it had been concealed under my clothing. Though I knew the gold and the silver dresses had not been adversely affected by being folded up in the wallet for so long, I was still anxious that the moon dress might have been damaged. After all, it had been through a storm at sea as well as the inhumanly freezing conditions of my trek northward. My fingers trembling slightly, I removed the dress from the wallet and shook it out.

I needn't have worried. There was not so much as a wrinkle in the exquisite fabric, and I marveled all over again at its breathtaking beauty, unbelieving as before that I had actually created such a wonder.

I set the dress aside for a moment and quickly pulled on an undergarment I had fashioned for myself in stolen moments. To protect myself from the cold (I would not be able to wear a reindeer-skin parka to the wedding feast or my duck-feather underwear), I had stitched together several layers of very fine silk into a full-length suit that fit close to my skin.

Then I put on the dress.

I crossed to a large oval mirror that the troll ladies had been using earlier to admire themselves in their gowns. It was the first time I had seen myself in a mirror since leaving the white bear's castle, and I was shocked to see my face. It was much thinner and paler, and there was a threadlike white scar on my right cheekbone, a souvenir of my brush with the bear in the ice forest. I also looked different in other ways—how I held my head, the expression in my eyes. I was not the same Rose who had left home almost two years before on the back of a white bear.

Anyway, it didn't matter how my face looked. I went to a corner of the room, and from under a pile of little-used cloths, I retrieved a small bundle. Carefully I un-wrapped it, revealing a mask. I had been working on this mask secretly for the past several weeks. It was made of fabric, though I had stiffened the material somewhat with a thin paste I had made of flour and water. It had been an immense task, and I had used every bit of skill I possessed for working with cloth. But the result was an extraordi-narily lifelike mask of a troll woman's face. Or rather my face, if I had had the white, ridged skin of a troll.

I put the mask on, fastening the ties under my hair, and once again gazed at myself in the mirror. It was amazing. I had been transformed into a young troll woman, if not as beautiful as the queen at least passably pretty. My mask would not have borne very close in-spection under human eyes, but I was counting on the trolls' poor eyesight to keep them from seeing through my disguise.

The gown had a high neck and long, flowing sleeves that hid my soft skin. And I had made white gloves with a ridged texture to cover my hands. On my thumb, underneath one of the gloves, I wore the silver ring the white bear had given me.

The day before, Tuki had presented me with a simple diadem of pearls, with trailing strands that wove into my hair. I did not want to accept the crown for fear he would get into trouble. But he would not take it back, making a maddening game, holding his hands behind his back and chuckling happily at my frustration. So I carefully arranged the diadem on my head, the strands of pearls looking like drops of pure moonglow shimmering in my dark hair.

Shoes had been my biggest problem; my big boots would hardly go well with a moon gown, but Tuki had once again come to my aid by finding me a pair of cast-off slippers. They were an old pair of the queen's, he told me, which she had given to Urda when the queen had tired of them. They were too small for Urda, but she had kept them anyway, in the back of her closet.

I slipped on the shoes, which were white and trimmed with tiny pearls. They fit. I don't know why exactly, but it was unsettling to me that the Troll Queen and I should have very nearly the same size feet.

I was ready. I had planned to time my arrival after the feast, when the dancing was to begin. I would be a late-comer, from a far-distant land, and would, hopefully, be able to slip into the throng without anyone noticing. I had practiced over and over in my head the troll words I would say if questioned. I was not sure if I would be able to capture the rough cadence of the troll voice, but the few times I had attempted it with Tuki, he had assured me that I would pass.

I think it was all a game to Tuki; he played along with all the eagerness and enthusiasm that he had shown when I'd used the story knife or we'd played the language game. I worried about him, though, and hated pulling him into my plot. Tuki was a simple soul, and guile did not come naturally to him. I prayed that I could keep Tuki from harm. I would not have been able to bear it if something were to happen to him.

I saw Tuki for just a moment that afternoon, and he whispered to me, when no one was near, that he had given Myk the unpowdered slank again the night before. It had been seven days since the white bear's last dose of slank laced with *rauha*. Tuki saw a difference in him.

I was sure that if only I could get near enough to look into his eyes . . . he would remember me. He had to.

Troll Queen

IT IS A TRIUMPH! The banquet hall is aglow with color and light, from the finery my people wear in my honor to the brilliance of the *revontulet,* the northern lights that stream rivers of color through the sky. Viewed through the crystalline walls and ceiling of my ice palace, it is extraordinary. A masterpiece.

Myk seems sleepy eyed, somewhat subdued. I suppose it is the effect of the double portion of powdered slank I gave him last night. But when he looks at me, he smiles.

I have never been so happy.

White Bear

MY QUEEN IS RADIANT. I can hardly believe it is me she wishes to wed. Tomorrow. How can I be worthy of such an honor?

Tuki is acting odd. All the time he gazes at the entrance, as though expecting someone to enter. He has hardly touched the delicious food.

I wish I did not feel so drowsy and dull witted.

Rose

ALL OF THE OUTLYING buildings, except the stables, were connected to the ice palace by tunnels, creating a weblike maze that caused at least one softskin a day to get hopelessly lost. There were trolls who were assigned the job of leading those wandering softskins to their proper place. Though it did not seem likely there would be trolls in the passageways on the night of the wedding feast, I did not want to take the risk. Even the most unobservant troll would think it odd to find a party guest roaming the passages leading to the servants' quarters. So I decided to circle around and approach the front entrance of the palace from the outside.

I put on my reindeer-skin parka over the dress, donned my old boots (putting the dainty pearl shoes in my pockets), and went outside.

The northern lights were extraordinary. I had never seen them so glorious, so richly hued and vivid. Though

I was not particularly cold in my layers, I began to shiver. The Troll Queen's power was immense. Did I really think that I, with nothing but a flimsy mask and a ring on my thumb, had any chance of taking away that which she desired above all else?

It was a long walk, skirting the outside of the ice palace, but eventually I came to the front. I slipped stealthily around the corner and saw palace guards busily meeting and attending to the sleigh of a group of late-arriving trolls. No one noticed me as I made my way up the sweeping ice stairway. Ahead of me a pair of trolls were just entering, and I trailed behind them. They, too, wore furs, which they hung on a treelike contraption made of ice—a coatrack, I guessed. There weren't many coats on it, as most of the visitors had arrived earlier and were staying inside the ice palace. I found a spot for my coat and placed my boots under it.

I entered the banquet room. The sight before me stopped my breath. It was an enormous hall, with glistening ice walls, a cathedral ceiling, and towering windows made of clear ice. Through the windows the northern lights were visible in all their overwhelming beauty. The ice refracted the pulsing blues, greens, and purples, causing color to swirl across every surface of the room. The radiance and perfection of it was almost too much to take in.

Hundreds of trolls were gathered, all dressed elegantly in brilliantly colored finery. The air vibrated with their guttural voices. Tables lined the outside walls, having been pushed aside after the banquet was done to make space for dancing. Many trolls were sitting at the tables, but most were dancing. What they danced to was barely recognizable to me as music. It was a rumbling, pulsing sound, combined with a higher-pitched noise, possibly from an instrument like a flauto, though there was little in the way of melody. The sound hurt my ears, but in some strange way fit with the pulsing of the northern lights. Probably the queen had arranged that as well, I thought grimly.

The trolls' dancing wasn't very much like the dancing I knew from back in Njord, either. Pairing off, they held on to each other by the elbows and moved their feet in a crabbed, sideways motion.

Then I saw him and all my other thoughts fell away.

I had not seen his face since that night when I had dripped hot tallow on him. I no longer was aware of the troll music, and there was a strange prickly feeling all along my skin.

He was dancing with a troll lady, and he had a stiff but genuinely polite expression on his face. His eyes looked tired.

A voice at my side startled me. *"Kaunis puku,"* it said. Taking my eyes reluctantly from the man who had been a white bear, I turned to find a male troll with a leering smile on his ridged face. He wore a turquoise jacket. *"Mutta miksi el varikas?"* he continued. I was not sure, but I think the words meant he thought my dress lovely but wondered why it had no color.

I smiled politely and, not knowing what else to say, croaked out in my best effort at troll language that I would love to dance. He looked a little puzzled at this but then said, *"Et saa tanssi,"* and, taking my gloved hand, led me out onto the dance floor. My heart pounding, I tried to follow what I saw the others doing. It did not seem difficult, though I managed to step on the troll's feet several times. Luckily, he did not try to converse with me. It was not long before he led me off the dance floor and then left me. Relieved, I hoped he would pass along the word that the troll lady in the colorless dress had two left feet.

I found a spot by an ice pillar from where I could watch the dancers. That my moon dress was not brightly colored made blending into the background easier.

I saw the Troll Queen at once. She was seated on a raised dais, on a throne that looked to be made of nothing but diamonds, and she was gazing out over the festive tableau with a serene, proprietary air. I noticed that most often her eyes were on the one she called Myk. And so were mine.

He was a stranger to me. And yet he was not. Though his form was that of a man, I could still see the white bear in him. Or perhaps he was the man I had seen in the white bear. But the way he held his head, the movement of his shoulders, the level gaze of his eyes. All those were familiar. And I remembered the days spent in the room with the red couch, my fumbling attempts at his music, the stories he had listened to me tell. The loneliness in his eyes, and the kindness. And as I watched the man who had been a white bear make polite conversation with a stout troll lady in an orange dress (one I had hemmed only the day before), I realized suddenly that this man, this stranger, was dear to me, as dear as one of my own family. Perhaps dearer, I thought, with a great rush of inexplicably strong feeling. There was a strange expectant beating of my heart that I had never felt before.

But just at the very moment I understood what this white bear–man was to me, I saw him gaze up at the Troll Queen. A look of warmth, knowing and affectionate, passed between them, and my stomach lurched. I felt as if Simka had kicked me there, hard.

Was it possible? Did he . . . *love* the Troll Queen? Had I come all this way to rescue one from a captivity he actually desired? My thoughts were jumbled, my hands sweating inside my white gloves. The ring felt slippery on my thumb.

Suddenly I saw Tuki. He was at the white bear–man's side and was speaking to him earnestly. The Troll Queen had been distracted for the moment by a delegation of particularly elegant trolls wishing to pay their respects.

Tuki had the white bear–man's hand and was pulling him across the dance floor. Toward me.

I watched them approach with a mixture of fear and excitement. *It all has come down to this moment,* I thought. *Journey's end.*

He saw my dress first and something flickered in his eyes, some dim spark of recognition, and I remembered the white bear watching me through the doorway when I'd tried the dress on. He hesitated, pausing in his approach. Tuki looked eagerly between us. But when the white bear–man looked up at my face, the spark faded. That polite, kind look I had seen him wear most of the evening replaced it. I could barely hear past the pounding of my heart, but I think Tuki introduced me in troll language as "Rose, who is visiting from distant lands."

"Would you care to dance?" he asked politely in stiff troll words.

I nodded. He led me onto the dance floor.

"I hope you are having a pleasurable evening," he said, again in troll language. He was not looking at me but keeping his eyes politely averted. *Troll small talk*, I thought wildly. My mouth felt dry, my tongue leaden.

"Your gown ..." He hesitated, that dim spark returning to his eyes. "It is ... unusual." He dropped one of my elbows and rubbed his forehead, as if trying to dispel whatever was clouding his thoughts.

"I have something to show you," I said in a low voice, using my own language and making no attempt to sound like a troll.

He looked genuinely startled by that, even alarmed. His eyes searched my face.

"Your voice ... And ..." I think he had seen that I wore a mask.

Quickly I slipped one glove partway off and removed the ring from my thumb. I pressed it into his palm.

His feet kept moving as he gazed down at the ring.

The edges of his eyes creased, as though he was puzzled. Then he gave his head a little shake and handed the ring back to me.

"It is very nice. But I cannot..."

"It is yours," I said urgently.

He shook his head. "I do not think so. But thank you." He wanted to get away from me, I could feel it.

I once more pressed the ring into his hand. "Look more closely," I said.

"You are kind," he said, "but I must return to my queen."

He reached toward me, to return the ring, but I backed away, curtsied, and said, "It is a gift. Please keep it."

Moving blindly I made my way back to my pillar and leaned heavily against it. I watched the man who had been a white bear move away from me across the dance floor. He put his hand into his pocket, and I guessed he had put the ring there. Then I looked up at the queen's throne and saw her eyes on me. I felt a shiver of fear. Had she seen? Had my mask slipped? But then her gaze shifted to the one she called Myk. I was not prepared for the look I saw on the pale queen's face. It was an expression of pure love. *Love.* Not ownership, or cruel manipulation, but wholehearted, even tender, love. And though I could not see his eyes, I guessed that her expression was reflected in his.

So that was it. They genuinely cared for each other.

Suddenly I could not stay there another moment. I had to leave. I wanted to run but forced myself to walk out of the banquet hall. Tears were already beginning to soak into the stiff fabric of my mask. The moment I was out of sight I began to run. I found my parka on the coat-rack, and my boots, and, hastily putting them on, headed for the palace entrance.

I slid sideways out the front; the trolls there were busy sharing some kind of steaming beverage that was making them laugh loudly in their coarse voices, and they did not notice me. The cold knifed into me, and the mask, damp from my tears, began to freeze to my face. Quickly I ripped it off and shoved it into a pocket.

I ran around the side of the palace and made my way to the stables. The trolls there were also drinking and talking loudly as they watched over a full paddock of the visitors' reindeer. I was able to sneak into a back stall, where I found one of my favorite reindeer, a sleek white beauty I had dubbed Vaettur. Taking his halter, I led him from his stall and out one of the back entrances to the stables. I mounted him and cautiously guided him to the nearest gate. All the gates had been left open to accommodate the troll visitors. As soon as I was some distance from the palace, I gave Vaettur a kick and we were off.

Vaettur was strong and fast, and I clung to him like a drowning person. I had no thought, no plan, except to get away from the ice palace. What a fool I had been. Every inch of that endless journey, the days, weeks, months . . . It had all been for nothing. And the worst of it was that I knew then what I had lost.

Throughout the journey to find the white bear I had

told myself I was doing it to make right the wrong I had done. It was a matter of honor, of responsibility. But that had been only part of it. The truth was I loved him. I loved him as a white bear, and I loved him still as the man who had been a white bear. I was no better than the Troll Queen, only I had cloaked my feelings in virtuous words.

And I had lost him. For the second time.

The cold seared through me, but it did not matter. Nothing mattered.

My heart felt frozen inside my chest. It was too cold a night for a broken heart, I thought irrationally. Where would I go, what would I do? "Go home," I told myself. Keep riding until I was back with Neddy, and Father and Mother. Then I railed at myself for behaving like a spoiled child who hadn't gotten the prize she wanted at a party. And it was absurd. As strong and swift as he was, I could not ride Vaettur all the way across the frozen land of Niflheim, much less back to Njord. I would need the right clothing, the rest of my gear. But I was not thinking clearly.

Suddenly the reindeer shied and then reared back. Lost in myself, I had not been paying attention to where we were going. I looked then and saw that we were on the lip of a steep icy slope. Vaettur had not wanted to take on such a descent at the pace we were going, and I didn't blame him.

As I looked down into the frozen valley, my eye was caught by a scattering of shapes that lay opaque against the frozen background of white snow. The northern lights were still illuminating the sky, though not as bright as before, and they gave teasing glimpses of the shapes below.

Despite the jumbled state of my feelings, I was curious. What could those objects be? I wondered. There were scores of them lit up by the lights above bursting into even greater brilliance. I urged Vaettur forward. Cautiously he began to descend the slope.

We reached a point more than halfway down where it was too slick for the reindeer to get a footing; in fact, I saw that there was a band of glittering ice about twice my height that ran around the perimeter of the valley floor.

But that was not all I saw. Dismounting, I stared into the valley, my eyes transfixed. Was it possible? . . . Vaettur snuffled at my pockets, looking for a treat, but I did not even notice. I just stared in disbelief and horror.

White Bear

AT LAST THE DANCING was done. I was so tired, my cheeks stiff from smiling at all those faces I did not know. I could not wait to leave and go to my bed.

My queen was well pleased with the evening. And even with all she had to do, was ever thoughtful of my comfort. When she saw how tired I was, she sent me off to bed, with Tuki attending. She said she would look in on me before going to sleep herself but that I needn't wait up for her, as she had to look after her guests. Before I left her my queen asked me about the troll girl in the moon dress. I told her she did not dance well but was pleasant. I did not tell my queen of the girl's odd behavior, of her voice and the language she spoke, and of the ring she thrust on me. And that she seemed to be wearing some kind of mask. I don't know why I did not speak of those things, except that I thought it might displease my queen in some way and the girl might be punished. I do not think the girl meant any harm.

Before getting into my nightclothes, I took the ring out and gazed at it. Why did it look familiar and yet not familiar? It made no sense. I placed the ring on my finger. It fit. Perhaps I had been wrong and it was mine, from long ago. And yet why would a troll girl I did not know have it? Or was she a troll? Her voice, and the mask... But I was too tired to think any longer.

I took the ring off and placed it in a drawer. My queen would know the answer. I would ask her in the morning, without telling her where I had gotten it.

Tuki brought my slank as usual. Then he, too, asked me about the girl in the moon dress. I repeated what I had told my queen and thought I saw a look of disappointment cross his face. I believe he wanted to talk more, but I was too exhausted. I told him to leave. I did not even care that his eyes looked bright with unshed tears at the shortness of my tone. I was so tired.

My bed felt inviting and I fell swiftly into a deep sleep.

I dreamed of the girl in the moon dress. We were dancing and I could not take my eyes from her eyes. Purple, like fleur-de-lis... In truth, I had barely noticed the troll girl's eyes while I danced with her, but in the dream they were bright and dark and full of some kind of feeling I could not put a name to. As we danced I felt happy, happier than I had ever thought possible. It was a different kind of dancing, too, flowing, moving in wide circles, my hands at her waist. I did not want the dance to end.

Then I looked down at my chest, and I was no longer sporting the handsome jacket I had been wearing that evening but instead a soft white shirt. I noticed there was a stain on the front of it and I was embarrassed, thinking I had spilled on myself during the banquet. I thought I would make an excuse so that I could go and change my shirt, but when I looked up into the girl's face to tell her I must stop dancing, I saw an unspeakable sadness in those dark eyes.

And then I woke up. There were tears on my face.

Absently I brushed at the wetness with my hand, and suddenly, out of nowhere, I remembered the shirt I had been wearing when I first came to the ice palace. In a daze I rose and crossed to my chest of drawers. At the back of the bottom drawer was a white shirt. It had a silver brooch of a flauto at the neck, and as I shook the shirt out, I saw that it had a stain on the front.

In wonderment I placed my finger on the stain. It was hard. Like dried tallow. My thoughts heaved. Suddenly I saw the girl, the girl in the moon dress, only her face was different. She was leaning over me, in a small golden circle of light. Then I felt a pain, a burning on my skin. But that was all; I could remember no more. I let out a groan, pressing my face into the white shirt. It smelt of soap and candle wax.

There was a light knock at the door to my room.

"Yes?" I said, quickly stuffing the shirt back into the drawer.

My queen entered. "You are still awake?" she said, curious.

"I was just a little restless," I replied.

"Have you had a nightmare?" she asked.

"No," I said evenly, thinking of the happiness in the dream. No, it was not a nightmare.

"Some slank will help you rest," she said, making a move toward the door.

"No, thank you," I said. "I had it earlier. I am fine."

"Very well." She crossed to me then and looked into my eyes. I kept my thoughts concentrated on her, on her beauty, her goodness to me, my queen who in a day would be my wife.

We embraced. And then she left the room.

I reopened the chest of drawers. I took out the white shirt, crossed to my flauto case, opened it, and wrapped the instrument in the soft white fabric of the shirt. Then I closed the case and returned to my bed.

Rose

KENTTA MURHA. The freezing field, or killing field, for that is what I came to know the words to mean.

This was where they brought the softskins who had outlived their usefulness.

It was like some horrible outdoor sculpture garden. Stiffened bodies, naked, frozen in all different positions, scattered across the wide valley. It had not snowed in some time, at least not since the most recent arrivals, and in the blazing light from the sky, I could see several faces that were familiar to me. The young girl with the cough that hadn't gone away. The elderly man who had lived on my corridor, who shuffled off every morning to his job in the dishwashing room.

The trolls took them out there, stripped them of their protective clothing, and then left them to freeze to death. It was cruel and barbaric, and I was filled with a bottomless rage at those monsters, those trolls. I shuddered to think how many bodies lay stacked up under the layers of ice and snow.

Human beings, taken from their families, their villages, the lives they knew. Then filled with poison that erased that which made them human but kept their bodies useful. And when their bodies were no longer useful, they were cast off in this forsaken place, to die.

At least it would be a quick death, I told myself. But that fact did not take away my rage.

Suddenly I thought of him, of the man who had been a white bear. Would he someday end up here, at *kentta murha*, when he had outlived his usefulness to the Troll Queen?

And then, with a sudden and intense certainty, I knew that the man I had come to know inside the skin of a white bear was not a man who could ever truly care for a creature who was capable of such cruelty. If he felt affection for the Troll Queen it was born of poisoned *slank* and of ignorance. He did not know of *kentta murha*. He could not.

And just as suddenly, it did not matter whether the man cared for me or I for him. The only thing that mattered was giving him his life back, as well as helping all the softskins whose lives had been stolen by the trolls.

I mounted Vaettur again, and we made our way up the slope to head back to the ice palace. I snuck in a back stable entrance, gave Vaettur a bag of oats, and then returned to the servants' quarters. The door to my room was shut, along with all the other doors lining the hall. I pulled open the heavy door and entered. I took off my coat, first removing the troll mask from a pocket and straightening and reforming it as best I could. Then, still wearing the moon dress, I slipped under the pile of fur-skins. I lay there, trying to make plans, to figure out what I must do, but I was too exhausted even to think. My eyelids closed.

When I awoke the next morning the door was still shut. Through the murky translucent walls I could tell the sun had climbed up fairly high in the sky. The wedding was to take place when the sun was directly above. The morning troll with his cart of slank was late.

Suddenly I remembered the tail end of a conversation between two trolls I had overheard the day before. I had only understood the words *"no softskins"* and *"wedding,"* and had thought that it meant that the Troll Queen did not want softskins present at her wedding. I had assumed we'd still be working behind the scenes. But the truth was clear now. We were to be kept shut up in our quarters until after the wedding.

I got out of my bed. Before putting on my coat, I gazed down at the moon dress. Despite my having slept in it, it looked as fresh and unwrinkled as it had the night before. I straightened my hair, put on the pearly shoes, and attached the mask to my face.

Placing one shoulder against the door, I pushed. Slowly the door opened. I stuck my head out, looking both ways down the hallway. It was deserted. Moving cautiously I made my way toward the palace. As I traveled that familiar path through the connecting passageways, I did not come across a single softskin or troll.

In fact, I did not see a living soul the entire way between the servants' quarters and the banquet hall. The softskins were shut in their rooms, and the trolls, every single one of them, from servant to highborn, were attending their queen's wedding.

I was still a short distance from the banquet hall when I heard the faint sound of music; not troll music but the lovely, clear notes of a flauto as it was meant to be played. The white bear was performing. I wondered how long he had been playing and when the wedding was due to begin. I quickened my pace, the haunting sound of the flauto beckoning me forward. Then I recognized the melody as his favorite, "Estivale," the one I had tried to play back in the white bear's castle. For the first time I heard how truly beautiful it was.

I entered by a side entrance, and the few who noticed did not give me a second glance. They were too entranced by the music. The vast room was packed with trolls. And above I saw that lining the walls were several layers of balconies—which, because they were made of the same translucent ice as the walls, I had not noticed the night before. The balconies were full of trolls in brightly colored clothing. The light from the sun shone through the ice, and the refraction caused shimmers of rainbow colors to dance along the walls. It was not as spectacular as the northern lights of the night before but gentler, and perhaps even lovelier.

I made my way around the edge of the room, where trolls stood shoulder to shoulder. Movement was not easy, and many of them gazed at me with displeasure; luckily, I was small and could squeeze through the tight crowd. There was room only for standing in the rear and at the sides, but eventually I spotted rows of chairs in the front, nearest the dais and throne, in which the more important trolls were seated. Determined to get as close as possible, I took a deep breath and wiggled my way through until I came to a small bare patch of floor beside the chair of a large female troll who wore a wide-brimmed red hat covered with opulent trimmings. The hat shielded me from view, but I had an excellent vantage point from which to watch what was going on.

When the white bear finished playing his song, there was a short silence. The Troll Queen stood and gazed sternly out over her people. And then, with a great swelling noise, the trolls began to shout and stamp their feet. The floor beneath me shook. Had I not been familiar with troll language and ways after living among them for so long, I wouldn't have known they were showing approval. But they were, and the noise grew and grew. I could tell the Troll Queen was very pleased. A wide triumphant smile curved her red lips.

I couldn't see the white bear–man's face well, but what I could see was unreadable, his features still and resolute.

Troll Queen

My people gave Myk a great ovation when he finished playing his flauto. As I knew they would. He has won them over and shall be a well-loved king.

Taking our places for the wedding ceremony, we stood facing my people, Tuki at Myk's side and Urda beside me. I opened my mouth to begin the words of binding, when suddenly Myk stepped forward, turning to face me. He got down on one knee and gazed up at me. This was not at all the order of events. I had gone over these with him many times and wondered if he had gotten confused.

"I have a very great favor to ask of you, my queen," he said loudly.

"Of course. What is it?" I replied. I heard a very faint murmuring from those trolls sitting in the rows closest to the front.

"There is an old custom in the land I come from,"

Myk said. "Will you humor me and allow me to ask you a question, before we say the words of binding?"

His words puzzled me. This must be from some old memory of his homeland that had suddenly returned. I did not understand why this should be happening now. But I smiled at Myk. "You may ask me anything," I said.

"Thank you, my queen," he replied. "In the land I come from, the question is asked so that a man may know if his intended bride will be a good wife to him. If she will care for him and the home they will share."

I nodded.

"Will you wash a piece of clothing for me, my queen?"

Wash a piece of clothing? I stared at him. *What sort of strange, outlandish custom is this?* I thought. It was irksome that he should have had this returned memory, now of all times. Probably some softskin servant triggered it. It is settled then—I shall get rid of all the softskin servants as soon as possible. They are more trouble than they are worth.

"My queen? Will you grant my request?"

The murmuring grew louder. My people knew this was out of the ordinary. They were waiting for my response. Myk's eyes were on me, too.

"Yes, Myk. I will honor this tradition of your land, and after I have done it, then we will proceed." It was annoying, but the proposition was a simple one. With my arts I could wash anything clean.

"Then you agree to honor my tradition—I shall marry the one who washes a garment of my choosing."

All eyes were on us. Tuki let out a little squeaking sound. His pathetic eyes shone with excitement. It was then I felt the first glimmer of unease. I did not see how Myk should have memories of wedding traditions of his homeland when he drank the slank every day. But I could not back down, not with my people watching. It would make me look weak. And I could not back down because of the foolish rules my father had imposed on me.

"I agree, Myk." After all, it was a small request, insignificant, one easily done.

Myk got to his feet and crossed to his flauto case. From it he withdrew a white bundle of cloth and carried it to me.

Gesturing at Tuki I said, "Bring me water and soap."

Tuki nodded eagerly and disappeared in the direction of the kitchen.

As we waited Myk again kneeled in front of me, taking my hand and looking up at me. "You are patient and kind, my queen, to indulge me in this tradition of my homeland."

I was reassured by his words and by the warmth in his voice. And yet there was something about him, I noticed suddenly, something different.

Tuki returned and handed Myk a bucket that was filled with warm water. Myk brought it to me.

I shook out the white cloth and held it up. It was a shirt with a dull gray stain on the front. Where had Myk gotten this shirt? I wondered. Something was not right.

But there could be no trick, no deception. The slank had never failed.

I took the bucket of water from Tuki and a bar of white soap he also handed me. I did not want to kneel over the bucket—that would not do—so I ordered a table brought. I set the bucket on the table.

"In the country of your future king," I said to my people, speaking loudly and with dignity, "they have a ritual before binding, and it is to honor him that I cleanse the shirt."

I dipped the shirt in the water, rubbed the stain with the soap, working it in until the fabric was covered with suds. In truth, I had never washed cloth in my life, for that is servants' work, but I had seen it done. The stained part was hard against my fingers, which puzzled me. But I concentrated, felt the tingling of power in my fingertips. Then I rinsed the shirt. Holding it up so the stain faced me, I saw that instead of fading away, the stain was, if anything, larger and darker than before.

Something bubbled in my brain. This was not right. It cannot be.

Calling on my arts, I immersed the cloth again. The soap churned white in the water; the surface of the soapy liquid swirled and foamed. Iridescent bubbles fizzed up into the air. All eyes were on me as once again I lifted the shirt from the water.

The stain had blackened, hardened. I let out a cry of rage. This could not be happening. Was it some sorcery? One of the southern trolls seeking to undo me? But why? My eyes found Myk. He was not looking at me but at someone walking toward him, wearing a dress that resembled the moon. I had seen it before. . . . She stepped forward.

"May I try to wash the shirt?" she said.

Then I knew. She wore a mask, but it was her. The softskin girl. She had come for my Myk. It was impossible. Yet there she stood, her face hidden by the mask, but her eyes filled with the most provoking bravery. Did she not know I could destroy her with little more than a thought?

I should have done so, right then, but everyone was watching, and it would have looked like weakness to refuse. If I with my arts had failed to clean the shirt, then so would she. Myk must see her fail once again. There would be ample time to destroy her *after* she had been defeated.

I saw Tuki cross to the softskin girl. She said a few words to him, and nodding eagerly, he darted away. Urda was speaking to me, buzzing in my ear, asking who the troll girl in the moon dress was. I told Urda she was a fool—this was no troll. Did she not recognize the softskin girl whom she had waited on in the castle? Urda recoiled, muttering under her breath.

I stared at Myk. His face was unreadable. Had he planned this? With Tuki? I could not believe it of him. Myk was mine, body and soul.

Tuki returned with several pieces of kindling, a large stone tile, a bar of white soap like the one I had used, and an iron pot with water in it. He gave these to the softskin girl. Urda ran to Tuki, taking him by the arm and hissing at him. He merely smiled at her, shaking her hand off gently, then gestured toward the softskin girl.

My people had been murmuring during Tuki's absence, but all grew quiet as we watched the softskin girl stack the kindling on the stone tile, light it with a striker Tuki had also brought her, and set the pot of water atop it.

Rose

I MADE THE SHIRT. I spun the thread from sheep's wool and white-bear fur. I wove the thread on the loom. I stitched the cloth into a shirt that fit the man who had been a white bear.

And I knew the way to remove tallow from fabric.

But the Troll Queen, with all her arts, had been unable to remove the stain. Was there really any hope that I should succeed?

I held the cloth in my hand, remembered well the feel of it in my hands as I folded it every morning and laid it on his side of the bed in the castle. And also the feel of it, wet and soapy, the many times I had washed it.

I dipped the shirt into the hot water, pulled it back out, then worked soap around and onto the stained, stiff area. When the water was boiling, I carefully lowered the shirt into it, then stirred the bubbling brew into a froth with a wooden stick Tuki had given me. I suddenly remembered the rhyme Estelle had taught me.

> *The old woman must stand at the tub, tub, tub,*
> *The dirty clothes to rub, rub, rub;*
> *But when they are clean, and fit to be seen,*
> *She'll dress like a lady and dance on the green.*

After a few minutes had gone by, I used the stick to lift the shirt out of the water. It gleamed white, steaming in the cool air of the ice palace. There was no stain.

A murmur swelled from the trolls standing closest to the front, then it grew even louder, working its way around the enormous room and up into the balconies.

Before anyone could move, Tuki bounded across to me and said in troll language, with a loud voice, "It is Rose—Rose will marry the prince from the green lands!"

I looked up at the Troll Queen then, and the ferocious and baffled rage on her face was a terrible thing to see. Instinctively I dropped the steaming shirt on the ice floor and reached for Tuki, thinking somehow to protect him, but too late, too late.

Troll Queen

I DID NOT THINK. I wanted heat, destruction. First Tuki. Then her.

I called on the sun. White hot, searing, blistering. Sent through my fingers. Straight, like a shaft of blazing flame, into his body, Tuki's body, obliterating him in an instant.

I heard Urda scream. My eyes were blinded by the heat and rage. I would kill Urda. I would kill them all. I rubbed my eyes.

Then I heard a deafening, rending explosion of sound. Beneath; below my feet. My eyes cleared and I looked down. Saw a jagged crack in the floor of my palace; followed it with my eyes to the place it began, the place I had sent the heat of the sun into Tuki.

My beautiful ice palace, splitting.

Then the ice crack opened up, yawning wide into nothingness. Immense, thundering sound filled my ears.

My palace, my glorious ice palace... Splintering, breaking apart...

Myk!

Rose

It WAS LIKE THE END of the world. The noise was massive, crashing, ear pounding, as the ice palace broke apart.

I saw it in only an instant. A scorching burst of heat, then the enormous crack in a moment spiderwebbing outward where Tuki had once stood. And the Troll Queen herself, teetering on the edge, only to be swallowed by the monstrous, gaping fissure.

I looked up. Saw the sheer windows shattering, turrets bending, toppling. I knew I was going to die.

As knifelike slivers of ice rained down, I ran. A large chunk of something slammed into my shoulder. I staggered, falling to my knees. More ice fell on me. I crouched, trying to protect my head with my hands, but ice continued to strike me, causing staccato bursts of pain. My head swam. Where was the man who had been a white bear? I had to find him—but I could not move.

Screams echoed all around. Balconies teeming with trolls fell through the air. Death was everywhere.

A strong arm grabbed my waist and dragged me out from under the ice. I was pulled along until I found myself in a tiny cavelike space. And the man who had been a white bear held me tightly. He was looking into my eyes. "Rose," he said urgently.

"Yes," I said groggily. Relief showed in his face.

We were lodged under a great slab of ice, part of the ceiling that had fallen at an angle, knifing sideways into the floor like an immense white sword. It was so thick and strong that it protected us as the ice palace crashed down around us.

I knew as I huddled there, the arms of the man who had been a white bear tight around me, that I would never forget the sound. It went on a long, long time— the cracking, grinding, slamming of fallen ice, and the screams of the dying.

I must have lost consciousness, for I suddenly became aware of his voice again saying, "Rose," in that same urgent tone, as if he was afraid I would not answer.

"Yes?" I said weakly.

"It's over, I think," he said.

We were crammed into a tiny space, only slightly bigger than our two bodies. And everything was silent except for an occasional cracking sound. The entire wreckage of the ice palace lay on top of us. I clutched at his purple waistcoat.

Then I remembered my mother's words as she'd told me the prophecy of the *skjebne-soke*. "Any north child I had would die—crushed by an avalanche of snow and ice."

Neddy

THE SHIP CALLED *Rose* was a fine one, the crew excellent. Father and I were kept busy learning all aspects of navigating the high seas. And Soren bustled about, consulting sea charts, an astrolabe, and cross-staff, and other familiar instruments of navigation. But he was most excited about a brand-new compass he'd gotten for the journey. It was a splendid instrument using an iron needle suspended in a small box, with a wind rose beneath the needle to indicate direction. He was as happy as I'd ever seen him, and I hoped Sara was prepared for a husband with an advanced case of wanderlust. (Surely Mother would have found out if he were a north-born!)

We had good luck with the weather, and the winds were favorable. It was early spring and we had more hours of daylight, even though we were heading north. And yet despite all the good omens, I was restless and uneasy.

On the seventh night of our voyage, I felt Rose again, beside me. I was by myself, on deck, gazing out at the sea, and again she laid her hand on my arm. All I could see around her was white. Immense and frozen, the whiteness seemed to be pressing down on her. She looked terrified.

I prayed that we would reach her in time.

Rose

SOMEHOW HE DUG us out. I don't know how. I helped as much as I could, but it was his strength and his will that saved us. I wondered if he still had a little of the power of a white bear in his body.

He had had a knife in his pocket and, when the ice palace had collapsed, had grabbed up his flauto. We used both to tunnel out. (The flauto was badly damaged, but he did not seem to care.) The ice slab we had sheltered under had fallen near the doorway from the banquet hall to the kitchen, and once we had dug our way to the kitchen, we found a clear passage. Then came more digging, upward, toward a faint light. Finally we broke through the ice above us and climbed up onto the roof of the kitchen.

Around us was a scene of utter devastation. The glittering, magnificent ice palace had collapsed in on itself and onto many of the buildings adjoining it. We were surrounded by an immense jagged pile of icy rubble. As I peered outward I saw that some outlying buildings, mostly servants' quarters, had escaped with only slight damage. And the stables, being the farthest from the palace, hadn't been affected at all.

We could not stop to gaze long, for neither of us wore any outer clothing and the freezing wind chilled us to the bone. I grabbed his hand and ran toward the building where my quarters had been. We entered without difficulty and I led the way to my room, where I retrieved my coat, boots, and other belongings. I gave him several fur-skins to wrap himself with. He looked around silently at the small place where I had lived for the past few months.

After leaving my room, we found a storage area with extra fur-skins and coats. He picked out a coat of thick white fur. As he bundled into it, he gave me a lopsided smile. And I was struck by the fact that the man before me, with his gold hair and sad eyes, was still a white bear to me. I knew of nothing else to call him. He could not be "Myk," for that had been the pale queen's name for him. White bear was mine, and so in my head, anyway, I continued to call him white bear. We dug around and eventually found mittens, boots, and other necessary items.

Then we set out to search for survivors. Gazing at the wreckage, I knew it was impossible that Tuki was alive. And yet I could not accept that. Tears freezing on my face, I began digging blindly into the icy ruins, but the white bear gently pulled me back.

"It's no use," he said.

And I knew he was right.

We circled the wreckage and looked for signs of life. We did not find a single living troll. If any had survived the destruction, they had long since fled.

We did find some forty or fifty humans in the outlying servants' quarters. They were all in their small rooms, passively waiting for their morning slank. Several had been injured by the collapsing palace. I'm not sure if either the white bear or I spoke it out loud; it just became a given that, somehow, we would take them with us, all of them, out of Niflheim.

The humans were, for the most part, dazed and unresponsive, but they were as docile as always and followed our pantomimed instructions without question or protest. First we made sure they were all outfitted with warm clothing, then we led them to the stables.

We rounded up eight sleighs, hitching five reindeer to each. Vaettur was in my sleigh's team. We set free those reindeer that we did not need, and they immediately galloped off. We stocked the sleighs with as much in the way of provisions as we were able to salvage. The kitchen had been completely destroyed, but we did find a cache of undoctored slank that we took with us. And we set out before the sun went down that night.

The white bear and I each commanded a sleigh, and we selected several of the most alert of the surviving humans to drive the remaining sleighs, telling them to follow our lead. The reindeer did the rest.

———

More than twenty-five of the humans perished on the journey out of Niflheim. Some succumbed to the cold, a few to their injuries, but most died because of the slank—or, I should say, of *withdrawal* from the slank doctored with *rauha*. Those who had been at the palace for years and had been fed a daily diet of it were not able to adjust to life without slank. The withdrawal was a terrible thing, causing a violent trembling of the entire body, vomiting, and eventually an abrupt halt of breathing. We left the dead in shallow, unmarked graves, and even that cost us valuable time and energy. Our only hope to survive was to keep moving.

By the time we reached the ice bridge, we were down to three sleighs. I had been dreading the bridge, thinking pessimistically that it mattered little if we survived getting there because we would be unlikely to be able to cross the cursed thing. But it turned out I needn't have worried. The reindeer navigated it with ease (I still don't know how), though there was a heart-stopping moment when one of the sleighs swayed dangerously close to the edge.

It was an enormous relief to be out of Niflheim, away from that unceasing wind. The sun shone in an icy-blue cloudless sky. The survivors of troll servitude were coming out of their stupor with a dazed sense of wonder; they had the blurry, blank-eyed look of newborn calves. Most had little or no memory of their life in the ice palace and were completely bewildered as to why they were in sleighs traveling through a frozen land.

At night we would upend the sleighs and huddle under them, kindling a small fire for warmth. Because we drove separate sleighs, the white bear and I were never together during the journey. Except once.

One night, after all the people in my sleigh were asleep, I crawled over to the white bear's sleigh. I found him awake, tending the fire.

"What is your name?" I asked abruptly. It didn't seem right to go on calling him white bear.

"I do not know," he replied with a small twisted smile that did not reach his eyes.

I nodded, not certain what to say. I looked sideways at him, then away. His face was pale and haggard, but it was a good face, a kind face, and I realized I knew nothing about what lay beneath the strained smile.

He had saved my life back in the ice palace. I knew I should thank him, but I couldn't speak. I was overwhelmed by the thought that this man before me—this stranger, really—had no name, no home, no life to return to. He'd told me the last time he had been a person was when he was a boy. He was going to need a world of time to discover his place in the world, I thought. I could not assume, should not assume, that that place would be with me. But I would be lost if it was not.

White Bear

SHE LOOKED STRICKEN, almost frightened. Of me? Did she see me as a burden, a great weight on her? I wanted to ask, to say something reassuring, but words were still difficult to find; they formed so slowly in my head.

She had journeyed all this way to find me. Surely...

But she held herself away. And she stared into the glowing embers of the fire, not at me.

Perhaps I would need to find my own way. Perhaps I should. I remembered so little of who I was. Only a boy, unformed.

But I was eager, hungry to live a normal life. To walk on two legs, to play the flauto, to eat with a spoon. Crack an egg with my fingers and cook it in a pan, an omelette with fresh herbs, brown at the edges... Drink a mug of good ale. I was free, after a very, very long time.

And to do these things with her, with Rose.

But, I told myself, I must be prepared to do them alone.

I turned to speak to her, but she was gone, returned to her sleigh.

BOOK FIVE

East

*They fled, as fast as they could, from the palace
that lay east of the sun and west of the moon. . . .*

Rose

ONCE WE WERE OUT of Niflheim, I thought everything would be all right. But I was wrong.

There was no Malmo to guide us. And spring had come. Which didn't mean green grass and flowers and birdcall, as it did in Njord. It meant meltwater and thin ice and the surface under our sleighs breaking apart.

That didn't happen right away, though, and I was able to lead us back to the frozen sea Malmo and I had crossed. At the edge of the sea was the ice forest in all its deadly beauty, the ice forest where I had faced the other white bear. The cracks in the surface of the ice I had seen before were larger and wider, and the groaning, creaking sounds were louder and more frequent. The sleighs were too heavy and we had to abandon them. The reindeer were eager to go their own way when we set them loose but three, including Vaettur, stayed with us.

As we made our way on foot through the maze of ice towers, fissures would narrow and widen unexpectedly, inches from our feet. It became a nightmarish dance as we darted and swerved and leaped to avoid the freezing water below. No one fell in, but by the time we got through the ice forest, we were all exhausted and wrung out. We encountered no white bears.

Crossing the flat expanse of frozen sea, I tried to remember what Malmo had taught me about melting—that you should pay attention to the puddles on the surface of the ice. Light blue water meant the underlying ice was thick enough to walk on; dark blue meant it was too thin. There were many dark blue pools of water.

But the man who had been a white bear knew how to live in a frozen world, in all its seasons, and he helped us to survive. He showed us how to walk like a white bear—legs spread out wide, sliding our feet quickly, never stopping.

When we reached the other side of the sea, we again came upon ice that was breaking apart. But the white bear led us across the ice floes and we made it safely to shore.

We had been traveling on land for a few days when an ice fog settled around us. At first it was beautiful. The sun was shining, and the sunlight reflected by the ice crystals created a shimmering golden curtain that enfolded us in its brilliance. It reminded me of the golden dress I had made in the castle in the mountain. But then the sun disappeared under clouds, and the golden curtain faded into a dense white fog. We could not see an inch in front of our faces.

We huddled together, thinking to wait it out, but the time stretched on and some grew restless. So we set out, moving slowly, feeling our way forward. This went on for what seemed days, until I thought I would go mad.

The fog finally lifted, but the sky was still overcast. I had no idea what direction we were heading. One of the women we had taken out of Niflheim slipped and fell, and she did not get up. We did all we could for her, but by the next morning she was dead. We slid her corpse into an ice crevasse and watched silently as it disappeared from sight. Then we resumed our journey, though there was still no sun to guide us. I began to picture us wandering endlessly through a frozen landscape, dying off one by one. The white bear came up beside me.

"We are lost," he said matter-of-factly.

"Yes," I replied.

"I wish I still had the senses of a white bear," he said. "Then I could lead us."

I nodded dully. Suddenly I remembered Thor's *leidarstein*. I fumbled in my pack and found the dull gray stone. Scooping up some meltwater in a cup, I rubbed one end of a needle with the *leidarstein* and floated it in the water. Lazily the needle swung back and forth, finally stopping.

"South," I said, pointing. The white bear nodded, relief in his eyes.

We had been heading due west, so we changed course. Knowing the direction helped, but I had no idea how far off course we had gotten. The slank was long gone and we were all starved and exhausted. There were several among us who were near death, and I didn't know how much longer any of us could keep going.

But we kept struggling on, and then one afternoon, as we crested an icy peak, I looked down and there was the impossible, unforgettable sight of Tatke Fjord. And anchored at the end of it was a ship.

Neddy

I SHALL NEVER FORGET as long as I live the sight of those huddled figures silhouetted against the brilliant blue sky. One of the sailors spotted them at the top of an icy cliff and called out to us belowdecks. We had just dropped anchor not an hour earlier and were organizing an expedition to go overland in search of Rose.

And there she was.

A party of us went ahead to meet her group as they descended. There looked to be about twenty, as well as three white reindeer, and even at a distance I could see that most of the people were barely able to set one foot in front of the other.

When I got to her I took Rose in my arms and did not want to let go. But then Father came up to us and I finally unloosed my grasp. Tears in his eyes, Father enfolded Rose, saying her name over and over.

White Bear

WHEN ROSE introduced me to her father and brother, she stumbled over the words, for she had no name to use. And I did not remind her that I had already met them before, under very different circumstances.

The ship was a fine one, and I saw how happy Rose's father and brother were to be reunited with her. I did not want to remember that it was I who had taken her away from them.

But it felt good to be warm again; I can't remember the last time I had been truly warm. And the food—good human food that I ate with human fingers and lips and teeth.

I should have been relieved that the journey was done, but I was not. For I did not know what was to become of me.

I have nothing to offer her. I do not even have a name.

Neddy

THE STORY THAT ROSE told was extraordinary. If I had not known Rose and known that she does not lie, I simply would not have believed her. Trolls, "softskins," shattering ice palaces, and something called *kentta murha*. Truly the stuff of nightmares.

The man who used to be a white bear was quiet and pale, and though clearly he was happy to be freed of his long imprisonment, there was still a lost look about him, as if he was not sure where he fit. He and Rose were awkward with each other, though I could tell there was much feeling between them.

On our way south we stopped at the village of Neyak. Malmo and a delegation of her people were waiting for us on the shore. It had been Malmo who had told us where to seek Rose.

We had found Malmo—or rather she had found us— as we were making our way north along the coast of

Gronland. She and several of her people came out in small two-person boats and gestured at us until we understood that we were to follow them. When we had dropped anchor and gone ashore, Malmo went directly up to Father and told him where to look for Rose.

I had no idea how Malmo knew we had come in search of Rose, or how she knew where to find her, but it did not occur to me to doubt her. She gave us "maps," carved out of walrus tusks, of the coastline. (Father later remarked that they were extraordinarily accurate, some of the best mapping work he had ever seen.) Malmo also indicated we should turn inland at something called Tatke Fjord. Which is where we found Rose.

Rose

AFTER ARRIVING IN NEYAK and being greeted by Malmo, I went to look for Thor. I found him working on his ship. He was assisted by two friendly young Inuit men, to whom he had taught all his favorite drinking songs.

An older handsome Inuit woman brought a substantial meal at midday, which they shared with me, and I thought I detected a shy sort of understanding between Thor and the woman.

He told me quite frankly that after I had left, he drank up every drop of ale remaining on the broken-down *knorr,* but that he hadn't had anything stronger than reindeer milk since. Initially he got quite sick, he said, his body not being used to an ale-free diet, but the people who had become his friends—especially the handsome woman, whose name was Rekko—had taken him in and seen him through the sickness.

"I've gotten used to it here," he said gruffly. "Think I'll stick around. And once I get the *knorr* fixed up, I might even start a small trading business, between Gronland and Iseland. Should keep me out of trouble. For a while anyway," he added with a grin.

I told Thor about Gest, that he had survived the storm (it was information from Gest that had led Neddy and Father to Gronland), and Thor was amazed.

"By Odin, I'd never have thought it possible! Well, that'll be my first voyage, then. Find the old scoundrel and see if he fancies going into business together."

I smiled.

I brought the white bear to meet Thor, and for some reason they took to each other right away. Maybe because both men had been lost for so long, Thor understood him better than any of us. The white bear even pitched in to help fix Thor's ship. He had never done work of that kind before, but he was strong and a quick learner, and it was clear he was glad of something to do.

It was an odd time, our short stay in Neyak. Father, Neddy, Soren, and I were preoccupied with figuring out what to do about the people we had taken away from Niflheim. There were seventeen survivors, and they were from all over the world. The two Njorden were the simplest to sort out, because they could tell us exactly where they had lived. And the same was true of the three from Fransk. But the others were more complicated. Malmo helped with the different languages, and the maps Father had with him were useful as well, but there were two whom we simply could not figure out. One was the young woman who had been on the sleigh with me when I had first gone to the ice palace, and the other was an older woman with flame-colored hair. These two, we decided, would simply come home with us (and they both were quite pleased with the arrangement), while we would make every effort to return the rest to their original homes.

Soren suggested that once we got to Suroy, the first big port in our southward journey, it wouldn't be too difficult to find each a passage to his or her home. And he was willing to pay all expenses. I saw then just how immensely generous Soren was, and I understood how lucky our family had been to meet up with him.

I did not know how those returning home would explain their disappearance. Who would believe the true story? Even the crew of Soren's ship—those who had seen us emerge from Tatke Fjord, a motley group in animal-skin coats speaking a wide array of languages and accompanied by some rather extraordinary reindeer—even they had difficulty believing our tale

At least, I thought, those seventeen people would most likely have homes of some kind to return to. And unlike the white bear, they knew their names.

White Bear

I HAD MADE UP my mind. I would go away.

In Suroy we were able to find passage for all but four of the people who had been enslaved. Three were from Fransk, and the fourth from a small inland country that had no coastal port. The man called Soren had been exceedingly generous. He reminded me of a good and gentle shepherd leading a herd of stray lambs back to their folds. The three from Fransk he decided to take home himself in the ship called *Rose,* traveling directly to La Rochelle before returning to Njord. And the one who lived inland, Soren supplied with provisions and enough gold pieces to make a good start toward his destination. I was sure he would do the same for me, but I could not ask without giving away my plans. And I did not want anyone to know I meant to go. Especially Rose.

I knew that if I was to look into those purple eyes, I would not be able to leave her.

In my days of wandering the world as a white bear, I observed much about the ways of men and women—and I knew that for me to start a life on unequal footing with Rose was to court disaster.

I must at least know my name.

Fransk was where I would begin my search. The one thing I knew about myself was that I had been a prince. The pale queen had told me one day when I said to her that I felt inadequate to rule the land of Huldre. "But you have royal blood," she said. "You were a prince in the green lands."

A prince in Fransk. More than a hundred years ago.

But I thought I'd be able to find someone in Fransk who knew of a long-ago king with a son who had "died" prematurely. I had been having more frequent flashes of memory the farther south we traveled, and I thought it was even possible that I might recognize the place where I had grown up.

I had no intention of trying to reclaim a royal title. I would have been thought a raving lunatic if I even attempted to convince anyone I was Prince So-and-So of the previous century, not to mention being ushered off to the nearest madhouse. Fortunately, my brush with potential kingship in Huldre had left me thoroughly disinterested in royalty of any kind. No, whatever form my life took, I wanted it to be a simple one.

I had decided to go to the castle in the mountain, though it seemed unlikely the castle would still be there. It was possible the Troll Queen had not taken me too far from where I had originally lived. Whether that was true or not, I thought it a good place to start.

My plan was to slip off the ship after it docked in La Rochelle. I would depart well before dawn and make a good start before anyone was awake. I wanted to leave a note for Rose, but when it came time I found myself unable to. What could I say? "Dear Rose, I go to find my name. Hope to return in a year or two. Yours truly, the man who was once a white bear."

No, I decided, it was better just to go. After all, she might be relieved.

I did not sleep well that night and thus had no problem rising before dawn. I gathered the few belongings I had decided to take with me—including my flauto—made my way through the silent ship, and descended the gangplank.

Rose

I AWOKE AT DAWN, which in itself wasn't unusual. What was unusual was the way I sat bolt upright feeling that I'd been smacked across the face.

I jumped out of bed and dressed with an urgency I didn't understand. I left my room quietly and made my way down the hall. Suddenly I stopped, not sure exactly where I was going. I stood like a hunting dog sniffing the air, trying to figure out the direction in which its quarry lay.

Then I knew. I made my way to the room where the white bear had been sleeping. Silently I opened the door. In the dim light from the porthole I could make out the slumbering forms of two sailors. But the third bunk, the white bear's bed, was empty.

In some odd way I had been expecting it. But I was flooded with despair anyway. He'd said nothing to me— no good-bye, nothing.

Then I saw something shiny lying on top of the neatly folded blankets of the empty bed.

I crossed the room. It was a silver ring, the one with VALOIS inscribed on it, the one I had worn on my thumb throughout the long journey. He had left it for me.

I grabbed it up, stuck it on my thumb, and left the room.

I returned to my quarters, got my cloak, then left the ship.

There were many people already on the docks, but none of them had seen a man with golden hair wearing a coat of white fur. How long ago had he left? Could it have been as long ago as the night before, right after the last person had retired for the evening? I felt suddenly cold and wrapped the cloak tighter around my shoulders.

Was I going to have to seek him all over again? I felt a rush of anger. Why would he disappear like that, in the middle of the night with no explanation or even a good-bye?

I stopped midstride. *Perhaps I should let him go,* I thought.

Then I remembered his face those past few weeks, strained and pale, and my anger softened. Maybe this was what he needed to do.

White Bear

AS I WAS WALKING along the road leading out of La Rochelle, an old farmer and his son came along in a wagon and offered me a ride. It turned out they were traveling in the same direction, and I was very grateful for their kindness.

The farther south we traveled, the more familiar the landscape began to appear. It was extraordinary how fast memories were returning. I was glad to be riding in the back of the wagon, for the farmer and his son would certainly have thought me quite mad if they had heard all my exclamations each time I was assailed by a new memory. Most were memories from when I had been a white bear, those endless years I had wandered the world looking for the one who would set me free. And some were memories from when I had been a child. What I had trouble remembering was how I had gone from boy to bear.

I asked the farmer about the history of the land, about who was king a hundred or so years before, but he and his son had no knowledge or interest in the past. All that concerned them was their lives at the time—how high the taxes were, what a wet spring they'd had, and so forth. I would need to go to a larger city to find scholars who made a study of the past. But for the time being I would continue south.

When their way turned east, the farmer and his son left me near a small village called Koln. Again I was fortunate enough to get a ride from a traveling merchant, who set me down at a crossroads not very far from the edge of the large forest that was known in the region to be haunted. Wouldn't the locals be amazed, I thought, to learn the true story behind the odd occurrences in that forest. Because the trolls working the farm had wanted their activities to be undisturbed by softskins, they had created the strange noises and lights that were seen coming from the forest. As for those who had been so bold as to stray too far into the forest, the trolls had killed them at once.

By the time I reached the mountain where the castle had been, I remembered everything.

The red ball. The beautiful pale girl with the voice like rocks. And my surprise at seeing her again when she had returned. The sound of bells and finding myself wrapped in furs, flying high in the sky. Arriving at the immense ice palace. Her father in a deadly rage. Watching stupefied as he berated her, setting out the conditions that took my life from me.

The terrifying moment when my body was transformed. The years of hopeless searching.

Rose.

Down to the last night and the last day. Finding the white nightshirt with the stain.

That night I did not remember, as I do now, about the last of her father's conditions:

Further, no request that he shall make of one of Huldre shall be denied. Except the request to be released from his enchantment. To be released from the enchantment, the white bear that was a softskin must abide by and satisfy a set of inviolable conditions. These conditions shall be made known to him in their entirety.

When I asked the pale queen to wash the shirt, I did not think of this last condition. Or perhaps there was some dim, buried memory spurring me on. I thought only of Rose. Of the story she had told of the careless husband and the tangled washing line—and of how we both had laughed. Of how she had made the nightshirt for me because I was cold. And of how she had washed it for me. I knew she would be able to wash it clean. And I knew the Troll Queen couldn't.

How odd to think that that stain of tallow had been both my undoing and my deliverance.

Rose

STANDING THERE ON the dock wondering if I should follow or let him go, I had been flooded with memories. A young sailor with a straggly mustache carrying an enormous spool of rope nearly knocked me over, but I hardly noticed as he recovered himself and continued on, hurling some colorful curses back at me.

The first journey on the white bear's back; "Are you afraid?"; the apologetic way he towered over me; the sigh through the doorway when he saw me in the moon dress; the way he covered his ears the first time I played the flauto; the relief in his eyes when I returned from visiting my family; his hand curled on the sheets; the polite, bored look on his face when we danced; and—I could barely let my mind think of it—the dazed look of wonder on his face when I held up the steaming, stain-free white shirt.

I would find him. I had to. And when I did, I would tell him all that was in my heart. We were no longer under an enchantment; there was nothing to keep us from speaking except our own ridiculous pride. If, after I had said what I had to say, he still wished to travel alone, then so be it. I would not shatter, nor would he.

I knew where he was going and I would follow.

White Bear

I STOOD IN FRONT OF the mountain for a long time. Surely, the castle inside was gone or, if not, was inaccessible to someone with no arts. The sheer rock face showed no sign of an entrance, but then it never had. I thought back to the many times I had gone in and out of that mountain. All I had had to do then was just picture the door opening and it did. Perhaps if I tried that now...

There was a grinding sound and to my amazement the rock face opened, revealing the interior of the castle. I rubbed my eyes, unbelieving. It was very dark inside, but the sun of the afternoon shed some faint light into the front hallway.

I entered.

There were no lamps burning, and therefore it was pitch-black. I kindled a flame in a lamp in the front hall with a striker I had with me. Carrying the lamp I began to explore the castle. It was very cool—the fires had not been lit for a long time—and there was an uncanny stillness about the place. I periodically lit lamps along the way, leaving a trail of light behind me.

Entering the music room, I gazed around at the familiar and well-loved instruments. That had been one of the worst parts of being imprisoned in a white bear's body; with no fingers or lips, I had been unable to play music.

I crossed to the flauto, the one I had preferred over all others, and picked it up. It had always been so familiar to me. I wondered if the Troll Queen had taken it from my previous life, or just re-created it for me. But why? Had she wanted to make me feel at home, or to torture me?

I put the instrument to my lips.

Rose

VAETTUR MADE GOOD TIME. I did not think I could be very far behind the white bear—that is, if I was right about his destination.

I must have caused quite a few people to stare as I rode Vaettur through the countryside of Fransk. I could tell that the reindeer was not comfortable in the warmer climate, but the early spring weather was still cool enough that he was not miserable.

The forest *"hanté"* was even denser than I remembered, and the empty farm just as eerie, but soon we had arrived at the base of the mountain. I found the open door right away and knew then that I had guessed correctly. I peered in the entrance, surprised to see that the castle was still there and that the white bear had managed to enter.

Vaettur followed me into the cool entrance hall but stayed there to munch on some oats I had brought for him in a small bag.

I followed the trail of lamps through the dim, echoing hallways, feeling surrounded by ghosts, whispering, sighing in my ears. I thought of Tuki; the pain of his loss was still a fresh wound. Seeing the place where we had first met and played our silly language game was like a blade twisting into me.

The lamps led me to the music room, but when I looked inside, it was empty. Then I heard it—the sound of a flauto. The music was far away, and I turned to follow it. As I made my way back through the hallways, listening closely, I recognized the song as the one he had been playing back in the ice palace when I had hurried toward the banquet hall. And the one I had long ago tried so pathetically to play. "Estivale."

As I moved closer I realized the music was coming from the room with the red couch. I approached the doorway, almost afraid to enter.

But I did.

And there he was, sitting on the red couch, playing his flauto. There was a large book of music open on the couch beside him.

He saw me and stopped playing. Our eyes met and he stood.

I crossed the room to him. "I love you," I said in a rush, afraid I would change my mind.

"Charles," he replied.

I stared at him.

"My name," he said with a smile that lit his face. Setting down his flauto, he leaned over and picked up the book beside him on the couch. Opening it to one of the blank pages at the beginning, he pointed to some words written in a flowing, cursive hand:

Charles Pierre Philippe, Dauphin

"I wrote this," he said. "My name. I am Charles Pierre Philippe." He set down the book.

And then he took both my hands tightly in his.

Father

MY DAUGHTER NYAMH... my daughter Rose married
Charles in a small ceremony in the front parlor of our
house in Trondheim. Her sister Sara's wedding to Harald
Soren had taken place several weeks before and was a
much grander affair. But Rose and Charles both insisted
on a simple celebration, and the joy in Rose's face shone
no less than Sara's; in fact, it was that much brighter for
being so hard won.

When Charles slipped the silver ring on Rose's thumb,
I thought he had gotten confused—or that it was a custom
peculiar to Fransk—but Rose seemed well pleased with
her thumb-ring, and anyway, my attentions were diverted
by the tears streaming down Eugenia's face. She had forgotten her handkerchief—or rather, I learned later, she
had deliberately not carried one because of some superstition that if the mother of the bride brings a handkerchief
to her daughter's wedding, a horrible tragedy will occur
within the first year of the marriage. Or some such nonsense. So I had to lend her mine.

Neddy

CHARLES PIERRE PHILIPPE was the fifth child of Charles VI, king of Fransk. My friend Havamal, the custodian of Master Eckstrom's library of books, helped me track down information about Charles's origins. It turned out that *Valois,* the word inscribed on the ring he gave Rose when they married, was the title of the line of royalty from which he was descended. Charles's younger brother was the dauphin whom the maid Jeanne d'Arc helped to put on the throne. But that is another tale.

All it says in the written history was that Charles, beloved son of Charles VI and Isabeau, was born around the time of a peace parley of Amiens and died at age nine. From what we have learned of his parents—his father was hopelessly mad and his mother greedy and traitorous—it is possible he was better off as a white bear. I do not know whether he would agree with that or not.

At any rate, Rose and Charles built a small home for

themselves in Fransk, not very far from that castle in the mountain. In fact, they took several wagonfuls of furnishings and other assorted items—mostly musical instruments and weaving paraphernalia, as far as I could make out—from the castle, and then they closed the entrance behind them for good. The spot on which they chose to build their house was close by Rose's friend Sofi and her young daughter, Estelle. At first we were all disappointed that they did not make their home in Njord, but the port of La Rochelle was not too distant, and we managed to visit back and forth at least once a year.

Charles dedicated himself to music and, in fact, invented a new design for flautos in which the mouthpiece cap contained a sponge to absorb the moisture from the player's breath. It was quite a success, and Charles became both a sought-after musician and an inventor. However, he never cared much for traveling, preferring to stay at home with his wife and children. They had four— one for each of the cardinal points of the compass, Mother said, although Rose vehemently denied it. They named their firstborn Tuki.

Rose could not give up her wandering ways entirely, though she was blissfully happy at home with her "white bear"—as she still sometimes called him. She occasionally got Charles to go on journeys with her, but her second-born child, Nena, was a north-born, so we all knew it wouldn't be long before Rose was kept busy running after her. Which seemed only right.

And Mother never gave up her superstitious ways.

She liked to point out that the *skjebne-soke* had been right all along about north-born Rose being buried in a deluge of ice and snow. The fact that Rose did not perish, Mother claims, was a minor detail, and probably due to the mitigating factor of being in proximity to a talking white bear. Or some such nonsense, as Father would say.

Neither Rose nor Charles liked to talk much of their adventures with the trolls, but some of the so-called "softskins" whom they had brought out of Niflheim, as well as the crew of the ship Soren had hired to go north to find Rose, must have spread the story, because for many years afterward, there were tales told of a race of trolls living at the top of the world.

Only Rose and her white bear know the whole truth of it.

GLOSSARY

Anglia — England

Arktisk — the Arctic

Danemark — Denmark

Finnland — Finland

Fransk — France (also French)

Gronland — Greenland

Huldre — the troll kingdom (also its people)

Inuit — a people who live in the far north of
    Greenland and Canada

isbjorn — ice bear

Iseland — Iceland

leidarstein — lodestone

Niflheim — frozen land of the dead

Njord — Norway

Njordsjoen — North Sea

Saami — a people who live in the far north of Norway

skjebne-soke — fortune-teller

Tyskland — Germany

ACKNOWLEDGMENTS

This book has been a journey of many years, and I, like Rose, had a great deal of help along the way from many people who were generous with their support and wisdom. Above all I would like to thank the "Havamals"—librarians who patiently and wisely led me through the byways of researching Norway, compasses, the Arctic, and white bears.

Many thanks also to Jean Emery and David Wilhelm, who led me to the fjords and were patient and forgiving when lost manuscripts needed to be retrieved (twice!); Sarah McPhee and Lennart Ericsson, who showed me the archipelago; Robin Cruise, who ferreted out all those spinning heads and "of courses," making my writing spotless; and my editor, Michael Stearns, who is Thor, Malmo, Sofi, *and* Neddy all wrapped into one—and who makes me laugh.

I also want to thank Vita, whose wanderlust and strength of character rival that of Rose, and the real Charles, who has been my north, south, east, and west from the beginning.

CHATTING WITH EDITH PATTOU

How long have you been writing?

I've been writing since I was a child. The first story I wrote, at age seven or eight, was called *The Adventures of Lipid Shortsock* and followed the exploits of a swashbuckling squirrel. At age eleven, inspired by the book *Harriet the Spy*, my best friend and I started spy notebooks, and I believe I've kept a notebook/journal ever since.

What is your writing process? Do you work at certain hours or on certain days, or under any special conditions?

I write my initial drafts longhand and then edit them on the computer. I don't stick to a strict schedule the way some authors do, but when I'm in the midst of writing a book, I write every day, usually in the morning. I've gone through periods when I find it difficult to concentrate at home (because of things like laundry and phone calls), so I write in restaurants. I have a few favorites, including a pub-style restaurant down the street and a pizza place in a nearby shopping mall. I wrote much of *East* in the café of a local bookstore.

Are your characters inspired by people you know?

It's unusual for one of my characters to be entirely based on a particular person, but there are bits of people I know in all of my characters. For example, Neddy was somewhat inspired by my husband and the strong love he had for his younger sister, as well as the sense of responsibility he always felt for her (although, as far as I know, he's never dabbled in writing bad poetry).

How do you come up with story ideas?

I don't seem to have trouble coming up with ideas. They come into my head all the time (hence the need to carry a notebook!) and they come from everywhere— newspaper stories, dreams, songs, watching a play, sitting in a car on a long drive. Which isn't to say that all these ideas are brilliant—far from it. There's a lot of sifting that needs to be done.

Rose's family is quite large. Did you grow up in a big family?

No. In fact, I am an only child. But when I was young I used to love reading a series of books about a very large, cheerful family called the Happy Hollisters, and I was always envious of friends from big families. When I got married, I was fortunate enough to marry into a large, wonderful family.

One unique feature of East *is the use of poetry as the voice of certain characters. What inspired you to do that? Do you write a lot of poetry?*

When it came time to give the white bear a voice—and I decided early on that one of the voices telling the story must be his—I initially made it stream-of- consciousness, just a flow of words with lots of dots between them. But each time I read over the words, they seemed wrong. I thought about what it would be like for a human voice buried inside an animal brain to try to find its way out. I decided the words would be very condensed and charged and sensory, which is how I think of poetry. So I decided to make each one of his chapters a poem.

But I don't write a lot of poetry. I won a school prize for a poem I wrote back in elementary school, and it's been downhill ever since (kind of like Neddy, who abandons *his* early efforts at poetry!). I did enjoy giving it a go in *East,* so perhaps one day I might rekindle that early spark.

Thus far three of your novels have been fantasies. What about the genre attracts you?

Ever since I discovered C. S. Lewis's Narnia books, I've been a lover of fantasy. As a child, I loved the way it took me away to a completely different world. When I got older, I became intrigued with the idea of actually constructing such a world. The first two fantasies I wrote were set in Eirren, a land based on Celtic mythology. But for *East*, although it is based on a fairy tale, I purposefully set the story in a very specific, very real time and place—Norway in the sixteenth century.

Along Rose's journey, she goes through a progression of different guides. Can you elaborate on this element of the story?

In the original fairy tale of "East of the Sun and West of the Moon," the heroine of the story gets to the far distant land of the trolls by riding on the backs of the East, West, South, and North Winds, an image I loved as a child. But as much as I hated giving up that image, I decided that in my tale I would turn those winds into people who would represent the four different points of the compass. So Sofi and Estelle are south and east, respectively; Thor is west; and Malmo is north, of course. Each one guides Rose along a portion of her journey, lending his or her own specific skills and support.

The compass motif is prevalent throughout East, *seemingly as a metaphor that one's life can go in many directions. But Rose's mother had the directions of her children's lives planned out from the day they were born. Did her expectations for her children shape their lives, or were their lives predestined by the points on a compass?*

That's an interesting question. Rose would seem to be an example of predestination, since she is much more guided by her birth direction than her mother's influence. But I guess I'd have to say that there is a little of both at work. I've always been fascinated by the question of fate and how the choices we make from day to day might drastically affect the direction of our lives.

In East, *Rose goes on a literal, physical journey as well as an internal, personal one. How do you think her adventure changes her inwardly?*

In the prologue Rose says about herself that over the course of her journey she learned "a little bit about patience," and that is certainly one of the main changes she undergoes. She also gains insight into her impulses, learning both how to curb them as well as how to use them to find her way toward her goal. She grows up and settles down, having learned how to love.

THE ORIGINS OF *EAST*

By Edith Pattou

The novel *East* is based on the Norwegian fairy tale "East of the Sun and West of the Moon." I first read the story as a child, in one of the Andrew Lang fairy books. I loved the heroine, a spunky unnamed girl who was brave enough to ride on the back of a great white bear and then ride the East, West, South, and North Winds. I admired her unyielding spirit, her tenacity, and the sureness of her love for the enchanted prince she was so determined to save. But I came to write *East* in a rather roundabout way.

I had been working for several months on a book that was to be a humorous, satiric fantasy about two kids who come across a portal that leads them into the landscapes of all the different fairy tales. I had the story mapped out but came grinding to a halt, suffering from an advanced case of writer's block. There was one part of the story that I kept returning to in my thoughts, the part when the two children enter the land of "East of the Sun and West of the Moon." And suddenly it struck me that *that* was the story I really wanted to tell.

When I started to write *East*, I had recently finished the book *The Poisonwood Bible* by Barbara Kingsolver. I loved her use of various voices to tell the story, and I decided that would be an intriguing way to tell the tale of *East*. (It turned out to be quite a challenge, trying to keep each voice distinct, and in the editing process, even more of a challenge to keep them all straight. I wound up having to storyboard the book on a large table in my basement to keep track of all the different threads of the story.)

I did a great deal of research in the course of writing *East*. I had to become an expert of sorts in many disparate areas, such as: weaving, compasses, mapmaking and its history, seamanship, Scandinavian languages, Norway in the sixteenth century, the Inuit people, Norse mythology, everything to do with the Arctic, and of course, polar bears. Our local zoo doesn't have any polar bears, so I traveled to Chicago to observe one. As I stood watching and taking notes about the large male polar bear, a family came up to the railing beside me and I heard one of the children say, "Oh, he looks so lonely!" Which summed up my white bear perfectly: lonely and waiting.

I also had the opportunity to travel in Norway while I was writing *East*, and I journeyed by ship through the fjords. It was summer rather than winter, but it gave me a sense of the grandeur and immense quiet of the fjords.

I visited a summer farm near Andalsnes, which provided a model for Rose's family farm. The trolls one finds in souvenir shops in Norway, as well as in traditional Scandinavian folklore, were nothing like the ones I created for my story. But in researching Norwegian folktales, I came across stories about a race of trolls called the Huldre, who were beautiful and clever rather than ugly and stupid, though they did have tails that they kept hidden under clothing.

The ending of *East* came together almost magically, like the final pieces of a difficult jigsaw puzzle. I had constructed the plot to take place in the 1500s, had located the castle in the mountain in France to which the white bear takes Rose, and had decided that the Troll Queen would substitute a shape-shifted troll to die in the place of a young prince of France one hundred years earlier. Though I was fully prepared to make up such a character, I thought it would be cool if by some chance there really was a French prince who died at a young age in that general time period. So I was looking through history books, and my eye was caught by a chance phrase in Barbara W. Tuchman's *A Distant Mirror: The Calamitous Fourteenth Century* referring to King Charles and Queen Isabeau's fifth child, a son born in 1392 who died at age nine. When I finally tracked down the name of this boy, it was Charles, which happens to be my husband's name. It was eerie the way it all came together, almost as if it was fated. But now I'm sounding like Rose's mother, and I can hear Rose's dad tell me it is all nonsense.

Edith Pattou is the author of *Mrs. Spitzer's Garden*, a picture book illustrated by Tricia Tusa, and two highly acclaimed teen fantasy novels, the first in the Songs of Eirren sequence: *Hero's Song*, an IRA Young Adults' Choice, and *Fire Arrow*, a *Booklist* Top Ten Fantasy Novel of the Year. She lives with her family in Columbus, Ohio, where she is hard at work on the third Eirren novel.